Corner
damage
back
cover
10-10
CIRCOK

P9-DWY-722
Bones of the
SF Wei
Silver City Public Library

# BONES OF THE DRAGON

# BONES OF THE DRAGON

MARGARET WEIS

AND

TRACY HICKMAN



TOR

A TOM DOHERTY ASSOCIATES BOOK

NEW YORK

This is a work of fiction. All of the characters, organizations, and events portrayed in this novel are either products of the authors' imagination or are used fictitiously.

BONES OF THE DRAGON



A Tor Book
Published by Tom Doherty Associates, LLC
175 Fifth Avenue
New York, NY 10010

www.tor-forge.com

Tor® is a registered trademark of Tom Doherty Associates, LLC.

Library of Congress Cataloging-in-Publication Data

Weis, Margaret.
Bones of the dragon / Margaret Weis and Tracy Hickman.—1st ed.
p. cm.
"A Tom Doherty Associates book."
ISBN-13: 978-0-7653-1973-9 (hardcover)
ISBN-10: 0-7653-1973-X (hardcover)
ISBN-13: 978-0-7653-2346-0 (first international trade paperback edition)
1. Heroes—Fiction. 2. Gods—Fiction. 3. Dragons—Fiction. 4. Magic—Fiction. 5. Quests (Expeditions)—Fiction. I. Hickman, Tracy. II. Title.

PS3573.E3978 B66 2009
813'.54—dc 22

2008038032

First Edition: January 2009

Printed in the United States of America

0 9 8 7 6 5 4 3 2 1

To Angel Jane Peterson from Grampa Hickman: Thank you for all my brighter tomorrows.

—TRACY HICKMAN

To my flyball team, the BC Boomerangs, and our dogs: Dixie, Joey, Bandit, Razor, Chloe, Riley, Scooter B, Scooter C, Feisty, Scotty, Figment, Scout, Fly, Shelby, Frasier, Shifter, Ginger, Shooter, Homer, Simpson, Jem, Skaner, Smush, Kanga, Solar, Luke, Squirt, Lunar, Stewie, Max, Streyeker, Mojo, Target, Nikki, Tempe, Ranger, Zoomer: Thank you for the fun and friendship!

—MARGARET WEIS

# WYRD

*The thread*
*is twisted and spun*
*upon the wheel.*
*Then I snip it,*
*and he dies.*

BOOK
1
THE OGRES

CHAPTER

# 1

The hunt had not gone well. The four young men had left their village six days ago, hoping to bring down game for their people. They had caught only a few thin and undernourished rabbits, which went to feed the hungry hunters. Discouraged, the young men had headed back home.

The Torgun were not generally hunters, except for sport. The clan raised cattle and sheep, ducks and geese, housing them in byres during the winter, feeding them grain grown during the summer months. But due to excessive rain, the grain harvest had been poor last fall. The winter, the dark months of Svanses, had been unusually long and bitterly cold, killing animals and people. Spring had brought hope to the Torgun, but the time of spring, Desiria, proved a mockery. The goddess Akaria's rains came early and then ceased. Now, in late spring, the young crops withered in the dry ground.

Even under ideal conditions, raising crops was always difficult in this land of cold and snow. The growing season was short, the ground rocky and difficult to farm. Despite the hardships, or perhaps because of them, the Vindrasi people had lived here and thrived for centuries. Not even the eldest among them could remember a time as bad as this.

On their return, the group of four friends split up, hoping to cover more ground in their efforts to find game. The brothers, Bjorn and Erdmun, took a different road to the village, using the northern route. Skylan and Garn took the south. These two young men walked in silence. Skylan did not react well to failure, and he was sullen and brooding. Garn was silent because he never spoke unless he had something to say that was worth saying.

The time was morning, near dawn. The young men had risen early, intending to find deer stirring in the gloaming and eating tender green grass or coming to the stream to drink. There were no deer, however, because there was no tender grass. As for the stream, lack of rain had caused it to dwindle to almost nothing. A small child could toddle through the water without wetting her knees.

Skylan watched the sun rise up over the hills, and he grew even glummer. Aylis, the Sun Goddess, was an angry goddess, burning away the clouds that might have brought much-needed rain.

The day would be clear and hot. Again.

"I am beginning to think Aylis hates us," Skylan said bitterly. "We prayed for the goddess's light during the harsh season of Svansol, and she was nowhere to be seen, leaving us to the mercy of Svanses and her snow and ice and bitter cold. Now, in the time of Desiria, we cannot rid ourselves of Aylis. We pray to the Goddess of the Waters for rain, but Aylis drives Akaria away, burns our crops, and dries up our water."

"One would think," Garn commented with a half smile, "that Torval could exert better control over his women."

"Perhaps Torval's women are like ours and do whatever they damn well please," Skylan muttered, thinking of one woman in particular.

He spoke lightly, but he touched the amulet—a small silver axe—he wore around his neck on a leather thong to appease the God of War in case he should take offense.

"But we should not jest about such matters," Skylan added hastily. "Torval might be insulted and take out his rage on us."

"I do not see how the god can cause us to suffer more than we already have," Garn returned dryly. "We endure the worst winter in memory and wait hopefully for spring. A time of new life, it brings drought and death."

Frowning, Skylan said nothing. He revered the gods, and he wished Garn would stop talking about them in such a disrespectful, almost mocking tone. Skylan might have said something, but he and Garn had been friends—more like brothers, for they had been raised together—since they were infants, and Skylan knew from experience that arguing with Garn would only encourage him in his irreverence. And so Skylan kept quiet.

Skylan's faith in the gods of the Vindrasi was simple and unquestioning, perhaps because—as Garn might have said—his faith had not been tried. At the time of his birth, Skylan Ivorson had been blessed by Torval, Chief of the Gods of the Vindras. A spark struck from Torval's war axe as he fought his enemies in heaven had flashed across the heavens at the very moment Skylan let out his first cry. When Norgaard, Skylan's father and Chief of the Torgun Clan, told Aldrif, the former Kai Priestess, about the spark and how all in the clan had witnessed it, she affirmed that the God Torval had indeed blessed the child, who would grow up to be a valiant warrior, a savior of his people. The sad fact that his mother had died giving him life made the sign more significant.

Everyone in the Torgun Clan believed in that blessing, especially Skylan. He was the strongest young man in the clan, the boldest warrior, the most skillful with sword and spear and axe. He was handsome, with eyes the color of the waves upon which the Vindrasi sailed their dragonships and hair the color of the golden rays of Aylis. His skin was bronze, his body well formed and well muscled. He carried himself with pride and confidence.

Skylan had taken his place in the shield-wall and killed his first man in battle at the age of fourteen. He had taken his first woman at about that same age, going on to lie with girls who were careless of their virtue or with low-born girls whose parents hoped that by coupling with the chief's son, their daughters would be provided for. As a result, there were several children about the camp who had sea-blue eyes and sun-gold hair.

Skylan cheerfully acknowledged his bastard children and gifted their mothers with presents from time to time, as was expected of him. He had no intention of wedding any of the women, however, and he had ceased his "tomcatting," as Garn had put it. Two years ago, when he was sixteen, Skylan decided he was in love. Her name was Aylaen Adalbrand, stepdaughter of his father's friend, Sigurd Adalbrand. She had been fifteen then. She was now seventeen years old.

The three of them—Aylaen, Garn, and Skylan—had been friends from the time their caretakers had laid them on blankets together. The three played together, which was unusual, for girls were generally kept at home to assist with household duties. Aylaen's father was dead, her mother could not control her, and Aylaen "ran wild," escaping from her chores to join Skylan and Garn in their play and in their fights. Skylan did not remember what he had done to anger Aylaen—perhaps he had roughly pulled her long red braids. Aylaen had rounded on him like a catamount, punching him in the face, splitting open his lip, bloodying his nose—and knocking him on his rump.

No boy in camp had ever bested Skylan in battle. He'd been so lost in admiration at Aylaen's spirited attack that he forgot to fight back, and she walked triumphantly off the field, sucking her small bruised knuckles, mantled with the honors of the day.

Two years ago Skylan had told Aylaen that he meant to marry her. True, she had stuck out her tongue and jeered at him, but he was not discouraged. Since that time, he had not slept with another woman. He had made an offer of marriage to her stepfather and Sigurd, after some bargaining, had accepted. Skylan was waiting now only to obtain enough silver to pay Sigurd the bride-price in order to marry her. Marriages were always arranged among the Vindrasi. A woman had the right to refuse a suitor, however, and Aylaen was forever swearing she would never wed him, but she said it in a teasing manner. Skylan was confident she didn't really mean it. He was the Chief's son, after all, a valuable catch for any family, as her stepfather well knew.

He should have earned the silver with wealth captured in raids, but things had not gone as planned.

Skylan still considered himself blessed—he was, after all, handsome, strong, healthy, and the most skilled and honored warrior in the clan. But it seemed nothing was going right for him or for the Torgun Clan these days, and Skylan couldn't understand it. The Torgun had been among the most feared clans of the Vindrasi. In years past, the Torgun's dragonship, the *Venjekar,* meaning the Forging, had come back laden with cattle, silver, grain, and the precious jewels demanded by the Dragon Kahg in payment for his services.

Now it seemed the Torgun were cursed.

First there had been the poor harvest, then the unusually cold winter, and now this terrible drought. Raids on their neighbors had not remedied the situation. The Torgun's neighbors had inexplicably been warned of the coming of the dreaded dragonship, and they'd fled into the hills, taking their treasure and their flocks with them, leaving behind nothing but stray cats and empty iron cooking pots.

Skylan and his warriors were forced to venture into unknown territory, and it seemed their luck had finally turned when they discovered a fat village of fat people and fat cattle. But when Treia, their Bone Priestess, prayed to the Dragon Kahg to join them in battle, the dragon did not answer. Skylan and his fierce band of warriors had not been concerned. They could take this village of blubbery cowards by themselves.

Unfortunately, another group of warriors had also spotted the village. The *Venjekar*'s lookout had spotted sails numerous as gulls squabbling over a dead fish on the horizon, driving toward them. Skylan had been amazed to recognize the triangular-sailed ships of an ancient foe, the ogres. Considerably outnumbered, Skylan had reluctantly ordered his single dragonship to take to the seas.

He had hated running from a fight, but without their dragon ally, the Torgun could not hope to battle both villagers and the brutish ogres. The faster, lighter *Venjekar* had skimmed the waves, and they were able to escape before the ogres caught them. Still, no one had celebrated. They had returned home, their ship empty, their warrior souls filled with shame.

"If only the Dragon Kahg had fought for us," Skylan complained. "We would now be rolling in silver and swimming in cattle. I wonder why the dragon refused to answer Treia's summons."

Garn was startled at this sudden change in subject, but he knew how his friend's mind worked, and thus he managed to make the bounding leap from talking of the gods to discussing the Torgun's last disastrous raid. He was about to comment, but Skylan didn't give him a chance.

"I want to go raiding again, but my father will not permit it. Norgaard says that until we know why the gods have turned against us, we will not take to the seas. I hate this!" Skylan exclaimed suddenly, slamming his fist into the trunk of a tree. "I hate sitting about like an old granny, wailing and doing nothing!"

"Norgaard speaks sense, though," Garn replied. "And no one can call your father an old granny. His warrior days may be behind him, but he has a warrior's heart still. And his valor lives in his son."

Garn clapped Skylan on the shoulder. Garn was Skylan's age, eighteen, his best friend, his cousin, his blood brother. The two had grown up in the same house together, for Garn had been orphaned at birth, his father having died in a raid, his mother dying of a fever. Because his mother had been Norgaard's half sister, Norgaard and his pregnant wife Edda took Garn to raise as their own.

He and Skylan had been inseparable. Many considered their friendship odd, for the young men were vastly different. Garn was the quiet one, people said. He was taller than Skylan, slender, not so muscular. Garn was an adequate warrior, not a great one like his cousin. He was fair-complected with brownish-blond hair and somber, thoughtful brown eyes.

As to their unusual friendship, Garn had given it thought, coming to the conclusion that it was their differences that drew them together, as iron to the lodestone. Skylan, by contrast, never questioned their bond. He knew that Garn was his friend as he knew the sun would rise in the morning.

Skylan was thinking about what Garn had said about his father not being an old granny. Skylan was not certain he agreed, though it made him sad and ashamed to have to admit it. The warrior exploits of Norgaard Ivorson, Chief of the Torgun, were legendary. Then, five years ago, during the heat of battle, Norgaard had leaped off a high stone fortification in pursuit of his enemy. He had landed wrong and broke his leg. The break did not heal properly, forcing him to walk with the assistance of a forked stick under one shoulder. Since then, he had lived in constant pain, though one could never tell by looking at his stoic face. The only indication of what he suffered came from the terrible moans that escaped him in his restless sleep at night.

Norgaard remained a strong Chief, however, with his son acting as War Chief. Skylan did not consider his father weak or cowardly, but he did secretly think that his father, an old man who had seen almost forty-five winters, had grown overly cautious. Skylan would never criticize his father aloud, but Garn knew what his friend was thinking.

"Norgaard is responsible for the welfare of the entire clan," Garn said, "and he dares not risk creating widows and orphans without knowing he will be able to feed them if their men do not come back."

"So rather than dying like warriors, we starve to death and will go to Torval with beggars' bowls in our hands instead of swords," Skylan returned.

"Perhaps if Norgaard asked for a meeting with the Kai Priestess of the Vektia, Draya could tell us if the gods—"

"He did so a month ago," Skylan interrupted tersely. "The priestess has not answered."

Garn looked startled. "I did not know that."

"No one does," said Skylan. "My father says Draya's silence is a bad sign, and he does not want to further discourage our people."

Garn did not know what to say after that. Matters were worse than he had supposed, and even he had no words of comfort now. The two young men continued along the trail that led back to their village. They walked across vast plains of burnt, brown grass that should have been green and lush this time of year. A few surviving cattle—thin and bony creatures—stood in the hot sun, looking miserable. The thin and bony boys who tended them languished in the heat, swatting at flies. They perked up at the sight of Garn and Skylan and ran to ask eagerly if their hunt had been successful. Their faces fell at the sight of the young men carrying nothing but their spears. Scuffing their feet in the dust, the boys went back to keeping watch on the cattle.

The young men left the plains and entered the thickly forested hill country. Though they could not see it from this vantage point, their village lay far below them, rows of houses scattered along the coastline. The location was ideal. The Torgun's swift-sailing dragonship could ply the waters in search of food and wealth, and when danger threatened, the women and children could seek the safety of the hills.

Garn breathed a sigh of relief as they entered the cool shade of the forest. Skylan scowled and increased his pace. He disliked forests. He felt smothered, surrounded by trees, unable to breathe the clean sea air. Then, too, fae creatures dwelt in the woods—faeries and dryads, wood fauns, fetches, and suchlike. The gods had no control over the fae folk, for the fae had been living in this world long before the gods found it.

The worst time of Skylan's life had been during his passage to manhood, when, at the age of twelve, he was sent out with other boys to survive a week in the forest, armed with only a knife. He'd had to avoid the Torgun hunters, who searched for him and the others, gleefully dragging back those they caught. These unfortunates would have to spend another year as "children" before being allowed to take the test again. In addition to those trials, Skylan had to avoid being seduced by a dryad or lured off to unhallowed revels by a faun, never to be seen again.

Skylan had prayed constantly to Torval to protect him, and Torval had done so. Skylan had not encountered any of the fae folk, though he had been convinced he could hear their revels in the night. Skylan had given Torval a fine gift for having protected him from the wicked fae.

Trudging along the dusty forest trail now, dry twigs and leaves snapping underfoot, Skylan remembered vividly how he had lain awake at night, gripping his knife in his hand as he listened to the squawks and squeaks, the screams and groans and snarls, picturing the fae folk gathering around him, eager to drag him down below the earth to their dark kingdom forever.

Hearing something—not a faery—Skylan came to a sudden halt. He raised his free hand, a gesture that brought Garn to a stop, as well. The sound was an odd one—a rumbling grunting and snorting. They listened intently. Something incredibly large was crashing about in the dry brush.

The two glanced at each other. The noises came from up ahead and to their left. Skylan was still thinking of fae folk, and he gripped his spear more tightly. He was afraid of nothing born of mortal man, but the thought of encountering a hairy troll made his blood run cold.

Neither young man had been particularly quiet or stealthy in his movements. So near to home, there was no need. But they grew quiet now, moving silently toward the thing making the noise. Skylan motioned for Garn to go off to his right as both left the trail, plunging into the forest, planning to converge on whatever it was from different sides.

Skylan was the first to spot the creature, and he stood in amazement laced with relief.

A wild boar.

Skylan had heard tales of these enormous beasts. Wild pigs with huge tusks, they could weigh as much as five stout men. He had never seen one, for boars did not live around here. The boar had likely been driven from its accustomed hunting grounds in the mountains by the drought, but Skylan believed Torval had sent it in answer to his prayers. The gods might be angered at the Torgun, but Torval loved Skylan still.

The boar had either heard or sniffed trouble, for it lifted its massive head, glaring about as though aware it was being outflanked. The boar's fur stood up in alarm, and it snarled a warning to keep away. The boar was a fearsome-looking beast. Its jutting, heavy head hung down from massive humped shoulders. It had two sets of tusks. One, the upper set, called *honors,* sharpened the lower, larger set, known as *rippers* for good reason. The lower tusks were designed to slash apart the flesh of a victim. Short, sturdy legs supported the heavy body.

Watching the boar, Skylan recalled the tales he had heard of hunters trying to bring one down. By all accounts, boars were fierce, vicious animals who would fight savagely to the death. His father had hunted boar in his youth. During one such hunt, a boar had slain a Torgun warrior, goring him in the stomach with its tusks. No one ever hunted boar alone. The warriors went out in parties, bringing nets to entangle the boar and dogs to attack and distract the beast, while the hunters closed in for the kill.

All this flashed through Skylan's mind, even as he determined that he would bring down Torval's boar by himself and haul it back to camp in triumph. The Torgun people would feast on boar meat this night and for many nights to come, and they would sing Skylan's praises. Aylaen would at last look at him with love light in her green eyes—not with the fond, tolerant, sisterly glint of amusement he had come to loathe.

Skylan eyed the boar and considered his strategy. Garn appeared in the shadows of the trees opposite. Guessing Skylan's intent, Garn waved his hands, urging Skylan to run away.

Skylan paid no heed. Spear raised, he advanced on the boar, motioning in turn for Garn to stay where he was. Skylan recalled his father saying that the boar carried a shield of cartilage atop its shoulders hard enough to stop a spear. He also remembered his father saying that one needed to make the first blow the killing blow.

Aim for the chest, the heart.

The boar smelled Skylan and fixed its eyes on him and lowered its head. He had been afraid it would flee, for boars had no honor to trouble them, and were content to run off and live to fight another day. This boar was hungry, however, and meat was meat, be it walking on two feet or four. With a savage snarl, the boar charged at Skylan.

Skylan had planned on charging the boar, and he was startled that the boar had taken the initiative and was charging *him*. The boar was the size of a boulder, and it seemed to grow as it thundered toward him. Skylan began to think he'd made an error in judgment. Garn was yelling for him to climb into the trees. Skylan briefly considered taking his friend's advice; then he thought of Torval watching from where the god sat at his feast table in the Hall of Heroes, roaring with laughter to see the young man scramble for his life up a tree, clinging to the branches while the boar rooted and snorted beneath.

Skylan ran to the tree, but he did not climb it. He set his back against it, along with the butt end of his spear. He had to withstand the force of the charge, or else the boar would slam into him and knock him to the ground, then gore him with its tusks.

Seeing that Skylan was determined to fight, Garn dashed out of the woods and hurled his spear at the boar, hoping to at least wound and weaken it. Garn was not so strong as Skylan, but he had a good eye and a steady hand, and he often beat Skylan in contests where accuracy counted more than strength.

Garn's spear struck the boar in the neck. Blood spurted, and the beast roared in pain, but it kept on going straight for Skylan.

"Torval, strengthen my arm and let my aim be true!" Skylan prayed.

A feeling of calm descended on Skylan. He had known such calm during battle, knew it to be a gift of Torval. Time slowed. Skylan focused on what he had to do, paying no heed to the crashing hooves and the horrible roarings and snortings or to Garn's shouts. Skylan heard the beating of his own heart, the rush of his own blood, like the crashing waves of the sea that filled his sleep at night. He dug his feet into the ground, braced himself against the tree trunk, and leveled his spear.

The boar's small red eyes burned with fury. Spittle flew from its mouth. Yellow tusks jutted upward from the outthrust lower jaw. Intent upon its prey, the boar rushed at Skylan. He drove the spear into the boar's neck.

Blood flowed. The boar gave a grunt—more of surprise than of pain. The shock of the blow slammed Skylan back against the tree, jarring his spear arm and almost hurling him off his feet. He fought to remain standing, fought to drive the spear deeper into the boar, for he had not killed the beast. To his shock and astonishment, the boar kept on coming. Roaring, thrusting at him with its tusks, the boar pushed its body along the spear's haft in a furious effort to destroy Skylan.

The boar was doing Skylan's job for him, driving the spear deeper into its body, but it was also closing in on Skylan. Its head thrashed, its yellow tusks slashed at him, and they were wet with his blood.

Skylan could do nothing except press against the tree and hold fast to the spear and pray to Torval it did not break. Sweat rolled down his face and into his eyes, half-blinding him. He shook his head to see. His muscles were weakening, starting to shake from the tremendous exertion. He had the dim impression that Garn had joined the fight, striking at the boar with his knife.

Blood flew; tusks slashed. Skylan held fast.

The boar, spitted on the spear, twisted and turned, more than once nearly yanking the weapon out of Skylan's hands. Gasping for breath, he threw the waning strength of his body into a last desperate spear thrust, driving as deep as he could.

With a slash of its tusks, the boar gave a gurgling grunt and crashed sideways onto the ground. It lay in a pool of blood, its flanks heaving and its feet twitching. Skylan held on to the spear until he saw the life gradually fade from the boar's eyes. The boar gave a shudder and lay still. Its hatred remained in the staring eyes even after death.

Skylan let go of the spear and collapsed beside the warm, bloody corpse. He lay in its blood and his own beneath the tree and dragged air into his burning lungs. He was dizzy, and now he felt the pain. He looked at his body to try to determine the extent of his injuries, but his clothes, ripped to ribbons, were sticking to the wounds, preventing him from judging their severity. His hands and arms were slashed, and blood and pain were everywhere.

Garn knelt beside him, his own arms bloodied to the elbow. He did a swift battlefield assessment, cutting away the cloth of Skylan's tight-fitting linen breeches and the long belted linen shirt.

"You have a deep gash in your thigh," Garn reported after examining Skylan from top to bottom. "But the blood is oozing, not pulsing."

That was good. Blood pulsing from a wound would have meant Skylan would bleed to death.

"You have lots of other wounds, but the thigh wound is the worst," Garn announced. He rocked back on his heels. "You are damn lucky," he added with a smile and a shake of his head.

Skylan smiled, too, through the haze of pain. He was not lucky. He was blessed. His wyrd, his fate, was bound with glory.

# CHAPTER 2

Though Garn wanted to carry Skylan back to the village immediately, to have his wounds tended, Skylan refused to leave the boar, fearing it would be devoured by wolves.

"Bjorn and Erdmun will not be far away," he said, sitting up, propping himself against the tree. "Summon them with your horn."

Skylan drank water from his waterskin and pressed the remnants of his shirt over the wound in his thigh to stop the bleeding.

He was a quick healer—another blessing from Torval. The wound burned and throbbed, but he did his best to ignore the pain. He was helped by the golden haze of triumph that acted as sweet medicine and eased his hurts. He rested his hand possessively on the boar's hairy, bloody flank.

Garn brought his ram's horn to his lips and gave three blasts, two long and one short, indicating that he needed help. He paced about restlessly, not so confident as Skylan that their two friends would be in the vicinity.

Bjorn and Erdmun arrived far sooner than even Skylan had expected, bounding out of the woods with their spears raised. Both skidded to a halt and stared in astonishment to see their friends covered in blood, next to the gigantic carcass.

"That was fast," said Garn.

"We heard the crashing and roaring, and it sounded like a battle," said Bjorn, unable to take his awed gaze from the boar, "and—"

"—we came to see what was going on," Erdmun said.

The brothers often finished each other's sentences.

The two moved closer, staring curiously at the boar. Bjorn was Skylan's age, eighteen. Erdmun was sixteen. Neither had ever seen such a beast before.

"Did the two of you slay it by yourselves?" Erdmun asked.

"Skylan killed it by *himself,*" Garn said, always honest, always quick to give praise.

"You stabbed it with your knife," Skylan said, heaving himself to his feet.

Garn laughed. "I think I only annoyed it."

Skylan stood up too quickly, staggered, and nearly went over backwards. He steadied himself against the tree until the dizziness passed, and then he made an attempt to walk. If he didn't keep moving, his leg would stiffen up. Pain tore through his injured thigh, causing his breath to come fast and sweat to bead his forehead.

"We have to haul the carcass back to camp," he announced through gritted teeth.

"Yours or the boar's?" Garn asked, grinning at him.

"We should rename you Joabis the Jester," Skylan grumbled, referring to the merry God of the Feast. "I am well enough. I just need a moment to rest, that's all."

Movement had caused the wound to bleed again. Garn tore up what was left of his ripped shirt, and Skylan used the strips of linen to further bind the gash.

Garn and Bjorn and Erdmun went to work. They had brought lengths of stout rope with them, hoping to use the rope to haul back a buck or a couple of fat does. They tied the rope around the boar's thick neck and front legs, and with Bjorn and Garn pulling and Erdmun pushing from behind, they dragged the carcass across the ground, leaving a bloody trail behind.

The road from the forest to the seacoast was downhill, but the carcass was heavy and clumsy to haul. The three were exhausted before they had gone very far. Skylan limped after them, his wound paining him more than he would admit. Eventually all the young men conceded defeat and halted.

Garn suggested that Erdmun run to the village to bring back help, leaving the others to guard the boar. He returned with twenty men and an equal number of small children and dogs, bringing with them a large skid used to haul boulders and stones from the hills down to the village. The men were singing a song of praise as they came, praise for Skylan.

At the sight of the young hero mantled in the blood of conquest, the men gave a hearty shout, while the children clustered around Skylan, each boy proclaiming an intention to be him someday. Skylan's heart swelled with pride, and he quickly touched the silver axe on his neck and loudly gave his own praise and thanks to Torval, lest the god feel his role in the battle was being slighted.

Skylan brushed off the accolades of the warriors, telling them how Garn had attacked the fearsome beast first with spear and then with only his knife. Garn described the battle in gory detail. The men listened in appreciation, nodding and clapping and, at the end, slapping Skylan on the back.

Skylan's young stepmother, Sonja, hearing of Skylan's wounds, had sent along a pot of healing salve, made by boiling and then straining a mixture of tansy, fish oil, the oil of pine known as pitch, wax, resin, and the plant called adder's tongue. Skylan was grateful to her, and he removed the bloody bandages and smeared the salve over his wounds, easing the pain almost immediately. The salve would also stop the flesh from putrefying.

While Skylan was treating his wounds, the men set to work wrestling and manhandling the heavy boar carcass onto the skid and lashing it securely so that it would not slide off. This took some time, and the sun was at its zenith, High Morn, before they were finished. Once the carcass was on the skid, the men hoisted Skylan onto the boar's back. He rode in proud triumph as they hauled the skid along the trail.

The ride was bumpy, and it jarred his wound painfully. The stench of the dead beast was nauseating, and both he and the bloody carcass were swarmed by flies. Still, Skylan would not have traded places with the Chief of Chiefs of the Vindrasi people. He was basking in his victory and leading the men in a song of praise to Torval when shrill cries and shouts brought the singing to a sudden, startled halt.

A group of Torgun women and children came running up the trail. The women carried bundles in their arms, and at the sight of their menfolk, they called out in alarm. Skylan had no idea what was happening. The excited women were all talking at once, making it difficult to understand what was wrong.

Skylan said a sharp word, and silence fell. He pointed to one of the middle-aged older women, Brynhildr, who had been a friend of his mother's. She was calm and sensible, about thirty years old, a leader among the Torgun women. He asked her what was happening.

"Three ships sailed into the bay at High Morn. Each ship has three sails that look like this"—Brynhildr formed a triangle with her fingers—"and hulls that sit on skids. The sails are striped, red and white."

"Ogres," said Bjorn.

Skylan's stomach clenched. Triumph turned to wormwood in his mouth, making him physically sick. He would not jump to conclusions, however.

"It cannot be," he stated. "We left the ogres far behind. I must see this with my own eyes."

He slid down off the boar's carcass and limped over to a point where the trees thinned and he could see Djvolk Bay. Garn and several of the warriors accompanied him. Standing on the ledge, they stared down in grim silence.

Three ships, each with striped triple sails and split-hull design, rode at anchor on the glittering waters of the placid bay.

"They followed us home," said Garn.

Skylan glared at the ships in angry bafflement. "They could not have! I made sure of that."

But he felt a twinge of unease as he spoke. Skylan believed, as did most Vindrasi, that ogres were loutish brutes, about as smart as your average rabbit. He had watched the triple-sailed ships dwindle to specks on the horizon and, having assumed that the ogres had given up the chase, had not kept careful watch on the way home or taken precautions against being followed or kept up the swift pace that would have left the slower ships far behind.

Instead, Skylan had stopped several times along the coast to lead his men in fruitless searches for plunder. They had fires at night, anchored their ship in plain sight by day. It had never occurred to Skylan that the ogres might sail after him.

"It must be Torval's will," Skylan announced, thereby absolving himself of blame. Now that the initial shock had worn off, he was eager to fight this formidable foe. "Our War God is with us. He sent the boar to me as a sign, and now the best and strongest warriors of the Torgun are here in the hills instead of being trapped by the ogres in the village. We will come fresh to the battle—"

"Fresh to *what* battle?" Garn asked.

"What battle?" Skylan stared at his friend and gestured to the three ships. "The battle against these sons of whores who dare—"

Garn shook his head. "I do not see a battle. I do not hear clashing steel or desperate horn calls or the beating of the war drums. I do not see our longhouses burning. Whereas I do see the smoke of a ceremonial fire rising from the Chief's Hall."

Skylan scowled. Everything his friend said was true, though it made no sense. Why raid a village and not raid it?

"The ogres have come here to talk," Garn continued, "not to plunder and kill. I find that odd, don't you?"

Skylan did not. Such actions accorded with what he knew of ogres, who were not only stupid, but also lazy and would do anything to avoid a fight.

"Then we should attack them," Skylan said.

"We should find out what is going on first," Garn advised. "Remember, the parley is sacred to Torval. He would take it ill if we broke faith."

"What he says is true," Brynhildr agreed. "The ogres came bearing laurel leaves."

Any enemy who came under truce to talk was protected by the gods. Skylan choked back his rage and tried to reflect calmly on what his friend was saying. Calm reflection was not easy for Skylan, who was impetuous, quick to take action and think later. He was proud of those traits in himself, considering them good qualities in a warrior. Let men such as Garn take time to observe, think over the situation. Garn thought; then he acted. Skylan acted—often recklessly—and only afterwards considered the consequences. He had sense enough to value Garn's wisdom, however, and sometimes he even allowed himself to be guided by it.

"I will take Bjorn and three warriors to the village to see what is happening," Skylan said. "Garn, you and the others wait here— Now, what is wrong with that idea?" he demanded, exasperated, for Garn was shaking his head.

"All the men should go," Garn said. "Norgaard will want the warriors present in the Chief's Hall as a show of force. We will all of us take the boar carcass back to the village. Even ogres will be impressed by the fact that you single-handedly killed a boar. And if they see us returning calmly from the hunt, they will see that we do not fear them. Whereas if we go rushing back, all in a boiling stew, they will think we are afraid—"

"Why can't you ever just give me a straight answer?" Skylan asked, cutting his friend off impatiently. Garn might be a wise thinker, but he was also a long-winded talker.

Skylan resumed his place astride the boar's bloody carcass. He would have liked to walk proudly in front, for the ogres to see him, but he secretly hoped he would be called upon to fight them, and he needed to conserve his strength. He ordered the women and children to take refuge in the hills, and they hastened past him, heading to the caves used by the Torgun on just such occasions.

Skylan watched them as they went, hoping to see Aylaen's tall graceful body and thick curling mass of fiery red hair. He burned to show off his prowess before her. Aylaen was not among this group, however.

He did see Sonja, his stepmother. She did not look well. She was heavily pregnant, and the climb had been hard on her. Ashen-faced, panting, she pressed her hand against her swollen belly. Brynhildr walked with her, supporting her. After Skylan's own mother had died in childbirth, Norgaard had taken another wife, hoping to father more sons, for Skylan was his only child. Sonja had borne Norgaard three children, but they had all been girls, and all had died in infancy.

Skylan liked his stepmother, and he spoke a word to cheer her as she passed. Sonja gave him a wan smile, and walked wearily on. Skylan gave the order to start, and the warriors heaved on the skid, boasting of the brave deeds they would do in the battle they were sure was coming.

Hauling on the ropes, they pulled and shoved the sled down the steep and winding incline that led from the forested hills to the seacoast. Their mood had changed from lighthearted pleasure to anger and determination—anger at the foe and determination to make the ogres pay for their effrontery.

The ogres lived in a realm far from the Vindrasi lands. They rarely ventured into Vindrasi territory. Few among the Torgun had fought them or knew much about them. The notion among the Vindrasi that ogres were stupid did not come from firsthand knowledge, as much as from the ogres' appearance.

Standing between ten and thirteen feet tall, ogres were massive, heavily muscled, and big-boned. Their heads were small and round, out of proportion to their hulking bodies. With their plump cheeks, small noses, large wide-set eyes, and pursed lips, ogres resembled human babies, and therefore the Vindrasi scornfully credited them with possessing the intellectual capacity of infants.

Chasing Skylan's dragonship all this distance required cunning, energy, intelligence, and skilled seamanship—none of which ogres possessed, or so the Vindrasi believed. Skylan concluded the ogres must have blundered onto the Torgun village by accident.

Pleased with his logic, he could now look forward to doing battle with this lumbering, dull-witted foe, and he was disappointed to find no ogre warriors roaming about the village. He had been nursing a hope for at least a small skirmish, if not an outright war. Parleys were sacred, but if an ogre insulted him . . . Torval could not blame Skylan for defending his honor.

The streets of Luda were empty, however. The village was made up of individual farms separated by fences and streets. The farm plots were of varying sizes, depending on the wealth of the landowner. Some were small, consisting only of the longhouse where the family lived and worked, the byre where the animals were kept, and a small plot of land for growing grain and vegetables. Others, such as the farm owned by Skylan's father, were larger, with a longhouse, byre, and many outbuildings, including a smithy. Men worked for Norgaard in exchange for shares in the crops and housing for themselves and their families. At least, that was how life had been up until this past year. With crops failing and cattle dying, there was scant food to share.

Skylan frowned to see the three ogre ships anchored in the Djvolk Bay, surrounding the *Venjekar*—the Torgun's most valuable treasure. Ogre warriors leaned idly over the sides, watching and waiting, probably as eager for battle as Skylan. Their commanders would be at the parley.

The men who had remained in the village while the others went to bring back the boar were now crowded inside the Chief's Hall, acting as witnesses to the parley. Most of the women and children had fled into the hills, though occasionally Skylan saw a woman's face peeping out of a half-open door.

The men hauled the boar's carcass through the streets to the door of the Chief's Hall, the largest structure in the village. The Vindrasi lived in longhouses, which were simple in design. Constructed of oak timbers, with a roof covered in thatch and straw, the longhouse was divided into several rooms. One room had wooden platforms on which blankets were laid for sleeping. Another was the kitchen, with a hearth for cooking and a domed oven for baking.

The central room was the main living area and housed one of the family's most important possessions—the loom—along with wooden chests for storage and a board for playing dragonbone, a favorite game of the Vindrasi. Other than these objects, and perhaps a few low stools, there was no furniture. People sat cross-legged on the earthen floor or on blankets. If there were windows, they were fitted with heavy wooden shutters, for the house had to be snug and tight to retain warmth in the winter. The interior tended to be smoky and gloomy as a result. Oil lamps and candles provided light.

The Chief's Hall was similar to a longhouse, except that it was far larger and open, not divided into rooms. The hall was the heartbeat of the clan. All business was conducted in the hall, as were feasts and celebrations. Judgments and criminal trials were held here and the regular meetings of the family leaders and, as now, parleys with enemies.

As was customary during a parley, four ogres and four Torgun warriors stood mutual guard outside the Chief's Hall. Skylan got his first good look at an ogre, and he had to admit they were impressive. Skylan had known the ogres would be tall and large, but he hadn't realized they would be quite that tall or quite that large. Skylan himself was of medium height, and his head was about level with an ogre breastbone. Skylan made up in girth what he lacked in height. His chest was broad, and his arm muscles bulged, as did the muscles of his calves and thighs. But he looked puny compared with an ogre, whose chest was half again as broad as his.

Ogres wore little in the way of clothing—leather breeches and belt. Harnesses strapped across their hairy chests held axes or swords. The weapons were enormous and looked to be of fair quality. Each ogre carried an oblong shield as large as the door to the longhouse. From the neck down, they looked fearful. From the neck up, the massive hunk of meat and muscle, bone and gristle was topped by a head as bald and a face as plump and smooth and guileless as that of a newborn babe.

Undoubtedly in an attempt to make their childlike faces more fearsome, the ogres had adopted the use of war paint, which had the added advantage of denoting rank. Each of these ogres, who were bodyguards for their commanders, had a broad blue stripe running from the back of the head up across the bald dome of the forehead, down the nose, across the lips, and down the chin. A broad red band ran over the nose and underneath the eyes. By contrast, the ordinary ogre foot soldier painted his head with a single brown stripe running from the back of the neck to the chin.

Skylan knew none of this, of course. He thought the paint made the ogres look silly and even more childish. He also discovered something else about ogres. They stank.

"Their stench is enough to knock a man on his ass," he remarked, not bothering to lower his voice.

The Vindrasi were a cleanly people who bathed often, even in the winter. The Vindrasi considered their bodies a gift from Desiria, Goddess of Life, and keeping the body clean showed appreciation for her gift. Judging by the smell, ogres must have thought their bodies came from the God of the Dung Heap.

Skylan raised his hand to halt the procession. At the commanding gesture, the men hauling the skid bearing the boar's carcass came to a stop. The ogre guards stared at the carcass and at Skylan and his bloody wounds, and their small eyes widened. As Garn had predicted, the ogres were impressed.

Skylan did not bother to try to conceal his limp as he walked boldly to confront the ogres. His wounds spoke to his courage. Ignoring the ogres, he approached the Torgun warriors who stood guard.

"I am Skylan, son of Norgaard, Chief of the Torgun," he announced. That was for the benefit of the ogres, the warriors outside the hall having known him from infancy. "I would speak with my father, the Chief. Is he within?"

"He has been asking for you, Skylan Ivorson, and said you were to be admitted when you arrived," the Torgun warrior replied with equal formality, though he winked at Skylan as he stood aside to allow him to pass.

Skylan nodded and, gesturing to Garn and the rest of the men to accompany him, he started to enter the Chief's Hall. The ogre warriors allowed Skylan to pass. They blocked the entrance of the others, planting their massive bodies in the doorway.

"You goat-fornicators, how dare you refuse to let these men enter their own hall?" Skylan demanded, taking this as a challenge.

His sword was halfway out of its sheath. The ogres were reaching for their weapons when Garn shouted loudly for everyone to calm down. He motioned for Skylan to come back to the entrance. Skylan rudely jostled one of the ogres aside and went to talk to his friend.

"Don't argue with them," Garn said in a low voice. "It's better that the warriors stay out here. They stand between the ogre ships and the Chief's Hall."

Skylan immediately saw the wisdom in his friend's idea. If the parley went badly and the ogres attacked, their warriors would come running from the ships, and these men were here to stop them. Though it galled him, Skylan sheathed his sword. He did so slowly, making a show of it, rattling the sword in its sheath.

"Garn comes with me," he said, clapping hold of his friend's forearm and hauling him close. "He is my brother."

The ogres seemed doubtful, but after a brief consultation—which consisted of a couple of grunts and a shrug—they allowed Garn to pass.

"The rest of you men remain here," Skylan called out loudly, "where the air is fresh." He sniffed, made a face, and pinched his nostrils together. "If we do not return, it is because we have died of asphyxiation."

His men laughed loudly. Skylan looked hopefully at the ogres. If they reacted to the insult with rage and attacked him, he could not be faulted for defending himself.

The ogres looked at him blankly. Skylan thought they were too stupid to realize they had been insulted. It never occurred to him that they might be too disciplined to fall for his ruse. Skylan glanced back at his men, grinned, and rolled his eyes. His men laughed even louder and nudged each other with their elbows. Their mirth did not last long, however. Some were starting to count the vast numbers of the enemy.

Norgaard Ivorson, Chief of the Torgun, was seated in a large ornate chair that stood at the north end of the Chief's Hall. He sat awkwardly, his bad leg extended straight out in front of him. He was constantly rubbing his leg, his hand moving up and down to try to ease the painful knots. The other members of the Torgun, the male heads of household, ranged along the walls of the longhouse.

There were also two women present. One sat in the only other chair that stood near Norgaard's. Treia, the Bone Priestess of the Torgun Clan, held a position of power and honor, for she interceded with the gods on behalf of the Torgun. The other woman, standing protectively beside Treia, was her younger sister, Aylaen.

The women were dressed formally in the traditional apron-dress of the Vindrasi. Made of wool, the apron-dress was worn over a linen smock. It was held together at the shoulders with two brooches, usually of gold or silver. As mark of her office as Bone Priestess, in addition to the dress, Treia wore long robes embroidered with runes, slit open at the sleeves and loose in the front. She appeared cool and detached, which was odd, for the hall was stifling in the heat of the day and she must have been sweltering in the heavy robes.

At first, Aylaen smiled to see Garn and Skylan. But her smile vanished and her eyes widened in alarm when she saw their blood-soaked clothing. Garn winked at her reassuringly, indicating all was well. Aylaen gave a doubtful nod.

"What is she doing here?" Skylan demanded in a displeased undertone, speaking to his friend. "She should have gone into the hills with the other women!"

"Aylaen run into the hills?" Garn grinned. "Remind me to introduce the two of you, Skylan, for you have obviously never met her."

Skylan grunted. "Such antics were funny when she was a child, but she is a grown woman now."

"You talk like her grandfather," Garn scoffed. "She's only a year younger than we are."

Skylan, having killed the boar and faced down ogres, was reveling in his manhood, and he decided that Aylaen should leave. He frowned sternly at her and made a commanding gesture toward the door.

Aylaen's lips twitched, and he realized she would have laughed at him outright if the situation had not been so serious. As it was, she deliberately looked away, pretending she had not seen him.

Skylan was angry. Aylaen should obey him. He was, after all, her betrothed—or as near to it as made no difference. He had only to come up with the bride-price for her stepfather. He would have said something to her, but Garn gave him a warning nudge. Everyone in the longhouse, including the ogres, was staring at him, and Skylan realized that his dramatic entrance had interrupted the proceedings.

"I heard we had guests, Father," said Skylan, "and I came as soon as I could. The boar I killed is outside," he added offhandedly, as though slaying boars were something he did every day, just for fun. He glanced at the ogres, who were seated on a bench that had been formed out of a large plank laid across several wooden trestles.

Two of the ogres were dressed much as the ogre guards outside, in leather harness and breeches. Their high rank was denoted by their face paint—white with a black stripe running from the neck to the chin, and another black stripe going over the nose and across the cheeks. The third ogre wore a tiger-skin cape draped over his shoulders. Since the other two deferred to him, Skylan marked him as their war leader. Each commander wore a greatsword—large, but not of the best quality, or so Skylan judged. Their shields, painted white with a black cross, rested against a wall.

The fourth ogre was dressed far differently. He wore a long cape made of glistening green and blue feathers and a large feathered headdress. His eyes were outlined in black. Skylan thought he looked like a raccoon, and he smothered a snicker. This ogre carried no weapons.

Norgaard listened to his son's boast, and he sighed. Norgaard was a sad man, an embittered man. Torgun men were supposed to die in battle, not survive as cripples. He lived in constant pain from his injury and constant fear for his people. He remembered a time in his youth when the Vindrasi had been a mighty nation. They had sailed the seas in their winged dragonships and returned laden with glory and jewels.

And now, all that was gone. The Vindrasi warriors no longer fought glorious battles against worthy foes. Their enemies these days were poor harvests, fierce winters, blazing summers, angry seas, and unfavorable winds. The gods had turned against the Vindrasi, and Norgaard did not know why. He had asked Draya, the Kai Priestess, but she was evasive and would not give him a straight answer.

The Torgun never guessed their Chief was suffering. His rugged, scarred face was like chiseled granite, revealing no emotion. He rarely spoke, but when he did, he spoke to purpose. His hair was iron gray, making him look older than his forty-five years. His back was straight, he was not stooped or bent, and he sat tall, with dignity, hiding his pain and his fear from his people as well as from his foes. He had likewise always hidden his pain and worry from his son, and now Norgaard was starting to wonder if that had been wise.

Skylan loved Norgaard as a son is required by the gods to love the man who gives him life. The young man had scant respect for the elder man, however, and Norgaard knew this. If Norgaard could admit that his son had a flaw, it was that the young man took his responsibilities as a future Chief too lightly. For that, Norgaard blamed himself. He had always held his shield in front of Skylan, guarding and protecting him from the jabbing spears of trouble and misfortune. The day would come—and it might come soon—when Norgaard had to leave this world for the next. Skylan would have to lead the clan.

Norgaard had lately tried to teach Skylan the duties and responsibilities of a chief. Whenever he launched into his lecture, Skylan would suddenly recall that he had to take a piss, or if he could not escape, he would listen to his father with undisguised boredom, his gaze roving restlessly about the longhouse as he swatted at flies or shoved about the pieces on his game board.

The thought often came to Norgaard that Skylan played at life as he played at the dragonbone game: He took huge risks, made bold and reckless moves. When he won, he won big. When he lost, it was disastrous.

Norgaard praised his son for killing the boar, then invited him and Garn to remain with him to hear the parley. Skylan took his place at his father's right hand and stared boldly and defiantly at the ogres. Garn stood beside his friend, crossing his arms over his chest and regarding the ogres with interest.

Norgaard started to return to the conversation. Skylan wanted his say first, however.

"What brings you to Luda?" Skylan asked the ogres, and he added brashly, "And when are you leaving?"

The Torgun men around the wall grinned. The ogres scowled. Ogres and Vindrasi spoke the same root language, as did all the people of the world known by the Vindrasi as Ilyrion. In ancient days, the various races had been ruled by one mighty seafaring empire. In order to govern his far-flung territories, the Emperor had decreed that everyone everywhere would speak the language of the Empire.

Though each race adopted the central language and made it their own, they added bits of unique vocabulary, pronounced the words with differing accents and shades of meaning, with the result that the ogre language was much different from that of the Vindrasi. The roots being the same, however, most ogres could carry on a conversation with most humans.

Legend had it that this ancient Emperor had hoped a shared language would foster peace and understanding among the races. Sadly, it had the opposite effect. They could all understand each other's insults.

Norgaard's lips tightened. His expression grew grim.

"Forgive my son, lords," he said to the ogres. "He is young and hot-blooded. I would speak a word with him, if you do not mind that we confer in private."

The ogres graciously acceded. By their grins, they guessed the young man was in for a tongue-lashing.

Skylan saw the grins and burned with shame. He had to swallow his ire, though. He was not often the recipient of his father's anger, and he could not understand what he had done wrong. He was also mindful of Aylaen's laughing green eyes.

Skylan walked over to his father and leaned across his father's shoulder to speak to him. "Why do you reprimand me before these brutes?"

"Because there are one hundred and seventy ogre warriors in those ships," said Norgaard, glowering.

The Torgun could muster perhaps seventy-five warriors—ninety, counting old men and boys. Skylan was not daunted, however. The fight with the boar had given him a taste for blood. Battle lust burned in him. He felt he could fight all 170 ogres himself.

"All men know that Torgun warriors are worth two of any ogre in battle," Skylan said.

"*I* don't know it," said Norgaard sharply. "And I have fought ogres. Have you, *boy*?"

"No, Father," Skylan said. Stung by the use of the term *boy,* he added sullenly, "Apparently I am not to have the chance."

"You may well get the chance," Norgaard said. "I do not know why the ogres have come, but I smell danger. These two ogres are commanders; the ogres term them *godlords.* The third is a shaman, and the fact that a shaman is present on a warship means this has something to do with their gods and is extremely important to them. They were about to tell me when you entered and insulted them. I remind you, Skylan, that the ogres are here under a flag of truce to parley. I invited them into the Chief's Hall, and as such, they are my guests. The parley is sacred; the guest is sacred. Torval watches."

Norgaard leaned nearer. "One thing more—did you see the ships when you came into the village?"

"Yes, Father," said Skylan.

"Did you happen to notice that they have our dragonship surrounded?"

Skylan stared at his father, stunned. He had seen that, of course. He had not thought of the implications. He began to consider that perhaps he had been in the wrong. Maybe he had earned his father's rebuke—at least some portion of it.

"I am sorry, Father," he said, subdued. "I was not thinking."

"You never think, boy," Norgaard said with a sigh. "You rush in, sword swinging. . . ."

"That is the way of the warrior," Skylan said proudly.

"But it is not the way of a Chief," said Norgaard. He gestured toward the ogres. "Apologize to our guests."

Skylan did as he was told. After all, Torval was watching. His apology was short and gruff and grudging, but the ogres accepted it. Now that the wise old dog had put down the boisterous young pup, they were ready to carry on with business.

"You were about to tell me why the ogres honor the Torgun with a visit," Norgaard said.

The two godlords looked with deference at their shaman and invited him to speak.

The ogre shaman rose to his feet. An imposing and outlandish figure, he was tall and thin, lacking the musculature of a warrior, and his headdress of long black glossy feathers made him appear even taller. In addition to the feathered cape, he wore a necklace of curved bones tipped in silver. His hairy arms were thick with silver bracelets. The black paint around his eyes emphasized his gaze, gave it strange intensity.

"We have come to tell the Vindrasi about a great battle that recently took place in heaven between your gods and ours," said the shaman. His eyes glinted. He didn't look so childlike anymore. "Our gods won this battle. Your gods lost. Your gods are dead."

The shaman calmly resumed his seat. Feathers rustling, he looked very much like a large and gangling stork settling into its nest.

## CHAPTER 3

There followed a silence so complete that everyone in the longhouse could hear the rustling of the shaman's feathers. Seeing that none of the Torgun had anything to say, the godlord wearing the tiger-skin cape rose to speak.

"Since the Vindrasi now have no gods, we are here to offer you our protection. In return, you will renounce your gods, who are dead anyway, and you will worship ours. In order to honor our gods, you will give us forty-three head of cattle, thirteen bars of silver, and seven men—among them your son—as hostage to your good faith. And you will also give us your dragonship."

Skylan was the first to find his tongue.

"You lie!" he cried savagely.

Drawing his sword, he tried to dash at the ogres, but his wounded leg gave out on him. He staggered and almost fell. By this time, Garn had hold of Skylan, grabbing his friend around his chest and dragging him to a halt. Skylan struggled to break free of Garn's grip. At Norgaard's sharp command, two more Torgun warriors ran to seize him.

"Torval would never flee!" Skylan raved, struggling in the arms of his captors.

"Torval pissed his pants and ran away," the ogre godlord said calmly. "Along with your Dragon Goddess and all the rest of the cowards."

Skylan surged at the ogres with such fury that he carried Garn and the two warriors along with him. His face flushed, his blue eyes blazed, spittle flew from his mouth. He roared as he went, looking and acting like a madman. The ogre godlords jumped to their feet and drew their swords.

Skylan charged straight at them, his feet driving into the dirt floor. Two warriors clung to his arms. Garn was still wrapped around his chest. Skylan made it halfway across the floor before the three men managed at last to wrestle him to the ground.

Even then, with his arms and legs pinned and one warrior sitting on him, Skylan continued to rail against the ogres. He cried out that they lied, until he lacked the breath to speak. Panting and gasping for air, he glared at the ogres and beat his clenched fists into the ground as though he were beating their heads.

He was not the only Torgun outraged by the ogre's statement. After their initial shock, every man in the longhouse was on his feet, each clamoring to have his say and determined to say it louder than the rest. The Torgun howled and raged and gesticulated, stamping their feet and banging their weapons on their shields. The walls of the longhouse shook with the commotion.

The warriors outside had not heard the ogre's pronouncement, but they could hear Skylan's furious roar and the warriors inside yelling. Thinking a fight had broken out, they rushed the door in an attempt to enter. The ogre guards raised their shields and shoved the Torgun warriors, who swore at the ogres and shoved back.

"Silence!" Norgaard thundered. "Cease this madness, all of you!"

He had been a War Chief once. Accustomed to issuing orders on the field of battle, forced to make himself heard over the clash of steel and the roars of battle lust, and the screams of the wounded and dying, he could make his voice slice through the clamor. He glared particularly at his son. The warriors holding Skylan eyed him dubiously.

"I'm all right," he said, shaking them off. "You can let go of me."

Skylan hoped it was clear to everyone, especially the ogres and Aylaen, that he was backing down only because he'd been ordered to do so by his Chief. He rose to his feet, angrily refusing help, and saw that his wound had broken open. Blood was running down his leg.

The hall was once more subdued, though not quiet. It was filled with an ominous and threatening muttering, like the lull in the stormy battles between the Goddess Akaria and her sister Svanses, who sometimes fought over the rulership of wind and water, whipping up great waves that sank boats and flooded villages. The warriors inside the longhouse returned to their places along the wall. Those outside backed away from the door. No one sheathed his weapon.

Skylan and every person in the hall looked at Norgaard, waiting for him to refute this outrageous claim and even more outrageous demand. There would be war, of course. Their Chief had only to give the order.

Norgaard remained grimly silent.

The truth was, he didn't know what to do. He had never been confronted with a situation like this. The ogres were not acting like the ogres he had fought. Those ogres would never have bothered to come to the humans with such a tale and demand a parley. The ogres he knew would have sailed into Luda, burned the village, slaughtered everyone, stolen everything, and sailed off.

Why the change? What was going on? These were dark and dangerous waters, and Norgaard had to wade into them carefully, feeling his way. He kept his mouth shut, scratching his bearded chin, and gazed thoughtfully at the shaman. As in the game of dragonbones, it was sometimes better to fall back, go on the defensive, allow the enemy to make the next move. He had tried teaching that to Skylan, to no avail.

"Why doesn't he say something?" Skylan demanded impatiently.

Garn replied with the old proverb. " 'A fool opens his mouth. A wise man keeps it shut.' Norgaard is trying to figure out what is going on. For example, why did the ogres not simply attack us? Why the parley?"

Skylan snorted. "Bah! They're ogres. They have cheese curds for brains. The old man has lost his nerve, that's all. I will say something if he won't."

"Stay out of it, Skylan," Garn warned. "Let your father handle this."

Skylan ignored his friend's counsel. He turned to face Treia, who had said nothing during the furor and was almost forgotten. Aylaen stood near her sister, her hand resting on Treia's arm. Both were watching Norgaard. Neither was paying any attention to Skylan, and both were startled to hear him speak.

"I call upon our Bone Priestess to refute these ridiculous claims," said Skylan. "Priestess, tell the ogres they are wrong. Ask Torval to give us a sign to prove to them he is alive."

Treia said nothing with her mouth. Her dark eyes glittered with anger. Her pale face remained impassive, giving no hint of her thoughts, but Norgaard noted her hands curling tightly over the arms of the chair, the knuckles white.

Skylan, pleased with his own cleverness, saw nothing of the Priestess's inner turmoil.

Norgaard saw, and hope died within him. Treia knew all was not well in heaven. She feared that if she called upon Torval for a sign, the god would not respond, and that would embolden the ogres, who—Torval knew—did not need emboldening.

At least now, Norgaard understood why the ogres had arranged for the parley. The knowledge that the gods had abandoned them would devastate his people, weaken their resolve. Undoubtedly that was why the ogres chose to talk instead of fight. The lives of the Torgun people depended on what Treia said and did, Norgaard realized, and he desperately wished that he knew her better, had some idea of how she would react.

Treia was newly arrived in the village. Although she was Torgun and had been born here, she had been sent away from home at the age of twelve, bartered to the Dragon Goddess by her mother, Holma, in hopes that Vindrash would spare her husband's life. Treia had gone across the bay to Vindraholm, the capital city of the Vindrasi nation, to study to be a Bone Priestess. Apparently the barter worked. Her father had lived many years afterwards. Unfortunately Treia did not know. She never again saw him.

Treia had remained in Vindraholm for sixteen years, during which time she had been initiated into the secrets of the gods. She had returned to the Torgun less than a year ago, when their Bone Priestess had died of eating tainted eels.

A morose woman, Treia was twenty-eight years old and still unmarried, with no man eager to seek her hand. She was not unattractive. She had pale skin and thick blond hair, a long narrow face, and a slender figure. Men might have been more interested in her if she ever smiled. Nothing pleased Treia or made her happy. Even during festivals, when everyone else in the village was celebrating, Treia regarded the merrymaking with disdain and would take the first opportunity to escape back to her dwelling.

Treia was extremely nearsighted, and she had developed a squint whenever she looked intently at something. Her squint and the uncanny ability she had of appearing to know what a person was thinking gave rise to the notion that she had the power to see through flesh and bone to the soul. Because of this, most of the people in the village—including the men—were daunted by her. After giving Skylan one irate look, Treia lowered her dark eyes, staring at the floor. Her sister whispered something to her. Treia shook her head.

Most of the Torgun warriors were watching Treia with smug smiles, confidently waiting for their Bone Priestess to scornfully deny the ogre's outrageous claims and call down the wrath of Torval upon them. But Norgaard noted that some were not so confident. Those men had been on the ill-fated expedition with his son, and all of them were remembering that during the raid, Treia had tried to summon the Dragon Kahg to fight for them and the dragon had not responded.

Treia had told them that Vindrash, the Dragon Goddess, was displeased with them. But what if Vindrash had not been merely displeased? What if the Dragon Goddess had been vanquished, driven out of heaven?

Treia did not speak, and now all the Torgun warriors were growing uneasy. Norgaard gave a low growl, indicating that Treia needed to say something and she needed to do it fast. The Priestess gave him a sidelong glance and then rose slowly to her feet.

Her movements were graceful, majestic. Her dark eyes shone with myopic luster. Her pale cheeks were stained red. She cast a sweeping glance around the longhouse, and her gaze came to rest on the ogres. Such was her proud and haughty demeanor that even they appeared respectful. She spoke directly to the shaman.

"I am going to the shrine of Vindrash. There I will call upon your gods and mine," said Treia. "I will wait to hear which gods answer me. I will be at my prayers all night. I am not to be disturbed."

Head held high, she walked out of the longhouse. As she passed Norgaard, Treia cast him a look that said as plain as speech, *I have bought you time. Use it well!*

The ogre guards, after a nod from their shaman, stepped aside and allowed Treia to depart the hall. The Torgun warriors fell back to give her room. One offered to escort her, but she scornfully refused.

Aylaen had been caught off guard by her sister's sudden decisive move. After a moment's hesitation, Aylaen hurried to follow Treia, who was already out the door. The ogres made no move to stop her, though they ogled her as she hurried past them, and one ogre made what was obviously a lewd comment to the other, who grinned.

Skylan did not hear what was said, but he could guess, and he reached again for his sword. Garn seized hold of his arm and whispered urgently in his ear, and for once Skylan listened.

The three ogre godlords consulted with their shaman. Norgaard remained silent, as did the Torgun warriors gathered in the longhouse. They did this ostensibly out of courtesy, but every man there had his ears stretched, trying to hear what was being said.

The ogres kept their voices low. Norgaard rose to his feet, and under the pretense of easing his crippled leg, he limped closer to hear better.

Absorbed in their talk, the ogres did not notice him.

The ogres spoke rapidly. Norgaard could understand only about one word in five, but he heard enough to realize that the ogres were confounded, uncertain what to do. The ogres had urged the Torgun to accept their gods, known as the Gods of Raj, and now the Torgun Bone Priestess had said she was going off to pray to the Gods of Raj. The ogres might or might not believe her (clearly one of the godlords did not), but the shaman insisted that they could not now attack the Torgun. The ogres had to give the Gods of Raj a chance to respond. Doing anything else would be an insult to the gods and, as the shaman pointed out, the ogres were a long way from home with miles of treacherous ocean to cross. It would not be wise to anger the gods.

That last argument convinced the godlords. Ogres did not love the sea, as did the Vindrasi, and the sea did not love ogres.

Having heard enough, Norgaard limped back to resume his seat.

After another few moments' conferring, the tiger-skin godlord spoke. "We are confident in the powerful and mighty Gods of Raj. We give your

Priestess time to pray to them. We will hear her answer—and yours—this night. In the meantime, we will tell you more of our gods at the great feast you will give this night in our honor."

Norgaard sighed. Feeding the ogres would deplete the Torgun's already meager food supply, but he did not dare insult them by refusing.

The ogre godlords made ready to take their leave, as did the shaman, his feathers rustling. Norgaard walked with them. At a gesture from him, his Torgun warriors remained where they were. The sight of all his men suddenly rushing at them might have alarmed their guests.

Norgaard escorted the godlords from the longhouse and sent four warriors with them.

"Make certain they return to their ships," he ordered the men. "Remain where you can keep an eye on them."

Norgaard watched the massive ogres walk ponderously away. He had what was left of this day to try to devise a plan to save his people.

Not much time, but it was better than nothing.

When the men reported that the ogres were back aboard their ships, Norgaard called a meeting of the Torgun Council, which was made up of all the heads of families, male and, in some cases, female if a woman's husband had died and she had not remarried. Skylan, as future Chief, was also in attendance, as was Garn, because he was always with Skylan.

Norgaard described the situation: "Tomorrow morning, we must either surrender to the ogres and give in to their demands, which means we must hand over forty-three head of cattle, thirteen bars of silver, seven men, including my son, and our dragonship. Or we fight—"

"Fight," said Skylan loudly.

"—an army that outnumbers us almost two to one," Norgaard finished, his voice grating.

"Where is the choice in this?" Skylan demanded impatiently. "Of course, we must fight."

"And we will be slaughtered," said Norgaard.

"We cannot lose," said Skylan. "Torval is with us." He reverently touched the silver axe he wore around his throat.

"Was Torval with you on your last raid?" Norgaard asked dryly.

The Council waited for Skylan's answer, though all knew what it was. Skylan's last raid had gained nothing and brought the ogres down on them.

"The god was not with us," Skylan said. "And now I know why. Torval and Vindrash were fighting a great battle of their own. A battle they did *not* lose, no matter what these ugly sons of ugly whores say!"

He added, with an irate glance at his father, "Are you saying we should surrender, give in to their demands?"

"It is true that if we fight, we may well die," said Sigurd, one of the Council members. "But if we give the ogres all our cattle, we will certainly die—of starvation. I choose to end my life clutching a sword, not my empty belly."

Sigurd was both uncle and stepfather to Treia and Aylaen. When Aylaen's own father, Myrdill, had died, Sigurd made his widowed sister-in-law an offer of marriage, not out of any care for her or her children, but to gain his brother's property. Aylaen's mother, Holma, had accepted because she needed a husband to assist with the labor involved in tending the farm. Not many people liked Sigurd. He was a dour, implacable man who openly kept a concubine, by whom he'd had two sons. He was good to them, whereas he treated his wife and stepdaughters like slaves. Aylaen loathed her stepfather and avoided him whenever possible.

The other Council members gave their opinions. All were loud and passionate in their agreement that the Torgun should fight.

"I am all for fighting," Norgaard said. "But I would like to have some chance of winning."

No one could argue that point. Skylan could boast that one Torgun warrior was worth two ogres, but the elders in the Council knew the boast was empty. Ogres might have faces like toddlers and smell like pigs, but when forced to fight, they were excellent warriors, savage and strong, and they were now backed by powerful gods.

Whereas the gods of the Torgun . . .

"May I speak?" Garn asked in low, deferential tones. He was not one of the Council, and thus had no right to participate in the meeting unless he was granted permission.

"Yes," said Skylan quickly to forestall anyone who might object.

Norgaard readily gave his assent. He had raised Garn, and he loved him like a son. Sometimes he loved Garn better than his own son, for which he often felt guilty. Norgaard had long hoped that Skylan might learn some of Garn's wisdom and patience. Thus far, his plan had not worked; Skylan was as impetuous and foolhardy as ever. Still, Norgaard was pleased that Skylan had sense enough to value Garn's good qualities.

"We should fight the ogres, but not alone," said Garn. "Help lies on the other side of the fjord."

The Gymir Fjord was a narrow stretch of deep water that cut inland between tall cliffs separating the Torgun from the mainland of Kharajis and the other clans of the Vindrasi. The Heudjun, the largest, wealthiest, and strongest of the eight major clans, lived in the lord city of Vindraholm, located on the other side of the fjord. Horg, the current Chief of Chiefs, the most powerful man in the Vindrasi nation, was also the Chief of the Heudjun Clan. His wife, Draya, was Kai Priestess.

"Horg has many dragonships and many warriors," said Norgaard thoughtfully. "His wife is close to the gods. They would answer her, if they are able to answer anyone."

Skylan grunted. "I hear Horg has lost his nerve and now searches for it at the bottom of a cider barrel."

"Horg is a warrior," Norgaard said sternly. The Chief of Chiefs was near Norgaard's age, and he could understand what youth could not. "His warrior's heart will not fail him."

"Whether Horg is or is not a drunken swine makes no difference," Sigurd said impatiently. "The ogres have seized our dragonship. We have no way to send for help."

Someone suggested swimming, but someone else pointed out that though the days were warm, the deep water of the fjord was chill. The swimmer would die of the cold before he made it halfway across. As for traveling overland, the fjord extended many miles inland; trying to walk around it would take days.

"Garn has a plan," said Skylan. "He would not have brought this up otherwise."

"Well, Garn? If you do have a plan, let us hear it," said Norgaard.

"We do not need ships or swimmers to summon aid. We will light the beacon fire."

An ancient means of summoning the clans to war, the beacon fire alerted the other clans to danger and called for help. Clans were bound by ancient law to respond to a beacon fire. Horg and his warriors would see it and know there was trouble.

There was one problem with this plan, however.

"It won't work, Garn," Norgaard said, sighing. He'd let his hopes be raised, only now to have them dashed. "Ogres also use beacon fires. They would see us gathering the wood and building the fire, and they would know we were trying to summon help. They would attack us on the spot."

"Not if their bellies are full of boar meat," said Garn.

The others stared at him, perplexed, not understanding. Skylan gave a great guffaw and slapped his leg, forgetting about his wound.

"Explain your plan to these slow-wits, brother," he said, pressing his hand against his thigh with a grimace.

"The ogres ordered us to give a great feast in their honor," said Garn. "We will serve them wild boar."

He paused, looking around, thinking that they must understand him now.

"Boar roasted over a great fire," said Skylan triumphantly.

The Council members grinned in sudden understanding, and several applauded. Norgaard, turning over the plan in his mind, could find no flaw. Ogres had voracious appetites, especially for meat. These ogres had been at sea a long time, probably forced to live on fish (which ogres detested) and cold peas, not the red meat they relished. He had noted them sniffing hungrily at the smells coming from the stewpots and ovens of the Torgun.

"A good idea, Garn," Norgaard said simply, and Garn flushed with pleasure at the praise.

Skylan was enthusiastic. "Horg and his warriors will see the beacon fire. They will sail before dawn, and when the ogres wake, *they* will find themselves outnumbered two to one. The water will be red with ogre blood. Their death cries will rise to the heavens, as will the smoke of their burning ships.

"Who knows," he added, grinning, "the ogres might even pitch in to help us build the fire that will mean their doom!"

The decision of the Council to approve Garn's plan was unanimous.

# CHAPTER 4

The ogre godlords were pleased with the invitation to feast on roasted boar meat. Garn, who went to issue the invitation on behalf of Norgaard, related that one of the godlords even began to drool at the thought. Garn appointed the time of moonrise, when Akaria, Goddess of the Waters and Ruler of the Tides, would lift her lantern.

The godlords said they would attend, and added that they would be bringing their bodyguards and their shaman with them. Garn calculated that this came to about fifteen hungry ogres. Norgaard sighed deeply. The Torgun did not have much food to spare, and what they did have was going into the bellies of their enemies. His one consolation was that on the morrow the ogres would be feasting in their afterlife.

Garn's next task, given to him by Norgaard, was to convince Skylan, who disliked being "prayed over," to have his wound healed. Skylan protested, but not so loudly as usual, and at last, he agreed to go seek out the Bone Priestess.

The truth was that the pain and loss of blood had caught up with Skylan during the last portion of the Council meeting. He'd come very close to passing out. Only a fierce determination not to show weakness before the other warriors kept him from succumbing to his injuries. The fear that he might be too weak to fight in tomorrow's battle drove him to seek what he generally tried to avoid—help.

Garn was going to accompany him to the Hall of Vindrash, but Skylan told him to go with the rest of the men into the forested hills to cut trees for the fire. "I will go, I promise," said Skylan, and he grasped the silver axe he wore around his neck. "I swear by Torval."

Reassured, knowing this was one vow Skylan would never break, Garn headed into the forest.

"There is just one problem. I have to find some explanation that will satisfy the ogres about why we have to build two fires," Garn said as he was leaving. "We cannot very well roast meat over a raging beacon fire."

Skylan laughed. "Tell the ogres one fire is for roasting the boar's head and the other the rump. They're ogres. They'll believe anything."

Wishing his friend well, Garn continued up the path that led into the hills. Skylan veered off toward the Hall of Vindrash, walking the empty streets, passing empty houses.

The silence was oppressive. Generally, this time of day, as the Sun Goddess, Aylis, started her downward descent into the sea, women would be making final preparations for supper. The air would be redolent with the smells of baking bread and bubbling stewpots. Children would be laughing and playing outside. The men would be coming home from tending the herds or toiling in the fields or forging iron or whatever each did to earn his place in the clan. They would gather in small groups, discussing the day's news and awaiting the summons to supper.

"It's as if everyone died," Skylan muttered.

Too late, he realized what he'd said. One did not speak of death on the eve of battle. He quickly touched the silver axe, asking Torval to avert the evil omen.

Each clan had its own Hall of Vindrash—generally small, not nearly so large or grand as the Great Hall of the Gods in Vindraholm. A simple structure, the Hall built by the Torgun was constructed along the lines of the Chief's Hall, only much smaller. Near the Hall was another longhouse, the residence of the Bone Priestess.

The Hall and the longhouse were located some distance from the village, in a small clearing in the midst of the forest. Both were kept in excellent repair by the men of the village. Treia had a small garden, where she grew herbs used in healing. Otherwise, the people of the village supported the Bone Priestess with gifts of food and hides, cooking pots and furs, and whatever else she might require.

Skylan found Aylaen pacing outside the closed door of the Hall of Vindrash. She smiled at him. He smiled to see her. He'd hoped to find her here, another reason he'd decided to ask for Treia's help. Her gaze softened when she looked at the bloody gash in his thigh.

"You are white as milk," Aylaen said. She eyed his blood-soaked clothing worriedly.

"Most of that blood is the boar's," Skylan said proudly.

Her concern was a pleasant surprise. Usually whenever Aylaen encountered him, she found some reason to mock or laugh at him. He was warmed to think she cared about him.

"Sit down on the ground. Let me see."

Skylan eased himself down. Aylaen gently tried to peel away the blood-gummed bandages that had stuck to the wound. He flinched and gasped with the pain.

"It looks bad," said Aylaen. "It's all inflamed."

"I have to fight tomorrow," said Skylan. "I need your sister to intercede with the Goddess Desiria for me."

Aylaen glanced doubtfully at the closed door. "Treia said she was not to be disturbed."

Aylaen's well-meaning ministrations had opened the wound again. Blood flowed freely. Skylan, now that he was sitting, was not sure he could get back up again.

"She must," he said. "I am the War Chief."

Aylaen nodded and went to knock gently on the door.

"Sister, I am sorry to disturb your prayers, but Skylan Ivorson is here. He is wounded, and he needs the healing blessings of the Goddess Desiria."

Skylan heard footsteps approaching the door. It opened a tiny crack. Treia peered out.

"I can do nothing for him," she said coldly, and started to shut the door.

"Sister, look at him!" Aylaen cried, seizing hold of the door and holding it ajar. She gestured to Skylan. "See how ill he is—"

Treia's nearsighted glance flicked over him.

"I can do nothing," she repeated, and she slammed the door shut.

"Your sister has never liked me," Skylan said. "I don't know why. I've never done anything to her."

Aylaen stood staring at the closed door, a dreamy haze clouding her eyes.

"It has nothing to do with you," she said. "The gods weep. Aylis hides her face in grief. Akaria screams and tears her hair. . . ."

"Aylaen," said Skylan sharply.

Aylaen looked at him and blinked. "What?"

"You are not a bard, and this is no time for storytelling," he said impatiently. "We have outgrown make-believe. Besides," he added, frowning, "the gods will take offense. Making up such stories about them is disrespectful."

"I don't mean to be. I like to think of them as a family." Aylaen's smile dimmed; her expression darkened. "Not as *my* family. A family that loves and cares for each other."

Skylan struggled to his feet, his hand pressed over his thigh.

"I will talk to your sister," he said, and he started for the door.

"I don't think that would be wise," said Aylaen hurriedly. "I have an idea. Owl Mother lives close by—"

"That old crone! Never mind. I am feeling much better. I must return to the village. Garn will need my help—"

Skylan took a step, swayed dizzily, and sagged to his knees. Aylaen knelt down beside him and slipped her arm around his midriff.

"Put your arm across my shoulder," she ordered.

Skylan was too weak to argue. He did as she told him.

Aylaen's body pressed against his, and with her help, he was able to stand. Skylan could feel the softness of her breast beneath the wool of her gown, the firmness of her thigh, the play of her muscles, and desire outdid his pain.

Aylaen was tall for a woman, above average height, and she was strong, for she had done hard physical labor on the family farm from childhood onward. She had no trouble supporting Skylan's weight. Her red mass of curls—so different from the silky blond hair of the rest of her family—brushed against his cheek.

No one else in the Torgun had red hair. There were whispers that the man who had been married to her mother was not her real father. Perhaps that was one reason Sigurd seemed to have so little fondness for his brother's wife.

"Owl Woman won't be in her dwelling," said Skylan huskily. The ache of desire warred with his pain. "She would have gone into the hills with the other women."

He'd never been this close to Aylaen, not since they were children and had played their rough-and-tumble games. He'd wanted to hold her, the gods knew! But he could never bring himself to touch her, which was odd, because he'd had no such inhibitions regarding other women.

He could still have his pick of those women, but he wanted only one, and that was Aylaen. He thought of her constantly, dreamed of her at night to wake with a groan of longing. He spent hours imagining what he would say to her that would cause her eyes to glow with desire for him. And yet, when he started to say the words, Aylaen would mock him and laugh at him, pretending she didn't understand.

She did understand; he was certain of it. He was convinced she wanted him as much as he wanted her. Women liked to tease a man, toy with him as fox kits toy with a dead rabbit.

Skylan slowed his steps. "Let me rest a moment with you. The two of us together, here, where it is quiet—"

His arm tightened suggestively around her shoulder.

"I have left my sister alone too long already," said Aylaen. "As for Owl Mother, she will be in her dwelling. She would never leave her animals. Just a little farther, brother—"

"Don't call me that!" Skylan ordered angrily.

"Why not?" Aylaen asked pertly. "That's how I think of you."

"I don't want you to think of me that way!" Skylan said. "You are my betrothed. Soon you will be my wife."

"You don't need a wife. You have too many women already," Aylaen said teasingly.

"I have not slept with anyone in two years!"

Aylaen's eyes widened. She was mocking him. "Truly?"

Skylan made a dismissive gesture. "I want you and no other."

"I was jesting," she said.

"I wasn't," he replied.

Aylaen flushed and lowered her eyes in confusion. "Skylan, there is something I must tell you—"

"Stop right there, whoever you are!" said a warning voice. "One more step, and I'll set the wolves on you."

The sound of a low, rumbling growl caused Skylan to draw his knife.

"We should leave!" he said.

Aylaen ignored him, as usual.

"It's Aylaen, Owl Mother, and Skylan Ivorson. He was gored by a boar. He needs your help."

"Let the gods heal him," came the scornful reply. "I have work to do."

"Perhaps you have not heard, Owl Mother. Ogres came to the village and—"

"I know about the ogres. The crows told me. What has that to do with anything?"

Aylaen and Skylan exchanged glances.

"The ogres said there was a great battle in heaven, Owl Mother," Aylaen replied. "They claim our gods were defeated—"

Her words were met by silence.

"We're getting out of here," Skylan said insistently.

Aylaen shook her head.

Skylan glared at her, exasperated. "I say we're leaving."

"And I say we're not," she flared, her temper as fiery as her flame-colored hair. "You don't tell me what to do, Skylan Ivorson. No one tells me what to do. And, in case you've forgotten, you may have to fight tomorrow. Look at yourself! You can't even walk without help!"

Skylan drew in a seething breath. He recalled what he'd said earlier in the day about Torval having difficulty controlling the women in his family.

"Let the son of Norgaard come forward!" Owl Mother said grudgingly.

Aylaen started to help him, but he shoved her away.

"I can manage on my own. Wait for me here."

Once again, Aylaen disobeyed. He looked back to see her walking along behind him. He shook his head. Things would be different once they were married.

Skylan emerged from the forest into a clearing. Here, he halted again, looking warily about, wondering where the old woman was and, more important, what she had done with the wolves. Skylan had never been to Owl Mother's dwelling. There had been no need. Desiria, Goddess of Life, had always thought well of him and given him her blessing. Skylan felt a flash of annoyance at the goddess for having forced him to resort to fae magic.

In the center of the clearing was a longhouse that was well constructed, small, and snug. There was a large garden, newly planted. Six deer stood grazing calmly on grass around the cabin. At the sight of Skylan, the deer fled, white tails flashing.

Six deer! And he and Garn had spent days searching and not seen one. Ducks waddled about the yard. Chickens pecked at the ground. Birds twittered and called.

Owl Mother was nowhere in sight, but the door to the cabin stood open. Moving closer, he saw animal pens in the rear of the house. A calf with a bandage around its leg, looking very sorry for himself, stood in one. A couple of goats were in another. Owl Mother was known for her skill in treating sick animals. People in the village would either send for her or bring the animals to her. A cat, missing an ear, strolled along one of the fence posts. The cat paused to lick its front paw and stare at Skylan. It didn't appear impressed.

Aylaen came to stand beside Skylan.

"Go home, girl!" Owl Mother yelled from the house. "You're not needed. This is between me and the son of Norgaard."

Aylaen looked uncertainly at Skylan. "Will you be all right?"

"Of course. Go back to your sister," he said.

"Don't be mad, Skylan," Aylaen said softly.

She kissed him on the cheek, as a sister might kiss a brother, and then she turned and walked back along the trail.

Skylan watched her until he lost sight of her among the trees; then he looked at the dwelling. He saw no sign of anyone. He was growing increasingly impatient; his wounds burned and throbbed.

"Put down the knife," said Owl Mother. "And then come inside."

Skylan did as he was told, dropping his knife onto the grass. The dwelling's interior was dark and shadowy. After the bright sunlight outside, Skylan was half-blinded, and he almost stepped on a large wolf that was reclining on the floor. The wolf reared to its feet with a snarl, hackles rising. Skylan stumbled backwards.

From somewhere in the darkness came a chuckle. "The wolf won't harm you. Not unless I tell him to. Just don't make any sudden moves or look him in the eye, and you'll be safe enough."

Skylan still could not see the woman.

"Don't just stand there like a lump, Son of Norgaard," Owl Mother said testily. "I have work to do, if you don't. Come into the kitchen where I can get a look at you."

Keeping one eye on the wolf, Skylan followed the sound of the voice. He entered a second room, which was dominated by a large fireplace. Owl Mother stood by the fire, stirring something in an iron pot.

Owl Mother was old, the oldest person in the village. She claimed to have seen seventy winters, and everyone believed her. Her hair was snow white, twisted in a long braid that extended below her waist. She wore a linen smock with a plain woolen gown over that, tied at her waist with a belt. With her hunched shoulders, beaky nose, and piercing eyes, she looked like a fierce old owl, though that was not how she had come by her name. She was called Owl Mother because of her way with animals.

"Sit," she said, and pointed a crooked finger at a three-legged stool.

Skylan had to first displace the stool's occupant, a squirrel, who raced across the floor and climbed a post that led to the rafters. He took his seat, looking about the shadowy longhouse, wondering uneasily what other creatures might be present. Owl Mother was known to consort with the fae folk who inhabited the woods.

Apparently the old woman was alone. He saw no gnomes lurking beneath the table, nor were imps cavorting around the fireplace. He did note that one corner of the room was concealed by a tapestry hanging from the rafters. The tapestry appeared to be very old, for it was worn and frayed in places. He regarded it with interest, for it portrayed a battle with warriors clad in strange-looking armor.

Owl Mother bent over him, examining the wound, sniffing at it and probing it with her fingers. She was not at all gentle. Skylan gritted his teeth and tried to keep silent, though now and then a grunt escaped him.

Finally Owl Mother straightened. "You had the good sense to use the salve. The wound will heal cleanly. Bathe in the sea every day, smear on the salve, eat red meat to restore the blood, and keep to your bed for three days. Do all that, and you will suffer no lasting effects."

"I thank you, Owl Mother," said Skylan respectfully. "But I don't have three days. We are lighting the beacon fire to summon the warriors of the Heudjun to come to our aid. There will be a battle with the ogres tomorrow, and I must lead the Torgun to war."

Owl Mother stood with her thin lips pursed, staring down her nose at him. "You want magic," she said at last.

Not really, Skylan thought, but he didn't seem to have much choice.

"I'm not sure," he said at last. "What does it involve?"

"It will cost you," said Owl Mother, crossing her arms over her breasts.

Skylan frowned. He had a few silver ingots and coins in his coffer, but he was saving all his wealth to pay the bride-price for Aylaen.

"I don't want your silver!" Owl Mother scoffed, seeing the doubt on his face. "You must agree to serve me for one day, do whatever I ask of you. Don't worry," she added dryly, "I won't ask you to dance with me naked in the moonlight."

Skylan's face burned. He didn't know what to say. He wanted to be polite, but he couldn't imagine a more repulsive sight.

Owl Mother laughed at him. "I need a man for only one thing these days, and that's to help me with chores. There's wood to be chopped and pens to be mended and—"

"I will serve you, Owl Mother," said Skylan hastily. He wanted to get this over with.

"Very well. I will do what I can. The magic is chancy, uncertain. I don't promise anything."

Owl Mother walked over to the part of the room concealed by the tapestry. She drew on a large leather glove and reached out her hand to pull the tapestry aside. Pausing, she glanced at Skylan.

"You must hold perfectly still," she warned him. "Do not speak or cry out, no matter what you see. She is a young one and startles easily."

Owl Mother disappeared behind the tapestry. He could hear an annoyed-sounding squawk and then Owl Mother's voice speaking softly, lovingly, clucking and cajoling. Owl Mother came out from behind the tapestry. Perched on her gloved arm was an enormous bird. Skylan thought at first it was the largest hawk he'd ever seen.

Owl Mother drew closer, bringing the bird into the light.

Skylan was so astonished, he started to rise off the stool, then remembered, too late, he was not to make any sudden moves. The bird was not a bird. The bird was a beast, and the beast was a wyvern. At Skylan's involuntary start, the wyvern reared back her head, flapped her wings, and screeched at him.

"I warned you to keep still, fool!" Owl Mother hissed angrily.

Skylan froze and forced himself to sit quietly, though his muscles shook with the effort. He liked to think he wasn't afraid of anything, but magic was different. The bravest, boldest warrior could be excused for fearing the power of those who had been old when the gods themselves were young. His stomach clenched and his bowels gripped.

The wyvern's red eyes glared at him. Her reptilian scales glistened orange in the firelight. Her wings, made of membrane stretched between the fine, delicate bones, were so thin he could see the light shine through them. Her long tail curled over Owl Mother's wrist. Two clawed feet dug into the leather glove.

The wyvern looked deceptively like a dragon, but there was no relation, as Skylan well knew. He was accustomed to dragons, who had long been allies of the Vindrasi. The spiritbone of the great Dragon Kahg hung from a nail on the mast of the dragonship. The spirit of the dragon sailed with them, and when summoned by the prayers of the Bone Priestess, the dragon would take on physical form to join Skylan and his forces in battle.

Dragons were thinking, reasoning, intelligent beings, gifted with miraculous powers bestowed on them by their Dragon Goddess, Vindrash, consort of Torval.

The Vindrasi believed wyverns were made of magic in mockery of dragons. Wyverns belonged to the Nethervold, the twilight world of the fae folk. Most of mankind could not see the Nethervold. But there were some, like Owl Mother, who had learned how to draw aside the curtain of moonbeams and stardust that kept the two worlds apart. She had now opened that curtain for Skylan, and he was sorry he'd ever agreed to come.

"I think I should go. . . ." He spoke through stiff lips.

"Don't move, and keep your mouth shut," Owl Mother told him. "Or you'll get us both killed."

Holding the nervous wyvern on her arm, Owl Mother dipped her fingers in Skylan's blood and traced a rune on his forehead and a similar rune on her own forehead. She placed her hand on the rune on Skylan's head and began to hum.

Her humming grew louder and louder, a single, jarring, off-key note that spread from her throat throughout her body. At the sound of her humming, the wyvern closed her eyes. She seemed entranced. Her wings folded at her sides. Her clawed feet eased their grip. She began to make a noise of her own, a high-pitched keening wail that was painful to the ears.

Except for a splitting headache, Skylan felt no different. He was disappointed and angered. All this fear and discomfort for nothing, and now he was bound by his word to do menial labor for this crazy old crone—

The magic burned him like a cauterizing iron, searing his flesh. He tried to bear the agony like a warrior, but he couldn't manage. He fell onto the floor, writhing with pain, and finally passed out.

He woke, choking on something, to find Owl Mother bending over him. Seeing he was conscious, she reached into his mouth to pluck out a wad of cloth.

"So you wouldn't swallow your tongue," she told him.

Skylan looked nervously about for the wyvern. The beast was gone. He cast a glance at the tapestry and saw it was closed again. Relieved, he sank back on the floor, drawing in welcome breaths, and realized, suddenly, that he was no longer in pain. Sitting up, he examined his wound in the firelight.

Owl Mother had washed off the blood while he'd been unconscious. The wound had closed, leaving a long jagged weal that was tender to the touch. He no longer felt weak. Elated, he jumped to his feet and immediately regretted the sudden movement. The wound still hurt when he put his weight on his leg. He would in the future continue to rely on Desiria's blessing. But at least he would be strong enough to slay ogres in the morning.

"Thank you, Owl Mother," he said.

Pleased and grateful, he kissed her weathered cheek.

Owl Mother chuckled and shook her finger at him. "Don't try to seduce me now. I don't have time. You had best be going or you'll be late."

Skylan looked out the dwelling's single window and was startled to see darkness. Night had fallen. Stars shone brightly.

"We are having a great feast tonight, Owl Mother," said Skylan. "I killed a wild boar, and we are roasting it. I would be honored if you came."

"I'm not much of a meat eater these days," Owl Mother said, picking up a basin filled with water. "I can't digest it."

"Let me carry that," Skylan offered, taking the basin from her and carrying it to the door. He tossed the water, stained red with his blood, out onto the grass.

"There will be a battle tomorrow," said Skylan as he prepared to take his leave. “We will win it, of course, but you may not be safe here. You should go into the hills.”

Owl Mother grinned and jerked a thumb to indicate the corner screened by the tapestry.

“My friends will take care of me,” she said complacently. “You should concern yourself with yourself, young Skylan.”

“They are only ogres,” said Skylan.

“Only ogres.” Owl Mother smiled derisively. “The thread of your wyrd snaps tonight, Skylan.”

He stared at her, shocked. When a man’s wyrd snapped, he died.

She poked him in the chest with her finger. “Tomorrow your wyrd is spun anew. Try not to screw it up.”

She left him, disappearing into the kitchen. He paused a moment, wondering what she had meant. It made no sense.

“Crazy old crone,” he muttered.

“I almost forgot,” Owl Mother yelled at him. “You must honor my mysteries, young man. Tell no one what happened here.”

“I will not, Owl Mother,” said Skylan. He had no intention of ever thinking about it again, let alone telling anyone. He clasped the silver axe. “I swear by Torval.”

“Torval!” Owl Mother cackled. “He’s got his own problems. Speaking of which, you had better leave now. The wheel turns.”

Bright orange light flared in the night sky.

The Torgun had lit the beacon fire.

## CHAPTER 5

In the lord city of Vindraholm, across the Gymir Fjord from the Torgun town of Luda, Draya, Kai Priestess of the Vektia, kneeled before the statue of the Dragon Goddess, Vindrash, and in a tear-choked voice beseeched the goddess to answer her.

The Great Hall of the Gods in Vindraholm embodied the soul of the Vindrasi nation. The Hall had been constructed many, many years ago, during a period of Vindrasi prosperity, and it was considered one of the marvels of the nation. Designed by the famous Chief of Chiefs Beocik Sundgridr, the Great Hall of the Gods was built in the shape of a Vindrasi dragonship; the only difference being that the enormous "ship" had two "prows"—each carved in the shape of the head of a fierce dragon. The Great Hall stood on a high point of land overlooking the sea, and the head of one dragon stared out across the waves while the other gazed back on land. Thus, it was said, no enemy could sneak up on the Vindrasi.

The outer walls of the Great Hall were decorated with the colorful shields of all the Vindrasi clans, placed as they would be placed on the rack along the sides of a dragonship. The roof was made of wood, not thatch, and the Great Hall had a wooden floor, resembling the deck of a ship.

The interior of the Great Hall was shadowy and windowless. A single opening in the ceiling above a fire pit allowed the light of the Sun Goddess, Aylis, to illuminate and bless the Hall. In the winter months, the Kai Priestess lit a small fire to keep her warm as she went about her duties. Such a fire would have been welcome to Draya now. The day had been hot, but the sun had set prematurely, the goddess hiding her bright face behind a scarf of clouds. The air inside the Great Hall was chill, and Draya shivered in her heavy robes.

She could have summoned one of the young acolytes to light a fire. She knew quite well it would be useless, to say nothing of the fact that the girl would look at her strangely for requesting a fire in the middle of the hottest spring anyone could remember. It was not cold that raised the flesh on Draya's arms and caused her hands to tremble as she clasped them in supplication. It was fear. Fear caused the tears to well up in her eyes, so that the statue of Vindrash blurred in the waning light. Fear choked Draya's voice as she begged the goddess to break her silence and once more speak to her devoted servant.

The statue of Vindrash, the Dragon Goddess, was the Great Hall's centerpiece. Carved of a rare and exotic stone known as jadeite, the statue was translucent emerald green. Beautifully detailed, down to each individual scale on the dragon's body, the statue had two large rubies for eyes, and fangs carved of ivory. The statue was prized beyond measure, for neither the stone jadeite nor ivory could be found in this part of the world.

The statue had been brought to Vindraholm by the same Chief who had designed the Great Hall, the legendary warrior Beocik. After the Hall had been built, Beocik stated that he would sail the world to find the perfect representation of the Dragon Vindrash, the patron goddess of his people. He set out on his dragonship with thirty men. Years passed, and he did not return. Everyone assumed, sorrowfully, that Beocik had perished. And then one morning, his dragonship sailed into the bay. It had no crew. The ship had been guided by the spirit of the dragon, and it bore the body of the

Chief wrapped in his cloak and covered with his shield, and the wondrous statue.

The statue was the length of a man's arm from elbow to fingertip, extremely heavy and so valuable that a special hiding place had been created for it, a large hole dug out of the ground beneath the floorboards of the Great Hall. When an enemy threatened, the statue could be lowered into the hole, which was then covered by wooden planking. The Great Hall of the Gods was the only building in the city of Vindraholm to have a wooden floor, and this was the reason.

Draya gazed into the statue's ruby eyes.

"Vindrash," she whispered, hoarse from days of fruitless pleading, "let me know if I have somehow offended you! If I did, I did not mean to. I will do whatever you ask of me to make amends. I would endure any pain, gladly suffer any punishment if you would only speak to me. I cannot bear your silence!"

Years ago, when Draya had been newly chosen by the Kai Moot as Kai Priestess, she had gone to her prayers with joy in her heart, as though meeting a dear friend. Draya and the goddess had formed a special bond, one that was unusually close. Other Kai Priestesses had placed ambition and love of power above their faith, but Draya was a devoted follower, sincere in her worship. She had dedicated her life to the goddess, and the goddess had rewarded her by speaking to her on an almost daily basis.

As the years passed and times grew hard for the Vindrasi, the goddess did not come so often. Draya blamed herself. She had been too importunate, constantly badgering the goddess to intervene with the other gods, imploring Svanses to ease the harsh winters or persuading Akaria to bring rain to end summer droughts. Draya had at last sensed Vindrash's sorrow and her helplessness, and the priestess quit making such demands. When the goddess came to her, neither of them spoke. They comforted each other.

But now a fortnight had passed, and in that time Vindrash had not appeared to Draya at all. The priestess was spending almost all her days and most of her nights in the Hall, neglecting her many duties, forbidding anyone to disturb her, even forbidding the other Bone Priestesses and acolytes from entering the Hall.

Draya had told no one about the goddess's refusal to speak to her, keeping the goddess's secrets as Draya kept her own. Draya was Kai Priestess, a position of honor many women coveted. If they had known the truth of her life, they would have pitied her deeply—and that was the very reason none knew the truth. Draya was too proud to let anyone see her suffering.

Thirteen years ago, the Kai Priestess had died, and Draya, at the age of seventeen, had been chosen by the Kai Moot to be their leader. Their choice had been presented to the gods for approval, and Draya received a clear sign of Vindrash's favor—on that night, a star fell from the sky. (One Bone Priestess had argued that a falling star was a sign of doom, not a mark of approval, but all knew she wanted the position for herself, and no one paid heed to her.)

Draya had been elated, and her joy was complete on the day she was married to Horg Thekkson, Chief of Chiefs. Draya had no say in her marriage; the Kai Priestess was always the consort of the Chief of Chiefs. She had not minded. She fancied herself in love with the bold and handsome Chief.

Horg Thekkson had been thirty years old then, and despite his age, he had been strong and brave and smart—or so he had seemed to the seventeen-year-old girl who knew little of life, having spent her years since the age of five in service to the gods. Sadly Draya soon came to learn that Horg was a sham—more cunning than smart, more brash than bold, more bully than brave.

Horg made it clear from the night of the wedding that he did not love her, nor was he even attracted to her. Horg liked plump, big-breasted women, and Draya was too thin and bony for his tastes. But Horg was thirty years old, and he still had no sons. So though he didn't like her, he used Draya like a breeding mare, coupling with her night after night, and then leaving her to spend the time more pleasantly with his latest concubine. Draya longed for a child herself, and she endured his brutish treatment without complaint.

Months passed, and Draya did not conceive. Horg blamed her. Draya blamed herself, until, shamed by his accusations, she began to make discreet inquiries. She discovered that Horg had never fathered a child by any woman, not even his numerous concubines. Life was difficult for Draya, but she took comfort in her duties as Kai Priestess. Then, about a year into their marriage, Horg was wounded in battle.

The wound—a spear thrust in his side—had not been bad. If he'd come to Draya and asked her to pray to Desiria to heal him, he would likely have recovered in a day or two. Instead, Horg had publicly spurned her. He had gone about telling everyone he did not trust the gods, who had given him a barren woman for his wife. He had sought treatment from one of his concubines, who claimed to have magical powers of healing. If she did, her magic had failed her. The wound festered. Horg was in terrible agony for many days, raving with fever. He finally recovered, but the wound had left deep and ugly scars on Horg's body and his mind.

He took to drinking hard cider, claiming that he did so to ease his pain. At least, he ceased his efforts to father a child with Draya. He no longer forced her to have sex with him. He beat her instead.

Horg blamed Draya and the gods for his problems and those of the Vindrasi people. He claimed he had lost faith in them. Draya suspected that this was just an excuse for him to take out his wrath on her. Horg hadn't lost his faith—a man couldn't lose something he'd never had. Draya hadn't lost faith, even though her prayers often went unanswered. Like a sailor washed overboard, she clung to her faith as to a piece of driftwood to keep herself from drowning.

Draya sighed deeply and sat back on her heels to gaze sadly at the statue. She felt closer to the gods than to people, and if she lost the goddess's trust and love, she did not think she could bear to go on living.

Draya heard raised voices and men shouting outside the Great Hall. Absorbed in her cares and her sorrows, she'd paid little heed. Only when one of her acolytes called for her by name did she rouse herself.

"Draya! Priestess, are you there?"

Draya wondered irritably why the girl didn't just enter; then she remembered that she'd forbidden anyone to come inside. The girl hovered in the doorway. She held a blazing torch in her hand, and Draya realized she had been sitting alone in the darkness all this time.

"Priestess?" the girl called again.

"I am here," Draya answered. "Wait a moment while I light the candles."

She had not known it was so late. The altar candles should have been lighted with the setting of the sun. The flame gleamed in the ruby eyes of the statue of Vindrash. Draya glanced at the statue and stood with her hand in midair, arrested by the statue's gleaming eyes. The ruby eyes stared at her, flickering as though alive. Their gaze was not warm and inviting. The eyes were cold and sharp, like the prickly light of a red star.

Draya stared so long, she forgot the lighted brand in her hand. The fire consumed the stick of wood, burning her fingers. She muttered in pain and dropped the brand and turned her attention to the acolyte. Draya could feel the statue's eyes still watching her.

"Yes, child, what is it?" Draya asked.

The girl was one of the young acolytes, about ten years old, and she was breathless from running and excitement.

"Trouble, Priestess!" the girl gasped. "The Torgun have lit the beacon fire!"

That was alarming news. The lighting of a beacon fire happened in only the most dire emergency, anything from plague to flood to an enemy invasion.

"Has Horg been told?" Draya asked immediately. "Has the Chief returned? Does he know?"

Horg had left a few days ago, telling her he was going to visit a neighboring clan. As Chief of Chiefs, he was required to travel among the clans, settling arguments before they turned into blood feuds, hearing grievances, handing down judgments. Disputes were constantly arising among the clans—fights over the shifting of a boundary stone, cattle stealing, a marriage arrangement gone bad.

Horg was supposed to keep disputes from devolving into war. Draya heard complaints by her Bone Priestesses that Horg was worse than useless. These trips for him were nothing more than an excuse for drunken revelry and a chance to sleep with any wretched female foolish enough to think she might gain something out of bedding the Chief of Chiefs.

Horg's failings meant that the Vindrasi nation was fractured, divided. Most of the clan chiefs had long ago lost respect for him, though they were careful not to show it. Horg might be too weak to do much good, but he was strong enough to do a great deal of harm.

"The Chief of Chiefs has returned," the girl reported. "He has gone to Torval's Rock to see for himself."

"Did Horg send you to fetch me?" Draya asked.

"No, Priestess," replied the acolyte innocently. "Some of the people wanted to know if you were coming. The Chief said you were at your prayers and not to be disturbed. He could deal with this. It was Priestess Fria who told me I was to fetch you."

Seeing Draya's face, the little girl faltered. "Did I do wrong, Priestess?"

"No, you did quite right, child," said Draya, curving her lips into the false smile that came so easily to her these days.

She took the torch from the girl and used it to light a torch of her own. She was leaving the Hall, just about to shut the door, when she heard a voice speak her name.

"Yes, child, what is it?" Draya asked.

"I didn't say anything, Priestess," said the girl.

Red light illuminated the Great Hall. The goddess's ruby eyes burned. Draya fancied she heard a breath whispering, "Make haste, Draya! Make haste!"

Draya did as the goddess commanded, walking as fast as she dared with only the torch to provide light. Draya would have been elated at once more hearing the goddess's beloved voice—if she had not heard that voice tremble with fear.

Vindraholm, the lord city of the Vindrasi nation, was many times larger than the Torgun village of Luda, for the Heudjun Clan, who had the honor of being the guardians of the lord city, was larger and wealthier than the Torgun.

But even the Heudjun were feeling the effects of a bad winter and the spring drought.

As Draya hastened through the streets, she saw a young woman seated near a longhouse door. The woman's eyes were sunken, her face pale and drawn. Draya knew her. The woman had recently lost her firstborn child. She stared at Draya as she hurried by. Draya had tried to save the child, but there had been nothing she could do except pray to Desiria, who had not responded. The tiny babe did not live to see the sunrise. Draya had tried to pray to the goddess to comfort the family, but her words rang hollow. After that, she had taken to sequestering herself in the Great Hall.

Torval's Rock was ablaze in torchlight. A large crowd had gathered to stare across the fjord at the beacon fire, speculating excitedly on what dire occurrence had befallen the Torgun Clan.

Horg was present, surrounded by his cronies. They stood clustered together in a small group, aloof from the rest. As Draya approached, she could hear Horg saying something in a loud voice. She couldn't understand him from this distance, but his remark was greeted with shouts of laughter from his cronies. The rest of the crowd, Draya noted, did not seem to think his remark funny. No one else laughed.

The people of the Heudjun Clan were unhappy and discontent. They had lost respect for Horg. They considered his judgments arbitrary, favoring those who could give him something in return. Many seasons had passed since he'd led the warriors in a raid. When the winter was over and the ships could take to the seas again, the warriors had waited in eager anticipation for this season's expeditions. Horg had refused to go, claiming that he'd received unfavorable signs from the gods.

Someone sighted her, and word went about that the Kai Priestess had arrived. The crowd parted for Draya. Everyone had words of greeting and respect for her. They might dislike her husband, but they honored her.

Horg turned to face her. His bloodshot eyes narrowed, warning, threatening. He wanted to strike fear into her, and she wondered uneasily why. What is going on? What is he doing? What has he done?

As she drew nearer to Horg, she could smell the sour stench of cider. The fury-filled eyes were bleary and having trouble focusing; he swayed slightly where he stood. Draya understood now why Fria had sent for her.

Draya found her friend waiting anxiously for her on the outskirts of the crowd. Fria gripped Draya's arm and hissed in her ear, "Horg is drunk!"

"I can see that for myself," Draya returned, deeply troubled.

The Vindrasi people worshipped Joabis, God of the Revel, and enjoyed the ale and cider that were his gifts to mankind. But they had small tolerance for drunkenness. Horg had been known to imbibe more than was good for him on occasion, but she had never seen him this drunk before.

Fria gripped her harder. "Horg says that ogre ships were sighted along the coastline, and he claims the Torgun are responsible and he refuses to go to their aid!"

Draya stared at her friend in shocked disbelief. "He will not answer their call for help? He will not fight? What is his reason?"

"Horg says the Torgun brought this on themselves by defying him and going raiding on their own. He says whatever befalls the Torgun is a punishment from the gods. Horg claims Torval told you that he was not to interfere. Our people don't like it, but if the god truly said that the Torgun were to be punished . . ."

Draya understood the problem. Clans often intermarried, and many Heudjun had friends or relations among the Torgun. Even those who had blood feuds with the Torgun did not like the idea of allowing the ogres to attack fellow Vindrasi. But if Horg was correct about the Torgun going against the will of the gods, then he was entirely in his rights to refuse to interfere. The people turned to Draya, to their Kai Priestess, for judgment in this matter, and she understood now why Horg was silently threatening her.

She knew the truth. She had not given Horg a sign from Torval. He was expecting her to go along with his lie. She had done so before, when he'd made such claims about the gods, to save herself from a beating. She had felt wretchedly guilty over it afterwards.

Most Vindrasi women could divorce a man who abused them. A Kai Priestess could not divorce her husband, the Chief of Chiefs, no matter what he did to her. Brought together by the will of the gods—the holiest woman matched with the strongest, bravest warrior—she and Horg were supposed to be above the failings of ordinary mortals. He was the leader of the temporal. She was the leader of the spiritual. The survival of the Vindrasi people was reliant on the stability of their union.

"Vindrash help us!" Draya prayed in agony. "Vindrash help me."

She clasped Fria's hand tightly, silently thanking her for the warning; then she left her friend and walked toward the knot of warriors. Since she did not immediately speak out against him, Horg assumed she was sufficiently cowed. He gave her a smug, knowing smile and took up his conversation.

"The Torgun should have listened to me when I ordered them not to go," he said loudly. "But Norgaard's spoiled whelp, Skylan, always does what he wants. He took his warriors out, and the raid was a disaster. The ogres pursued them, and now the boy finds himself in trouble and he comes running to me, begging me to pull his fat from the fire! This is the gods' punishment upon the Torgun," Horg repeated. "I will not interfere!"

"But if the ogres slay the Torgun, lord, they will attack us next," said one of the young warriors. "What do we gain by refusing to help our cousins?"

Horg snorted. "The Torgun warriors may have their noses bloodied and their heads cracked, but they will defeat the ogres."

The crowd agreed with this reasoning, for all knew ogres were no match for Vindrasi. Horg should have stopped then, but he blundered drunkenly on. "And if the Torgun *are* all killed, we know how lazy ogres are. Once their ships are loaded with Torgun cattle and silver, the ogres will sail back to their homeland. They will not attack us. We are safe. Go to your beds."

Faces flushed in anger. No one moved and no one spoke, not even Horg's cronies. The Torgun would defeat the ogres, of course. They were Vindrasi, after all. Still, even Vindrasi warriors lost on occasion, and every person could picture the scene of ogres rampaging through the Torgun village, burning and looting, slaughtering their kinsmen and friends. They stared balefully at Horg.

"What is the matter?" Horg glowered at them. "I told you! It is Torval's will! His punishment! Do you go against the will of the gods?"

"No Vindrasi warrior ever walked away from a fight, lord," Sven, one of the older warriors, stated. "I cannot believe Torval would order us to do so now. I want to hear this from the Kai Priestess."

Horg's eyes shifted to Draya. His message was clear.

*Support me, woman, or you will regret it.*

Draya shuddered beneath her fur cloak. Horg was cunning in his torment. People would talk if the Kai Priestess were suddenly to appear among them with a bruised face. Horg hit her in places that left no mark. In the distance, the beacon fire burned bright as the fire in the statue's ruby eyes.

"Look at Horg, Draya. . . . Look closely. . . ."

The goddess's voice was a whisper, barely heard above the mutterings of the crowd.

Draya looked intently at Horg. She saw nothing new. A large man, big-boned, well-muscled, though the muscle was buried beneath layers of flab. He was clean-shaven, as were all warriors during raiding season. A beard gave an enemy a handhold. Men shaved in the spring, grew their beards back in the winter, to protect against the cold. His hair was a nondescript color, more gray than anything else, worn down his back in a single braid.

He wore a long leather tunic and breeches and boots—no cloak, for Horg was hot-blooded and never minded even the most extreme cold. He had been handsome, and some women still considered him good-looking—though the once-firm jawline was starting to blur, and the flesh of his face sagged into jowls that were beginning to swallow the golden Vektan Torque he wore around his neck, a mark of his rank.

Everything about him seemed the same, yet something *was* different. She studied him more closely, trying to think what had changed since she saw him last.

Horg scowled. He had expected her to go along with him, and her silence was making him nervous. Drunk as he was, Horg could sense his clansmen's angry mood. He needed Draya to affirm his decision. Raising his massive fist to his face, he made a show of scratching his chin with his thumb. Draya had been hit by that fist often enough to understand the threat.

"Well, Priestess," said Horg. "Tell them Torval's will."

He smiled, sure of himself, and lifted his many chins to stare down his nose at her.

Then she saw. Then she knew what was different.

The Vektan Torque, the most sacred artifact of the Vindrasi people, worn by the Chief of Chiefs, was a ring of heavy gold formed in the shape of two dragons, their tails intertwined, their heads staring at each other. The two dragons held, in their front claws, the spiritbone of a dragon, ornately carved, adorned with a beautiful sapphire, one of the largest ever discovered.

The torque was ancient, dating back to the time of creation, when Torval's consort, the Dragon Goddess Vindrash, bestowed it on the first Kai Priestess with orders that the Kai Moot was to revere it, keep it safe, and never, never try to summon the powerful dragon whose spirit resided in the bone. For the dragon—one of the Five Vektia dragons—could tear apart creation itself.

Of course, giving a human being possession of a powerful artifact was certain to arouse temptation even in the heart of the best person—or god. Long ago, Hevis, the God of Deceit and Trickery, had gotten into a dispute with Sund, God of Stone. Hevis plotted to summon one of the powerful Vektia dragons and send the dragon to war against Sund. The god seduced a Kai Priestess and urged her to summon the dragon.

The dragon had run amok. The Kai Priestess had not been able to control it, nor could Hevis. The dragon killed the Priestess in a raging inferno. The fire had spread, destroying many homes and taking many lives. The angry Chief of Chiefs had seized the Vektan Torque, removed it from the care of the Kai, claiming women could not be trusted with such a valuable artifact.

Ever since then, the Vektan Torque had been in the care of the Chiefs, handed down from one Chief to the next, much to the ire of the Kai Priestesses, who claimed that the Goddess Vindrash herself was offended. The torque was a sacred relict, indicative of the goddess's love for her people. It was also immensely valuable, worth more than all the wealth of all the Vindrasi clans put together.

And it was gone. Horg was not wearing it. And he was trying to deceive people into thinking he was. A gold torque was buried in the folds of his neck, but it was only a plain circlet, such as Chiefs gave to reward valiant warriors.

Fear such as Draya had never known squeezed her heart. She couldn't breathe, and she felt faint and dizzy. She was terrified for a moment that she was going to pass out. Her heart started beating with a lurch, and the horrible sensation passed. She drew in a shivering breath.

Half-hidden between the folds of flesh and his leather tunic, the torque was difficult to see. Draya herself would not have noticed anything was amiss if she had not been warned to look for it. She was willing, even eager, to give him the benefit of the doubt. Perhaps he had taken it off when he traveled, put it away somewhere safe.

Horg betrayed himself. He saw Draya's eyes fixed on his pudgy neck, and he went white, the blood draining from his face all at once, turning as pale as a dead fish's belly. He sealed his fate by raising his hand to the golden torque and trying clumsily to thrust it beneath his tunic.

Draya did not know what he had done, but she knew it must be awful. She could not confront him there, not before the people. He was their Chief. They must continue to have some confidence in his ability to lead; otherwise, there would be dissension, quarrels, rebellion—a clan at war with itself. She had to remove Horg from the crowd in order to question him alone and find out the truth.

"The Chief and I will go to the Great Hall to pray," Draya said, trying to remain calm. "We will ask the gods for their verdict."

Horg blenched, licked his lips, and swallowed a couple of times. He might have lost his faith in the gods, but he still harbored a superstitious dread of them. He managed a sour smile.

"Undoubtedly the gods have better things to do than listen to us, but if you think it right, Priestess, we will go speak to Torval *again*." He laid emphasis on the last word.

Draya bowed in silence, afraid to trust herself to answer. She turned and walked back toward the temple, the crowd parting to allow her passage. Horg caught up with her. Under the guise of offering her assistance, he took hold of her arm and gave it a painful squeeze.

"You'll be sorry," he breathed in her ear.

"I am certain of that," Draya returned coldly.

She stared at him, unafraid, until he let loose and, muttering something about needing another drink, stalked off toward the Great Hall on his own.

# CHAPTER 6

Back in the village of Luda, the beacon fire blazed, lighting up the night sky. Women who had volunteered to leave the safety of the caves supervised the roasting of the boar on a spit over a much smaller fire. The spit was crude, for it had been hastily constructed; meat for the household was generally boiled, not roasted.

The feast would be held in the Chief's Hall. Men hauled in trestles and placed them at intervals down the length of the hall, then laid large planks on the trestles to form a single long table, with wooden benches ranging along either side. Other women returned to their homes to bake round, flat loaves of bread and to dish up meat and vegetables from the family stewpots that were always kept bubbling over the kitchen fires. Men carried in casks of foaming ale and lit the torches, both outside the hall and within.

Akaria, Goddess of the Waters, held up her lantern, shedding silver light on the waves that were her province. The warriors gathered in the Chief's Hall. They were dressed in their finest, wearing the silver and gold torques, armbands, and bracelets that had been given to them or their fathers as reward for courageous actions in battle. The women, who under normal circumstances would have graced the feast, had fled back to the hills, where they fed the beacon fire and tended to Norgaard's young wife, Sonja, who had gone into early labor.

Though the warriors were decked out for a celebration, their mood was far from festive. Every member of the Torgun Clan was acutely aware of the beacon fire blazing atop the cliffs. Norgaard had cautioned the warriors not to draw attention to it by staring at it, but they could not help themselves. They roamed about outside the Chief's Hall, their eyes drawn continually to the leaping orange flames, as each asked himself the same questions: Will the Heudjun see it? Will the Heudjun come?

Skylan was late. He had to return to his dwelling, strip off the bloody clothes, change into his best, and deck himself out proudly in the silver adornments and the family sword, which had been his mother's wedding gift to his father.

His arrival caused a stir among the warriors, who were waiting for their Chief and their Bone Priestess. He showed off his healed leg by walking without a limp, and they greeted him with a cheer, pleased and reassured to see him healthy and whole.

"The goddess healed you," said Garn. "That is a good sign."

"Keep your voice down. That is not exactly what happened," said Skylan.

Garn would have questioned Skylan further, but they were interrupted by the arrival of two of the ogre godlords and their shaman, all of them hungrily sniffing the air, which was redolent with the smell of roasting meat. Skylan started to greet them in his father's absence. Garn stopped him and drew him aside.

"Neither of these two is the commander. The one who wore the tigerskin. Ask them where he is," Garn said.

"I don't know how you can tell one of the bastards from the other," Skylan muttered. "They all look alike to me. But I'll find out."

He walked over to greet the ogres, taking his time, allowing the torchlight to shine on his sword and on the numerous silver armbands that marked his valor.

"Welcome to our Chief's Hall," Sklyan said proudly. Glancing about, he said, "But there are only two of you. Where is your commander?"

The two godlords shrugged.

"He will be along," said one.

"Or he won't," said the other.

The shaman stood behind them, blank-faced and dumb.

Skylan thought he'd never known such stupid creatures. He wondered how their race had managed to survive for so long.

"My father, the Chief, has not yet arrived," said Skylan. "But you are welcome to enter our hall."

The two godlords, smacking their lips, took him up on his invitation and shouldered their way past him. Their bodyguards accompanied them. The shaman in his feather cape did not immediately enter. He stood in front of the door, staring up at the blazing bonfire. Garn flashed his friend a look of concern.

"A large fire," Skylan remarked to the ogre. "For a large boar. The boar was a gift from our gods," he added pointedly. "Our gods who are still very much alive."

The shaman's round childlike eyes flickered with amusement. He took hold of the silver axe Skylan wore around his neck and laughed in his face.

Skylan grasped his sword's hilt.

"Let go," he ordered through clenched teeth, "or I'll cut off your hand!"

The shaman chuckled and gave the axe a flip, causing it to strike Skylan on the chin.

"Don't, Skylan!" Garn warned, grabbing hold of his friend's arm. "He's baiting you! Look around!"

The shaman's bodyguards were standing behind Skylan, their weapons in their hands. Behind them, the Torgun warriors stood ready to come to his defense.

One hundred and seventy ogre warriors waited on board the ships.

Skylan slammed his sword back into the sheath.

The ogre shaman, still chuckling, entered the hall. The guards slung the axes into the harnesses they wore on their broad backs.

"We will wait for my father inside," said Skylan, and he led the way into the Chief's Hall.

The ogre godlords took their seats at the head of the table. The Torgun warriors, at a glance and a nod from Skylan, crowded into the hall and took their seats at the long table.

"Look at him. Smug bastard. I should have cut off his head," Skylan said.

"Time enough for that tomorrow," said Garn. He was watching the ogres, and his expression was dark, troubled.

Norgaard arrived, and Skylan, as leader of the warriors, went to embrace his father. Norgaard looked unhappy, haggard. He had heard that his young wife had gone into early labor. The baby was not due for a month, at least. Unless the women could stop the birthing process, he might lose yet another child.

"I am sorry to hear about Sonja, Father," said Skylan as he accompanied his father into the hall. "Desiria will be with her, and by morning you will have a fine son."

Norgaard gave a wan smile, something he did rarely, for there was not much in his life to smile about. He rested his hand on Skylan's shoulder.

"You mean, I will have *another* fine son," he said quietly. "Come with me a moment. I would speak with you in confidence."

Norgaard motioned for Skylan to join him, and the two left the hall.

"Where is Treia? She should be here. You spoke with the Bone Priestess this afternoon. Do you know why she hasn't come?"

Skylan remembered Treia's cold face peering at him from behind the closed door and the flat tone of her voice refusing to help him.

"Who knows why Treia does anything? She's a strange woman, Father. Perhaps it has something to do with me. She doesn't like me. I don't know why. I've never done anything to her."

Norgaard gave him a puzzled look. "What do you mean Treia doesn't like you? Why would that matter?"

"She refused to heal me," said Skylan. "I had to go to that horrible old woman, Owl Mother—"

"The Goddess Desiria refused to heal you?" Norgaard interrupted, aghast.

"The goddess didn't refuse. Treia refused. She never even spoke to the goddess. I told you, Father. Treia doesn't like me—"

"That can't be the reason," Norgaard muttered. "A Bone Priestess is required to heal her worst enemy if the gods command it. This bodes ill for us."

"Do not speak words of evil omen, Father," Skylan urged him. "The beacon fire burns. The call has gone out. Tomorrow morning, Heudjun warriors will be here to help us teach the ogres that the Gods of the Vindrasi are very much alive!"

"And yet, it was Owl Mother and her fae magic who healed you," said Norgaard grimly, and he limped inside the Chief's Hall to take his place at the head of the table.

Skylan accompanied him into the hall.

"What did Norgaard have to say?" Garn asked.

The warriors were handing around the drinking horns and pouring the ale. The noise in the hall increased, and though the two young men sat at the front of the table, not far from the ogres, they were able to talk without worrying that their words might be overheard.

"Nothing of importance," said Skylan, filling his own drinking horn from a pitcher. "My father is being an old granny."

He related his conversation, adding, "The gods have their reasons for not revealing their power yet."

Garn shook his head somberly.

"Not you, too!" Skylan exclaimed, exasperated. "Don't tell me you're worried about the gods, as well."

"Not the gods so much as the ogres," Garn said quietly. He glanced back at them. "They're too smug, too pleased with themselves. And where is their commander? Why didn't he come with the others?"

Skylan shrugged. "Maybe he's sick. Maybe he has the trots and they don't want to admit it."

One of the godlords raised his voice. "Where is your shaman? Ours is here. Where is yours? She was supposed to bring us an answer from your gods."

"Perhaps she is having trouble finding them," suggested the other godlord, and the two ogres laughed.

Norgaard said something evasive. Catching sight of Skylan and Garn, he motioned to them.

"You heard them? I need Treia here. Now," Norgaard said.

"I will go fetch her," said Skylan.

"No, your absence would be noted," said Norgaard. "I must commence the feast. The ogres tell me we should not wait for their commander. I do not like this, any of it. Garn, summon Treia and then see if you can find out what the ogres are up to. Skylan, come sit in front with me."

Garn gave a nod and departed on his errands.

Skylan took his place at his father's right hand. The two ogre godlords and their shaman sat on the bench at the head of the table along with Norgaard. Ogre bodyguards stood behind their commanders.

At a signal from Norgaard, men entered the hall bearing large wood platters filled with roasted meat. Others brought in stew in wooden bowls and the round, flat loaves of bread.

The ogres did not appear concerned over the absence of their commander, nor did they wait for him to arrive before they commenced eating. Spearing large hunks of meat with their knives, they piled it on their plates along with bread and bowls of steaming stew.

Skylan watched food that would have fed the Torgun for weeks filling ogre bellies, and he burned with anger. He contained himself, however, thinking of the dawn and imagining slitting those bellies wide open.

Once each godlord had a full plate, he gestured to a bodyguard, who reached over to the godlord's plate, tore off a piece of meat, stuffed it into his mouth, chewed, and swallowed. The bodyguard did the same with the bread, eating a portion of it, and using it to sop up gravy from the stew.

Skylan paused in his own meal to stare at this practice in astonishment. "Why do your men eat *your* food?" he asked one of the godlords.

The ogre blinked at him, not understanding the question. Then, comprehension dawned. The godlord grinned and nodded and jerked his thumb back at his bodyguard.

"If the food is poisoned, he dies, not me," said the godlord.

Skylan leaped to his feet, drawing his sword from the sheath. The ogres reacted immediately. Their blades flashed in the torchlight. The Torgun warriors, already tense and excited, jumped to their feet and started to shove back the benches.

"Hold!" Norgaard roared.

Everyone stood still, weapons poised. Norgaard looked to his son for an explanation.

"These bastards think we're trying to poison them!" Skylan cried, pointing at the ogres.

The Torgun growled in anger. A warrior fought his foe face-to-face, looked him in the eye. Poison was the weapon of weaklings, cowards. The Torgun had been insulted.

Norgaard heaved a sigh and shook his head. "It is their custom, Skylan. It has nothing to do with us."

Seeing that Skylan remained unconvinced, Norgaard added, "Assassination is one way of advancing in rank."

"That is true," the godlord affirmed. "It is not you Torgun I fear." Grinning widely, he pointed to his fellow godlord. "It is him."

The ogres appeared to find his words hilarious. Both godlords and their guards burst out laughing, hooting and banging the table with their large hands, causing the wooden plates to jump and the horn mugs to rattle. The shaman did not join in. He glowered at the two godlords in displeasure.

As for the Torgun, they had never heard of anything so barbaric, and they regarded the ogres in silent wonder. Vindrasi Chiefs were chosen by the gods, not by murder. Shaking their heads and muttering in low tones of amazement, the Torgun warriors sheathed their weapons and resumed their seats.

Once the godlords knew their food was safe, they began to eat, stuffing their mouths with huge chunks of meat. They chewed and talked at the same time, spitting bits of food.

"It is a wicked custom," said the shaman. "Left over from the Dark Times."

"Our leader got his position that way," stated one of the godlords defensively. Gravy dribbled down his chin.

The shaman fixed the godlord with a withering glare. "Times are changing. Our new gods, the Gods of Raj, demand we put a stop to it. You see that no one tastes *my* food!"

From the baleful looks the godlords gave their shaman, Skylan thought the shaman might want to reconsider that practice. The godlords said nothing, but both continued to hand their bodyguards bits of food before they ate it, and they made them drink ale from the horn mugs, as well.

Knowing the duties of a host, Norgaard asked the shaman polite questions about the ogre gods, the Gods of Raj. The shaman was eager to answer. Skylan should have been conversing with their guests, as well, but he was hungry, and he left entertaining the ogres to his father. He was still a little weak from the loss of blood, and he would need his strength in the morning.

He would also need a clear head, as would his warriors. Skylan was careful to drink no more than two mugs of ale, and he frowned at the men who were laughing or talking too loudly or were seen filling their drinking horns too often. Catching his warning look, they put down the horns. The Torgun would go to their beds this night relatively sober.

The ogres had no such worries. All of them, including the shaman, drank vast quantities of ale, nearly emptying the cask. The ale seemed to have little effect on them, however, except to make the shaman more and more effusive in his praise of their gods.

Skylan paid scant attention. In his mind, he was on the other side of the fjord in Vindraholm. He could picture the excitement and alarm. Everyone would be rushing about, making preparations to go to war. Warriors would be examining their shields to make certain there were no weak spots and sharpening swords and spears and axes. Those fortunate enough to have chain mail would be going over the shirts by the firelight, making certain no links were missing. Those who did not have mail would be donning leather shirts made of deerhide, which were almost as tough as chain.

Skylan had work to do himself. He had inherited his father's chain mail, and though hardly a day went by that Skylan did not examine it to make certain every link was sound, he planned to go over it again tonight. He would sharpen, clean, and oil his sword, though it did not really need it, for the sword, named Dragon's Tooth, was Skylan's pride.

He pictured the battle tomorrow and the glory he would win for himself. He imagined fighting alongside Horg, the Chief of Chiefs. He imagined saving Horg's life and Horg offering him rich reward in gratitude. Cattle, perhaps, or silver or even gold. Skylan would at last have enough to pay the bride-price, and that turned his thoughts from battle to love. He wondered what Aylaen had been about to tell him this afternoon before they were interrupted by Owl Mother. It seemed to have been important. He would have to remember to ask her. Perhaps he would see her tonight, if she and Treia came to the feast. . . .

Bjorn kicked Skylan in the shins hard enough to make him wince and rouse him from his reverie. Something had happened. Something was wrong. A deathlike silence shrouded the hall. Every man, including Norgaard, had turned to face the entrance.

Alarmed, Skylan gripped his sword and turned, as well.

The ogre commander stood in the doorway. He was an arresting sight, for he wore a shining breastplate that gleamed brightly in the firelight. But why, Skylan wondered, was everyone staring at him as though he'd fallen from the skies? Plate armor was worth a Chief's ransom, but the Torgun had fought men in plate armor before.

Then Skylan saw that Norgaard's appalled gaze was not staring at the armor, but at some point above the breastplate. Skylan looked more closely.

His eyes widened. His hand, gripping the sword's hilt, went numb. He could not believe what he was seeing. He had only to look at his father for confirmation of the unthinkable truth.

Gold glinted. Sapphire glittered.

Around his fat neck, the ogre godlord wore the sacred Vektan Torque. He rested his hand on it and grinned.

"You can douse your beacon fire," said the godlord. "No help is coming."

In the silence that quivered tense and taut as a bowstring, the godlord walked over to the table, shoved aside the bench with his foot, sat down, and began to calmly fork meat onto his plate.

# CHAPTER 7

Aylaen sat on the ground with her back against the Hall of Vindrash and watched the flames of the beacon fire flicker through the tree branches. Night had fallen, and her sister was still inside, still refusing to answer Aylaen's periodic questions. Was Treia ill? Was she in need of water? Should Aylaen run to fetch Norgaard?

Not a word in response. The last Aylaen had seen or heard from Treia was when she opened the door to tell Skylan she could not heal him. Aylaen, putting her ear to the door, couldn't hear her sister moving about inside.

Aylaen began to worry that some accident had befallen Treia. She tried to enter the Hall, even though she wasn't supposed to disturb Treia when she was at her prayers, but Treia had used something to block the door. That in itself was strange. The Hall of Vindrash was supposed to be open to all, day or night. Aylaen had given the door a healthy shove, and she could not cause it to budge.

Darkness fell, and the hours passed, and Aylaen grew more and more uneasy. Perhaps she should fetch Alfric to help her force the door open. Alfric was the strongest, largest man in the village. He had once picked up Skylan, hoisted him over his shoulder, and carried him around as effortlessly as if Skylan were a babe. But Aylaen was loath to leave her sister alone in the wilderness, especially with ogres roaming about.

The longer Aylaen sat in the darkness, with only the moon and the stars for light, the more worried she grew. She went again to the door and called to her sister.

No reply.

What if Treia was lying there hurt, unable to move or cry out? Maybe she was subject to foaming-mouthed fits? That was possible. Aylaen didn't know that much about her sister, who had been away for so many years. Treia was still a stranger. Aylaen was about to leave to obtain help when she saw torchlight and heard someone walking along the path.

Aylaen picked up her axe. All Vindrasi women were trained to fight. If an enemy overran the men of the village, it was left to the women to defend themselves and their children.

Aylaen was strong, and she was a skilled warrior. Having grown up with Skylan and Garn, she was more boy than girl, as her mother never tired of telling anyone who would listen. Aylaen did a man's work on the farm. She hated being cooped up inside the house, doing women's work: cooking and weaving and the like. She had learned from Skylan and Garn how to handle weapons. She even knew how to use Skylan's most prized possession—his sword.

Aylaen had no sword. Few men in the village owned one. But she had an axe, and was not afraid. Whoever was out there was making a great deal of noise. An enemy would move silently, try to sneak up on her.

"Who is there?" she challenged. "Make yourself known to me."

"Aylaen, you can put down the axe!" came the laughing call. "It's Garn."

Aylaen sighed in relief and dropped the axe to the ground. Garn, bathed in yellow torchlight, came into sight. Aylaen ran to him, threw her arms around him, and pressed her head against his broad chest.

"Thank Vindrash you've come! I've been so worried."

"What is it? What's wrong?" Garn asked, alarmed. "Where is Treia? She's supposed to be at the feast."

"She's in there. In the Hall. She won't answer me—"

Garn gave a sigh of relief. "So she is safe. You are safe."

He put his arms around her, clasping her close to him. They pressed together, heartbeat to heartbeat, warm and comforting. And then, gently, he pushed her away.

"We shouldn't," he said. "This is wrong."

"Wrong to love each other?" Aylaen asked, and she raised her lips to be kissed.

Garn glanced at the Hall. Though the building had no windows, Treia might be watching through a chink in the wall. He shook his head.

"Skylan is dear to me," he said. "Dearer than a brother."

"And he is dear to me, as well," Aylaen said gently. "Dear to me *as* a brother. We should tell him we are in love. I almost told him today."

"You mustn't, Aylaen!" Garn said. "You must never say anything to him."

"I don't see why not," Aylaen said. "He has to know sometime."

"No, he doesn't," said Garn quietly. "Promise me you won't say a word to him or to anyone."

Aylaen tossed her head defiantly.

"You would hurt Skylan deeply, Aylaen," Garn told her. "He adores you. And he trusts me. Promise me you won't tell him. . . ."

"Sometimes I think you care more about him than you do me," Aylaen said petulantly.

"I hope I never have to choose," said Garn.

Aylaen heard the sorrow and pain in his voice, and she regretted her hurtful words. He loved her, loved her deeply and dearly, as she loved him. The two had not meant to fall in love. It had just happened. It seemed they had grown up loving each other. The threads of their wyrds were bound together. Yet she was as good as betrothed to Skylan.

"I'm sorry," Aylaen said remorsefully. "I promise I won't tell him. But I won't marry him!" she added with a flash of her green eyes.

Garn shook his head. "Not even the gods can see the future. Norgaard sent me to fetch your sister. The feast has started, and her absence has been noted."

"I tried to go inside," said Aylaen. "Something's blocking the door."

Garn looked grim on hearing this, and Aylaen's heart lurched. Treia was not an easy person to get to know, much less to love, but Aylaen was doing her best. She liked having a sister. Having grown up with the boys, she had never made friends with girls her age. Most of the time, Treia was stiff and cold, but sometimes, in rare moments, she would relax and forget the grudge she bore the world, and she and Aylaen would talk confidingly as sisters talk. They discussed their mother and her problems, shared memories of their dead father, and acknowledged the hatred both felt for their stepfather. Aylaen cherished these moments, and she was afraid for her sister now.

"Treia!" Garn called, knocking respectfully on the door. "Bone Priestess, the Chief requests your presence at the feast. It is important that you attend."

He waited, but there was no response.

Garn handed the torch to Aylaen, who put it into the iron sconce on the wall. He put his shoulder to the door and shoved. The door moved a little, opening a crack. Aylaen put her eye to it and tried to see inside, but all was dark.

"It will take both of us," said Garn. "Put your weight into it. Now—"

"No, stop," came Treia's cold voice. "I will let you inside."

They heard something heavy being dragged across the floor, and then the door swung open. Treia had been sitting in the darkness, apparently, for no light burned inside. Her face was stark white in the torchlight.

"Treia, what's wrong?" Aylaen asked, alarmed. "What's the matter? Have you been here all this time in the dark?"

She took hold of her sister's hands, rubbed them with her own. "You're freezing! Where's your cloak?"

Garn carried his flaring torch inside. The flame cast a pool of light around them, leaving the rest of the Hall in shadow.

"Treia, Norgaard requires your presence at the feast," Garn said.

Treia stood stiff, unmoving. Her face was drawn and haggard. She did not respond. She gazed at the firelight, did not appear even to have heard him.

Garn and Aylaen exchanged perplexed glances. They had no idea what to do. Garn could not very well drag Treia to the feast, yet it was of vital importance that she attend.

"Treia, dear sister—," Aylaen began in soothing tones.

"Look!" cried Treia suddenly, savagely. She pointed a quivering finger at the altar. "Look! Look there!"

Garn held his torch closer, and light flowed over the altar. Aylaen blinked, not certain if she was seeing things. The flickering light of the torch was causing the shadows to dance, playing tricks on her eyes. Garn drew nearer still, holding the torch directly above the altar. Aylaen sucked in a horrified breath. The statue of Vindrash had split in two. The goddess lay in pieces on the floor.

Every clan had a statue to honor Vindrash, generally reproductions of the beautiful jadeite statue of the goddess found in the Great Hall of the Gods in Vindraholm. The Torgun's statue of Vindrash was carved of wood, larger than the jadeite statue, coming to about a man's waist. Vindrash was portrayed as a dragon rearing up on muscular hind legs. Her long spiked tail wrapped gracefully around her scaled body. Her wings thrust out from the shoulders, and her head was raised in fierce dignity, the fanged mouth gaping wide in a silent roar.

The statue was said to be nearly as old as the original statue, and now it lay broken. A crack ran lengthwise, dividing the head, sundering the body. One of the wings had fallen off when the statue hit the floor, and it lay to one side.

"The ogres are right," said Treia in a shaking voice. "The gods are dead. This proves it!"

"Nonsense!" Garn said sharply. "This proves that the statue was very old and fragile and it fell apart. Nothing more."

"Nothing more . . . ," Treia murmured. She continued to stare at the statue.

She has been here all this time, Aylaen realized, sitting with the broken statue, believing the gods are dead.

"Listen to me," said Garn, gripping Treia's arms and giving her a shake. "That statue was older than the hills. It's been out in the rain and the snow and the freezing cold. The wood rotted, as it was bound to do eventually, and the statue broke."

The statue of Vindrash was present at the launching of the dragonship, where she was doused with seawater. She attended weddings and funerals in sunshine and rain. She presided over the harvest festival and came out of her warm Hall into the fierce wind and cold to celebrate the winter solstice.

"The true miracle is that the old wooden statue has survived this long," said Garn.

He was being logical, as always. Still, looking down at the broken statue, Aylaen wasn't certain logic made her feel any better. She remembered being afraid of the statue when she was little. The dragon seemed to glare down at her as she stood in the Hall beside her mother, and she had nightmares about the teeth snapping at her, the claws reaching out to tear her apart.

Her mother had sought to reassure her, telling her that Vindrash loved her people. Her fangs and claws were used to protect the Torgun, not harm them. Aylaen tried hard to believe that was true, but the childhood fear never truly left her. She had always felt a little tremor pass through her when she looked upon the statue of Vindrash.

Now, as she stared down at the two halves of the broken statue, she was reminded of her dead father. She remembered seeing his corpse laid out in the funeral boat, and she remembered feeling bewildered and confused. That wasn't her father, lying there, any more than these broken pieces were Vindrash. Her father had been a hale and hearty man with a ready laugh. She had worshipped him, adored him. The disease-ravaged corpse with its frozen grimace of pain and its wasted, shrunken limbs was a stranger. Someone she didn't know.

She had refused to believe her father was dead, and she had run away to hide in the woods until the funeral had ended and the blazing boat carrying his body had been shoved out to sea. And though she knew in the bleak empty darkness of her heart that her father was dead, she kept stubbornly insisting he was merely gone on a raid and would someday return. That was one reason she had been so furious with her mother when she had married Uncle Sigurd.

Aylaen felt the same now, bewildered and confused. This was not Vindrash. This was a stranger.

"We will build a new statue," Garn was telling Treia. "A better statue, adorned with jewels to honor the goddess. This is what you will tell our people. This is what you will tell them *tomorrow*"—Garn emphasized—"*after* we defeat the ogres. You will say nothing about this to anyone tonight."

Treia's eyes flashed. "I am the Bone Priestess! How dare you give me orders? I will say what I must say. The ogres are right. Our gods are dead—"

"If you tell the people that, you will send our warriors to battle tomorrow with dread and fear in their hearts instead of courage and pride," Garn said. "And if we are defeated, the fault will be yours. Not the gods'!"

Treia glared at him, but she did not refute his words. Aylaen could not guess what her sister was thinking. Treia hid her thoughts behind a cold, pale mask. At last she stirred and rubbed her thin arms.

"You claim the statue broke because the wood rotted." Treia gazed up at Garn and smiled a thin, bitter smile. "Is *that* what you would have me say to the people? That our goddess rotted?"

Garn made an impatient gesture. "It's a piece of wood shaped like the goddess, Treia, not the goddess herself. If the lintel above the door split, would you read in that the end of the world? Don't say anything to anyone, Treia. Not until after tomorrow's battle."

Treia gestured to Aylaen. "Bring me my robes."

Aylaen was quick to respond. Catching up the embroidered robe that marked her a Bone Priestess, Aylaen draped it around Treia's spare shoulders. Aylaen put her arm protectively around her sister, for, though the night was warm, she could feel her shivering.

The two walked out of the Hall. Garn shut the door and followed, bringing the torch. He was heading for the path toward the village when Treia stopped him. She laid her chill fingers on his arm.

"What is, is what is. I cannot change it, and neither can you." Treia huddled more deeply into her robes. "I will not attend the feast. I will go home. Aylaen will come with me."

Garn hesitated. Norgaard had wanted her there, but if she went in her present mood, there was no telling what harm she might do.

"A wise decision, Priestess," Garn said at last. "What do you want me to tell Norgaard?"

Treia stared at him, and then she laughed—strange, harsh laughter that was the most terrible sound Aylaen had ever heard.

"You still don't understand, do you?" Treia said, the laughter bubbling in her throat. "There will be no need to tell Norgaard anything. By now, he already knows!"

# CHAPTER 8

The wind rose in the night, causing the ogre ships to rock as they lay at anchor in the bay and sending whitecapped waves rolling in between the high cliffs of the fjord. The wind tore at the beacon fire, catching up sparks and flinging them into the air. The logs that fed the bonfire collapsed, fell in on one another, sending up a shower of ashes. No one bothered to add more fuel. The warriors who had tended the fire stared grimly at the dying flames and saw in them their own future. Word had come from Norgaard, carried by swift messenger.

"Help is not coming."

Across the fjord, the young warriors of the Heudjun watched in silence as the beacon fire dwindled. They did not speak, or look at each other. They were ashamed.

The beacon fire finally went out. The Heudjun warriors returned to their homes. Some of them had decided amongst themselves to prepare for battle. Despite Horg's assurances that the ogres would not attack, the Heudjun did not trust either him or them. Many hoped the ogres would attack Vindraholm.

Battle would ease the Heudjun's shame.

Horg had worked himself into a rage by the time he reached the Great Hall. He was Chief of Chiefs, after all. His fists clenched. He muttered imprecations and swore beneath his breath. He had a right to do as he had done. The plague take anyone who thought otherwise, and that included the gods.

Draya had never seen him in such an ugly, belligerent mood, and she began to think fearfully that she should have confronted him in the open when there had been people about. Not even Horg was drunk enough to publicly raise his hand against a Kai Priestess.

But she had to find out the truth about the Vektan Torque, and the only way to do that was to bring Horg before the gods, even if it meant placing her life at risk. Horg might lie to the people. He might lie to her. He could not lie to Vindrash.

Draya opened the door to the Hall and went inside, carrying a torch with her. The light shone on the statue of the Dragon Goddess, Vindrash, and caused her to leap out of the darkness. The dragon's eyes glowed in righteous anger, her fangs gleamed, her claws were extended, ready to rend his flesh. Horg staggered back a step or two in drunken terror. He stood on the threshold, refusing to enter, staring at the statue with blenched face and quivering gut.

Draya's fears vanished—at least her fear for herself. She was in no danger from this sweating, sodden coward.

"Come inside," she ordered.

Horg hesitated; then he lurched across the threshold.

"Well, woman, I'm here. What do you want?"

Draya could not reply. She felt smothered, unable to fully catch her breath. Fear clogged her throat.

Not fear of Horg. Fear of what Horg had done.

Vindrash, give me courage, Draya prayed, and her voice came back to her.

"Where is the Vektan Torque?"

Horg gave a blustering laugh. "Is that what all this fuss is about? I thought you suspected me of murder at the very least!"

"The torque," said Draya. "Where is it?"

Horg shrugged. "I put it away for safekeeping. I never wear the torque in battle." He yawned massively and scratched himself. "I'm going to bed."

"You said there would be no battle." Draya spoke to his sweat-stained back. "You said the ogres would not attack us. Where is the Vektan Torque?"

Horg took another step; then he halted. He paused a moment, turned too fast, and almost stumbled over his own feet. He pulled himself upright and said with massive calm, "I gave it to the ogres."

Draya pressed her hand over her thudding heart. "Vindrash save us!" she gasped. "What have you done?"

"What have I done?" Horg repeated, and his face flushed in anger. "I have saved us from death—that's what I've done. The ogres came with their ships. Their sails filled the skies—"

"So many that no one else saw them," said Draya caustically.

"I was riding alone! They would have sent their warriors ashore, but I met with their godlords, made a deal—"

"You gave them the sacred torque," said Draya. "But that wasn't enough. They wanted blood, and you gave them our kinsmen."

"We were outnumbered!" Horg bawled, raising his fists and shaking them in the air. "They would have destroyed us!"

"The Vektan Torque belongs to the gods. You have given what was not yours to give. Torval's curse will fall on you!" Draya's voice trembled. "His curse will fall on us all!"

"Torval's curse!" Horg laughed and struck himself on the chest. "Look at me, bitch. I'm going to tell you something about Torval."

"Get out!" Draya cried. The smell of cider and his sweaty, filthy body sickened her. She averted her face, gripped the altar with her hands. "Get out of my sight, you drunken coward!"

"I'll go," said Horg. "I have a new woman to warm my bed and a cask of cider to drink. But first, bitch, you're going to listen to what I have to say for a change. Torval won't curse me. The old fart couldn't curse a cat! The ogres told me. There was a war in heaven, and our gods lost."

Draya laughed. "How ludicrous!"

"You don't believe me?" Horg sneered. "Ask your precious Vindrash. *If* you can find her."

Draya started to angrily refute him, but the words died on her lips. She didn't believe him—or rather, she didn't want to believe him.

"You are shamed, dishonored, no longer fit to be Chief of Chiefs. I will tell the people what you have done."

Horg shrugged. "Go ahead. And I'll tell them what I know about the gods." He smirked at her. "Where does that leave you, Kai Priestess? If the gods are dead, who in the name of Hevis needs you anymore? Certainly I don't!"

Horg made a lunge for her. She tried to escape, but he was too fast. He grabbed hold of her, gripping her by her chin and digging his fingers into her jaw. Draya moaned in his grasp. He held her so tightly, she was afraid to move for fear he would shatter her jaw as if it were an eggshell.

He laughed again, then snarled at her. "Here's what I think of you. And here's what I think of your fucking gods."

He flung Draya to the floor. She landed heavily on her hands and knees. She tasted blood. Her teeth had cut the inside of her mouth. Her eyes burned with tears. She kept her head lowered, determined not to let him see that he had made her cry.

She heard Horg's footfalls thud across the floor, felt them vibrate through her body. He slammed the door, and she flinched at the sound.

Draya remained where she was, afraid to get up. Finally, she glanced around. Seeing that Horg had truly gone, she sighed and leaned weakly against the altar. The awful calamity had stunned her. She touched her hand gingerly to her face, felt the bruises Horg's gouging fingers had left behind.

"It's not true," she said bleakly. The tears spilled over and ran down her cheeks. "It's not true!"

"I'm afraid it is, my dear," said a gentle voice. "We who are immortal. We who cannot die. We watched Aylis cradle her dying child, Desiria, in her arms. Her wyrd had snapped, and now the tapestry of all our lives is starting to unravel."

The wyrd.

The Vindrasi believed that when the thread that ties a babe to the mother is cut, the thread of that child's wyrd begins. The wyrd is spun by the Norn, three sisters of the God Gogroth, who came at Torval's summons to plant the World Tree. His three sisters sat beneath the tree, one twisting the wyrd on her distaff, one spinning the wyrd on her wheel, one weaving the wyrds of gods and men on her loom. Every person had his own wyrd, as did each god. The wyrds of both men and gods together formed the tapestry that is life. A single thread is fragile. The tapestry itself is strong. Before now, Draya would have said indestructible.

"We lost the battle," Vindrash said. "The Gods of Raj and Aelon, Lord of the New Dawn, are young gods, and they are powerful. They proved too strong for us. Desiria, Goddess of Life and Healing, is dead. Her twin sister, the Sea Goddess, has gone mad with grief, and there is no telling what she will do now. Skoval threatens. Hevis plots. Sund advises caution. The God Joabis basely fled the battle and has disappeared. I myself dare not linger in one place long. My enemies seek my destruction.

"Since time's beginning," the goddess continued, "mortals have come to the gods seeking our help. Now, at what may well be time's end, we gods are forced to go to mortals. I need your help, Draya."

Draya remembered a time when a raging wildfire had swept through the small village where she'd grown up, destroying everything, leaving nothing standing. She felt now as she'd felt then, overlooking the charred remains of what had once been a town. Now she stared out over the charred and blackened remains of what had once been her world.

"I am honored by your trust, Blessed Vindrash. Whatever you ask of me, I will do," Draya answered through her tears. "I would give my life, if it would help you."

Vindrash was silent a moment. When the goddess spoke again, it was with sorrow.

"Long ago, Torval foresaw the day of our doom. He made preparations—though, in our arrogance, none of us truly thought we would be forced to resort to them. Sadly, the day of doom has come. The Bones of the Vektia Five must be found and brought together."

Draya sat upright, staring at the goddess in dismay.

The Old Gods had once ruled the heavens from their thrones in the realm of Edonai. A great battle erupted among the gods, and Edonai had been destroyed. The gods and the mortals who worshipped them had been scattered throughout the heavens. Roving the universe, searching for a world of his own, Torval came upon a world beautiful as a jewel. He had never seen anything so wondrous and wanted this world for his own.

But the world was guarded by the Great Dragon Ilyrion, and she refused to give it up. Torval declared he would not relinquish the gem, and he challenged the dragon to a fight. Torval and Ilyrion fought for many thousands of years. During their battle, the two enemies came to respect and admire each other, even as they sought to kill each other.

At last Torval slew Ilyrion. As she lay dying, the dragon forgave the god and bequeathed a final gift to the world she was leaving. Her bones and teeth, claws and scales rained down upon the world and buried themselves deep in the ground, taking the form of precious gems, each endowed with a portion of Ilyrion's soul.

Knowing his rival gods still roamed the universe in search of worlds, Torval feared the day would come when he would be called upon to defend his prize. He summoned other gods, those he could trust, to assist him in protecting his conquest. Sund came, God of Stone, a thoughtful, contemplative god. Gogroth came to plant the seed of the World Tree. Freilis came, Goddess of the Tally, to rule over the dead. Joabis came, bringing wine to celebrate.

When the gods were assembled, Torval used Ilyrion's crest to create the Five Dragons of Vektia, immensely powerful dragons who would be the guardians of the world. To keep them hidden from their enemies, Torval secreted the spirit of each dragon inside a bone taken from Ilyrion's own skeleton.

All that was left of Ilyrion was her blood. Torval poured the blood into his drinking horn, and from this sprang Vindrash, Goddess of Dragons. Torval loved her on sight and made her his consort. He gave her the spiritbones of the Vektia Five as a wedding gift. Vindrash, in turn, divided the five spiritbones among the other gods, ordering them to hide the spiritbones away and keep them hidden. This they did, though none of the gods ever believed the bones of the Five would be needed.

The tale ran through Draya's mind, and she was overwhelmed by the magnitude of the task.

"Vindrash," Draya cried helplessly, "I do not know where to find the spiritbones of the Five."

"You know where one of them is," said Vindrash, and her voice was cold and pitiless as the dead of winter. "Your husband gave it to the ogres."

# CHAPTER 9

Garn saw Aylaen and her sister safely enter Treia's dwelling, and then he hastened back to the feast. Treia's dire statement that Norgaard "already knew" worried Garn. Priestesses were always deliberately vague when it came to such pronouncements. That way, no matter what happened, they were never wrong.

Garn believed in the Gods of the Vindrasi, but he did not believe that the gods were constantly peering over a man's shoulder. Garn believed that as a child plays with a top, so the gods had set the world spinning and now watched it wobble around creation.

Skylan, on the other hand, believed that Torval was always listening to him, always watching him, always prepared either to reward Skylan or slap him up the side of the head. Their differing viewpoints led to some heated arguments, for Garn liked to speculate about such things. Skylan did not, and once he realized which direction the conversation was tending, he would always end it.

Garn looked toward the cliffs and saw, to his concern, that the beacon fire was being allowed to die. True, the fire had done its work, sent its message. Horg and his warriors would be making preparations for battle, perhaps even setting sail. The beacon fire should continue to burn—in defiance, if for no other reason. But all that was left was a sullen red glow atop the peak.

When Garn reached the Chief's Hall, his uneasiness became alarm. Torches blazed inside and out. The ogre guards were gone, which meant the godlords had returned to their ships. Garn should have heard laughter and raucous voices raised in stirring songs of battle, accompanied by feet rhythmically stamping the floor, hands slapping the table. He should have heard boasting about the great deeds the warriors would perform tomorrow. He should have heard Skylan, the War Chief, leading his men in a war chant.

Instead, there was quiet—and no Vindrasi feast was ever quiet. Even funerals were riotous affairs.

Garn broke into a run. The thought came to his mind that the ogres had poisoned everyone. Half-expecting to find his friends slumped over dead, Garn burst into the hall. He came to a halt, staring.

The warriors, alive and well, sat in silent gloom around the table. Drinking horns lay empty. Plates filled with food had been thrust aside. The face of every man was shadowed and grim. No man looked at another. Each stared into some private hell.

Norgaard's head was lowered, his arms resting heavily on the table. His face was gray and drawn. He had aged years in the time Garn had been gone.

Skylan sat hunched on the bench. He had fresh hurts—his jaw was swollen, and blood trailed from a split lip. He was staring at the table in silence; then suddenly he slammed his fist down and jumped to his feet.

"We cannot sit here like dead men," he said. "Dead men who have died dishonored! We have to act."

No one responded. A few grunted and some glanced at him and then looked away. Most didn't even do that.

"What has happened?" Garn demanded. "What is wrong?"

Skylan rounded on him. "Where have you been?" he asked accusingly. "I needed you!"

"The Chief sent me to fetch Treia—"

"Is she coming?" Norgaard lifted his head and looked at Garn, hope flickering in his eyes.

"No, Chief," Garn said. "She is not."

He tried to think of some reason that was not the truth, yet not an outright lie. He hesitated too long, however, and Norgaard saw through him.

The Chief shook his head and slumped back into his misery.

"Skylan . . . someone tell me!" Garn insisted.

"The sacred Vektan Torque!" Skylan said, choking on his rage. "One of their goat-screwing, shit-eating godlords was wearing it around his fat neck!"

Garn staggered, knocked off balance by the astonishing news.

"No help is coming," Norgaard said. He stared down at his gnarled hands, which lay limply on the table, and repeated, "No help is coming."

"The Heudjun are all dead, then," said Garn, dazed. "Horg, our cousins, our clansmen. The ogres have slain them—"

"Not according to the ogres," Skylan said, seething. "As they tell it, the ogres had no plans to raid us. Why should they? We are a piss-poor clan with nothing they want. They were going to raid the Heudjun. Horg called for a parley. He gave them the Vektan Torque in exchange for their promise to leave the Heudjun in peace."

"The ogres are lying," said Garn. "Horg would never do such a thing."

"That's what I said," Skylan said.

"And what did the ogres say?" Garn asked.

"They asked—had we heard Heudjun horns calling the clans to battle? Had we seen the smoke of their beacon fire summoning us to help them? Did we see the flames of burning houses? Are the ogre ships now filled with Heudjun cattle and Heudjun slaves? The answer to all is no."

Garn stared at his friend in silence. He tried to think of some logical explanations, but none came to mind.

"How did you get a bruised jaw?" he asked at last, though he could guess.

"Sigurd had to knock some sense into him," Norgaard growled. "He would have fought all the godlords single-handed and got himself killed."

Skylan shrugged. "We'll be dead by morning anyway. I am not afraid to die in battle. Every warrior prays that when he goes to Torval, he will stand before him with a sword in his hand. But I go into this battle tomorrow with one regret."

The warriors shouted in anger. They knew what he was going to say.

Skylan raised his voice. "My regret is that I will not have the chance to slit open the coward Horg's belly and throw his yellow entrails to the dogs!"

"Not my dog," shouted Alfric the One-Eyed. "I think too well of that mutt to poison him!"

The other warriors laughed and pounded on the table in agreement.

"Then I say we do not lose the battle tomorrow," said Garn. "No, wait! Hear me out, lord."

He turned to Norgaard. "We are outnumbered—that is true. But if the Dragon Kahg were to fight for us, that would more than even the odds."

"And if shit were gold, I would be a wealthy man," said Norgaard impatiently. "The ogres have captured our dragonship. It rides at anchor among their fleet. Their ships have it surrounded. Ogre spearmen would cut us down before we came near it."

"One man might well succeed where an army would fail," Garn replied. "After all, we do not need the dragonship. We need only the dragon."

Skylan's eyes flared with blue flame. "This is why you are my brother!" he cried, pleased. He turned to Norgaard. "You must admit it, Father. Garn's plan will work! I will swim to the dragonship, board it, and bring back the spiritbone. No one will see me in the darkness."

Norgaard's graying brows twitched. His lips creased in a rare smile. "It might work," he conceded, and that grudgingly. The Chief leveraged himself painfully to his feet, took hold of his crutch. "I will go inform the Bone Priestess, tell her to hold herself in readiness—"

"I'll do that, lord," Garn said hastily. The last thing Norgaard needed now was to see his Dragon Goddess lying on the floor in pieces. "You should remain here with the warriors. In case anything goes awry."

"Very well," Norgaard agreed readily. He sank back down thankfully into his chair. The walk to Treia's dwelling was a long one.

Skylan was already stripping off his clothes, preparing for his swim. He started to pull off his trousers. The movement caused him to draw a sharp breath. The gash inflicted by the boar's tusk ran the length of his thigh, a long red weal, and though the flesh had closed, it was obviously causing him discomfort.

"Skylan, you should let someone else go," Garn ventured to protest.

"I am War Chief. I would never order another man to face danger in my place," Skylan said.

Garn glanced about the hall. The other warriors were talking excitedly among themselves, making plans for the morrow. Garn moved closer to speak to Skylan in private.

"A War Chief must also put the good of the people above his own needs and wants. Your wound may be healed, but it obviously causes you pain, and you are weak from loss of blood. No man would say that you were shirking your duty if you asked someone who is strong and fit to undertake this."

"Like yourself?" Skylan returned. "So that you can grab all the glory?"

Garn made no reply to Skylan's remark. He folded Skylan's tunic and placed it on the table, then bent down to pick up his trousers.

"Garn, I'm sorry," said Skylan, resting his hand on his friend's arm. "I didn't mean what I said. It's just—I am the only one I can trust."

Skylan wasn't being arrogant. Even weak and wounded, he considered himself the best man for the job. But Garn knew something about Skylan that Skylan would never admit—Skylan could not bear seeing another man lay claim to the glory. Never mind that if Skylan failed, the Torgun would not have another chance to gain the spiritbone. The Torgun would pay for Skylan's failure with their lives. Garn could have said all this to his friend, but he knew what Skylan would say in return. The very words he was saying now.

"Trust me, my brother. Torval is with me. I cannot fail." Skylan went on issuing orders. "Tell the Bone Priestess to meet me in the Hall of Vindrash—"

"No," said Garn. "Not the Hall."

"Why not the Hall?" Skylan asked, pulling off his shirt. He looked out the neck hole, startled. "The Hall is the most suitable place for the ceremony."

"And that will be the first place the ogres will come looking when they find the spiritbone missing," said Garn.

"Of course, you're right," Skylan said. He smiled at his friend. "You see. I *do* listen to you. Tell Treia I will bring the spiritbone to her dwelling."

Garn breathed a sigh of relief. He had been fairly certain Skylan was too excited to see the flaw in the argument, and he'd been right. The ogres, being strangers in this part of the world, had no way of knowing where the Hall of Vindrash was located.

"I'll go talk to the Bone Priestess now," Garn offered. "Make certain she is prepared."

"A good idea," said Skylan. "And if Aylaen is there, tell her I am thinking of her. I will carry her love with me as a talisman."

Garn flinched and muttered something. Fortunately, Skylan was not paying attention.

Skylan tossed his shirt onto the table. His strong young body was seamed with marks of his valor. The scar on his thigh was only one of many.

Garn smiled, moved by true affection for his friend and admiration for his courage. Whatever Skylan's faults might be, cowardice was not one of them.

"You are the best person for this mission," said Garn.

Skylan clapped his hand on Garn's arm. "You think too much, my brother. Thinking is good, but sometimes acting is better. Don't worry. Torval is with me."

Is he? Garn wondered as Skylan left the hall, accompanied by the blessings of his father and his comrades.

Or does Torval also lie in pieces on the floor?

# CHAPTER 10

The ogre ships rocked gently in the dark water of the bay. The wind continued to freshen. The sea was choppy and restless. Sklyan watched in scorn as the ungainly ogre ships, silhouetted against the light of Akaria's silver lantern, wallowed about like grunting hogs in muck, bobbing up and down one minute and pitching side-to-side the next. By contrast, the Torgun dragonship rode the waves with a graceful motion, dipping and gliding as the waves slid beneath its keel. The dragon's fierce head reared up defiantly, dominating the gaggle of ogre ships that surrounded it.

Sklyan frowned at Akaria. He could have done without her moonlight, and he scanned the skies in search of clouds. A few drifted across the stars. Skylan tracked their progress, hoping they would cross the moon, douse the lantern's silver glow.

"Give me the knife," Skylan whispered, and Bjorn silently handed over an extremely sharp thin blade used for gutting fish.

Tonight, thought Skylan, it will be used for gutting ogres.

He tied the blade's handle onto a leather thong and slung the thong around his neck.

The three young men crouched in the shadow of the sand dunes, which were covered with brown sea grass.

"Wait for me here," Skylan ordered Bjorn and his brother. "No matter what happens, keep quiet and stay out of sight."

"What do we do if you don't come back?" Erdmun asked.

Skylan glanced at Bjorn, who rolled his eyes. His brother was a worrier, always expecting the worst.

"I will come back," said Skylan, and he added with a shrug, "They are ogres."

"Torval be with you," Bjorn whispered.

"It's just that—," Erdmun began. His brother jabbed him in the ribs, silencing him.

Skylan touched the silver axe around his neck. He was naked except for the god's token and the knife. He took one more look at the ogre ships. There would be lookouts, and they would have posted guards on the dragonship. He took hold of the knife, put it between his teeth, and bit down on it. He had braided his long hair to keep it out of his face. The most dangerous part would be running across the beach toward the water. Silhouetted against the white sand, he would be seen by every ogre in the universe. He waited, watching a cloud that was sliding nearer and nearer to Akaria's lantern.

"Torval, douse the light!" Skylan prayed. The cloud blotted out the moon.

Crouching low, Skylan dashed across the beach. He ran clumsily, slowed by the gash in his thigh that pained him more than he would admit. He kept an eye on the sky. The cloud was not large, and it was moving rapidly. Already the edge of the moon peeped out. Fortunately the tide was rising. Skylan thanked Akaria for that much, at least.

The waves broke over his feet, and he was in the water, gasping a little at the sting of the salt in his wound and the shock of plunging into the cold. Though the sun warmed the air by day, the temperature dropped when the sun set, and the sea retained the night's chill. Skylan was accustomed to much colder water, however. His people lived in the sea, bathing in seawater so cold that ice formed on their hair when they emerged.

This section of beach formed a shelf that dropped off precipitously. Skylan took only a few steps, and he was in water up to his shoulders. He began to swim, his strong arms gliding beneath the waves, taking care not to break the surface of the water with his strokes.

He hoped the chill water would ease the pain in his leg. Each time he kicked his legs was like jabbing himself in the thigh with a spear. The pain hampered his swimming, and the unwelcome thought came to him that Garn might have been right. Maybe he should have let some other man undertake this. The thought made Skylan angry, and he gritted his teeth, champing down hard on the knife's blade, and deliberately gave a strong kick, like that of a frog's, to challenge the pain.

Akaria brushed aside the cloud, and moonlight glinted off the waves. Skylan would have to swim close to the ogre ship in order to reach the dragonships. He scanned the deck as he swam near. He could not see the ogres who stood on watch, but he could hear their voices. There were two of them, by the sounds of it, and they were playing at some sort of game to keep themselves awake. The rest of the crew would be wrapped in their blankets on the deck, getting what sleep they could before tomorrow's battle. As stupid as ogres were, they were smart enough to know that the Torgun would not give up without a fight.

Skylan swam silently around the ship, keeping in its shadow, which drifted over the water.

The dragonship loomed in front of him. Akaria's light lovingly gilded the dragon-head prow with silver. The ship was painted blue to honor the Dragon Kahg, whose spirit guided the dragonship on its voyages. Kahg's spirit resided in one of his bones, which had been given long ago by the Goddess Vindrash to the Torgun in the Hall of Vektia, on the famed Dragon Isles.

The spirit of the Dragon Kahg powered the dragonship, so that it could travel the seas without need for oarsmen or sails. When summoned by the prayers of a Bone Priestess, the Dragon Kahg could take on physical form and fight the Torgun's enemies. Many of the clans had dragonships, which were a mark of a clan's rank and power. The Torgun might be poor, but so long as they had their dragonship, they remained a force among the Vindrasi.

In return for the dragons' guidance and protection, the Vindrasi people pledged to give all the jewels they captured to the dragons. The dragons sorted through them, kept the gems they wanted, and returned the rest as a reward to the warriors.

The Vindrasi had no idea why the dragons wanted the jewels. It might be supposed that the gems the dragons kept would be the most valuable, but that was not case. Skylan himself had seen Kahg select a small emerald, badly set and crudely cut, and hand back a large ruby with a heart of fire.

The Vindrasi did not know what happened to the jewels the dragons took with them. Legend spoke of vast hoards stashed away in secret caves on the

Dragon Isles, kept safe by a curse placed on them by the Goddess Vindrash. There were always, in every generation, a few greedy and irreverent men who would defy the goddess and set out in search of the dragon hoards. Such warriors always came to a bad end. Their stories and their gruesome deaths made for cautionary tales told during the long winter nights.

The Vindrasi imagined that dragons were like crows—fascinated by anything bright and shiny. None ever came close to understanding the truth, for that was a secret the dragons had kept for centuries and intended to keep for centuries more.

Skylan thought of all this as he swam through the water, his gaze fixed on the dragon's fierce head. Treia had said the Dragon Kahg had not answered her summons because he was angry with the Torgun for not keeping their end of the bargain. Last year's raiding season had brought only a handful of jewels, all of which the dragon had tossed aside in disdain. This year's raid had brought no jewels at all, only ogres, and now the loss of the Vektan Torque, which contained a sapphire said to be of immense value. The Dragon Kahg might well be so furious that even if Skylan succeeded in bringing back the spiritbone, the dragon might refuse to fight for them.

"Perhaps you would like to see us impaled on ogre spears," Skylan remarked, speaking to the dragon's head, whose red eyes seemed to glare down on him with a baleful expression. "I am not saying that we have not deserved your wrath. But keep this in mind—if the ogres defeat us, there will be no more jewels for you, ever."

Trusting that the dragon would take this reasonable view of the matter, Skylan treaded water near the prow of the dragonship and concentrated on listening, hoping to be able to judge how many ogres guarded the ship and where they were located. He heard the tread of heavy footfalls. One ogre at least walked the deck. Skylan, staring upward, was startled to see a bald head outlined against the stars, leaning over the side, gazing down.

Skylan ducked beneath the waves and remained there, holding his breath as long as he could. He surfaced some distance away, snatched a gulp of air, and looked. The ogre's head was gone. The heavy tread of boots was moving on. Skylan did not hear any voices, and he hoped the ogres had posted only one guard on board. Skylan himself would have posted three, but then, these were ogres.

He didn't dare take any more time to investigate. The chill of the water was starting to sink into his bones. He heard the ogre walking away from him. He swam silently to the prow, where the dragon's long, gracefully curving neck formed the ship's stem. The wooden carving that represented the Dragon Kahg was beautifully rendered. Each scale—and there were hundreds, each about as large as a man's hand—had been carefully delineated. The grooves in the wood outlining the scales had been carved deep enough so that Skylan could dig his fingers into them and use them to assist him in climbing up the neck. One of his jobs when he was nine years old had been to "scale the dragon." He had climbed the long neck, then clung precariously to the swaying head and acted as lookout, watching for everything from enemy ships to dangerous shoals.

Skylan's fingers were no longer those of a nine-year-old child. They no longer fit into the grooves, but the irregular surface allowed him to establish a handhold. His arm muscles ached with the strain; his wound throbbed. The water had been cold, but the air was even colder. The breeze raised gooseflesh on his naked body. His teeth would have chattered, but he still held the knife between them.

The ogre guard had walked to the ship's stern. Skylan, clinging to the dragon's neck, was just thanking Torval for this blessing, when a large head, bullish neck, and massive shoulders reared up from the deck not five paces away. Skylan froze, holding his breath, careful not to move or even shiver. The guard stretched and yawned cavernously; apparently he'd been napping. He scratched his belly and peered in a bored manner around the ship.

Both ogres had their backs to Skylan. Neither had seen him. Torval had given his enemies into his hands, but Skylan had only seconds to act. He climbed silently over the hull and jumped down, landing lightly on the balls of his feet, and immediately crouched, hiding in the shadows. Skylan eyed the ogre nearest to him. He had to fell this ogre and do it quietly. If the guard had been human, Skylan would have wrapped his hand over the man's mouth to prevent him from screaming as he plunged the knife into his heart.

The ogre was too large for that. Skylan would have had to jump on the brute's back to reach his hand around the head, and then he wasn't sure his knife was long enough to find its way through the blubber and bone to the brute's heart.

The ogre blinked, yawned again, and stretched his arms over his head. Any moment, he might call out to his friend, who would turn around and see Skylan.

Skylan glanced swiftly around the deck for another weapon besides his knife. Men were constantly working on the dragonship when in port, making repairs and keeping the ship fit and trim. Woodworking tools littered the deck. Grabbing hold of an adz, Skylan padded soft-footed up behind the ogre, and using all his strength, he swung the adz and bashed the ogre in the back of his head.

The adz's sharp point pierced the skull and sank deep into the ogre's brain. Skylan yanked. The tool came out, trailing blood and brains. The ogre's body jerked spasmodically. His knees buckled, and he started to fall backwards. Skylan caught the heavy body in his arms, nearly collapsing himself under the dead weight. Grunting softly, Skylan lowered the body quietly onto the deck.

Skylan had kept as silent as he could, but the other ogre had either heard something or sensed something that alarmed him. He whipped around, his large body moving faster than Skylan would have thought possible. The ogre's eyes widened in astonishment to see a man, dripping wet, naked as the day he was born, standing on the deck.

The ogre reached for his axe, opening his mouth to shout the alarm. Skylan had to shut him up, and he flung the adz at his foe as he would have thrown an axe in battle. Unfortunately, the adz was lighter than a battle axe. It struck the ogre a glancing blow on the forehead. The ogre stumbled a little and blinked his eyes as blood poured down his face, but he did not fall.

Skylan broke into a run, racing across the deck, bounding over what tools he could avoid, treading barefoot on others. The ogre was dazed from the blow, and Skylan barreled into him. He slammed his right shoulder into the ogre's gut, driving the breath from the ogre's body. The two crashed against the hull.

Though he was gulping for breath, the ogre continued to struggle and, what was worse, to make noise. Skylan plunged his knife into the ogre's side, not caring where he hit. The ogre grunted in pain, and Skylan stabbed again and again and at last the ogre quit moving and bleating. Skylan sank back on his heels, sucking in air and looking around to see if anyone on the ogre ships had heard the commotion. He waited tensely for flaring lights and voices shouting in alarm.

Nothing happened, and Skylan heaved a sigh. He groaned as he rose to his feet. He limped like his father across the deck, his injured leg throbbing, his feet cut and bruised from treading on the tools. Skylan was elated, however, and he laughed to himself to think how easily he had defeated his enemies. He touched Torval's silver axe in thanks.

The sacred spiritbone—a fingerbone from Kahg's front claw—hung on a wooden peg that had been driven into the ship's curved prow. Unlike the Vektan Torque, the spiritbone was not decorated with gold nor was it adorned with jewels. A pewter band wrapped around the knuckle portion of the fingerbone held it suspended from a plain leather thong.

As a child, Skylan had been bothered by the fact that their spiritbone was not so magnificent as the gold-and-sapphire Vektan Torque. He felt that the

Torgun were being disrespectful of their dragon, and he had vowed to his father than when he was Chief, he would set Kahg's bone in the finest gold and surround it with jewels.

Norgaard had explained why Skylan would do no such thing. Skylan took hold of the leather thong and gently and reverently removed the spiritbone from the peg. He remembered his father's words, and now he saw the old man's wisdom.

"An enemy who seizes our ship and sees a bone hanging from a peg will not look at it twice. An enemy who sees a bone decorated with gold and jewels will do what with it, Skylan?"

"He would steal it," Skylan had said then, and he said the same softly now.

Ogres did not worship the Dragon Goddess. Their shamans had no way to summon dragons, and even if they did, the dragons would not stoop to serve ogres, or at least so Skylan liked to think. Seeing a bone decorated in gold and jewels, the ogres would have taken it for the wealth alone. As it was, they had probably not even noticed it.

He removed the leather thong and was hanging it over his head when he heard the sound: a booted foot, trying to move quietly, had stepped on an auger lying on the deck. The tool had rolled out from underneath, causing the foot to slip and scrape on the deck.

A third guard. Right behind him.

The ogre let out an immense roar, sounding the alarm. Enormous arms wrapped around Skylan's body. Clamping both arms to Skylan's rib cage, the ogre hoisted Skylan off his feet and began to squeeze the life out of him.

Warned by a split second of the coming attack, Skylan had his knife in hand, but with his arms pinned, he couldn't use it. He flexed his arm muscles, pushing against the ogre's arms, hoping to break the brute's grip. Feeling Skylan wriggle, the ogre gave a grunt and tightened his grasp.

Skylan was finding it hard to breathe. His head pressed against the ogre's massive chest, he could hear him grunting and smell the stink of unwashed flesh.

Skylan flailed about with his feet, trying to find the deck in order to gain purchase. The deck was nowhere near, but the prow was. Skylan lifted his knees and, with a desperate lunge, thrust out his legs. Hitting the prow with his feet, he pushed himself backwards straight into the ogre, whose feet went out from under him. The ogre landed heavily on the deck with Skylan floundering about on top of the immense belly. The stupid brute refused to let loose.

Skylan jammed his foot into the ogre's crotch. The ogre groaned in pain and let go of Skylan to grab himself. Skylan scrambled to his feet and cast a quick glance around at the ogre ships.

Lantern light flared. Ogres milled about on the decks, trying to see who had raised the alarm, determine the threat. Several of them caught sight of Skylan and began yelling and pointing at him. A spear thudded into the prow not a hand's span from his head.

Skylan grasped the spiritbone. Feeling it secure around his neck, he ran to the ship's hull, swung himself over the side, and dropped into the water. He would have to swim between two ogre ships to reach the shore. Looking up, he saw an ogre holding a trident and peering down. Skylan made a desperate dive. The trident splashed into the water beside him, a narrow miss.

Skylan swam underwater as long as he could hold his breath, until at last he was forced to surface. The ogres had been watching for him. Sighting his head, they raised a shout. Spears plunked into the water all around him. Skylan had to search for the shoreline; he'd grown confused in the darkness. A spear struck him in the leg, but its flight was slowed by the water, and it did little damage. Akaria, his blessing on her, held her lantern high. The beach gleamed white silver in the moonlight, and Skylan sucked in a breath and dived down once more.

He thought he heard more spears strike the water, but he couldn't be sure, and by now he no longer cared. His strength was flagging. The waves carried him forward, and at last his feet struck the sandy bottom. He lurched up out of the water and staggered toward the shore and heard the ogres yell. Spears thunked around him, and he fell to his knees and began to crawl. He was about finished. He could not make it much farther.

Two men rose up out of the dunes. Bjorn and Erdmun, braving the spears, dashed across the sand. Each grabbed hold of Skylan by his shoulders and, lifting him up, hauled him bodily across the beach and into the shadows of the dunes.

Skylan shook with the cold. Bjorn flung a cloak around him, began rubbing him down.

"Did you get the spiritbone?" Erdmun asked worriedly.

"I would not . . . have come back . . . without it," Skylan said through chattering teeth.

CHAPTER

# 11

Skylan sank into a deep sleep, his hand clasped around the spiritbone, while Bjorn and Erdmun worked unsuccessfully to warm him. They tried to wake him, but he remained unconscious. They tried to pry Skylan's fingers from the spiritbone, but even in his sleep, he refused to let it go. Eventually, not knowing what else to do, they picked him up and carried him back to the village, where they were met by a contingent of armed men.

Having heard the ogres' shouts, they thought the battle had started. They cheered when they saw Skylan and heard he had the spiritbone. When he did not rouse at the cheering or at the sound of his father's voice, they grew concerned. They loaded him onto a wooden plank and carried him to the dwelling of the Bone Priestess.

Garn waited with Aylaen and Treia in the small longhouse. Hearing the shouts, Garn picked up his axe.

"Is it ogres?" Treia asked calmly.

Garn listened carefully. "I don't think so. But something's happened. I'll go see." He ducked out the door. "I'll be back," he called over his shoulder. "Wait here!"

Aylaen looked at her sister. Treia did not appear at all frightened. She remained seated on a stool, her hands folded in her lap. If anything, Treia sounded almost relieved.

"It's Skylan!" Garn cried exultantly.

Aylaen met him in the doorway.

"He has the spiritbone!" Garn told her. "Norgaard says your sister should make preparations for the ceremony to summon the dragon."

"Is Skylan all right?" Aylaen asked, noting Garn looked worried.

He shook his head. "I don't know. Something is wrong. He has fallen into a strange sleep, and he won't wake up. I'm going to him."

Before Aylaen could say a word, Garn dashed off. She turned to her sister. "Did you hear?"

Treia nodded. "Shut the door."

Aylaen stared at her. "But they will be coming—"

"I said shut the door." Treia's voice grated.

Aylaen did as her sister asked and pulled the heavy door shut.

The only light in the dwelling came from the fire, and that had been allowed to burn low. Treia's face was a pale glimmer in the shadows. Aylaen sat down beside her sister. She reached out, clasped Treia's hand.

"Treia," Aylaen said softly. "What's the matter?"

Treia did not look at her. She sat gazing into the darkness.

"The last time I tried to summon the Dragon Kahg, on the raid, the dragon would not come," said Treia.

"You said he was angry," Aylaen reminded her. "The warriors had not found any jewels—"

Treia shook her head. "I lied. Vindrash won't speak to me. How can I summon the dragon if the Dragon Goddess won't answer my prayers? And then there's the statue. . . ."

"Treia, it broke—"

"It broke," said Treia, "when I touched it."

Aylaen was shocked, but she tried to devise an excuse. "As Garn said, the statue was old—"

Treia made an angry, impatient gesture.

Aylaen loved and admired her sister, but she was also intimidated by her. Treia was so smart, so clever, always thinking deep and serious and complex thoughts. Aylaen wanted life to be simple. She wanted only to love Garn and be loved by him in return. The gods wanted life to be simple, too. Aylaen had always felt close to the gods, perhaps because as a little girl she had liked making up stories about them and telling them to her friends.

An unhappy child—bereft of the father she had adored, mistreated by her stepfather, and generally ignored by her grieving mother—Aylaen found a father in Torval, who would protect her from Sigurd's thrashings, and a loving mother in Vindrash. The dragon would let Aylaen ride upon her back, between her wings, and carry her off to heaven.

Aylaen could hear voices outside. The men were coming, bringing with them the unconscious Skylan and the sacred spiritbone.

Treia made no move to rise.

Aylaen sighed. She squeezed her sister's cold hand and said quietly, "Skylan risked his life to recover the spiritbone. You have to try to summon the dragon, Treia."

"And let them see me fail again?" said Treia bitterly.

"You won't fail," said Aylaen. "The gods know we are in trouble. They will come to our aid."

Treia shifted her bleary-eyed gaze toward her. Aylaen had often tried to imagine what it would be like to see the world through imperfect eyes. Treia had once told her she saw everything a blur, as though someone had wiped a wet rag across the world.

"I was twelve years old when the Kai Priestess took me away," said Treia, the words pouring from her in an ugly, bitter torrent. "Only twelve. And I was alone in a strange place, living with strange people, none of whom gave a crap about me. Nothing I did was ever good enough for Draya. All she thought and talked about day and night were the gods. Her husband, Horg, is a drunken pig. He was always trying to force himself on me. Once, when I was fourteen years old, he had his filthy hands all over me.

"I worked like a slave, scrubbing and cleaning and cooking. And all the while, I had to listen to stories of the gods. Draya droning on and on until I wanted to scream. And the sick people! I had to help the Priestesses heal them, which meant I did all the horrid work while they prayed. I can still smell the stink of rotting flesh and the puke and the pus oozing from putrid wounds. I wanted them to die. I wanted them all to die—"

"Treia, stop!" Aylaen cried, frightened.

Treia fell silent. Aylaen could hear the men muttering outside. Having found the door closed, they wondered what was amiss.

Garn raised his voice. "Bone Priestess, open the door." His tone was respectful, but there was an edge to his voice.

"I'll let them in, shall I, Treia?" Aylaen asked hesitantly.

Treia sat with her hands clenched in her lap. Her face was like granite, her lips tight. Suddenly she rose to her feet. Pushing past Aylaen, Treia walked to the door and flung it open. She stood on the threshold, gazing out at the warriors, at Skylan, unconscious, lying on his cloak on the plank.

"Bring him inside," Treia ordered.

The warriors lifted Skylan and carried him into the dwelling. They laid him on the bed—a platform made of wood covered with cushions.

"Return to your homes," Treia told the warriors. "There's nothing more you can do this night."

"The Priestess is right," said Garn. "Go back to your homes. Get what sleep you can before the battle."

The warriors departed, some to sleep, but most to make ready for the fight.

Treia frowned at Garn, who settled himself in a corner.

"I'm staying," he said in answer to her look.

Treia shrugged. Kneeling down beside Skylan, she ordered Aylaen to bring a light. Aylaen lit a candle and held it above Skylan. His lips had a bluish cast. Every so often, a tremor shook his body. His hand was still wrapped around the spiritbone. Treia rested her head on his chest.

"His heart is weak. He needs warmth," she said. "Build up the fire. Cover him with furs and blankets. I will mix a potion to heat his blood."

Garn cast a troubled glance at Aylaen. She avoided his gaze, pretending to be busy in gathering up blankets. Her sister's outburst had left a raw, bleeding gash in her soul. Aylaen had always pictured her sister's life in Vindraholm as one of serene tranquillity. She had imagined Treia being honored, loved, and cherished—for the Bone Priestesses were revered among the Vindrasi. In a few brief and bitter words, Treia had destroyed Aylaen's illusions, portraying instead a life of loneliness, fear, and deprivation.

Aylaen was consumed with remorse. Her life with her stepfather had not been easy, for Sigurd was a hard man. But Aylaen had been fortunate to have friends, like Garn and Skylan. For Treia, there had been no one.

Treia crouched over a kettle, engaged in combining various ingredients and stirring them together. Aylaen rested her cheek against her sister's and put her arms around her. At first Treia stiffened in Aylaen's embrace and seemed about to rebuff her. Something in Aylaen's softened expression touched her sister. A faint smile flitted over Treia's thin lips. She touched Aylaen's hand, and then she went back to her work.

Garn returned with wood and built up the fire until the room was almost too hot to bear. Aylaen piled furs and blankets on top of Skylan, wrapping him snugly. He remained sunk in the strange sleep.

"He's still so cold," she said.

She smoothed back Skylan's wet hair with a gentle hand, looking with deep concern at the pallid face of her friend. Skylan was dear to her, taking second place only to Garn in her heart.

"Treia should ask the gods to help him," said Garn.

Aylaen cringed and glanced around, but Treia was absorbed in her work and did not seem to hear.

"I'm certain she knows best," Aylaen said, and changed the subject. "What Skylan did was very brave. And very foolish." She shook her head in fond exasperation. "He should have sent someone who didn't have a gash in his thigh."

"Skylan is War Chief," said Garn. "It was his right to accept the danger."

Aylaen could tell by his tone that he secretly agreed with her, but he would let himself be sliced open and turned inside out before he would say anything against his friend.

"Which is why I love you," Aylaen whispered, and she brushed her lips against his shoulder as she rose to go see if she could assist Treia.

"Hold this," said Treia, and she handed Aylaen a drinking horn.

Liquid clear as water simmered in the kettle. Treia filled a ladle and poured the contents into the horn mug.

Aylaen regarded it dubiously. "What is it?"

"It is called bread wine," Treia said. "It is wine made from grain, not grapes.

The process is secret, known only to the Kai Priestess. Draya gave me some to bring with me."

"It looks just like water," Aylaen said. "Are you sure it will warm him?"

"It will warm everything inside him," said Treia dryly. "Taste it, if you like."

Aylaen tipped the mug gingerly to her lips and swallowed a small mouthful. Tears stung her eyes. She couldn't catch her breath, and she choked and gagged. Treia was right. The liquid burned from her tongue down her throat and into her belly.

"Lift his head," Treia ordered Garn.

Treia shoved the horn mug into Skylan's mouth and expertly tilted back his head, forcing the liquid into his mouth and down his throat. Skylan gagged much of it back up, but Treia was persistent and kept pouring it down him.

When the drinking horn was empty, Garn laid his friend back down on the bed.

"Now what?" he asked.

"He wanders the Nethervold," said Treia, shrugging. "He will either find his way back or he won't."

Dark waves washed over Skylan's head. He swam and swam, but he could not reach the shore. He was cold, bitterly cold, and exhausted and in pain. He kept swimming because he had the spiritbone and his people needed the dragon. He swam until he was so cold that he could no longer feel his arms and legs. He was tired. Very tired. It would be easier to die. He started to sink. . . .

His feet touched sandy bottom. He almost wept with relief as he waded out of the water. The sun blazed down on him, warmed him. He had landed on a strange shore, one he did not recognize. White cliffs soared high above him. He had to crane his neck to see to the top. Eagles circled in the blue sky.

Naked, Skylan walked the shore, searching for a ship, a boat, a raft—anything. He had to return to his people before it was too late.

At the bottom of the white cliffs was a cave. Outside the cave, a man sat on a boulder. He had his back to Skylan, who walked toward him. The man was a warrior, and an important one at that. He must be a lord, the Chief of some wealthy clan. He wore a helm adorned with dragon wings, and he was clad in plate armor and chain mail, bright and shining in the sunlight. His shield, painted blue and gold, lay on the ground. A beautiful two-handed sword hung at his side.

"Hail, noble sir!" Skylan said, calling out so that the lord would not think he was sneaking up on him.

The lord turned his head, and Skylan was startled to see the noble lord bent over a hot flat rock, cooking fish.

Skylan stood touching his hand to his breast in a mark of respect, but he couldn't help staring.

The armor the man wore was costly. The sword alone could ransom a king. So what was this noble warrior doing sitting alone on an empty stretch of beach cooking his dinner like a poor fisherman?

The warrior had long gray hair and was clean-shaven. He had a beaked nose and far-seeing eyes, a strong jaw and jutting chin. He was old, far older than Norgaard, who was the oldest man Skylan had ever known. The lord's eyes, shadowed by overhanging brows, glittered with an inner blue fire. The eyes pierced Skylan through and through.

"Forgive my nakedness, sir," Skylan said, ashamed. "I was shipwrecked, lost at sea. Can you tell me where I am and where I can find a boat? My people are going to battle against the ogres, and I must fight for them."

"I know all about your people," said the old warrior, grunting. "I know about the ogres, Freilis take them and feed them to her demons. And I know you, Skylan Ivorson. You obviously do not know me, though you wear my axe around your neck and your prayers din in my ears daily."

Skylan's jaw dropped. He stared, gaping. "Torval!" He couldn't help but add in disbelief, "Cooking fish?"

"What of it? I can't stomach them raw." The god eyed Skylan. "You're an arrogant young dog, aren't you?"

Skylan flushed, not sure what to say. Torval, Warrior God of the Vindrasi, should have been sitting at ease in his chair in the Hall of Heroes, drinking and celebrating with those valiant warriors who had died in battle and would fight with Torval in the last great war at Time's end. Instead, he was here alone on a empty beach, roasting fish.

"I worship you, Torval, and honor—," Skylan began.

Torval rubbed his chin. "You claim to have faith in me. But I'll wager you have more faith in yourself."

Skylan's flush deepened. His dearest wish in all the world was to stand before Torval, and here he was, saying, doing, and thinking all the wrong things. "I swear to you, Torval—"

"Forgo swearing." Torval sighed. He looked suddenly very old and very tired. "We don't have much time together. My enemies pursue me, harry me. I cannot remain here long. I cannot remain anywhere long."

"Then what the ogres claimed is true!" Skylan said, dismayed. "The Gods of the Vindrasi lost the battle—"

"I did not piss my pants and run!" Torval roared. "Nor am I dead, as they claim. Though I did lose Desiria, who was dear to me."

His eyes grew moist as he spoke. He clenched his fist in anger, and the fire burned away his tears.

"We gods will continue the fight. Or at least some of us will; I have no idea where that craven coward Joabis is hiding. I've had my eye on you, Skylan Ivorson. Most of what I've seen I've liked. Not all." He shrugged. "But most."

Skylan fell to his knees. "I am yours, Torval."

"You must fight in the battle for the Vektan Torque tomorrow," said the god. "The very survival of the Vindrasi is at stake, and so I'm going to do for you what I've never done for any mortal. I'm going to make you whole again."

"Thank you, Torval!" Skylan was elated. "I will justify your faith in me."

The god grunted. "We'll see about that. I am not an easy master, as you will soon find out. Here, drink this."

He handed Skylan his drinking horn. Inside was a clear liquid. Skylan drank and choked and coughed and kept coughing, his eyes watering so he could not see. When he finally caught his breath, Torval had disappeared.

"What is it? What's happened?" Garn asked, waking with a start.

He had not meant to fall asleep, but he was worn out from the day's exertions. He'd leaned his back against the wall near Skylan's bed, planning to keep watch over his friend. Sleep had crept up on him and captured him without a fight. He glanced outside. The sky was still dark. The stars still shone brightly. Morning was yet some distance away.

"He's breathing normally," Aylaen said. "His skin is warm to the touch! Treia was right. Sister, look!"

Treia came over to the bed. She bent down, placed her hand on Skylan's head and then on his chest. He smiled and let go of the spiritbone.

"Torval," he muttered, "I am yours!"

"Your prayers worked, Treia!" Aylaen said softly. "What the ogres claimed is not true! The gods are not dead. The broken statue was just a broken statue."

"I didn't pray for him," Treia said.

Lifting Skylan's head, she removed the spiritbone from around his neck. "I am going to the Hall of Vindrash," Treia announced, taking up a torch. "Alone," she added, guessing that Garn would offer to escort her. "I will be safe. After all, the gods are with me."

Aylaen winced at her sister's mocking tone and hoped Garn did not notice.

"I will take the good news to Norgaard, and then I will be back," Garn said. He looked very grim.

He left, heading for the village at a run. Treia walked into the darkness, carrying the spiritbone, clutching it tightly, her fingers curled over it as though she secretly longed to crush it. She kept her head lowered, forced to peer, squint-eyed, at the uneven ground beneath her feet to avoid tripping and falling. The torch flame wavered in the wind.

Aylaen watched from the doorway until she saw the torchlight vanish and she was certain Treia had reached the Hall safely. Sighing, Aylaen shut the door. She drew the blanket up around Skylan's shoulders and tucked it around him and added more wood to the fire. The room was warm; the heat was making her drowsy. She needed something to do to keep herself awake. Skylan would be hungry when he woke. Garn had brought along some of the boar meat. Aylaen tossed it in the stewpot and began chopping up vegetables. Intent on her work, she was startled to feel that someone else was in the room with her. The presence was not threatening. It was reassuring, warming as the bread wine.

"Treia? Is that you?" Aylaen asked. She turned abruptly and almost cut herself with the sharp knife. "I didn't hear you come in—"

The door was shut. The room was empty.

Aylaen looked at Skylan, but he lay sprawled comfortably on his back, fathoms deep in easeful slumber.

Aylaen finished her task and sat down. She thought back to a time when she was a little girl and she had run away from Sigurd and his fist and had ended up getting lost in the woods in the night. She had been terrified and had started to cry, and then she had felt a presence as she felt now, gentle and loving. She had imagined wings folding around her, holding her close, keeping her safe. She had fallen asleep. . . .

Aylaen woke with a start.

"Vindrash," Aylaen whispered, "I am not one of your Priestesses. I know it's not my place to ask, but as you love your people, please grant Treia's prayers this night!"

CHAPTER

# 12

Skylan woke before dawn feeling groggy, his head pounding, as though he'd spent the night carousing, not dodging spears and fighting ogres. He reached immediately for the spiritbone, and not finding it, his eyes flared open and he sat up, alarmed.

"Relax," said Garn, smiling. "Treia has the spiritbone. She has gone to summon Kahg."

Skylan sighed in relief. He swung his feet over the side of the bed and winced.

"How's your leg?" Garn asked.

"Stiff," Skylan admitted, adding in a puzzled tone, "It's not my leg that aches. It's my head. I feel as though I'd gone swimming in ale, not seawater."

"It must be the bread wine Treia gave you," Garn said.

"The stuff tasted foul," Aylaen said. "It sent you into a deep sleep. You called on Torval in your dreams."

"I never dream," Skylan returned contemptuously. "Ask Garn."

"He doesn't," Garn agreed with a shrug. "Or if he does, he never remembers them."

Aylaen was skeptical. "Everyone dreams."

"I don't," Skylan said firmly. He glanced around at his surroundings, dim in the gray light. "Where am I?"

"My sister's house," said Aylaen, and she handed him a bowl of stew along with a hunk of bread.

Skylan sniffed at it dubiously. "Did you make this?" He winked at Garn. "Perhaps I should have you taste this first, like the ogres, to make sure you haven't poisoned me."

"Fine. I'll take it back," said Aylaen, reaching for the bowl.

Skylan yanked it out of her hands. He dipped the bread in the gravy, stuffed it hungrily into his mouth.

Aylaen handed Garn a bowl of stew. As he took it from her, their hands touched.

"Torval be with you this day," she said softly.

"He will be," said Skylan, scooping meat into his mouth with the bread.

He looked up to find Aylaen standing close to Garn, her hand resting lightly on his shoulder. Seeing Skylan watching, she flushed and moved her hand. Garn cleared his throat and stepped a pace away.

Skylan quit eating to stare at them. "You two . . ."

"What?" Garn asked in a tight voice.

Skylan smiled. "The three of us together this morning. My brother and my betrothed. It makes me happy, that's all."

He handed Aylaen the empty bowl.

"A good thing I'm not marrying you for your cooking," he jested.

Aylaen's face went crimson. She took the bowl and laid it aside, hardly knowing where she put it. Garn opened the door and stood breathing deeply. Aylis the Sun Goddess had not yet risen from her bed, but the light of her blazing torch could be seen above the treetops, brightening the sky in the east, causing the stars to grow pale in homage.

"A fine day for a fight," said Skylan.

He wrapped the blanket around his waist and rose from the bed, putting weight on his leg. The wound was sore, but his leg bore his weight without complaint.

"I brought you some clothes." Garn gestured to the foot of the bed. "And your weapons, your armor, and your shield."

"Why so grim, brother?" Skylan bantered as he pulled his tunic over his head. "Cheer up! We do battle this day!"

He dressed swiftly, pulling on his trousers and then his boots, lacing them securely around his legs. Garn assisted him with his armor. Skylan buckled his sword around his waist. He put on his helm, which had belonged to his father, and picked up his shield. Last, as he always did before a fight, he reverently touched the silver axe and pledged himself to Torval.

"I will join the other warriors," he announced to Garn. "You go to the Hall of Vindrash, escort the Bone Priestess to the battlefield."

Garn nodded silently. Skylan thought his friend was unusually quiet. Skylan clapped his hand on Garn's shoulder.

"Aylaen said I spoke Torval's name in the night. Even though I don't dream, it is undoubtedly a good omen," Skylan said, trying to cheer his friend. "The Vektan Torque will be ours this day."

His voice hardened; his expression grew grim. "And once I have it, I will take it to that whoreson Horg and shove it up his arse!"

"You should use your spear for that, *not* the sacred torque," Garn said.

Skylan laughed. The two embraced.

Skylan tried to persuade Aylaen to give him a farewell kiss, but she shoved him away.

"I'm coming with you," she said.

"No, you're not," said Skylan firmly. "It is too late for you to go to the hills with the other women, but you will be safe here."

"Skylan's right—," Garn began.

Aylaen's lips tightened, her chin lifted, her jaw set. Her red hair seemed to lift and stir as though it were alive. Her green eyes flickered dangerously. The two young men knew the signs, and they glanced at each other.

"I can fight her or I can fight ogres," Skylan said to Garn. "I don't have time to do both. Keep her with you and keep her safe."

He hastened off, walking without a limp. He was in excellent spirits, and as the flames of the Sun Goddess's torch began to lick the clouds, Skylan raised his voice in a war chant.

Garn began to walk rapidly toward the Hall of Vindrash. He moved so fast that he caught Aylaen off guard, and she was forced to run after him. She could not take his hand, because he was carrying a spear in his right hand and his shield in his left. She caught hold of his forearm. He moved his arm from her grasp.

"You should go back to Treia's house," he said.

"You're mad at me, aren't you?" Aylaen asked.

Garn kept walking, moving rapidly, for the torch of the Sun Goddess was spreading a golden sheen across the blue sky. The warriors would be assembling, preparing to take their places in the shield-wall.

Aylaen looked up into the glorious sky and said quietly, "Without the dragon, you cannot win. Not even Skylan can change that. You will die."

"You nearly gave away our secret," Garn said abruptly.

"I didn't mean to—"

"Didn't you?" He glanced at her.

Aylaen flushed. She was about to continue denying the charge, but then saw no reason why she should.

"Very well. And why not?"

She rounded on Garn with a sudden savagery that took him aback. "Am I the only one with any sense? Skylan sings war chants and talks of dying with glory. I talk of dying, Garn! You could die today! I am not a fool. The ogres outnumber you. I know that if Kahg does not fight, you and Skylan and the rest of our warriors are doomed. I know that this time might be the last time we are ever together. I could lose you today, my love, and I can't bear the thought."

Garn's expression softened. Aylaen wrapped her arms around herself, kept them tight beneath her cloak.

"And if the warriors all die, what happens to us women?" she said bitterly. "You men never think of that! You join Torval in his Hall to spend the afterlife singing war chants and reliving your glorious battles. This night I might be lying on my back with my hands bound with some grunting ogre on top of me—"

"Aylaen, don't!" Garn said swiftly. He dropped his weapons and his shield and put his arm around her. He felt her shivering.

"You know it's true," she cried, pulling away from him. "You know the women are not safe in the hills. The ogres will pursue us. They will kill the children and the old people and enslave the rest of us. They will carry us off to their land, where we will be beaten and raped to death. And you and Skylan go into battle singing!"

She wanted him to suffer, and she'd succeeded. Garn went extremely pale. He had been on raids. He knew, better than Aylaen, the cruel fate suffered by women at the hands of raiders. In the old days, the Vindrasi had taken slaves, a practice that they discontinued. Slaves were a nuisance to deal with on a voyage, requiring constant guarding and gobbling up meager supplies. Even now, though, a victorious warrior could take his pleasure with a captured woman, do with her as he pleased, then abandon her.

"That is why I would rather be near the battle than skulking in the hills," Aylaen stated.

She drew aside her cloak. She had brought the battle axe with her, the head tucked into the leather belt she wore around her slender waist. She smiled at him. "Do you think Torval will let me into his Hall?"

Garn could not speak; his emotion swelled his throat and choked off his voice. He drew her close and kissed her forehead. "I'm sorry I was angry," he said.

"I want the world to know of our love," said Aylaen. "I don't want to have to stand guard on my lips, fearful of letting the wrong word slip out. I don't want to have to slip away to meet you in secret—"

She stopped suddenly, sniffed the air. "I smell smoke!"

The two looked at each other in alarm, then looked at the Hall of Vindrash. They could see smoke rising, but they could not tell what was burning.

Garn picked up his weapons. He and Aylaen broke into a run, heading for the Hall. The same thought was in both of their minds: The ogres had somehow found the Hall and set it on fire. Aylaen cried out her sister's name, but there was no answer.

Reaching the Hall, Garn and Aylaen stopped and stared in shock and dismay. The statue of Vindrash was going up in flames. Treia stood beside the fire, watching the statue burn, her face impassive.

Garn ran toward the fire with some wild thought of trying to save the statue, snatch it from the flames. He could see that he was too late. Not only was the wood old, but it had also been soaked in oil, for part of the Priestess's daily ritual was to rub it and polish it lovingly. The flames crackled. The Dragon Goddess withered.

"The statue was broken," said Treia, not looking at either of them.

Aylaen put her hand to her mouth to stifle a cry. She looked at Garn.

"It is time," he said harshly. "Past time. We must make haste."

He told the two women to walk in front of him. He followed behind, his weapons in his hands. Treia held the spiritbone pressed against her chest.

"Have you ever been in a battle?" Aylaen asked.

Treia shook her head.

"Neither have I. We have been lucky, Mother says. No enemy has attacked us on our own soil in many years, not since before I was born." Aylaen hesitated, then said, "Did Vindrash answer your prayers?"

Treia's lips tightened. She stared straight ahead, then said, "Why do you think I burned the statue?"

Aylaen's mouth went dry; her stomach clenched. A tremor of fear ran through her. Without the dragon to help even the odds, the Torgun could not win. Aylaen had talked of being taken captive by the ogres, but she had said that mainly to hurt Garn, not because she'd truly confronted the awful reality. Now she did so, and she was sick with fear. Her hands shook; her palms were wet with sweat. She gripped the axe tightly to keep the handle from slipping out of her grasp.

"I prayed to Vindrash, that she would answer your prayers," Aylaen said softly, thinking this would please her sister.

Treia's face went livid. "Because I am a failure."

"No, sister, truly!" Aylaen faltered. "I never thought that!"

"Who asked you to come, anyway? I don't want you. Go home where you will be safe," Treia said, and she stalked off.

Aylaen stared after her, dismayed.

"Did you hear?" she asked Garn. "The goddess didn't answer!"

"Don't tell the others," he said.

Skylan led the Torgun warriors from the Chief's Hall. He took with him a scouting party and sent the rest out to form the shield-wall on the ground he had selected for the battle. He and his small troop of men topped a ridgeline overlooking the bay. The ogres were leaving their ships, coming ashore. Unlike the dragonships of the Vindrasi, which were lightweight and steered by a uniquely designed rudder that allowed them to sail almost up onto a beach, the heavy ogre ships had to remain in the deep water, forcing the ogre warriors to jump into the sea and swim.

The Torgun paused to watch the ogres floundering in the waves, which were breaking over their heads. The seas were rough this morning, and he worried that the angry Sea Goddess might drown his foe, robbing him of his battle. Akaria seemed content with tormenting them, however, slapping them with waves while a vicious undertow sucked at their ankles, trying to drag them under.

Although ogres disliked water, they were strong if clumsy swimmers, and they reached the shore without too much difficulty. The first to arrive took up positions along the beach in order to protect the rest of the army. They brought with them a small boat piled high with their weapons, armor, and shields, and while some ogres stood guard, others armed themselves for battle.

Also in the boat was the shaman. Akaria's breath ruffled the black feathers of his cape. He was holding a large gourd, painted and decorated with feathers, which he would shake at the ogre warriors as they came ashore. Some of the ogres glanced askance at the shaman and rolled their eyes or glared at him in disgust. Ogre shamans did not fight, and some ogres, who followed the old religion, considered them cowards who hid behind the skirts of their gods. Many of the ogres bowed their heads, however, and reached out to reverently touch the gourd.

Skylan laughed and made a crude comment about the gourd and what it resembled. The warriors chuckled at Skylan's lewd jest, all except Erdmun.

"There are a lot of them," he observed gloomily. "They outnumber us four to one."

"Not so," said Skylan. "We outnumber them. One Torgun warrior is worth five ogres. The fight seems so one-sided, I am considering reducing our army by half."

Erdmun looked alarmed and opened his mouth to protest.

"He's joking," his brother told him, and added, "We could attack them now, Skylan, while they're disorganized."

Skylan had been considering that idea, then rejected it. One Torgun might equal five ogres, but his scouting party was too small to do much damage. They would waste their strength and their spears with little to show for it. Better to meet the enemy on the battlefield, standing shoulder to shoulder in the shield-wall.

"Norgaard said the shaman doesn't fight, but what if he comes onto the battlefield?" Erdmun asked. "He could cast his holy magic on us, strike us blind or wither our arms—"

Skylan laughed and nudged Bjorn with his elbow. "Your brother has been spending too much time with Owl Mother. He's starting to believe her wild tales! Best be careful, Erdmun. The black stork might shake his 'gourd' at you!"

Skylan grabbed his crotch to make his meaning clear. The men sniggered, and Erdmun flushed, chagrined and angry.

Skylan led the way to the strip of ground he had chosen for the battle. Like him, the other young men were in high spirits, looking forward to the fight. Death was a possibility, of course, and none of them wanted to leave this world, but every man must die sometime, and each wanted to stand proudly before Torval and join the other warriors in the Heroes' Hall.

"Keep your mouth shut," Bjorn scolded his brother. "You shame us both!"

"Skylan isn't a goddamn god," Erdmun muttered, but he said it below his breath.

## CHAPTER 13

The warriors gathered on the battlefield—a ridge of grassland not far from the village. Below the ridge, the ground rolled down into a slight depression, curved upward to form a smaller ridge before tumbling in a rocky torrent down to the sea. Skylan chose this ground because it was deceptive. An enemy standing on the opposite ridgeline could not readily see the slight depression. Their godlords would think they could send their warriors racing across a level field. Only when the ogres had run into the depression would they realize they had to fight while charging uphill.

The Torgun greeted Skylan with cheers. Skylan acknowledged them with a grin and raised his sword in salute; then he went to greet his father. Though Norgaard had to rely on a crutch to walk, he insisted on being present at the battle.

"Better to die standing with an axe in my hand than having my throat slit while hiding in a cave."

Norgaard embraced his son, and Skylan was touched to see tears of pride in his father's eyes. The Torgun cheered the two of them and then lifted their voices in a rhythmic war chant. Their blood was up, their spirits roused.

The Torgun were angry at the ogres, but they were furious at Horg and the Heudjun. The Torgun meant to fight the battle Horg had basely fled, and they meant to win it. Until the day he died, each man would remember the shame he felt witnessing the ogre godlord standing in their Chief's Hall, smirking at them, his filthy fingers toying with the sacred Vektan Torque.

Under Skylan's direction, the Torgun warriors formed the shield-wall.

Somewhere in this world of Ilyrion, generals spent hours studying maps, devising devious strategies. Somewhere in the world, but not in the land of the Vindrasi.

Battle was a simple affair. The Torgun warriors drew together to form two lines. Veteran warriors stood in the back row, prepared to take up the fight should the enemy break through the front ranks of the shield-wall. Men such as Sigurd and Alfric the One-Eyed carried spears, several at a time, and huge battle axes requiring two hands to wield them. These men could not hold shields and their weapons at the same time, so they took shelter behind the front line, made up of younger warriors eager for blood These men stood close together, shield overlapping shield, protecting the men in the row behind them.

The men in the second line hurled their spears at the enemy and then waited for the chance to rush out from behind the shields, wielding their axes, hacking at legs, chopping off arms, and cleaving open skulls.

The veterans in the second rank were also there in order to "encourage" those in the front who might suddenly lose their nerve. The veterans behind made sure those in front of them did not break and run, but kept on fighting. Some men had been known to do their "persuading" by jabbing reluctant warriors in the backs with their spears.

Norgaard, Chief of the Clan, stood on a rise some distance behind the shield-wall, surrounded by his bodyguards. The goal of the battle for both sides was simple: Capture or slay the Chief.

The Bone Priestess usually stood with the Chief, whose guards protected both of them. Treia had not yet arrived, and the Torgun were starting to wonder nervously if something was amiss.

As the Torgun warriors were forming their shield-wall on the hillside, they jested with each other, making the nervous jokes of men trying to bolster their own courage and show their comrades they were not afraid. The veterans recalled deeds of bravery from previous battles. The green youngsters vowed in their trembling hearts that they would find such glory for themselves this day.

The warriors good-naturedly jostled and shoved each other in an effort to find the best place. Skylan walked up and down in front of them, haranguing the young warriors, yelling at them to keep their shields up and not let them drop down around their knees. He was facing his men, had his back to the sea. All laughter and jesting suddenly ceased. Skylan turned to see what was the cause.

The ogre army had arrived.

The Torgun had not realized quite how many ogres there were. As more and more ogres came straggling up from the sea, some of the appalled Torgun thought the entire ogre nation had come to do battle.

Skylan was considerably daunted by the sight of nearly two hundred ogres forming a shield-wall. The ogres in the front rank were enormous. Their shields alone were as big as a Torgun man, and they were armed with war hammers, battle axes, and swords. Those in the second rank were even larger than those in front. Each ogre held fistfuls of spears. The line bristled like a quill-pig. The ogre shield-wall spread out along the ridgeline, extending far beyond the smaller Torgun shield-wall. Skylan saw the godlords' plan of attack, and his heart sank. The ogres would charge forward in a sweeping arc, like a crescent moon, outflanking Skylan's men, hitting them from the front and the sides at the same time.

The only thing that would save them was the Dragon Kahg.

"Where is that damn Bone Priestess?" Skylan shouted angrily, turning away from the sickening sight. "Why isn't she here?"

He was immediately annoyed at himself for giving vent to his feelings. Several of the young warriors were pale with fear, and even some of the veterans were looking nervous.

Skylan glanced at the ogre lines and said loudly, "Yes, they are big brutes. That only makes them a better target! Even you, Alfric, cannot miss hitting one of them!"

That drew a laugh. Alfric had lost an eye in battle, and he was notorious for bumping into trees and posts. A close friend of Norgaard, Alfric was proud to stand as one of the Chief's bodyguards. The truth was that no one wanted him in the shield-wall, where his wild swings with his battle axe made him more dangerous to friend than to foe.

The ogres were taking their time. The godlords charged into the ranks, ranting and raving, bullying and shoving, and sometimes even kicking their warriors until they had shuffled into proper position.

This is part of their strategy, Skylan realized dourly. The longer the bastards take to form their shield-wall, the more time my men have to think about dying.

His warriors needed something to give them hope, and Skylan whispered his thanks to Torval when the call rang out that the Bone Priestess had arrived.

The warriors craned their heads to see her. Skylan went to meet Treia himself. He smiled at Garn and frowned at Aylaen, who was standing beside her sister.

"You should go home," Skylan said.

"And you should go soak your head in the slop bucket," Aylaen returned.

Skylan could not help but smile. He was secretly proud of her courage and her loyalty to her sister. She must have been terrified, but she did not show it.

Treia carried with her the spiritbone Skylan had risked his life to obtain. She lifted it into the air, and the warriors, taking heart, cheered loudly. Skylan cast a triumphant glance at the ogres, who had no idea what was coming.

Skylan ordered the two women to take up positions alongside Norgaard, well behind the shield-wall, out of range of enemy spears yet still within sight of the enemy. Being in such close proximity to the battle was dangerous, but necessary. The warriors needed to see the Bone Priestess, needed to know that their Dragon Goddess, Vindrash, was with them.

Treia stood staring at the ogres or what she could see of them with her weak eyes, which was a large, dark, homogeneous mass—a gigantic worm undulating on the green grass. Her face was coldly pale, expressionless. She made no response when Skylan spoke to her. He had no idea what she was thinking or even if she was thinking. She might have been a doll carved out of bone.

Aylaen's eyes widened at the sight of the ogres, and she gave a little gasp.

"There are so many! We are too close," she said, rounding on Skylan. "My sister will not be safe!"

"Of course she will," said Skylan dismissively. "My father is here and his bodyguards." He shrugged. "Besides, the Bone Priestess is under the protection of Vindrash. The goddess will protect her servant."

Aylaen went white at the lips and glanced fearfully at Garn, who looked troubled.

"What is it?" Skylan demanded, glancing from one to the other. "What is wrong?"

"Nothing," said Treia, casting a chill glance at her sister. "Nothing at all."

Relieved, Skylan turned to look back at the ogre lines. The godlords were finally taking up their positions, each going to stand with his bodyguards behind the shield-wall. Skylan focused on the godlord who had been sporting the Vektan Torque. He knew him by his tiger-skin cape. It was hard to see him. Aylis rose from the east, shedding her morning light on the bay, which meant Skylan was staring directly into the sunlight. Even so, he could not see the torque, and he gnashed his teeth in bitter disappointment. He had been counting on decapitating the godlord and snatching the torque from his bloody neck. It had not occurred to him until now that the whoreson might have stowed it away for safekeeping during battle.

"I will pry their ships apart board by board until I find it," Skylan vowed, and he put his hand to the small silver axe.

He ran his gaze over his men and was proud to see them standing shoulder to shoulder, shield to shield, straining forward, yelling insults at the enemy. He was about to tell Treia it was time, when he saw the shaman, preening his black feathers, go striding up to stand beside the godlord. The shaman held the feathered gourd in his hand and he stood at his ease, gazing about with interest, a cunning look on the childlike face. Norgaard had said the shamans did not use their dark magicks in battle. Skylan wondered if that was true. He was amused to see the godlord move away from the shaman, leaving him to stand alone.

Skylan made a mental note to tell his spear-thrower to take special aim at the shaman, and then he turned to Treia.

"It is time to summon the dragon."

"I need seawater," said Treia composedly. "Kahg is a water dragon. I need seawater to summon him."

Skylan gaped at her and extended his arm in a sweeping gesture. "Two hundred ogres stand between us and the sea!"

Treia blinked at him. "No one told me where we would be fighting. I assumed we would be by the sea."

"Skoval's balls!" Skylan swore furiously.

"Don't yell at her, Skylan!" Aylaen cried. "She's nervous and frightened. This is her first battle."

"And probably her last," Skylan returned grimly. "The last for all of us unless she can summon Kahg!"

"Sister," said Aylaen suddenly, "can't you use earth—?"

Treia flashed her a furious glance, and Aylaen stammered and fell silent.

"Your sister's suggestion is a good one, Priestess," said Norgaard, limping over to join the conversation. "You can use earth to form the dragon. I've seen it done. Possibly, this being your first battle, you did not think of that."

Treia's lips pressed together tightly. Her eyes narrowed. "Perhaps."

"I will take the Dragon Kahg in any form, Priestess," Skylan said through gritted teeth. "I don't care if he's made from mother's milk! Just summon the dragon, and be quick about it! The sun is risen."

Sunrise was the traditional time for the Vindras to commence battle. No one fought at night. The warriors wanted Torval to be witness to their courage and bravery.

"I have to go—," Skylan said.

"I'm coming with you," said Garn.

Skylan stopped him. "No, my brother. You stay here to guard Treia and Aylaen. If the ogres break through, you must help them escape."

Garn frowned. "Let one of Norgaard's men do that. I will take my place with you in the shield-wall as always."

Skylan shook his head. "The bodyguards' duty is to my father."

He lowered his voice, drew Garn to one side. "You are the only man I trust with Aylaen's life, my brother. Promise me. Swear by Torval, you will keep her safe. And her sister," he added as an afterthought.

Skylan knew he was asking his friend to make a sacrifice. If the ogres broke through the lines, Garn would have to flee with the women. He would not be there to avenge his friends. He would not have the honor of dying in battle.

"I swear," Garn said at last.

Skylan gripped his friend by the arm, then went to take his place in the shield-wall, in the second row with the veteran warriors. He would gain glory this day, smashing headlong into the enemy's ranks, driving through to do single combat with the godlord who had taken the sacred torque.

"Hand me a spear," said Skylan. Several men thrust their spears forward. He clasped one, hefted it.

"For Torval!" he roared, and he hurled the spear at the ogre lines, throwing it as far as he could. The spear sailed over the heads of the ogres in an arc, thudding into the ground behind them. Thus he dedicated his enemy to the god.

"For Torval!" the Torgun warriors cried.

The ogres responded, hurling their spears and chanting something that sounded like, "Raja Raj, Raja Raj!"

The ogres launched what seemed a veritable forest of spears.

Skylan drew his sword. The warriors in the front ranks lifted their shields and braced themselves for the onslaught. Some landed short. Some flew long. Some found their targets. Near Skylan, a warrior named Gregor screamed horribly. He lay on the ground, twisting about on a spear that had gone through his belly and pinned him, like a pig on a spit. Skylan turned away. No one could do anything for Gregor, not even take time to end his suffering with a merciful sword thrust. The fallen had to take care of themselves. No man dared break the shield-wall.

"Hold firm!" Skylan cried, seeing some of the excited young warriors starting to lurch forward. "Make them come to us!"

Under most circumstances, his army would have rushed at the enemy. The ogres would have rushed at them, both armies meeting with a bone-crushing crash in the middle. Garn had suggested this alternative strategy during the Council meeting. The Vindrasi would utilize the dip in the ground, forcing the ogres to run across the expanse and then fight uphill.

"Won't they just wait for us to charge them?" Skylan had argued.

"The ogres are arrogant, overconfident," Garn had replied. "They will throw everything at us at once without thinking, counting on ending the battle swiftly."

"The brutes are massive, but they have no stamina," Norgaard had added. "They wear heavy armor and carry heavy weapons, and they count on smashing an enemy into the ground with a single blow. If they fail to do this, if they are forced to keep fighting, they soon grow tired and lose heart. The longer we can make the battle last, the more we stand a chance of winning."

Skylan had reluctantly agreed to Garn's plan, keeping his doubts to himself. He could always order the shield-wall to advance, which is what he expected to do.

Erdmun, who stood in front of Skylan, lifted his shield to block a spear. It bounced off and fell to the ground. Sigurd plucked a thrown spear out of midair and hurled it back at the enemy. Sigurd was an expert with spears. He could throw two at once, one in each hand. He fought with a wide grin on his face; the only time anyone ever saw the dour man smile was during battle.

"Where's Kahg?" Erdmun demanded suddenly, twisting around to look. "Where's the dragon?"

His brother, Bjorn, stood at his side. This was Erdmun's first time in the shield-wall, and Skylan had put him in the front row. Bjorn, who had fought in shield-walls before, insisted on standing next to his brother.

As to the dragon, that was a good question. Skylan looked back to see Treia on her knees on the ground, using a knife to dig up the dirt. Aylaen stood protectively beside her sister, staring at the ogre lines. Skylan saw a spear land on the ground near her. She did not flinch, barely glanced at it. She merely shifted her stance slightly, taking a firmer grip on her axe. Catching Skylan's eye, she smiled encouragement. Skylan loved her so much, his heart ached with his loving.

Treia began daubing the spiritbone with soil.

"The Dragon Kahg will help us," Skylan said confidently.

Treia was a Bone Priestess. She knew her business. He was a warrior, and fighting was his business.

The ogre godlords waited for the Torgun to run toward them. When that did not happen, the ogre warriors—hot, sweaty in their heavy armor—grew angry and impatient. Several of their number had been felled by Torgun spears. Their shaman had been forced to hike up his black feathered robe and scramble for his life.

The Torgun began hurling insults, taunting them. The ogres could stomach only so much. A smattering of humans stood between them and gold, cattle, and women. An ogre broke out of the shield-wall and went lumbering across the grassy expanse. The godlords shouted and raged, but soon the entire ogre army was on the move. Brandishing axes, swords, and hammers, the ogres charged at a ground-thudding run.

Garn's plan worked. The ogres were deceived. They thought the distance they had to cover was short until they came to the dip in the ground and realized they had to cover more territory. Torgun spears slammed into their midst. Many ogres fell. Those on their feet were huffing, blowing out their fat cheeks, mouths gaping, gasping for breath.

The Torgun did not celebrate. Half the ogre army could keel over dead and they would still outnumber them. The massive brutes came thundering at the Torgun shield-wall. The ground shook with their coming. Skylan braced himself for the blow.

He had time for one quick glance at Treia. She held the spiritbone in her hands, and it seemed to him she was not praying so much as desperately pleading. If the Dragon Kahg was going to answer her appeal, he would have done so by now.

Skylan sighed, and then he shrugged.

At least we will die bravely. We will stand before Torval with honor. And if it is my last act on this world, I will slay that whoreson who has the torque.

Skylan divided his gaze between the onrushing ogres and the torque-bearing godlord, who was running after his men, his face purple with rage, shouting commands no one heeded. The godlord frantically and repeatedly gestured toward the end of the ranks of the Torgun warriors, attempting to tell his warriors to move to outflank the foe, get in behind their shield-wall, surround them.

The ogre warriors paid no attention. They kept coming straight at the Torgun, stumbling clumsily over their own feet or tripping over the bodies of their own dead.

The ogres had been shouting insults, but they were now forced to save their breath for running. Their chubby faces were red from the exertion and hardened in resolve. They resembled little children playing at war, except they were armed with axes and swords, not sticks.

The ogres lifted their shields. Using them like battering rams, the ogres slammed into the front ranks of the Torgun warriors with such force that men in the front ranks were lifted off their feet and bowled over backwards by the shock of the impact.

The Torgun shield-wall disintegrated.

Blood spattered. Men grunted and screamed and shouted and swore. Skylan heard the crunch of breaking bone, and he smelled the stench of war—blood, urine, and excrement—as men lost control of their bladders and bowels in the desperate struggle.

Bjorn, who had been standing in front of Skylan, suddenly wasn't. Erdmun had been pushed back into the second line by an ogre warrior, who began slashing wildly at him with an axe. Erdmun floundered, holding up his shield to absorb the blows, unable to return the attack, which seemed to come at him from every direction at once. Sigurd grabbed hold of Erdmun and dragged him out of the way, then jammed his sword through the ogre's gaping mouth.

The ogre's head seemed to explode, spattering Skylan with blood and brains. He fell, but another ogre thundered up to take his place, heedlessly trampling the body of his comrade. This ogre rushed at Sigurd, who had no more spears. The two collided and stumbled back, fighting hand-to-hand. Skylan lost track of them. He had his own trouble—an ogre charging straight at him.

The ogre's face twisted in a snarl. He didn't look ferocious, more like a toddler throwing a tantrum. Skylan would have laughed, but the ogre's eyes were grim and intent on his death.

The ogre lifted his enormous shield, planning to bash it into Skylan, knock him down, and then hack him to pieces with his battle axe. Skylan waited until the ogre was directly in front of him; then he ducked, hunching his body, keeping his head down. Unable to stop his forward momentum, the ogre tumbled over Skylan, who leaped to his feet and, grabbing the ogre's legs, heaved upward, upending him. The ogre landed on the ground. Three spears pierced him seconds before Erdmun chopped off his head.

The battle swirled past Skylan, leaving him, for a moment, in the clear, and he looked about to take stock of the situation. It was grim. The shield-wall was no more. The Torgun were being pushed back. Garn stood protectively beside the two women. Aylaen was arguing with Treia, urging her to abandon her prayers and flee. Treia stubbornly resisted. She remained on her knees, the spiritbone in her hand. There was no sign of the dragon.

Norgaard stood with his bodyguards, his sword in one hand, his crutch in the other. His bodyguards had gathered around him, ready to defend him. They would be the last to die.

A bitter taste filled Skylan's mouth. The taste of failure, defeat. Some men see their lives flash before their eyes in the moments before death. Skylan saw the future. The Torgun would be no more. They would be wiped out as a clan. And all because of Horg, the Chief of Chiefs. To save his own skin, he had sacrificed the Torgun, given them to their enemies.

Despair and fury clouded Skylan's vision. He seemed to be seeing everything through a haze of blood.

He climbed up on top of the body of a dead ogre to search for the godlord with the torque, but couldn't find him. An ogre struck at Skylan with an axe. Annoyed—the whoreson was blocking his view—Skylan cleaved open the brute's skull. He swung his sword again, took down another ogre—at least Skylan supposed it was an ogre. His eyes burned. Everything he looked at seemed drenched in blood.

He couldn't find the godlord with the torque.

The Sun Goddess had taken refuge in a bank of clouds. Aylis was not afraid. She was waiting for the moment to part the clouds and blaze forth. And when she did so, a bright flash caught Skylan's eye.

There was the godlord, standing right in front of him. The sun struck him in blazing, terrible splendor, illuminating the Vektan Torque. He wore it beneath his armor, trying to keep it hidden. Aylis had found it, however, and she revealed it to Skylan.

Rage seared his brain, consuming fear as the beacon fire consumed oak.

He rose from the ashes of the blaze with one clear purpose—to slay the godlord and recover the Vektan Torque.

"Torval!" Skylan prayed, kissing the amulet around his neck. "I give myself to you."

And Torval blessed him.

Skylan heard nothing except the roar of the god's voice in his ears. He felt nothing except the hilt of his sword in his hand. He saw nothing but his enemy, and Skylan struck at anything that stood between him and his target, not knowing if he was killing friend or foe, not caring.

He knew the Torgun were doomed. He knew he was going to die. He would stand before Torval proudly, holding the Vektan Torque in one hand and the head of the ogre godlord in the other.

# CHAPTER 14

Skylan was not the only one to see Aylis's light shining on the Vektan Torque. Other eyes saw it, as the goddess intended. Eyes that had been gazing off in an entirely different direction.

The Dragon Kahg was not angry with the Torgun, as they imagined. He had been busy, preoccupied with fear and worry. The dragon heard the prayers of the Bone Priestess, but they were faint, distant—an annoyance, like gnats—and he paid scant attention. The humans were off on another raid, summoning him to go harass a bunch of goat-herders.

Kahg had other worries, other cares and concerns that were far more important. His goddess, the Goddess of All Dragonkind, the blessed Vindrash, had vanished from the world. Her disappearance had thrown her dragons into turmoil. The dragons had heard rumors of a war in heaven. They had heard rumors that their gods had lost. The dragons did not believe these rumors. They sought out Vindrash to refute the claim, going to the sacred Hall of Vektia, located on the Dragon Isles.

The dragons were shocked and horrified to find the Hall had been attacked by some unknown foe. The dragons who served Vindrash and who should have been guarding the Hall had vanished, both from the Realm of Stone and the Realm of Fire.

Dragons were creatures of magic, created by the dying Dragon Ilyrion when she gave herself to the world. Ilyrion came from the Realm of Fire, as did the fae folk who populated the world. The gods and all races of men (including the races of ogres, Cyclopes, and so forth) came from the Realm of Stone.

The dragons, with their powerful magicks, discovered that since the dying Ilyrion had given herself to the world, which lay in the Realm of Stone, they could live in both realms simultaneously. By leaving a physical part of themselves (the spiritbone) in the Realm of Stone, their spirits could remain safely hidden from their foes in the Realm of Fire. Through the spiritbone, they could manifest themselves physically in the Realm of Stone.

The dragons needed to be in the Realm of Stone, for it was only in this realm that they could find the "shards of Ilyrion," which were used to create new dragons and perpetuate their race. These shards, made of the scales and teeth of the dying dragon, took the form of gemstones. The dragons scoured the world, searching for gems, taking those they found that were dragons back to the Realm of Fire for nurturing.

The task was long and laborious. To their dismay, the dragons discovered that men coveted these gemstones, not for the fact that they might hold the spark of dragonlife within them, but because they were pretty, because they were rare, because they were valuable.

The dragons might well have gone to war with men over the gemstones (joining the fae folk in the battle that was known as the First War), but their Dragon Goddess, Vindrash, who had presided over their creation, taught them how the humans could be useful to them in their search.

Dragons could move about the Realm of Stone in their spirit form or in their physical shape. In the spirit form, they could not interact with the world. They could not eat or drink or pick up a ruby in their claws or fight an enemy. In their physical form, they could do all those things, but there were drawbacks. Dragons in the physical form were heavy. They had wings and they could fly, but not very far or very fast. That made it difficult for them to traverse the world hunting for the gemstones.

Vindrash proposed that dragons give their spiritbones into the hands of her chosen people, the Vindrasi. She would make the Vindrasi into a nation of seafarers, a nation of raiders, who would sail the seas of the known world in search of gold and silver and jewels. The Vindrasi would take the dragons along on their questing. The dragons would imbue the ships with their spirits, guiding the ships, giving them wings, as it were. The dragons could also assist the Vindrasi in battle by taking physical form and attacking their foes.

The beauty of this plan was that the Vindrasi would be ignorant of the fact that they were the unwitting tools of the dragons, transporting them over the seas in the never-ending search for jewels. The Vindrasi would imagine the dragons were serving them, whereas the dragons knew it was the other way around.

The dragons who volunteered to work with the Vindrasi gave a piece of bone to the Bone Priestesses, who could use the bone to summon the dragons should they have need. The dragons were free to answer or not as he or she chose. Generally it was in the dragon's interest to respond. The Vindrasi became known and feared throughout their portion of the world for the dragonships and the dragons who fought for them.

Then came these new gods, young gods, seeking to rule a world of their own. The Gods of Raj, they called themselves, and a single god, Aelon, Lord of the New Dawn. The old gods had not foreseen their coming. Caught by surprise, they had been defeated, vanquished. One of their number had been slain.

Emboldened by their victory, the worshippers of these gods had attacked the Hall of Vektia. They had come by night—come silently, by stealth, for the giants who were Torval's servants and kept watch over the Isles claimed they had never seen them.

The Hall of Vektia had been ransacked. Whoever had attacked the Hall was not after treasure, but had been looking for something else. Urns made of pure gold lay overturned on the blood-covered floor beside silver pitchers and jewel-encrusted candleholders, all of which looters would have carted off. The ancient statue of the Dragon Goddess had been ravaged, decapitated.

And then the dragons discovered what was missing—the spiritbones of the dragons who were supposed to have been guarding the temple.

Here was a mystery. Why had the dragons failed in their duty? What had become of the bones? Who had taken them and why? Only the Bone Priestesses could summon the spirits of the dragons, and the Priestesses resided among the Vindrasi. They came to the Hall of Vektia to present the goddess with treasure or on other special occasions.

The dragons searched for clues to the nature of the enemy. Generally soldiers would discard something that gave some indication of where they were from—a torn leather strap, a leaky waterskin, a half-eaten apple. This army had left behind nothing, no trace. They had even taken care to hide their bootprints.

The dragons were baffled until they came across a lone spiritbone lying on the floor below an immense tapestry. The spiritbone was broken in two. The dragon whose spirit it held was dead. The dragons had started to pick it up, to give it a reverent burial, when one of them happened to notice that the two pieces were seemingly pointing at the tapestry.

The dragons studied the tapestry and saw, to their dismay, that it portrayed the story of the creation of the Vektia Five, born from the crest of the Great Dragon Ilyrion.

The dragon, grievously wounded, had chosen this place to die, knowing that his spiritbone would be found here. He had taken a risk, for the enemy might have removed the spiritbone. Perhaps he had waited until after they departed, or perhaps they had not bothered with a spiritbone they knew to be dead.

This, then, was the answer—or so the dragons believed. The enemy had come in search of the Five Bones of the Vektia. Which meant that the enemy knew about the Five, though not where they were hidden, apparently, or how to distinguish them from other spiritbones, for the bones they had captured were those of ordinary dragons.

Or perhaps not. The dragons came to the terrible realization that the intruders had escaped with one of the Five Vektia spiritbones, which must have been hidden in the Hall. But which of their enemies had taken it? And, more important, did they know that the spiritbone could transform into one of the most powerful dragons ever created?

The Dragon Kahg was the leader of the dragons who served the Vindrasi. Like others of his kind, he had been searching for his missing goddess until the dragon elders gave him the task of ensuring the safety of the Vektan Torque.

Returning to the Torgun, Kahg at last heard the pleading prayers of the Bone Priestess, and he became aware that the Torgun were in a desperate struggle for their lives against raiding ogres.

Kahg was at first annoyed. He'd gone on an urgent mission to check on the Vektan Torque, and now he was going to have to waste time snatching the Torgun fat out of the fire. Undoubtedly this was the fault of that young hothead, Skylan Ivorson. Kahg was grumbling to himself, taking his time materializing to teach them a lesson, when the angry Goddess Aylis struck the ogre godlord with a shaft of sunlight. Kahg saw the bright flash of gold and the sparkle of sapphire and realized in an instant that the ogre wore the Vektan Torque.

Kahg had no idea how the ogre had come into possession of the sacred torque, but he could guess. Kahg did not like Horg, who refused to go raiding, much to the ire of all the Vindrasi dragons. The Heudjun's dragon had left in a rage, first seeing to it that Horg's dragonship struck a rock and foundered. Feeling his stature as Chief of Chiefs was diminished by his lack of a ship, Horg had tried to persuade the Torgun to give him the *Venjekar*. When Norgaard refused, Horg sent a raiding party to steal the dragonship.

The Dragon Kahg had angrily smashed their boats, forcing them to swim back. The Torgun never knew anything about Horg's attempt to steal their dragonship, or there would have been war between the clans.

Kahg could picture Horg bartering the torque for cattle, silver, or even to save his own skin. The reason did not matter now. The torque held the spiritbone of one of the powerful Five, and Kahg had to help the Torgun recover it. The task was made more urgent by the implication that another of the Five was already in enemy hands.

"Vindrash, hear my prayer." The words of the Bone Priestess dinned in the dragon's ears. "Tell the Dragon Kahg of our desperate need."

Kahg roared into being, astonishing both friend and foe as he burst into life directly above their heads.

Fighting was now hand-to-hand, warrior pitted against warrior. Surprisingly, after that first terrible onslaught had caused their shield-wall to crumble, the Torgun were holding their own. The ogres had brawn and brute strength on their side, but those had been assets only at the start of the battle. Weighted down by their heavy armor, massive shields, and enormous weapons, the ogres were being forced to fight a protracted battle, and they didn't like it. Their arms were starting to ache. Their leg muscles burned. Their clumsy blows went wide, missing the mark.

Ogres were deemed lazy by humans, but the truth was, as Norgaard had said, they lacked stamina. Ogres were practical-minded, with no concept of honor. Unlike the Vindrasi, they did not consider dying in battle a glorious end. They liked a good fight, so long as they didn't have to expend too much effort in order to win. These stubborn humans, who were apparently made of iron, not flesh and blood, were taking all the fun out of warfare.

The ogres were not ready to give up yet. Or rather, their godlords were not, and the ogre warriors were more afraid of their commanders than they were of the enemy. The Torgun, locked in a desperate struggle for their lives, greeted the dragon's arrival with ragged cheers. The ogres gaped at the dragon in openmouthed amazement that swiftly devolved into horror. Most had never seen a dragon or even known such creatures existed.

A dragon took on the appearance of the elements from which he was created. If the Dragon Kahg had been formed of seawater, he would have been glistening blue green with a white crest, like foam-spattered waves. Created out of dirt and desperation, he was an earth dragon. His scales were a dull brown mottled with green. His crest was the gray of jagged mountain peaks, his tail the red color of clay. He was hampered by the fact that he'd come to the battle late. With warrior battling warrior, the dragon dared not use his fiery breath, for fear of harming the Torgun.

Kahg's first concern was for the ogre who had possession of the Vektan Torque. The dragon saw Skylan running to confront the ogre, and Kahg might have intervened, but Skylan shone with a holy radiance, and Kahg realized the young man had given himself to the god. The Madness of Torval was upon him. Kahg decided to leave the ogre to the human warrior. He swooped down on three ogre warriors fighting Norgaard's bodyguards and snatched them up in his clawed feet.

Kahg soared skyward, clutching the howling ogres. When he was high above the trees, he opened his claws and dropped two of them. The screaming ogres plummeted to the ground, their heavy bodies landing on their comrades, smashing them into a jellied mass of blood and bone, brains and blubber.

The third ogre hung on to Kahg's claw for dear life. Annoyed, Kahg shook his claw, trying to dislodge the ogre. The ogre clung to the claw, wrapping arms and legs around it. Kahg at last stuck the claw in his mouth, sucked up the ogre as though he were a splinter, crunched him to pulp, then spit him out.

Some of the ogres decided they'd had enough. They were already weary of this fight, and now they were being attacked by a fearsome monster, a creature from a nightmare. These ogres threw down their heavy weapons, turned, and began to lumber back toward the sea. The others fought on, but they were rapidly losing heart.

The dragon's body blotted out the sun. His fierce eyes glared down at his foe. He made another dive, snagged several more ogres, and hurled them onto the ground. Their bodies split wide open, spewing blood and guts. Even the godlords, who had been urging their warriors to stand and fight, were appalled at this gruesome sight. The godlords fled Kahg's fury, and they took their warriors with them. Within moments of the dragon's coming, the entire ogre army was stampeding madly for their ships.

Skylan saw none of this. The Madness of Torval was upon him.

# CHAPTER 15

The ogre godlord watched the human warrior come charging at him across the battlefield and stood waiting for him, not because he relished the idea of a battle of heroes, but because he was bitter, angry, and frustrated. What should have been a resounding victory was turning into a disastrous rout. His men were thundering past him, running for their miserable lives. The only ogre who was staying with him was the shaman, and the godlord wished he would get swallowed by the dragon.

The godlord considered the shaman with his black feathers and his stupid gourd bad luck. He ordered the shaman to go, but the black-feathered bastard remained rooted to the spot. The godlord planned to retreat with his men, but he had not made any kills this day; he'd been too busy trying to beat some sense into his warriors, and he could not leave the field of battle without having drawn blood. The other two godlords, who were always watching for a chance to demean him, would report such "cowardice" to his superiors the moment they returned home.

This young human with the sun-gold hair and the sky-blue eyes was the Chief's son. He was the one who had wanted to fight them all at dinner. The one who had sneaked aboard the dragonship and slain two ogres and escaped. The one who had killed the boar. This would be a good kill. The godlord would bash in the young pup's skull and then depart.

The godlord cast a dark glance at the dragon. The ogre was fifty years old, and he had faced dragons before. He knew that the dragons of the Vindrasi had something to do with their famed dragonships, though he was not entirely sure what. He had the vague idea that the ship turned into a dragon, and so he had made certain that the Torgun dragonship was safe in ogre hands.

Then had come the daring raid in the night. The surviving ogre guard could not say exactly what the Torgun warrior had removed from the ship, but it must have had something to do with the dragon, for the ship was still surrounded by ogre vessels, and here was the dragon carrying off his warriors as the eagle carries off rabbits.

Seeing that the dragon posed no threat to him, at least for the moment, the godlord turned his attention back to his foe. The young human advanced on the godlord unafraid, carrying his sword and a dented shield he had taken off a dead man. His long fair hair shone in the sunlight, seeming to surround him with light. His blue eyes were hard and glittering with battle rage.

Some god must love him, the ogre thought sourly, and he strode forward to do battle.

Skylan was caught up in the Madness of Torval, and he did not see the dragon, or the ogres, or his own men. He saw only his foe—the ogre godlord who wore the Vektan Torque around his neck. It seemed to Skylan as if Torval had lifted the two of them up off the earth and dropped them both down on some distant shore where they could fight together, isolated and alone.

Some thought the Madness of Torval sent men careening headlong into battle, witless as raving lunatics. That was not true. Torval had more sense. The madness opened a warrior's eyes, gave him insight into his foe—how he thought, how he would react, which way he would move.

Ogre and human used far different fighting techniques. Ogres had little use for developing weapons skills. They saw no need. Ogres counted on strength and brute force to strike down an opponent, generally with a single blow. Their weapons of choice tended to be war hammers and battle axes.

Skylan, by contrast, had started learning to fight at the age of four, when Norgaard put a wooden sword into the child's hands and showed him how to use it. Not a day had gone by since that Skylan did not practice, first with a wooden sword, then with a real one, learning the Vindrasi technique of dividing an enemy's body into quarters and striking first at one quarter and then another, forcing the enemy to constantly shift position.

He and the godlord squared off. Skylan had to remain constantly on his guard, not allow his foe to hit him. A single blow from the godlord's war hammer would bring the battle to a quick and bloody end.

Skylan adopted a balanced stance, left knee forward, right leg braced behind, his shield held parallel to the shield of his opponent. Skylan raised his sword above his head, blade pointed down. Fighting a human, he would have been prepared to strike at the face. With the ogre, he was going for the chest.

The ogre held his shield roughly parallel to Skylan and slowly swung the hammer, giving Skylan no indication where he meant to strike. Skylan shifted his weight and made a quick sword thrust at the ogre's chest. As he had hoped, the ogre raised his shield to block the blow, leaving his legs exposed. Swiftly Skylan lowered his sword, stabbed the blade into the ogre's unprotected thigh, swinging his shield outward at the same time to sweep aside a blow from the hammer.

If the ogre had struck Skylan's shield with full force, he would have broken his arm. As it was, the ogre's leg buckled when Skylan drove his sword into the thigh muscle. The ogre didn't fall, but he was thrown off balance, and the hammer swing hit Skylan's shield a glancing blow. Skylan's shield arm tingled from wrist to shoulder, and he fell back to catch his breath, expecting his opponent to do the same. This was how humans fought. A flurry of five or six attacks and counterattacks and then a fall back. Skylan was astonished, therefore, to see the ogre godlord come after him. Blood flew from the ogre's wound; saliva drooled from his mouth. The hammer swung at Skylan's head.

Skylan aimed his sword again at the ogre's leg. The godlord, anticipating this attack, lowered his shield to block. Skylan kicked the shield aside, which left the ogre wide open, and drove his sword into the ogre's hip joint, severing tendons and muscle. The ogre godlord crashed to the ground. Howling in pain and rage, he rolled about in agony, wallowing in his own gore.

Skylan flung aside his shield. He shifted his sword to his left hand and bent over the ogre to wrest the Vektan Torque from the godlord's fat neck.

Pain lanced through Skylan. The godlord had stabbed him in the shoulder with his knife. Skylan slammed the hilt of his sword into the ogre's face. He felt and heard bone crunch, and the ogre quit moving. Skylan's fingers closed around the golden circlet that was half-buried in the ogre's flesh and yanked it free.

He saw, out of the corner of his eye, the shaman flapping his black-feathered arms like an irate bird, waving his gourd at him and chanting strange words. Skylan paid no attention to the shaman. He heard Norgaard's voice shouting to kill the shaman, but he paid no attention to his father either.

With the torque safe, Skylan drove his sword into the ogre's neck, cleaving the head from the body. He raised the torque into the air in triumph. He was about to shout a prayer of thanks to Torval, when he was suddenly deluged with warm blood. Blood flew into his eyes. Blood filled his mouth. He tried to wipe the blood from his eyes, but he couldn't. He tried to spit the blood out of his mouth, but he couldn't do that either. He couldn't move his lips or his tongue. He couldn't move his hands. He couldn't shift his feet. All he could do was stare at the black-feathered shaman.

The shaman had known better than to try to stop the fight between the godlord and the human. The shaman was permitted to bless the warriors before the battle, but he was strictly forbidden, on pain of death, to take part. In the old days, not so long ago, shamanistic magic among the ogres was known as "death-magic." Ogre shamans did not necessarily have to kill something for their magic to work, but they did have to make a sacrifice of some kind. Ogres were pragmatic. They knew that life was hard and you never got something for nothing. In the dark days, when they worshipped dark gods, ogre shamans who wanted to raise a dead ogre did so by killing off one of his relatives. Ogres healed sickness in one by inflicting the illness onto another.

When the Gods of Raj took over, they had been appalled by such behavior. Pragmatic themselves, they saw that their worshippers were eventually going to kill themselves off. The Gods of Raj persuaded the shamans to use symbolic sacrifice to replace blood sacrifices. Break a gourd, not a head. The shamans were still in the practicing phase of trying to learn this new magic, which meant their spell-casting tended to be erratic and unreliable, resulting in some spectacular failures. Ogre warriors feared their own shaman far more than they did the enemy, and so shamans were not permitted to join the fighting.

The shaman now had nothing to hold him back. The godlord was either dead or dying, and the human was about to recover the Vektan Torque.

The moment the shaman had seen the torque around Horg's neck, he had sensed its power. He was the one who had urged the godlords to accept Horg's bargain, take the torque, and leave him and his people in peace. The shaman had been irate when the godlord claimed the torque for himself. The shaman wanted the torque as he had never wanted anything in his life.

And now it was going to be his.

The shaman drew a knife and lopped off the top half of the gourd. Mumbling the words to his spell—or at least what he hoped were the words to the spell—he scooped up the dead godlord's blood in the gourd and flung the blood into Skylan's face. Somewhat to his amazement, the shaman saw the spell work. The young human was paralyzed, unable to move. The shaman reached out, plucked the Vektan Torque from Skylan's frozen fingers, and turned and ran for the sea.

Disaster struck so swiftly that the Torgun had no idea, at first, that disaster had struck at all. Elated by their victory, the men laughed out loud to see the ogre shaman fling blood on Skylan and then run off, his feathers flapping around his bony knees.

Norgaard was not laughing.

"Stop him! He has the torque!" Norgaard thundered.

Garn saw the flash of gold in the shaman's hand, and he realized what had happened. He gave a shout and dashed down the hill in pursuit. Torgun laughter changed to curses as the others joined Garn in his frantic chase.

Ogres could move fast when there was need. Terrified of the dragon, the ogres had surged through the water and were swarming up ladders to board their ships. By the time the shaman reached his ship, his fellow ogres had already pulled up the ladder and were raising the sail. They lowered a rope, and one of the godlords helped drag the shaman aboard.

As Garn and his men reached the sea, the ogre sails caught the wind. The outraged Torgun flung off their armor and plunged into the waves, intending to swim to their dragonship and sail after the ogres in pursuit. The Torgun learned then, if they had not learned before, that ogres were not stupid. Those waiting onshore cried out in anger and dismay to see clouds of smoke rise from the *Venjekar,* accompanied by orange tongues of flame. Unable to steal the dragonship, the ogres had set it ablaze.

"Kahg!" Norgaard bellowed at the dragon, who was circling above them, glaring at the ogres. "Go after them! Sink them! Burn them!" He jabbed his finger at the departing ogres.

The Dragon Kahg only shook his head and continued to fly above them in gloomy circles.

"He cannot," said Treia. "The Dragon Kahg fears that if he attacks, the ogres will destroy the Vektan Torque. He dares not risk it. According to the dragon, the ogres spoke the truth, at in least part. There *was* a great battle in heaven, though only one of the gods, Desiria, was slain. Unfortunately, she was the Goddess of Life. With her death, we have no ability to heal."

Norgaard stared at the woman, unable to grasp the enormity of what she was saying. Bewildered and still angry, he lashed out at her. "You are awfully calm about this, Priestess!"

Treia shrugged. "I am just glad to know it wasn't my fault."

Having lost the chase, Garn returned to Skylan, who remained spellbound, unable to move. Taking off his helm, Garn dipped it in the seawater. He washed the blood from Skylan's face, and the spell was shattered.

"Get out of my way!" Skylan cried, almost knocking Garn down. "I'm going after the torque."

"Skylan, stop," said Garn. "The *Venjekar* is on fire. There's nothing you can do."

"I can swim!" Skylan said, wrestling with his friend. "I'll swim around the world if I have to—"

"We cannot recover the torque," Garn said swiftly. "But we can avenge its loss. And we can avenge our dead," he added with a grim glance at the bodies strewn over the bloody battleground.

Skylan relaxed. His muscles twitched. His lips compressed. His blue eyes met Garn's, and he spat a single word, "Horg!"

# BOOK 2

## THE VUTMANA

# CHAPTER 1

The Norns spin the threads of our wyrds on the day of our birth. This does not mean that a man's wyrd—or a woman's—cannot be changed. Each man's wyrd is affected by the wyrds of others, when their threads cross his. Not even the gods remain untouched.

The morning the Torgun fought for their lives against the ogres, their clansmen, the Heudjun, gathered at Torval's Rock. Draya joined them.

After her disastrous confrontation with Horg over the Vektan Torque, she had spent the night praying in the Great Hall of the Gods. She had not returned to her dwelling. Horg would be off somewhere, grunting and sweating with one of his concubines, but when he was finished with his lovemaking, he would return to his own bed to sleep.

This night, he would find his bed empty. She would not be there. Not this night. Not any other night. She loathed him. She could not stomach the sight of him. Her hatred was so deep, it drowned fear.

That said, what was she going to do about him? Horg was not fit to be Chief of Chiefs. He was not fit to empty the pisspot of any brave warrior. Yet she dared not challenge him openly.

Horg was cunning. If he went through with what he had threatened, telling the people that the Gods of the Vindrasi were dead, the entire Vindrasi nation would be thrown into turmoil. People would come to the Kai Priestess, demanding answers, and what would she say? The gods lost a great battle, one of their number is dead, Torval is lying low, and Vindrash has gone into hiding. The people would be thrown into despair.

Draya would have to tell the Vindrasi some version of the facts eventually. They were already starting to wonder why the Bone Priestesses had lost their ability to heal the sick and injured. But as a mother keeps a brutal truth from a child, so Draya wanted to keep the worst of what she knew from her people for as long as possible. Which meant she had to find a way to deal with Horg.

Draya spent the night in agony, restlessly pacing the length of the Hall, seeking answers to her dilemma. She prayed to the goddess, but Vindrash did not respond.

Day dawned. Across the fjord, the Torgun were forming their shield-wall, each warrior aware that he might not live to see the twilight.

The Great Hall of the Gods had no windows, but the blazing ire of the Sun Goddess seemed to burn through the walls. The Hall was stifling, driving

Draya out into the fresh air. She had been awake all night, and she was exhausted. Lack of sleep, strong emotion, anxiety, and fear had drained her. Her thoughts plodded round and round in the same circle like a hobbled horse. Perhaps a walk would clear her mind.

Almost immediately she realized she'd made a mistake. The moment people saw her, they looked alarmed. They came to her, trepidatious, fearful. What had happened? Was she all right?

*I must look terrible,* Draya realized, and she pressed her hands against her cheeks. Her skin was fevered to the touch. Her eyes burned, half-blinded by the bright light.

Draya needed refuge, she needed to talk, she needed to rest. As if in a daze, she found herself standing on the threshold of the home of her dear friend and fellow Priestess, Fria.

Fria was not within, however. Her little son told Draya that his mother had gone to Torval's Rock. The child was on his way there himself, along with several of his friends. He was armed with a wooden sword.

"My papa and I are going to kill ogres!" the little boy announced proudly.

Alarmed, Draya accompanied the child and his group of excited companions to Torval's Rock, where a crowd had gathered to hold silent vigil. Among them were the Heudjun warriors, armed and ready for battle. Draya searched for Fria, but could not find her. The child ran off, playing at war with his companions.

A thin, pitiful trail of smoke was all that was left of the beacon fire. Every man there was present only in body. In spirit, he was with the Torgun warriors. They would know by now that they fought alone, that their clansmen were not coming. Draya noticed one grizzled veteran dash a tear from his cheek. He wept from shame.

The Heudjun could not see the fight, for the Torgun village was located on the other side of the fjord, below the cliffs, near to sea level. But they hoped to be able to hear the sounds of the battle, for the air this early morning was clear and still, as though the gods themselves watched with held breath.

Suddenly several warriors cried out and pointed, though in truth there was nothing to see except the cliffs and the restless sea. The warriors claimed they had heard the crash of shield against shield. Draya heard nothing herself, and she doubted the men did either. They were hearing what they wanted to hear. They could picture the fight, the Torgun outnumbered, the ogres smashing into the wall, the slaughter. . . .

Draya could picture the slaughter quite clearly. Once the ogres overran the small band of Torgun, they would head for the village. She would soon see the smoke rising from burning homes and crops. They would butcher the little children, who would fight with wooden swords. . . .

Draya felt suddenly sick. She pressed her hand against her mouth, doubled over, and retched.

"My dear, what are you doing here? You should be at home in bed!" Fria came out of nowhere and slipped her arm around Draya's waist. "You're not well."

Fria was a large woman, big-boned and strong-willed. She was thirty-two years old and had brought fourteen healthy children into the world, all of them large and big-boned like her and her husband. Six of her sons stood with their father, Sven Teinar, himself a skilled and valiant warrior.

"I can't go home," Draya mumbled, her lips too numb to form words.

Fria's own lips clamped together. Fria knew Horg beat his wife, but she never said a word to Draya about it. Such a conversation would have been embarrassing for both, and it would have served no purpose. Chief's Law, the law governing all the clans, would not permit a Chief of Chiefs and a Kai Priestess to be divorced. These two people, leaders of their nation, were supposed to be above human frailties and weaknesses. All Fria had to offer her friend was fierce, angry sympathy.

"You must come to my dwelling, then," said Fria. "I will fix you something hot to eat."

Draya smiled faintly. Food was Fria's answer to all life's problems. Draya was not hungry, but she was too tired to resist. She allowed Fria to lead her away from Torval's Rock, where the warriors stood listening.

"Has Horg . . . Has anyone seen him this morning?" Draya asked the question reluctantly, almost choking on his name. She could not even talk of him without tasting bile in her mouth.

Fria glanced at her. "There was trouble this morning. You didn't hear about it?"

Draya shook her head. "I was at prayer. What happened?"

"Some of the warriors planned to defy Horg and sail off to fight with the Torgun, my husband and sons among them. They were boarding the ships before dawn when Horg's toadies saw and ran bleating to Horg. He came roaring down to the sea and ordered the men to return home. The ogres might attack us next, he said, and the warriors would be needed to help him defend the town."

"And so the warriors did not sail," said Draya.

Fria gave a deep sigh. "How could they, my dear? Horg spoke the truth. My man knew it, they all knew it, much as they hated to hear it. How could they sail off and leave us defenseless? And so, in the end, they came back."

The two women had reached Fria's house. Draya paused on the threshold, turned to face her friend. "What will Sven and the others do, Fria?"

"You mean about Horg?" Fria cast a sharp glance up and down the street. "Come inside, my dear. We're being watched."

Draya was not surprised. She saw one of Horg's cronies lounging in a doorway across the street, his thumbs tucked into his belt. He did not even bother to dissemble, to pretend he had business there. He stared meaningfully at Draya.

Casting the man an irate glance, Fria led Draya into the dwelling and slammed the door.

Once inside, she fussed over Draya, giving her a stool near the fire, offering her hot stew, bread, ale, dried apples—anything she wanted.

Draya shook her head. Her stomach roiled. Anything she ate would only come back up. She did finally accept ale and sipped a small amount. Fria drew up a stool and, seated close to her, spoke in a soft undertone.

"There will be angry talk among the people about Horg. Curses and threats. But in the end, it will come to nothing. Horg is strong and he has friends, not only in our clan, but in the others, as well."

Fria cast a loving gaze around her large and comfortable dwelling place. "I have five young ones still at home. Could Sven and I afford to lose our dwelling? Our land, our cattle?"

Draya clasped her friend's hands. "No, of course not. I understand. It's just . . ."

Draya paused. She toyed with the idea of telling Fria about the Vektan Torque.

"Just what?" Fria asked.

Draya shook her head. There was nothing Fria or her husband could do about Horg. As Fria had said, they had their family to think about. In his position as Chief of Chiefs, Horg was responsible for settling disputes among clansmen. All one of his cronies would have to do, for example, was to claim that he had a right to Sven's farmland. He could swear that Sven's great-grandfather had promised the land in return for several head of cattle. Sven could dispute it, of course, but Horg would be the final judge.

Draya made an excuse. "I was awake all night, Fria. I'm so tired."

"You must get some sleep," said Fria. "Lie down. With the men gone, the house will be quiet—"

"Mother!" The little boy came shouting and banging through the door. His face was flushed, his eyes bright with excitement. "You can see the dragon! Come quick! He might still be there!"

The two women stared at the boy in astonishment.

"Is this one of your tales, young Fari?" Fria demanded.

"No, no, Mother!" The boy seized hold of her hand, tried to pull her along. "I saw the dragon. Father says to come quickly."

"What dragon?" Draya gasped.

"The Torgun's dragon! Father says the dragon is helping the Torgun fight the ogres." The boy tugged on his mother's hands. "You must come see. The dragon is green and brown, and he flies around in a circle and then dives like an eagle."

The two women looked at each other, the same thought coming to each.

Draya clasped her hands together. "Blessed Vindrash, thank you!" she whispered brokenly.

Fria promised to go and then shooed her son out the door, sending him back to his father.

"The Torgun have a chance now!" Draya said, almost in tears. "With Kahg to fight for them, they may yet defeat the ogres!"

And recover the Vektan Torque! Please, Vindrash, let them find the torque and bring it back! she prayed silently.

Draya realized suddenly that Fria did not share her joy. Her friend looked grim and stern. She stood with her hands on her hips, arms akimbo.

"Draya," said Fria sharply, "don't you realize what this means?"

Draya shook her head. She was too tired to think.

"If the Torgun defeat the ogres, what then? They lit the beacon fire asking for our help, and help did not come. The Torgun will come to Vindraholm demanding answers. They will come in anger. We may have escaped ogres only to fight the Torgun."

Draya stared at her friend in dismay; then she groaned and sank back down onto the stool.

Blood feuds, clan wars, just what she had worked all her life to prevent. Few of the Heudjun liked Horg. Few had agreed with his decision to refuse aid to the Torgun. But he was their clansman, and he was their Chief. His honor was their honor. They might mutter against him among themselves, but they would close ranks around him and stand together to protect him.

"What can I do?" Draya asked helplessly. "I can do nothing!"

"The one thing you can do is rest. You'll make yourself ill otherwise, and we need you. Come, lie down."

Draya did not think she could sleep, but she was too weak to resist. Fria led her to the sleeping platform and helped her into bed. She tucked the blankets around her and stood over her, smoothing Draya's hot forehead with her hand.

"We will ask Vindrash to help us," Fria said softly. "The gods will not turn their backs on us now."

Draya closed her eyes, pretending to sleep, and Fria left, going to join her family at Torval's Rock.

When she had gone, Draya slipped out of bed and knelt in prayer. But no voice answered.

Horg pretended to be glad when people brought him the news that the Dragon Kahg had joined the fight against the ogres.

"You see there," Horg told the warriors, who had assembled in front of his dwelling place. "All that excitement for nothing. Take off your weapons and pick up your tools. The crops won't tend themselves."

He shut the door and stood for long moments in the shadowy darkness of the windowless dwelling. Then he slammed his fist into one of the support beams, causing the longhouse to shudder.

"Goat-fucking sons of whores!" he swore. "Witless arseholes! I warned the godlords. 'Capture the dragonship and set fire to it,' I said. 'Leave nothing but ashes floating on the water.' The greedy bastards didn't listen. They wanted the ship for themselves. It was that whoreson shaman. I saw the gleam in his eyes when I spoke of it."

Horg sucked his bruised knuckles and thought things over. There was the chance that the ogres could still win the battle. Dragons weren't invincible. They could be killed, same as any other creature. Or perhaps the dragon had arrived late, after the battle had been lost and all the Torgun were dead.

Horg brightened at the thought. He hated the Torgun, who spent the fine summer months sailing the seas in their dragonship—the ship that by rights should have been his—in search of gold and glory, fighting battles Horg refused to fight. True, such raids had gained the Torgun little these days, as Horg was continually pointing out to his disgruntled warriors. That was why he no longer led the Heudjun in raids. Their time was more profitably spent in tilling the fields and tending the cattle.

Horg heard the whispers. He knew some of his people despised him as a coward. Horg's spies were quick to bring him the latest rumblings and seemed to relish telling him the foul things people said about him.

Horg had another reason for hating the Torgun. Skylan Ivorson, the Chief's son, had not shown Horg the proper respect. Two years ago, the Heudjun's dragonship had been wrecked off the coast in a storm. Many warriors had drowned, as well as the ship's Bone Priestess. The sacred spiritbone had been lost at sea and never recovered, which meant that the Heudjun had no dragon.

Horg and several of his cronies had gone to the Torgun to demand that

Norgaard give him the *Venjekar*. During the meeting, the whelp Skylan had stated that it was his belief the gods had sent the storm to deliberately wreck the Heudjun dragonship as a punishment for their cowardice. That rash statement had angered the Heudjun and had almost resulted in war.

Norgaard had reprimanded his obstreperous son and insisted that Skylan apologize. Skylan had done so, though to Horg's mind the young man hadn't really been sincere. Horg had confidently expected Norgaard to hand over the dragonship, for the Torgun Chief was a broken old man who dared deny his Chief of Chiefs nothing.

Norgaard had refused, however, much to Horg's ire. He was Chief of Chiefs. He deserved a dragonship. He deserved to have a dragon serve him. Horg had been angry enough to fight, but at the thought, his stomach curled up in a tight little ball. He decided that he would send his men on a raid to steal the *Venjekar*. The damn dragon, Kahg, had thwarted that plan.

Horg had waited for his revenge, biding his time until he could find a way to inflict harm on the Torgun and, especially, on Skylan.

Horg was a gambler. He believed in luck, not in the gods. He considered himself lucky. He attributed his rise as Chief of Chiefs to luck. His marriage to that cow, Draya, had not been lucky, but a gambler could always find ways to explain away a bad fall of the dragonbones.

The ogres had come to Horg as a lucky throw of the dragonbones. Horg had been dallying with one of his women in a secluded part of the beach when he had seen the ogres' ships sailing under a flag of truce, heading for Vindraholm. He had been tempted to wait until they reached the city, where he would meet them surrounded by his warriors. Some god had whispered to him that he should meet with them alone, and he had rowed out to intercept them.

The ogres had given him the news that the Vindrasi gods were dead, defeated in a great battle. The godlords declared that the Vindrasi must worship the Gods of Raj and pay them tribute. Horg had been proud of his own cleverness. He had made a pact with the ogre godlords. The ogres would leave the Heudjun and the other clans in peace. In return he had given them a moldy old dragonbone and the Torgun. As to worshipping the Gods of Raj, Horg had been as happy to pray to them as to any other gods. Faith was all a lot of horseshit anyway.

But luck had turned on him.

His plans should have worked! Horg couldn't understand how it had all gone awry. First his meddling bitch of a wife had discovered he no longer had the Vektan Torque. He'd dealt with her. He'd seen the fear in her eyes when he'd threatened to tell the people that her beloved gods were dead. She would never dare betray him.

Just as he thought he was safe, now this. What would happen to him if the Torgun survived the battle? They would be puzzled that their plea for aid had been ignored. Their first thought would be that the ogres had already attacked and defeated the Heudjun. They would sail over to investigate and find the Heudjun squatting comfortably over their cook fires.

That was always presuming they didn't know the ogres had taken the Vektan Torque. If they did . . .

Horg broke out in a cold sweat and began to feverishly calculate how fast the Torgun could reach Vindraholm. The day was fine. The sea was calm. The battle had taken place at dawn. . . .

He sent men to the shore with orders to keep watch. He filled a mug with cider and paced his lodging, waiting for news.

The day passed. Night fell. No ships were sighted, and Horg's hopes revived. The Torgun must have been slaughtered. Otherwise they would have been here by now, howling with rage and threatening to rip off his head.

Horg was in such good spirits that he summoned his latest concubine to come to him, rather than sneak off to meet her. He was Chief of Chiefs. He could have any woman he wanted. Let Draya come home to find him taking his pleasure. He'd be glad to let her watch. She would see for herself that some women enjoyed being in the arms of a strong, powerful man such as himself.

He drank more cider and more after that.

# CHAPTER 2

The Torgun were eager to confront Horg, but even the enraged Skylan realized that they could not immediately leap into their ships and sail off to what might be war with their fellow clansmen. The Torgun owed a debt to their dead, whose souls were waiting, impatient to commence their journey to join Torval in the Hall of Heroes. In addition to honoring the dead, the Torgun had to make repairs to their dragonship. Norgaard meant to arrive on his clansmen's shores in full dignity and might.

The number of dead was surprisingly few. Most had died in the initial clash, when the ogres had crashed headlong into the Torgun shield-wall and left it in shambles. Fighting one on one, warrior to warrior, the Torgun had discovered, like Skylan, that ogres were relatively unskilled with their weapons. Bjorn had survived with only a cracked head.

But it was the Dragon Kahg who had saved the day. The Torgun honored the dragon and sang songs in praise of him.

The Dragon Kahg generally disliked such displays, and he would ordinarily have left immediately after the battle. He felt some small remorse for having initially ignored the Bone Priestess's desperate prayers, however, and the dragon deigned to graciously receive the Torgun's homage. He did not stay long, for he had to report the disastrous loss of the Vektan Torque to the dragon elders. Kahg planned to return that night. He intended on being present when the Torgun confronted Horg. The dragon was keenly interested to hear what Horg had to say for himself.

The Torgun reverently carried the bodies of their dead to the beach. Warriors who had died in battle were placed in boats with their weapons, their armor, and their shields, along with food and ale to sustain them through the long journey. The boats would then be set ablaze, the bodies cremated.

The women had already started to come down from the hiding places in the hills, some to hear the news that they were now widows. The women brought sad tidings themselves. Norgaard's wife, Sonja, had lost her baby, a little boy. He'd been born too early to survive outside his mother's womb. Sonja herself was now fighting for her life in a cave in the hills. She was too ill to be moved.

"I am sorry, Father," said Skylan, resting his hand gently on the older man's arm. "If there is anything I can do—"

Norgaard had lost men close to him this day. He had lost his hope for the future, and he might yet lose the young woman who brought joy into his life. He had been told by the Bone Priestess that the gods were themselves fighting for their survival. He had watched the ogres sail off with the sacred Vektan Torque.

His eyes were red with tears, yet a flicker of flame blazed in the blue depths.

Norgaard gripped his son's hand with crushing strength. "I will make Horg pay!" he vowed. "I swear to Torval! I will call for the Vutmana!"

Skylan gaped. He was about to say, Father, don't be ridiculous! when Garn leaned close to whisper, "Tread softly!"

Skylan took his friend's counsel and closed his mouth on his hasty words. Norgaard was serious. He was determined, resolved to challenge Horg to a fight to the death.

Perhaps the old man wanted to die in battle and this was a way to do it. Or perhaps grief and anger had acted as flint and tinder to rekindle a fire in the old man's belly.

Whatever the reason, it was Norgaard's right, as Chief, to challenge Horg, the Chief of Chiefs, in the Vutmana.

Dating back to the days of the great Clan Chief Thorgunnd and his legendary war against the Clan Chief Krega, the Vutmana was an institution created by the Bone Priestesses as a means of ending the ceaseless feuds between the clans. In those days, clans had gone to war and men had lost their lives over the theft of a chicken. With the Vutmana, one man could challenge another to fight to resolve the issue. The Vutmana could be made by any warrior against another, but only a Chief could challenge the Chief of Chiefs; the winning combatant could then claim the right to be Chief of Chiefs.

Skylan drew Garn to one side. "What do we do, my friend? A hog has more right to be Chief of Chiefs than Horg. Yet, how can Norgaard fight him? Horg is a big man, strong as an ogre. Norgaard is a cripple."

"Torval judges the Vutmana," Garn reminded him. "The god must be furious at Horg's treachery."

"That is true," Skylan conceded, "but sometimes Hevis plays cruel jokes on both men and gods. Hevis might devise some trick to allow Horg to win."

Garn admitted that was true. Hevis, God of Deceit and Trickery, was always plucking at the thread of a man's wyrd, seeking to unravel it.

"Skylan," said Garn suddenly. "There is a way." He spoke quietly in his friend's ear.

Skylan regarded him dubiously. "Are you certain?"

Garn smiled and said dryly, "Unlike you, I stay awake during the annual recital of the Chief's Law."

Skylan's eyes shone with fierce joy. He embraced Garn. "You have given me a great gift, my brother."

Skylan drew his sword, which was red with ogre blood, and walked over to stand before his father. Skylan knelt down on one knee. He thrust the blade into the ground in front of him.

"Revered Father," said Skylan. He spoke humbly, and he was sincere in his humility, for he could see the raw grief and terrible anger in his father's face. "Your honorable wounds, which are a testament to your skill and valor, give you the right to select a warrior to fight the Vutmana in your place. If the Heudjun agree to the challenge, give me the privilege. Let me fight Horg for you. I will make you Chief of Chiefs!"

Skylan clasped one hand around the blade and rested his other hand on the silver axe. "I vow to Torval."

A pale smile flitted across Norgaard's lips. Looking down on Skylan's upturned face, Norgaard saw true admiration and respect in his son's eyes.

This was a day to cherish. Much that was bad had happened, but now it seemed something blessed might come of it. Norgaard would be Chief of Chiefs, and he believed in his heart he would be a good one. He felt new life stir in him at the thought. He would lift the Vindrasi people out of this ugly bog in which their boats had long been mired, and he would guide them into a safe and prosperous harbor.

Norgaard clasped his hand around his son's. Then he seized the sword's hilt, drew it from the ground, and raised it high into the air. He handed the sword back to Skylan. The warriors lifted their voices in a cheer.

Aching from bruises, the blood still oozing from fresh-bandaged wounds, the men and women returned to their tasks, some tending to the dead, others to the wounded, and still others working to repair the harm done to their dragonship.

The Torgun would spend the night honoring their dead.

They would sail with the dawn to avenge them.

Draya spent another sleepless night in fruitless prayers. When the sun rose, she left the Great Hall and walked down to the shore. Armed Heudjun warriors had gathered on the shore, along with many women and children, all watching and grimly waiting. The Heudjun were acutely aware that if the Torgun had survived the ogre attack, they would come to find out why their clansmen had refused their summons for help. A low growl rumbled through the crowd when the Torgun's dragonship, the *Venjekar,* was sighted sailing around the cliffs.

"Someone should alert Horg," said Sven, Fria's husband and the War Chief for the Heudjun Clan. Sven's voice was flat, noncommittal. As Chief of Chiefs, Horg should be with his people. No one knew why he wasn't.

Horg's cronies stood huddled together in a knot on the fringes of the crowd. None of them made a move, and Sven wondered if Horg was even still in the city. Perhaps he had fled during the night. Sven glowered at them and then gestured to his eldest son. "You go."

Sven ordered the warriors to make a show of force, let the Torgun know they could not come uninvited onto Heudjun territory, even if they did have a legitimate complaint. The warriors held their weapons in plain sight and raised their shields. They did not form a shield-wall, though they were prepared to do so should it come to that. The Torgun were fellow clansmen, and they had a grievance. They would be permitted to tell their side of the story, but only from a distance. Their dragonship would not be permitted to land.

Draya watched the *Venjekar* draw steadily nearer. Everyone saw her, knew she had arrived. They cast her hopeful glances, wanting her reassurance, wanting her to tell them the gods were on their side. Her pallid face and stoic silence made them uneasy. The dragon's-head prow turned toward land. Draya could see the fiery gleam in the Dragon Kahg's carved eyes. She left the beach and ran back to the Great Hall and threw herself before the statue of Vindrash.

"Please tell me what I should do!" she begged.

Someone was banging on the door. Horg woke from a stuporlike sleep with a jerk that almost knocked his partner out of the bed. She grunted, rolled over, and went back to sleep.

Horg wrapped his naked body in a blanket and flung open the door. Half-blinded by the bright sunlight, he blinked and squinted, trying to see.

"Yes, what is it?" he demanded surlily, recognizing Sven's son.

"The Torgun," said the young man.

Horg blinked again. His cider-soaked brain stumbled about a moment, trying to remember why he should give a fart. Then it all came back to him.

"How many ships?" he asked.

"Just one, the *Venjekar*."

Horg nodded. "Assemble the warriors."

"We have already assembled, Chief," said the young man. "My father has command. He said I should let you know."

Horg cast a sharp glance at the young man, who met the glance with a frozen stare.

Horg grunted. "Tell the men I will be there shortly."

"I'm sure they'll be elated to hear that," the young man muttered.

"What did you say?" Horg barked.

The young man grinned and ran off.

"If your turd of a father won't teach you manners, I will!" Horg yelled savagely.

He slammed the door and, walking over to the sleeping platform, kicked at the woman lying beneath the blankets. He cuffed her when she did not immediately respond.

"Fix me something to eat. And fetch me more cider," Horg told her as she dragged herself out of bed.

His head throbbed. His mouth was dry as dirt. The cider was cold and tasted good and eased the pain. He drank it thirstily. As his head cleared, it occurred to him that two nights had passed and he had not seen Draya. She had not come home. He was angry. A wife belonged with her husband.

Horg did wonder, a bit uneasily, what he would do if she refused. Her defiance would make him look bad. People would say he could not control his wife.

An idea came to him, struck him like a thunderbolt. His idea was so amazing and wonderful, it sent tingles of excitement through his blood, as exhilarating as the cider.

Horg chuckled and made haste to dress and arm himself. He would go to the beach, but first he intended to have a talk with his wife.

Draya was rising unsteadily to her feet when the door to the Hall flew open with a bang.

"Bitch!" Horg roared. "You did not come home last night!"

Draya stilled her trembling heart and slowly turned to face him. She had gone two days and nights with almost no sleep and nothing to eat, and she was taut as a bowstring. She didn't feel fear. She didn't feel anything. She could smell the cider.

"I am not coming home," she told him. "Ever. I loathe the very sight of you."

"I don't take any great pleasure in looking at you, Wife, what with your small tits and bony ass," Horg said crudely. He had drunk just enough to give himself courage. "But you're my wife, and you'll do as I say."

"We will not speak of this now. Leave the sacred Hall. Your presence angers the gods."

"Gods!" Horg gave a whoop and a great guffaw. "What gods?"

Draya gasped. "Are you mad? Keep your voice down!" She tried to sidle past him, heading for the door. "The Torgun are here. You should be with the warriors—"

Horg seized her arm in a bone-crushing grip and twisted it. She moaned and tried in vain to break free.

"I got to thinking about what the ogres told me," Horg said, breathing cider fumes into her face. "About the gods being dead. Do you realize what this means, Kai Priestess? You have no power over me! No rutting Priestess does. I can get rid of the whole bloody lot of you!"

"You are wrong, Horg," Draya said, her numb lips barely able to move. "The gods are not dead—"

"C'mon, Vindrash!" Horg bawled, still hanging on to Draya. "Strike me down! Prove to me you're alive!"

Horg laughed again, his foul-smelling breath hot on her face, nearly gagging her. The blast of a ram's horn sounding the alarm cut short his mirth.

"The Torgun." Horg spoke with a disdainful curl of his lip. "Norgaard has come to whine that they've been mistreated."

"They have just cause for complaint," said Draya. She paused to try to keep her voice from trembling, then said defiantly, "And so I will tell the people."

Horg grunted. "You'll keep your mouth shut if you know what's good for you."

He gave her arm another twist; this one nearly wrenched her elbow from the socket. Pain flared, white-hot. Draya cried out and sagged in his grip. She was afraid she would pass out. Horg drove her to her knees and squatted over her.

"You will back me up, Draya. If you don't, there will be war, and it will be your fault. The blood of your people will be on your hands!"

"I have a duty to the people! I am still Kai Priestess!" Draya cried.

Horg smiled an unpleasant smile. "Not for long." He walked off, slamming the door behind him.

Draya remained crouched on the floor, cradling her injured arm. She had underestimated Horg, underestimated his cunning and tenacity. Horg had the power to destroy the Kai. If he did, he would bring about the fall of the Vindrasi nation.

Draya raised her eyes to the statue of the goddess.

"You must stop him, Vindrash!" Draya breathed.

The eyes of the goddess might have flickered—Draya wasn't sure.

She picked up her ceremonial robes and gingerly wrapped them around her shoulders, favoring her injured arm, then left the Great Hall, heading for the beach. Horg was in front of her, swaggering and lifting a waterskin filled with cider to his lips.

## CHAPTER 3

By the time Draya arrived, the dragonship of the Torgun, with its shallow draft, was very close to shore. The helmsman was maneuvering to bring the *Venjekar* to within hailing distance. The prow, with its figurehead of the dragon, faced the beach. The dragon's eyes flamed red. The Dragon Kahg had not manifested himself, yet he was present. In all the long history of the Vindrasi, the dragons had refused to take sides in a clan war. But then, up until now, the dragons had never had provocation.

The morning was still, cloudless. In the breathless air, the waves were little more than rivulets that rolled ashore and then departed with a soft sigh, leaving behind smatterings of foam bubbles. The Sun Goddess glared at them from across the sea. The warriors on the ship and on the beach sweat beneath their heavy armor.

Norgaard stood at the ship's prow. Beside him was his Bone Priestess, Treia. Draya immediately recognized the young woman's tall, spare form. Draya had tried very hard to love Treia, but when her affection was met by nothing except sullen, smoldering resentment, she had given up.

Draya had sent Treia back to the Torgun with misgivings. She'd had doubts about how well the bitter young woman would serve her people. Treia was Torgun, however, and it was her right to return to her people upon the death of the old Bone Priestess.

Now Treia stood in a place of honor, proudly wearing the spiritbone around her neck. Draya was glad for Treia's sake that the Dragon Kahg had answered her summons. Perhaps this would give the young woman needed confidence, strengthen her belief in herself and in the gods.

No one had started talking yet. The ship was not quite close enough. Men on both sides needed to be able to hear each other clearly, so that there could be no claim of misunderstanding. Horg stood at his ease on the beach. He appeared relaxed, confident, and was even joking with some of his cronies. As Kai Priestess, Draya's place was at Horg's side, as Treia stood beside her own Chief.

Draya took up a position on top of a sand dune, deliberately choosing the highest point on the beach. The people had their backs to her. They were watching the dragonship and did not notice her. None of the Heudjun knew she was there. Only the gods saw her.

Her gaze went to the *Venjekar*. A young man had come to join Norgaard and Treia at the prow. He rested his hand on Norgaard's shoulder and said something to him, and Draya recognized Skylan, Norgaard's son. She had not seen the young man in years, but she had heard many tales about him, and she regarded him with interest.

The young man was the clan's War Chief, now that his father's injury had left the elder man incapacitated. She had heard stories of Skylan's prowess and courage in battle. She had also heard—from Horg—that Skylan was wild, reckless, and headstrong. She wondered where the truth lay. Probably somewhere in the middle.

The dragonship was in position now. The Torgun lowered the heavy stone weight that would anchor it. Horg began the conversation. Draya shifted her gaze back to him.

Horg took the role of the injured party, demanding to know why the Torgun had come in a belligerent and warlike state to Heudjun shores. The Heudjun had no quarrel with their clansmen, but if the Torgun wanted a fight, they could see for themselves that the Heudjun would be happy to accommodate them.

Leaning on his crutch, gripping the rail to steady himself against the rocking motion of the ship, Norgaard responded. The Torgun had been attacked by a large army of ogres, he said. The Torgun had kindled the beacon fire, asking their kinsmen for help to fight the foe. As Chief of Chiefs of the Vindrasi, Horg had sworn a sacred oath to take all the clans to war should any one clan be threatened. Horg had sworn vows of brotherhood to the Torgun. Why had he broken these vows?

Draya had known Norgaard for many years. She liked and admired him. She always made it a point to converse privately with him when he came to the annual Clanmeld. Mostly the two of them discussed the Torgun people and their problems, but sometimes they spoke of personal matters.

Draya knew Norgaard to be everything Horg was not. The gods had permitted Norgaard to survive his terrible wound, but they had, for reasons of their own, left him crippled and in pain. Draya saw the suffering in his eyes, yet he never spoke of it, never complained. He was considered a good Chief, fair in his judgments. He was said to be a good husband, a good father. He was intelligent, wise. And he was playing Horg for the fool he was, lulling his enemy into complacency, luring him into a trap.

Horg thundered back. "I did not come to your aid because the gods forbade it!" He pointed at Skylan. "Your son brought the ogres down on you! Your son led them to your shores! It was up to your son to fight them. My warriors remained here to defend our homes and families should the ogres attack us."

Norgaard was silent. The Torgun in the *Venjekar* were silent. The Heudjun people gathered on shore were silent. The only sound was that of the waves washing up against the hull of the dragonship.

And then Norgaard spoke. "You lie, Horg Thekkson. You knew the ogres would not attack the Heudjun."

Skylan reached down at his father's feet. He picked up something and held it in the air. At first, Draya could not make out what it was, and then she gasped. Skylan held in his hands the head of an ogre. He held it long enough for everyone to see, and then he flung the head at Horg. The grisly object plopped into the sand at Horg's feet.

Horg stared down at the head, whose eyes—frozen in death—seemed to be staring up at him, and he turned a ghastly color, almost as pale as the bloody head.

"I see you two recognize each other," said Norgaard.

Draya's blood tingled. Her stomach clenched. Her heart raced; her palms were sweaty. She had heard warriors describe similar sensations as they stood waiting in the shield-wall for the order to attack.

Horg licked his lips. He was not about to give in without a fight. She could see him scrambling about desperately for some way to weasel out.

*Vindrash, help me!* Draya prayed. *Give me courage.*

Standing atop the dune, alone and apart, Draya called out to Norgaard. "Does this mean, Chief, that you have recovered the Vektan Torque?"

A collective gasp swept through the crowd. Heads jerked in her direction. Eyes widened in shock, jaws dropped, mouths gaped. Among those staring at her was Horg. He scowled, his hands clenching to fists.

"Kai Priestess." Norgaard bowed low, in respect. "It grieves me deeply to say that we did not recover the sacred torque, though my son was almost killed in the attempt."

Norgaard raised his voice, which wasn't really necessary. The crowd was so quiet, so attentive, he could have whispered and they would have heard every word.

"The godlord whose head lies at the feet of this craven coward"—Norgaard pointed at Horg—"came to us flaunting the sacred Vektan Torque. He claimed that the gods of the Vindrasi were dead and the fact that he had the torque proved it. He demanded that we worship his gods and pay him in silver and cattle to leave us in peace. We answered that we would pay him in blood!"

The Torgun cheered. The Heudjun shifted uneasily and glanced at each other, their faces darkening.

Norgaard resumed speaking. "The ogre godlord had the temerity to wear the Vektan Torque into battle, hoping to demoralize us. Instead, it gave us courage. Our Bone Priestess"—he indicated Treia, who stood at his side—"summoned the Dragon Kahg. The dragon, too, was furious at the loss of the sacred torque. He attacked the ogres, and with the Dragon Kahg's help, the Torgun routed the ogres, sent them running for their ships like whipped dogs."

"If you defeated the ogres and killed their godlord, where is the torque?" demanded Sven in a stern voice.

Norgaard rested his hand proudly on Skylan's shoulder. "My son challenged the godlord who wore the torque to fight in single combat. Skylan killed the ogre and took the torque from the whoreson's neck. But the ogres do not fight with honor. They had brought one of their foul shamans into battle. The shaman used evil magicks on my son and froze him where he stood, so that he could not move a muscle. The shaman took the torque from my son's hand and ran off with it to his ship, which immediately set sail."

"Why didn't you pursue them?" Sven asked, frowning.

"The ogres had set our dragonship ablaze, leaving it damaged. We spent all night repairing it. Some of my warriors tried to swim after them," Norgaard added with pride, "but that proved impossible."

"What of the Dragon Kahg?" Draya asked. "Why didn't he take the torque from the ogres?"

Norgaard looked to Treia. All dealings with the Dragon Kahg were referred to the Bone Priestess.

Treia seemed reluctant. She had a thin, reedy voice that could sometimes be shrill. She knew this, and she had never liked to speak in public.

"The Dragon Kahg—" Treia's voice cracked from nervousness. She swallowed and started again. "The Dragon Kahg feared that if he attacked the ogre ships, the ogres would destroy the torque."

The carved eyes of the dragon gleamed red. Perhaps it was merely the position of the ship, but the eyes seemed to be glaring at Horg. Because of him, the ogres were now in possession of one of the powerful Five Dragons of Vektia. Draya heard the terrible news with equanimity. She had allowed herself to hope for a brief moment that disaster had been averted. The gods had deemed otherwise, though whose gods were doing the deeming was open to question. For the moment, the Gods of Raj appeared to be on the ascendant.

Horg tried one last bold move. "Lies!" he sneered. "All lies. I will tell you the truth. Several weeks ago, I was riding to visit one of the Steppe Clans. During the night, I was attacked by thieves. I fought them, but there were too many, and they took the torque from me. I did not tell anyone about this, for I was determined to find the thieves myself and have my revenge. And now I can put a name to the thief. Skylan Ivorson! *He* and Torgun raiders stole the torque! *He* gave it to the ogres when it became clear that the Torgun would lose the battle—"

The Torgun on board the ship howled in rage. Several of the warriors leaped into the water and started toward the shore. Norgaard barked a sharp command, and they floundered to a halt.

The Heudjun were confused. Clearly they did not know whom to believe, and they started arguing among themselves. Horg's cronies were loud in his support. Others like Sven were troubled and eyed Horg darkly. Norgaard was respected among the Heudjun. Horg was not. Few trusted him. Yet, he was their Chief. Their own honor was at stake. They wanted to believe him.

Norgaard shifted his gaze to Draya, giving her fair warning of his next move. She understood, and she gave a slight nod in return.

"Since it is our word against the word of the Chief of Chiefs, we seek the judgment of the Kai Priestess," said Norgaard.

Everyone, including Horg, turned to Draya. Horg wore an expression of confidence that was not entirely misplaced. Never before had Draya crossed him.

She fears me, he would be telling himself. She won't dare betray me. She knows what I'll do to her.

Draya drew in a deep breath. No one stood beside her. She was alone on the dunes. Yet she felt the supporting touch of an immortal hand.

"Norgaard, Chief of the Torgun, tells the truth." Draya spoke loudly, clearly. "It is Horg who lies. He admitted to me on the night of the beacon fire that he gave the Vektan Torque to the ogres in return for a pledge that they would sail off and leave us in peace. And as part of the deal, Horg also gave the ogres the Torgun. That is why the Heudjun did not go to your aid, Norgaard. He promised the ogres we would not."

Horg flushed in rage. His thick brows contracted. He would have spoken, but Sven forestalled him. Stepping out from the line of warriors, Sven faced Draya.

"You knew the sacred torque was missing, Kai Priestess," he said in accusing tones. "Why didn't you make the truth known to us before now?"

Draya felt half-suffocated. The hand on her shoulder tightened its grip.

"I was afraid of Horg and what he would do to me," Draya replied. Shoving up the sleeve of her robe, she showed him the bruise marks. "I was ashamed."

Draya lifted her head, stood tall and proud.

"As Kai Priestess, I swear by the blessed Vindrash that I am telling the truth." She raised her hand to touch the silver dragon amulet she wore around her neck. "Norgaard Ivorson, I call upon you to swear to Vindrash that you are telling the truth."

"I swear by Vindrash," said Norgaard firmly. "And I swear by Torval, who gave us victory and delivered the ogres into our hands."

"He is the liar," Horg cried loudly, "and so is my wife! They're in this together! She paid the Torgun to steal the torque. You all know the Kai have long been angry that it was taken from them!"

Draya looked at Norgaard and saw a smile touch his lips. There could be only one response to this terrible charge, and she realized suddenly that Norgaard had been digging this trap ever since his arrival. Horg had not merely stumbled into the pit. He had jumped in feetfirst.

"The honor of the Torgun has been called into question," Norgaard said. "There is only one way to settle this. I call for the Vutmana! Let the gods be my judge."

He turned to his warriors. "Are the Torgun prepared to back me in this challenge?"

The warriors answered with a mighty shout that caused the *Venjekar* to rock in the waves.

"I accept the challenge!" Horg shouted. He glanced around confidently at his warriors. "The honor of the Heudjun is at stake! The Heudjun will back me!"

When the Kai Priestesses had first laid down the Law of the Challenge known as the Vutmana, they had wisely understood that the practice was open to abuse. Unless checked, any ambitious young buck hoping to become a Chief could issue a challenge. A Clan Chief might well find himself forced to spend most of his time fending off rivals.

The Kai had therefore declared a Chief could ask his clansmen to fight with him. For their part, the clansmen of the warrior making the challenge had to be prepared to back up his challenge with their blood. In addition, the challenger had to stake his own wealth on the challenge. If the gods went against him, he would pay a substantial sum to the winner for the insult. Issuing a challenge was thus a very serious matter, not to be undertaken lightly.

Horg was confident. The Heudjun warriors would never back down from a fight, no matter whether they believed him or not.

But long moments passed and no one spoke. Horg turned, glowering, to Sven. "Well? Why do you wait? You are not afraid of these yapping dogs, are you?"

Sven's lips tightened. He stared grimly at Horg. "I do not know what others will do," Sven declared. "For myself, I will not fight to save the skin of a man I consider to be a liar, a drunk, and a bully. A man who has brought shame on us all."

Sven threw down his battle axe. The weapon landed in the sand at Horg's feet, not far from the ogre's grisly head.

Horg's eyes bulged. He seemed to swell with fury. "You do not fight, Sven Teinar, because you are a coward!" Horg glared around at the others. "What about the rest of you? Are all of you craven?"

In answer, Sven's sons proudly threw down their weapons. Other warriors joined them, tossing their weapons at his feet. Their women cheered and called out support. Horg's latest concubine clapped her hands wildly.

At last, only Horg's cronies remained. They held on to their weapons, hedging their bets, but they sidled away from him. None would look at him.

Horg was angry and he was puzzled. He should have kept quiet, but he had drunk a good deal of cider, and the spirits seized hold of his mouth.

"Sons of whores!" he raved. "I saved your sorry arses! Two hundred ogres there were! Two hundred monsters who would have come howling down on you in the night, slitting your throats, raping your women, and burning your homes! I gave them a moldy shinbone, and the ogres sailed away and left you—"

Horg came to a stammering halt. He had just realized what he was saying.

Sven eyed Horg balefully. "You admit it, then. You gave the ogres the sacred torque, and you lied when you claimed it was stolen."

"I admit nothing,' Horg said sullenly. "Except that all Heudjun are piss-pants."

Sven turned to Norgaard. "Chief of the Torgun, our shame is very great. We ask the spirits of your dead to forgive us. You are free to challenge Horg Thekkson to the Vutmana. We will not oppose you."

Sven walked off across the sand. His sons followed him, as did the rest of the warriors. Their womenfolk walked with them, putting their arms around their husbands in sympathy and ordering excited, clamoring children to keep quiet.

Horg looked dazed, like a man who feels pain in his back and looks down to find the head of a spear protruding from his gut.

The Torgun steered their dragonship in to the shore. Men jumped over the sides to assist in the landing. Norgaard did not jump into the water with the others. He was forced to walk down the ship's gangplank. Horg's eyes glittered. The old look of cunning was back. He turned to his cronies and grinned. Draya could not hear his words, but she could guess them.

"I'll be fighting a cripple," he said.

His cronies laughed and clustered around him, pleased that they had placed their bets on the right man.

Splashing through the waves, heading into shore, Skylan and Norgaard looked at each other; then Skylan threw back his head and laughed.

A thrill of excitement surged through Draya.

One of the rules of the Vutmana was that a Chief may select a champion to fight in his stead

A rule Horg had apparently forgotten.

"Thank you, Vindrash!" Draya whispered.

# CHAPTER 4

Draya returned to the Great Hall of the Gods and was thankful to find it empty. Soon, she would have to assemble Fria and the other Bone Priestesses, and the acolytes would also assemble to prepare for the Vutmana. But for now, she was alone with Vindrash.

Horg would not face the crippled Norgaard. He would have to fight Skylan, the strong warrior son. Horg had forgotten the provision about champions, apparently. Or perhaps he didn't even know it. The Law of the Challenge was recited every year during the annual Clanmeld, but Horg generally paid scant attention to the recitations, which admittedly went on for days. He spent the time jesting with his friends or catching up on his sleep to be ready for the nightly revels.

The Gods of the Vindrasi judged the Vutmana, determined which man was best suited to be Chief and gave that man the victory. But were the Gods of the Vindrasi fit to judge?

Draya pondered this question in an agony of doubt.

The Vindrasi Gods had been too weak to hold on to the Vektan Torque, allowing it to fall into the hands of one of the Vindrasi's most feared enemies. Draya's one poor consolation was that the ogres did not know what they had or how to use it. They might learn over time, however, and that could not be allowed. The spiritbone of the Vektia Dragon had to be recovered.

A daunting task! An old man of the Luknar Clan, who claimed he had seen eighty winters, told tales of having visited the ogres' realm as a boy, during the glory days when the Vindrasi had been a mighty people, ruling the oceans as their gods ruled the heavens. But that was long ago. Many years had passed since the Vindrasi last crossed the seas to ogre nations. Vindrasi glory was now nothing more than an old man's fading memory.

No one knew now how to find the ogres' realm. The Vindrasi dragonships would have to sail seas strange to them, and they would need a strong, wise, intelligent Chief of Chiefs to lead them on what could be a desperate voyage for their own survival. Half the time Horg was so drunk, he could not find his own slop bucket. Draya remembered his threat to get rid of the Kai, to get rid of her.

Could the gods be trusted to make the right judgment?

Draya's faith was her reason for being. As her own life grew more wretched, she clung to Vindrash for support, turning to the goddess for comfort and consolation. Now it seemed Vindrash clung to her.

Torval had fought a great battle and lost. The goddess Desiria was dead. Vindrash was in hiding, unable to respond to the prayers of her people for fear her enemies might find her. If the Gods of the Vindrasi were vanquished, the people who depended on them would be left weak and vulnerable, exposed to powerful enemies. For centuries, the Vindrasi had been conquerers. Now they would be the conquered, their land occupied by strangers, forced to bow to strange kings.

Which left Draya with a terrible decision to make. Could she entrust the future of her people to gods who were fighting for their very existence?

Kneeling before the statue of Vindrash, Draya brought her question to the goddess and waited, trembling, for the answer.

The eyes of the goddess were empty. There was no life in them.

"Don't do this to me!" Draya cried out. She beat on the floor of the Great Hall with her fists. "Tell me that I can trust you!"

She heard the hiss of the wind through the chinks in the wooden walls. She heard the laughter of children and the squabbling cries of seabirds quarreling over a dead fish. She heard the scream of a swooping hawk.

Draya curled in on herself, wrapped her arms around her knees, and moaned. She was so very tired. The darkness was so very dark. She was so very alone.

"Give me an answer!" she prayed.

The response was silence.

Draya sat back on her heels.

Perhaps that *was* the answer. . . .

That evening, the Heudjun Priestesses assembled in the Great Hall of the Gods. The young acolytes were excited. They did not understand the terrible import, and they viewed the Vutmana as a holiday. The older women were more subdued, for they recognized that whatever the outcome, life for the Heudjun would never be the same.

"If Horg is judged innocent, we are in trouble," Sven told his wife. "He will take the opportunity to avenge himself on those of us who opposed him, and there will be nothing we can do to stop him."

"You did what you had to do, Husband," Fria said practically. "Horg gave the sacred torque to our enemies to save his own flabby skin. You could not condone such a heinous crime."

She gave her husband a hug. "No matter what happens, my love, I am proud of you. You did right, and so the gods will judge."

"I did right when I married you," Sven told his wife fondly, and he kissed her on her forehead.

The Great Hall buzzed with conversations, each woman relating what she knew of the ceremony. Draya had never presided over a Vutmana. Neither she nor any of the Bone Priestesses of the Heudjun had ever seen one. Horg had become Chief of Chiefs upon the death of his father, the former Chief. There had been no challengers. Too late they realized their mistake, and now they were paying for it in shame and humiliation. Horg's dishonor was their dishonor. The possibility that the Torgun, the poorest clan among the Vindrasi, would gain ascendancy over the Heudjun, their Chief becoming Chief of Chiefs, was a bitter draft to swallow.

Vindraholm had been chosen lord city long ago by the fabled Kai Priestess Griselda the Man-Woman to settle a feud between the Heudjun Clan, who resided in Vindraholm, and the Svegund Clan, who wanted their city,

Einholm, to receive the honor. Griselda had traveled to each of the cities. On the day she arrived in Vindraholm, the sun shone brightly. When she went to visit Einholm, the city was hit with one of the worst storms in recent memory. The will of the gods was clear.

The Heudjun Clan would remain the guardians of their ancestral homeland, but they would no longer be the city's dominant clan. That honor would go to the Torgun. If Norgaard won, he would move from Luda into the Chief's longhouse in Vindraholm, bringing with him his household and many warriors. Already the Heudjun were getting a taste of what this would be like, for the Torgun were setting up camp on the beach. Torgun warriors would soon be swaggering through the streets.

"We must hold the Vutmana as soon as possible," Draya told the assembled Priestesses, "or there will be trouble."

The Priestesses were in agreement. They were aware of the mood of the people. Almost every woman there had been forced to listen to the angry rantings of husbands and sons, brothers and fathers.

"I do not condone what the Chief of Chiefs has done," Fria said, rising to speak. "Far from it. Still it would be best for the Torgun if they returned home until it is time for the ceremony. Our men have promised they will not fight them, but that promise will be hard for some of them to keep, especially if the Torgun warriors go about the city like young bucks flaunting newly sprouted horns."

Draya agreed, and as the first order of business, she sent Fria as messenger to Norgaard to explain matters.

Norgaard sent back word that he understood completely. He and the Torgun would sail home with the tide.

Draya was pleased at his response. Norgaard was a man of sense. He would make a good Chief.

"And," said Fria, squeezing Draya's hand and whispering excitedly into her ear, "I found out that Norgaard is now a widower. His young wife died last night in childbirth. That is sad, of course, but it makes things easier. Now there will be no messy entanglements, no divorce."

"I grieve to hear Norgaard's wife died," Draya said. "But what else do you mean? Was there talk of divorce between them?"

Fria stared at her, amazed. "Don't tell me you haven't thought of this, Draya! If the gods are just, you will have a new husband."

Draya gasped. She had been so caught up in worrying about how the change to a new Chief would affect her people, she had not remembered that the Vutmana would have a profound effect upon herself.

The Kai Priestess was required to marry the Chief of Chiefs. If the Chief was already married, as Norgaard had been, the law required that he divorce his wife. Such a divorce was most honorable. The woman received substantial compensation and could either remain in her own home or return to live with her family. Norgaard, now a widower, would be looking for a new wife anyway.

Draya considered Norgaard as a husband. He was her elder by some ten years or more; she liked him, but she knew him to be a disappointed man—a somber, cheerless man with a crippled leg who was always in pain. She suppressed a sigh.

"He would be a good husband for you, Draya," Fria told her. "He can give you children. And he won't beat you."

Was that the measure of good husband? Draya wondered. That he didn't beat you?

In a society where marriages were always arranged between families, few married for love. Songs celebrated love found *after* marriage, and Draya had only to see the way Sven and Fria looked at each other to know that the words of the poets were not empty. Men and women who had scarcely known each other before they lay together in the bridal bed often found deep and abiding love came after they had said their vows.

Draya longed for such a bond. Instead she saw herself moving from one loveless bed into another. She must hope for a child. That would be her consolation.

"We need to set a date for the Vutmana," said Draya, addressing the Priestesses. "How soon can all the clans be notified? The other Clan Chiefs will want to attend to serve as witnesses for their people."

The Bone Priestesses calculated how long it would take messengers to travel from Vindraholm to bring the news to the other clans and how long the Chiefs would need to undertake the journey to Vindraholm. Fortunately the weather was fine for sailing. Most would travel by sea. Add a day or so to take into consideration the possibility of bad weather, and Draya judged they could safely schedule the Vutmana to occur within a fortnight, the last week of the month of Desiria.

Desiria, the month of spring, the time of hope and rebirth, named to honor the Goddess of Life. What dreadful irony! Draya thought. That reminded her of another unhappy task. She would have to tell the people the terrible news about the gods. Now was not a good time, not with all the upheaval and turmoil. Yet she feared Horg would tell them if she did not. He had threatened to do so, after all.

And then Draya realized Horg didn't dare carry out his threat. If he should win, he would claim Torval's protection. Horg would be a fool to go around telling people Torval was dead.

Draya sent word to Norgaard that the Torgun should return in a fortnight's time. She sent a messenger to Horg, as well. The girl returned with word that Horg was gone. He and some of his cronies had gone on a hunting trip.

"Likely stalking the woods in search of the wild cider jug," said Fria tartly. "A good thing he left, given the way people feel about him."

Draya felt an overwhelming sense of relief. Hopefully he would stay away, far away, until time for the Vutmana. She did not want to have to speak to him or think about him or set eyes upon him until the day she stood before him during the ceremony.

After that . . .

Hopefully there would be no after that.

# CHAPTER 5

Long, long ago, a Clan Chief named Thorgunnd Sigrund declared war upon a rival Clan Chief, Krega of the Steppes. The war started innocently enough. Chief Krega sought the hand of Thorgunnd's eldest daughter in marriage, hoping to ally his clan with the more powerful clan of Thorgunnd. The young woman refused the marriage, as was her right, for Krega had the reputation of being a savage brute.

Krega was angry and affronted, and he urged Thorgunnd to force his daughter to marry him, but Thorgunnd would not do so. A short time later, Thorgunnd's youngest son, his father's favorite, went walking in the woods and vanished. When he did not return home, Thorgunnd sent men to search for him. They found the boy on Krega's land. The boy was dead, an arrow in his back.

Furious, Thorgunnd demanded a blood-price for the life of his son. Krega refused, claiming the boy's death was an accident. Men had been out hunting and mistaken the lad for a deer. Krega further stated that the boy had trespassed; he had no business being on his land in the first place.

Thorgunnd suspected that Krega had murdered the boy and then dragged his body onto his land, but he could not prove it. Since Krega would not pay the blood-price, the clans went to war.

Each Chief called upon his allies to fight for his cause. The Djevakfen fought alongside Krega. The Martegnan joined forces with Thorgunnd. Not content with victory on the field of battle, warriors burned and looted the homes of their fellow Vindrasi, raped their women, and sold their children into bondage. Every battle engendered another, as relatives of the dead demanded revenge. Soon every clan had been sucked into the terrible maelstrom.

The Kai saw the valiant young men, the future of the Vindrasi people, lying dead on the field of battle. The Kai heard the screams of ravished women and the cries of orphans. The Kai saw their enemies watching, biding their time, waiting for the Vindrasi to destroy themselves. When that happened, they would swoop down, like carrion birds, to pick the flesh from the carcass.

Fearful that this war threatened to fell the World Tree, the Kai Priestess, a valiant woman named Ingunn, undertook a perilous journey. Ingunn traveled to the Nethervold to beg the Goddess of the Dead, Freilis, to end the strife.

Freilis was moved by the pleas of Ingunn, and she left the Nethervold—a thing unheard of. She sailed in a ship drawn by ravens to Torval's Hall of Heroes. She found the God of Battle carousing with the souls of valiant warriors, listening to them relate their heroic deeds. Freilis reproached Torval with the vast number of dead. She pleaded with him to end the strife before the Vindrasi people ended up destroying themselves.

Torval roared his refusal. The warriors had died with honor. Their deaths brought them glory. Freilis asked him bitterly what glory there was in a woman lying slaughtered in a pool of her own blood or in Vindrasi children being carried away to slavery.

"I say these so-called valiant warriors are cowards with *no* honor," Freilis declared angrily. "They fear to fight each other. Instead they kill defenseless women and old men and helpless children."

Torval was furious. He thundered that he would stake anything Freilis named upon the courage and valor of his warriors.

"If I am proved right, then you must end this war," Freilis said.

"I take your wager," said Torval, pleased, for he was convinced he would win. "How shall it be settled?"

"The two Chiefs, Thorgunnd and Krega, started this war. Let them meet in single combat," Freilis declared. "This will not be a fight to the death, for we have seen death enough already. Whoever draws first blood will be the victor."

Both Clan Chiefs agreed, and they met in single combat. Torval favored Thorgunnd, for Torval knew the Chief's cause was just. As for Freilis, she had tricked Torval, for she knew Krega's heart was black, and she was certain he would not fight according to the rules.

She was proved right. Thorgunnd drew first blood, slashing Krega across his cheek. Krega dropped his sword and walked forward to congratulate the winner. But when Thorgunnd sheathed his sword and lowered his shield, Krega drew a knife from his boot and stabbed Thorgunnd in the heart.

Shocked and outraged, Torval conceded he had lost the wager. He cursed Krega and caused him to be expelled from his clan. Krega was forced to become an outlaw—one who lived outside the law. This meant that his life was forfeit. Anyone who came upon him could slay him, and the killing would be deemed justified. Krega had many enemies who sought his blood. Hunted like an animal, he lived a miserable existence and ended up being torn apart by bears—an animal sacred to Torval.

With the war at last at an end, the clan of Thorgunnd Sigrund prospered. They renamed their clan in his honor, calling themselves the Torgun. Their many dragonships sailed the seas, venturing into distant lands, performing deeds that were forever after known as the Thorgunnd Sagas.

Admitting Freilis's wisdom, Torval decreed that henceforth the Vindrasi would settle disputes through the Vutmana, the Law of the Challenge.

The Vutmana was centuries old, and the Vindrasi still adhered to many of its ancient traditions. Draya had been present at the Clanmeld year after year, listening to the Talgogroth recite the Law of the Challenge.

Since the Vindras had no written language, the Talgogroth—the Voice of Gogroth, God of the World Tree—was a man whose only task in life was to memorize the laws of the Vindrasi and recite them during the Clanmelds, meetings held annually in each clan. Every man fifteen years and older was required to attend the Clanmeld to hear the recitation. Thus no man could claim he was ignorant of the law.

For the first five days of a Clanmeld, the Talgogroth recited all the laws of the Vindrasi nation. Chiefs attended the Great Clanmeld held in Vindraholm every year. Men of the clans attended the Lesser Clanmelds held yearly when the Talgogroth, traveling from clan to clan, came to give them the law. Bone Priestesses were also required to attend the Clanmeld, for a Clan Chief might ask for the assistance of the gods if he felt uncertain on how to rule.

The day after the Torgun's departure, thirteen days prior to the Vutmana, Draya paid a visit to the Talgogroth, to ask him to relate the Law of the Challenge, ostensibly to make certain she did not offend the gods by leaving out an essential part of the ritual. In truth, Draya needed to ask the Voice of Gogroth an important question.

The Talgogroth was named Balin, and he was about thirty-five. He had learned the law at his father's knee, for his father had been the Talgogroth, as had his father before him. The Talgogroths were highly regarded among the Vindrasi. The Talgogroth was the only man exempt from fighting, for his knowledge was deemed too valuable to risk. Whenever the Chief of Chiefs sat in judgment, Balin stood at his side.

Balin had been expecting Draya, and he welcomed her cordially to his longhouse. He offered her food and drink, which she accepted to do honor to his house. She listened silently and patiently as he recited the Law of the Challenge and then went into all the details about where it was held, who could attend, how long the ceremonial cloth should be, what it should be made of, the roles of all the participants, and so on.

"Each fighter has three shields, kept for him by an unarmed shield-bearer who takes no part in the battle but provides replacement shields if a shield is broken," Balin declaimed. "Each fighter strikes a single blow in turn, with the challenged party delivering the first blow. The fight continues until first blood is drawn, whereupon the Kai Priestess ends the fight, proclaiming that Torval has issued his judgment."

Draya frowned slightly and raised her hand to stop the flow of words. "How is 'first blood' to be determined? I assume this does not mean a scratch on the cheek."

"The Kai Priestess is the one who decides when first blood is drawn. Traditionally, the blood must be sufficient to spatter the cloth at the warriors' feet."

"I see." Draya remained thoughtful.

"You must remember, lady," Balin said gently, "that the Vutmana was established by the Kai to *avoid* the shedding of blood."

"Yet the Vutmana is not the same now as it was when it was first established," said Draya.

"The Vutmana we know today is very different from those described in the old songs," Balin agreed.

"How exactly?" Draya asked. "I want to be clear on this."

"For example, when the Vutmana was first established, two men could fight for any reason under the sun. The idea of a trial by combat became so popular, the Priestesses were doing nothing but watching warriors take swings at each other," Balin told her.

"The Clan Chiefs were not happy about this. They were supposed to judge disputes, but increasingly the Chiefs were being bypassed by those wanting to bring their petty grievances to Torval. And then there was the problem that if anyone disagreed with a Chief's judgment, the warrior could challenge the Chief to the Vutmana to try to overthrow him.

"After a few years of such chaos, the Kai decreed that the Vutmana would be used *only* to settle disputes that might lead to war *and* to determine who was to be the new Chief. Further, the challenger has to be willing to stake a goodly portion of his wealth on the outcome, to be given to the challenged if Torval rules in his favor."

Balin reached for his lyre. "For example, in the lay known as 'Gonegal's Heart' there is a verse that goes—"

"Perhaps another time, Balin," Draya said politely, rising to take her leave.

Balin was a bard, as well as Talgogroth, and if permitted, he would spend the rest of the day singing his songs.

"I enjoy your music, as you know, sir," Draya added, to take the sting out of her words, "but I must forgo all such pleasures until this important matter is settled. You do understand, don't you?"

Balin inclined his head and regretfully laid his lyre aside. "I hope I have been of help to you, lady," he said, rising in turn.

"Your help has been inestimable, sir. I thank you for your time." Draya glanced at the lyre that resided in a place of honor near the fireside and said politely, "I hope you will compose a song in honor of this Vutmana, so that it will be remembered by our children."

"That will depend, lady," said Balin after a moment's hesitation.

"On what?" Draya asked, smiling. "You bards make everything into a song."

He regarded her sadly, then said, "Perhaps our children will not want to remember."

The day of the Vutmana dawned clear and bright. The Sun Goddess Aylis seemed to leap out of the ocean, as though eager to watch the contest. Akaria was reluctant to lower her lantern; the moon was loath to set, but remained a pale orb in the sky until long after the sun had risen, before sinking down reluctantly.

The Torgun had arrived at Vindraholm the night before. No one was on the beach to greet them, but no one was there to oppose them, either. Norgaard understood. The hearts of the Heudjun were sore and bitter. Norgaard and his warriors camped on the beach and he'd placed strict limits on the amount of ale they consumed.

Horg and his cronies had also returned to the city. Horg had spent the time in the forest brooding over his perceived wrongs and reviling his unfaithful clansmen. His friends had soothed him and flattered him, assuring Horg he had been in the right. Sven was a coward, they said. Norgaard was an ambitious rival who would stop at nothing, while his whelp Skylan was all clamorous bark and no bite.

Horg's friends had been quick to disabuse him of the pleasant notion that he would be fighting a cripple.

"Ten to one," they said, "Norgaard will have his warrior son fight in his place."

Horg shrugged it off. He would have liked to fight Norgaard, not only because of the physical advantage, but also because of their clash over the dragonship. Horg had never forgiven Norgaard for withholding what Horg believed to be rightfully his.

Horg did not mind fighting Skylan. Thinking it over, Horg decided he preferred it. Norgaard was a sly old fox who would know all Horg's little underhanded tricks and undoubtedly have a few of his own. Skylan was young and inexperienced, a notorious hothead who would make mistakes. Skylan lacked Horg's advantage in height, nor was the young man as strong. Horg had been renowned during his days as a warrior for his ability to shatter a man's shield with a single axe blow.

Horg's hatred was a fire burning in his belly, a blaze so fierce and warming that he lived on it and forwent cider. He stoked the fire of his hatred by feeding it Draya and Sven and Norgaard and Skylan and all the other whoresons who conspired against him. When he was victorious, he would avenge himself on all of them. Horg spent his days practicing his skill with his axe.

Horg had not touched a drop of strong spirits in fourteen days, and he was in relatively good shape when he woke the morning of the Vutmana. He had shed some of the fat around his belly. His jawline had firmed and tightened. His eyes were clear, keen, focused. He was determined, resolved, and cold sober. He meant to win the Vutmana.

No man—and certainly no god—was going to stop him.

# CHAPTER 6

The Vutmana to determine the Chief of Chiefs was held in a place sacred to all the Vindrasi, a small grassy island located in a cove northwest of Vindraholm next to the estuary of Akaraflod. On this piece of ground, Thorgunnd had fought Krega, or so legend told. The island was known to this day as Krega's Bane.

High cliffs surrounded the island, providing an ideal vantage point for spectators who would line the tops of the cliffs to watch the challenge taking place on the island below. The cliff's steep rocky walls served to deter any overly enthusiastic supporters who might be tempted to join the fight.

Crowds had been gathering at the site for many days in advance of the event. Some people had walked or ridden miles in order to be present. The Chiefs of all the clans were there, escorted by their household guard, their honored warriors, and their Bone Priestesses. Dragonships and boats lined the beaches for miles. Each clan had established its own campsite, and their colorful banners floated in the strong sea breeze. The fierce Martegnan, Warriors of the Spear Steppes; the proud Svegund, Warriors of the North Shore; the clever Djevakfen, Warriors of the Land; the bold Olfet Margen, Warriors of the North Sea; and the skilled Luknar, comprising two clans who had joined together: Warriors of the South Bay and the Forge Masters.

The Clan Chiefs, as witnesses, were given the best vantage points. They took their places near the cliff's edge, where they could look down upon the island. The Bone Priestesses gathered nearby, their embroidered robes making a bright splash of color against the gray rock.

The leading warriors of the Heudjun and Torgun Clans were given places of prominence. The two groups stood as far apart as possible, neither acknowledging the presence of the other. Sven Teinar led the Heudjun contingent. Sigurd Adalbrand headed the Torgun.

Bone Priestess of the Heudjun, Fria Teinar, and Bone Priestess of the Torgun, Treia Adalbrand, stood in between the two groups of men. Their presence was indicative of the Kai solidarity. They were also there to stop any trouble that might erupt between the two clans.

The Heudjun were grim and silent, struggling with conflicting feelings. The Heudjun disliked Horg intensely and would have been glad to see him lose, but, at the same time, they did not want the Torgun to win. For their part, the Torgun were in good spirits. Torval was on their side.

There had been some grumbling among the Torgun to the effect that because the Kai Priestess was also Horg's wife, Draya would be prejudiced in favor of her husband and might give the fight to him. Men brought their complaints to Norgaard. He was angry and denounced those who doubted her.

"I have known the Kai Priestess for many years, and I know Draya to be a woman of honor," he stated. "Draya is dedicated to the gods. She is Kai Priestess first and Horg's wife second. She will uphold the judgment of the Torval. She must uphold it, or be god-cursed herself."

This quieted the talk, if it did not quiet men's doubts.

The remainder of the Vindrasi people who had come to see the fight found places for themselves wherever they could, crowding the tops of the cliffs, shoving and jostling to get a better view, so that a small boy slipped and nearly fell to certain death on the rocks below. He was saved by a warrior's quick-thinking grab. The Bone Priestesses, taking heed of this near tragedy, ordered men from each clan to form a cordon along the top of the cliffs, warning everyone away from the edge.

The crowd was in a festive mood, greeting friends and kinsmen from other clans they had not seen in years, relating joyful news of those who had been born and sad news of those who had died. Everyone was dressed in their finest. Weapons were prohibited, but the men wore their silver armbands and golden chains, which spoke to their valor. Women pinned their apron-dresses with their finest brooches. Children ran about underfoot. Dogs barked and chased the children. Ale skins were passed from hand to hand. Then all talking and laughing stopped. The *Venjekar,* bearing the Kai Priestess, the two combatants, and their shield-bearers, came into view.

The ship used in the ceremony would ordinarily have belonged to a neutral clan, but according to Treia, the Dragon Kahg insisted on being present and, given his anger over the loss of the Vektan Torque, none were inclined to argue with him. The dragon's eyes, gleaming fire, cast a red pall over the crowd and impressed upon them the serious nature of this contest. Women ceased their gossip and latched on to their children. Men dropped the ale skins to the ground and stood with their arms folded across their chests. Silence fell, tense and uneasy. The scraping of the keel of the dragonship against the rocks could be clearly heard.

Draya stood at the ship's prow, her hand upon the curved neck of the dragon. The warriors stood behind her. She looked ahead, not behind, careful not to acknowledge any of the combatants. The reason she gave for this was that she did not want to be accused of favoritism. In truth, she could not bear looking at Horg.

The *Venjekar* made landfall upon the small island, the Dragon Kahg guiding it to a gentle landing. Draya made ready to leave the ship, for she had to prepare and sanctify the ground where the two would fight. The shield-bearers, Garn and one of Horg's friends named Rulf, lowered the gangplank and stood by, ready to assist Draya to descend.

She stared at the gangplank, which was nothing but a long wooden board, in dismay. She had not sailed with a dragonship for many years. Her stomach was queasy, she was unsteady on her feet, and the gangplank, resting on the rocks, shifted with the motion of the ship. Sea spray blew into Draya's face and stung her eyes. She would have to walk along the narrow plank, encumbered by her long skirts and the heavy ceremonial surcoat. She pictured herself slipping and falling into the sea, the waves catching hold of her and smashing her body against the sharp rocks. She went cold and sick with dread.

Draya clung to the rail and stared down into the gray-green foam-spattered water. The ship edged back and forth, the keel surging forward, striking the rocks, then receding. Draya placed a foot on the gangplank, which was slick with sea spray. She had to find the courage to do this.

"Vindrash, help me!" Draya prayed, and she was about to fling herself forward when she felt strong hands take hold of her.

"The sea is rough, Kai Priestess," said a voice. "Allow me to assist you."

Such was Draya's confusion that she didn't know which man had spoken. Whoever it was launched himself over the ship's side. He landed on the rock island, and then, turning around to face her, he extended his hands.

"Take hold of my hand, Priestess," Skylan told her. "Do not be afraid. I will not let you fall."

Draya looked down at him, the young man who had chosen to fight the Law of the Challenge in his father's stead. She had seen Skylan before, but she had not, until this moment, truly seen him.

Sun-gold hair fell to his shoulders. His chest was broad, his back straight, his body strong and muscular. His eyes were sea blue, his skin burnished bronze. Silver bands glinted on his arms. He was the stuff of legend, the hero of girlhood dreams, the embodiment of all the great Vindrasi warriors celebrated in story and song.

"Some god must love him!" Draya breathed.

Skylan looked up at her and smiled. He braced himself and extended his hand.

Draya caught hold of his hand and was walking down the gangplank when her foot slipped and she lurched into him. Skylan caught her, his hands around her rib cage, his fingers brushing her breasts. He lifted her off the gangplank and lowered her gently to the ground.

"Are you all right, Priestess?" he asked solicitously, keeping hold of her until she found her footing.

She could only gasp in answer.

His hands on her were firm and strong, and desire swept over her, its sweet, painful flame melting her heart, burning her blood, consuming her flesh, till there was nothing left of her.

Skylan let go. Inclining his head, he brushed off her confused thanks and left her, running up the gangplank, returning to board the dragonship.

Draya stood on the island alone. No one was allowed on the island until she had prepared for the Vutmana. She was aware of the crowd, tense and hushed, lined up along on the top of the cliff, watching her expectantly.

She was aware of the men in the dragonship, waiting the judgment of Torval.

She was aware of the Dragon Kahg, his red eyes watching.

She was aware of the gods, but only dimly. Whether that was her fault or theirs, she could not say.

She was aware of all of this, yet she was most aware of Skylan's touch, the sky-blue light in his eyes.

Draya lifted her head and raised her arms, as though she were praying, then turned to the task at hand—preparing for the Vutmana.

"What does she wait for? Why doesn't she get on with it?" Skylan demanded.

Impatient to start the contest, which he was confident he would win, Skylan was frustrated with all the ritual and ceremony. To him, the Vutmana was simplicity itself: Two champions do battle. Give him a sword and a shield, and let him fight.

Skylan had taken part in three Clanmelds. Three times he had listened to the recitation of the Law of the Challenge, but he had paid scant attention. His mind tended to wander, making plans for a future raid or inwardly chuckling at some jest he'd heard the night before. Thus he had been astonished and appalled to hear the rules of the Vutmana, as related to him by his father.

"You mean I have to stand there and let Horg hit me?" Skylan had asked.

"You can defend yourself," Norgaard had told him. "You cannot strike back. Not until it is your turn."

If that is true, then even you could fight! Skylan had thought scornfully. He hadn't said the words aloud, but Norgaard read his son's mind.

"Standing alone, waiting, unflinching, for your opponent to aim a deadly blow at you takes courage, requires self-control." Norgaard eyed Skylan grimly. "Qualities people want in a Chief *and* in a Chief's son."

Skylan thought this over. "What you say makes sense, Father," he had conceded, adding magnanimously, "In that case, I have no objections."

"I'm sure Torval will be pleased to hear it," Norgaard had stated dryly.

Skylan had chafed at the fourteen-day delay. He had been ready to fight Horg the day he had challenged him. Though he understood the need for the other Clan Chiefs to be present, he did not see why it should take them a fortnight to assemble. They should drop everything and rush off. And he was highly annoyed at his father, who made him spend the night before the Vutmana in isolation. The other clans had gathered for a feast and a bonfire. Skylan, sitting alone on the beach, could hear the laughter and shouts, and he longed to be among them, listening to the boasts of the other warriors, making his own boasts in turn.

Norgaard had attempted to explain to Skylan how his presence this night would be salt in the wounds of the Heudjun, perhaps end in fighting and bloodshed, the very outcome they were trying to avoid. Skylan supposed his father had a point, but he had gone to bed in an ill humor.

He had been up before the dawn, rousing everyone and hurrying his father and Garn on board the *Venjekar*. They could have had their sleep after all, for they had been forced to wait for Horg and his shield-bearer, and after that there was another wait for the Kai Priestess.

At last the Kai Priestess had arrived, bringing with her the sacred cloth rolled up and tucked under her arm, as well as a basket containing a wineskin and two drinking mugs made of rams' horns and decorated in silver. Skylan asked his father what the drinking mugs were for, but Norgaard couldn't say. The Priestesses always added some touch of their own to the ceremony.

The men had bowed in respect as the Priestess boarded. She had very carefully avoided looking at or speaking to any of them. She made her way forward to take her place near the figurehead, where hung the spiritbone of the Dragon Kahg. She remained there, unmoving, throughout the voyage.

Skylan had found the journey to the island long and tedious. He was not permitted to talk to his opponent, but no one had said anything against making a few cutting remarks, ones Horg would be bound to overhear. Every time Skylan opened his mouth, however, Norgaard frowned fiercely at him. Garn was subdued and had whispered tersely to Skylan that he should take this seriously.

Skylan had been offended. He was taking this seriously. He was the one doing the fighting, after all. Torval was on his side. True, Hevis had been known to play his tricks upon both men and gods, but Skylan was young and strong, courageous and confident. He could overcome anything.

After what seemed an interminable length of time, the dragonship arrived at the island known as Krega's Bane. Skylan saw the people crowding the cliff, more people gathered in one place than he'd ever seen in his life. He was awed. For the first time, the true import of the Vutmana struck him. Here, on this island, the great Clan Chief Thorgunnd had fought and died. Here Torval had cursed the treacherous Krega. Here countless other men had fought and gone on to glory.

Skylan looked up to see the people—his people—looking down at him, and his heart swelled with pride. He felt himself invincible and he saw himself standing in the center of the sacred cloth, the cheers of the people resounding in his ears. He saw his father, limping into the ring, named Chief of Chiefs.

Chief of Chiefs. Norgaard, the old man, the cripple, Chief of Chiefs.

The *Venjekar* had anchored alongside the island, which was too small to permit the ship to land onshore. Skylan had dashed to the side, prepared to jump off, only to be stopped by Garn.

"The Kai Priestess goes first," Garn had told him.

Skylan had seethed at yet another delay. Garn and Rulf, Horg's shield-bearer, lowered the gangplank.

Skylan had waited impatiently for the Priestess to descend, but the woman stood at the rail, staring over the side. She looked faintly green, and Skylan had wondered irritably if she was seasick.

Norgaard had hissed in Skylan's ear, "Draya is afraid, my son. You should assist her."

"I thought I wasn't to set foot on the island until the old woman prayed over it," Skylan had returned.

Norgaard had glowered at him. "You young fool! Draya holds our fate in her hands. Make haste to help her before Horg thinks of it!"

"Torval holds my fate," Skylan muttered, but he had understood what his father meant. It would do no harm to be of service to the Kai Priestess.

Skylan had vaulted easily over the side of the ship and extended his hand to assist Draya in walking down the slippery and unsteady gangplank.

He had noted that the woman was of slender build, with pale hair, a pale complexion. A worry line creased her forehead. Her lips were thin and compressed, accustomed to keeping secrets. Her eyes were her best feature, being large and luminous, though they were marred by crow's-feet.

She must be thirty-five if she is a day, Skylan had reflected. If my mother had lived, she would be about the same age.

Remembering that this woman was old, Skylan had caught Draya as gently as he could, so as not to break any bones. He had taken care to lower her easily and respectfully to the ground. She had stood there for some time, staring at him, as if she were in some sort of trance. She had been about to speak, but he had not lingered to hear her thanks. The sooner he was back on board the ship, the sooner she could set to work, and the sooner he would have his chance to fight.

Now Skylan watched impatiently as the Kai Priestess measured out the Holmhring, a square patch of land roughly fifteen feet by fifteen, on which the Vutmana was fought. Inside this square, the priestess laid down the Vutmana cloth, which was nine feet by nine feet. The cloth was sacred, she said, for it had been blessed by Vindrash.

When this was finally done, the Kai Priestess summoned Garn and Rulf, the shield-bearers, who were now permitted to come ashore. Under her direction, the two men drove stakes into the ground at each corner of the cloth, anchoring it. The shield-bearers then hammered wooden posts into the ground at the corners of the Holmhring and tied ropes around the posts, defining the outer edge of the field of combat.

The shield-bearers, each with three shields, took their assigned places outside the rope. The shield-bearers were permitted to hand their champions fresh shields as needed, but they were prohibited from taking part in the combat.

At last, Draya indicated that all was in readiness. The snow-white cloth, made of linen, was staked in place. The shield-bearers had taken their positions. Now it was time for Norgaard to come ashore. Proudly refusing help, Norgaard descended the unsteady gangplank. His crutch slipped, his bad leg collapsed, and he fell. His face twisted in pain and anger, he lay floundering in the water at the foot of the gangplank.

Garn and Rulf hastened to assist him, but Norgaard pushed them both away. He managed to stand on his own. Leaning heavily on his crutch, he limped over to take his place alongside Garn. The watching crowd murmured in admiration. Courage of all types was admired.

On board the dragonship, Horg glanced sidelong at Skylan and chuckled. "You really think Torval will make a cripple Chief of Chiefs?"

Skylan flashed Horg a furious look and seemed about to make a scathing retort, when Draya beckoned to both men that it was time to begin. Skylan started to disembark, but Horg roughly shoved him aside.

"The man who is challenged goes first," Horg stated contemptuously; then he added with a grin, "Or perhaps I should just say the *man* goes first."

Skylan went pale with fury at the insult. His sword was halfway out of its sheath and he was going for Horg when both Norgaard and the Kai Priestess called sharply for him to stop. Fuming, Skylan sheathed his sword.

"I will slit your fat belly and feed your entrails to the fish!" he said.

"Yeah, you do that, *boy,*" said Horg, and as he passed Skylan, he lashed out with his foot, kicking him in the kneecap.

Skylan gasped in pain at the unexpected blow. Horg had timed it perfectly. No one on the ground had seen him.

"That is cheating!" Skylan grimaced as he tried to put weight on his sore knee.

"So go crying to Mama, boy," Horg retorted, and he laughed as he launched himself over the side.

He made a show of selecting his place on the cloth. If the battle had been held early in the morning, this might have made some difference, for Horg would have put his back to the sun, forcing Skylan to fight while staring into the glare. But Draya had fussed over her blasted cloth and her stakes and ropes so long that the sun was no longer a factor.

Horg defiantly faced the crowd of onlookers. Let them see he was not afraid, not ashamed.

When Horg indicated he was ready, Draya summoned Skylan. Horg looked back at the dragonship and sniggered to see the young man trying to conceal the fact that he was finding it hard to walk on his injured knee.

Horg had no fear Skylan would accuse him of cheating. The young man was far too proud to admit he'd been such a witling as to fall for that old trick. Horg watched Skylan limp down the gangplank, hoping to see him fall, like his father the cripple. Skylan disappointed him. The pain must have been excruciating, but he kept careful control of his face, gave no sign that he was in pain.

Skylan looked at Horg with ice-blue eyes, and he looked at no one else as he walked to his place with his very slight but very visible limp. His father asked him if he was all right. Skylan paid him no heed. Skylan looked at Horg. His shield-bearer, Garn, asked him what had happened. Skylan did not respond. He looked at Horg. Skylan did not answer the Kai Priestess, who was bleating about something. Skylan looked at Horg.

Horg, irritated, looked away. I'll have Skylan's body strung up, he decided, and let the crows pick out those damnable blue eyes!

All was now in readiness. The wind died. The crowd hushed. The waves stilled. The ocean was flat, dead calm. The red eyes of the dragon watched.

"Horg Thekkson, Chief of Chiefs of the Vindrasi, come forward," Draya called. "Skylan Ivorson, son of Norgaard Ivorson, Chief of the Torgun, come forward."

Horg sauntered over to her. Skylan limped.

Draya lifted a jeweled drinking horn from her basket and filled it with wine—a rare delicacy, for wine was costly and drunk only on festive or sacred occasions. She held out the horn to Skylan.

"By drinking this sacred wine, you pledge yourself to obey the rules of the Vutmana as set down by the gods. You pledge yourself to Torval."

Skylan solemnly took the drinking horn in his right hand and clasped the amulet he wore around his neck with his left. He raised the horn to the sky and said, "Torval, be witness to my faith."

Skylan drank a sip of wine and handed the horn back to Draya. His blue eyes fixed, once again, on Horg.

Draya wiped the rim of the horn with a white cloth and gave it to Horg. He took hold of the horn, tilted it to his mouth, and quaffed the remainder of the wine, gulping it down. He wiped his lips with the back of his hand and, grinning, handed the horn back to Draya.

"Let's get on with this," he said.

As Draya took the horn from him, she moved a step nearer, so that she faced him directly. Her back was to the crowd and to the shield-bearers. She spoke to him alone. Her voice was low, and she put a long and deliberate pause between each phrase.

"There are gods, Horg. The gods are not dead. The Gods of the Vindrasi curse you!"

Perhaps it was the way Draya said the words—calmly, coldly, and with absolute certainty. Or perhaps it was the terrible light of truth in her eyes.

Horg wondered suddenly, with a gut-clenching feeling of panic, What if she is right!

# CHAPTER 7

Garn reached across the rope barrier to hand Skylan the first of his three shields. Each shield was round in shape, made of planks of wood, and was large enough in diameter so that it protected him from shoulder to knee. The shield was trimmed in leather, which gave it added strength, for when the leather shrank, it bound the wooden planks together. An iron boss in the center protected Skylan's hand. He grasped the shield's wooden crosspiece, sliding his hand into the domed underside of the boss.

"What happened to your leg?" Norgaard asked, seeing Skylan favor it.

Skylan cast a dark glance at Horg. "The whoreson kicked me in the knee as he was leaving the ship!"

The kick wouldn't have been so bad, but Horg had unknowingly struck Skylan's weak leg. The wound inflicted by the boar had healed cleanly, but the muscles were still sore, and Horg's kick had aggravated the injury.

"He called me 'boy,'" Skylan continued furiously. His lips twisted in a snarl. His heart thudded in his chest. A red mist clouded his vision. His hands were wet with sweat, and he tasted blood in his mouth. "He acts as though he's fighting a child!"

Norgaard gripped his son by the shoulder.

"Listen to me, Skylan," he said fiercely. "Why do you think Horg kicked you and insulted you? Not to hurt you! He could have broken your kneecap, but he didn't. He's goading you, hoping you'll forget all you know and fight stupidly, like a child."

Across from Skylan, on the other side of the expanse of white cloth, Horg calmly slid his large fist through the handgrip of his shield. As he did so, Rulf, his shield-bearer, made some jest. Horg was supposed to laugh, but perhaps he didn't find it funny. He muttered something and turned away. Rulf looked at him, puzzled.

"This is not the shield-wall. You cannot call upon the Madness of Torval," Norgaard was saying. "This fight requires patience and cunning and watchfulness and the need to make every blow count. Do you understand, my son?"

Skylan closed his eyes, blotting Horg from his sight. He drew in a breath of salt-tinged air and let it cool his overheated blood. His vision cleared. He felt empty, light, and pure.

"I understand, Father," he said, and he gripped his father's hand. "I will make you proud of me."

Norgaard eyed Horg, who was arming himself.

"He's chosen to use a battle axe, not a sword. That means he'll aim blows at your shield, trying to break it."

Skylan nodded. He understood this tactic, for it was one he himself had considered. When a warrior has used up his three shields, he was left with only his weapon.

"Horg will try to end this fight quickly," Norgaard said. "For he knows that although he is stronger, you are younger and you have more stamina. He'll put everything he has into his first blows. You have to grit your teeth and take it."

Again, Skylan nodded.

"Remember, you can defend yourself, but you cannot attack him until it is your turn. And watch where you put your feet. Don't move a toe off the cloth, and whatever you do, don't let yourself be pushed outside the ring!"

Stepping off the cloth was known as "flinching." Stepping out of the roped-off ring was called "fleeing." Both were marks of a coward.

"I know all this, Father," Skylan said, somewhat impatiently.

"I know you *know* it," Norgaard replied grimly. "Now you must live it."

The Kai Priestess took her place outside the roped-off area. It was time to begin.

"Horg Thekkson of the Heudjun, are you ready?" the Kai Priestess called.

"I am," Horg returned sullenly, but he didn't look it.

"Something's happened to him," Norgaard said, frowning. "Garn, did you see anything?"

"I saw the Kai Priestess speak to him when she handed him the wine," Garn returned. "She spoke so softly, I couldn't hear what she said."

All of them could see that a change had come over Horg. On board ship, he had been swaggering, boastful, confident. Now his face was dark, his expression grim, his manner sullen. Though the morning breeze off the sea was cool, a trickle of sweat rolled down his cheek. Large patches of sweat stained his tunic beneath his arms. He glowered at the Kai Priestess, who paid him no heed.

"There is no love lost between those two," Norgaard remarked. "She said something to him that took the wind out of his sails. This bodes well for you, my son."

Skylan didn't care. He was eager to start.

"Skylan Ivorson, son of Norgaard, are you ready?"

"I am!" he shouted, exultant.

Norgaard handed Skylan his sword. "Torval be with you, my son!"

"He is, Father," said Skylan, breathing deeply of the sea air. "He fights at my side."

Skylan walked to his place on the white cloth. Once there, he took a moment to look up at the cliff top, his gaze sifting rapidly through the people until he spotted Treia. He did not care two straws for her, but he knew the one he sought was certain to be at her side. He found Aylaen, and he raised his sword to her. She smiled and waved her hand.

Skylan turned to face his opponent. He held his shield in front of his body, his sword ready to knock aside Horg's axe. Skylan was dressed in tunic and trousers and boots, his silver armbands, and of course, the amulet of Torval. Horg was dressed much the same. Neither man wore armor or a helm. Each was supposed to rely on his wits, his courage, and his skill with weapon and shield to win the contest.

Skylan braced himself. As the one challenged, Horg had the right to make the first attack. He was a big man, and he moved slowly, conserving his strength.

Standing unmoving, waiting for Horg to attack him, was the most difficult thing Skylan had ever done in his life. He gripped shield and sword and spread his feet and softened his knees to absorb the shock. He watched Horg's eyes, hoping for some indication of where Horg would strike. He could not attack with his sword, but he could use his weapon to deflect the blow.

Horg held his own shield in front of him to ward off just such an attempt by Skylan and raised his battle axe. The blade of the axe trailed fire in the sunlight as it came sweeping down. Horg was clever, his eyes gave away nothing.

Skylan lifted his shield as Horg's axe thudded into it. Splinters flew. The powerful blow bruised Skylan's knuckles and jarred his arm. The axe bit so deeply into the wood that Horg had to expend some effort to yank it free, which gave Skylan an opening. He brought up his sword, only to hear Garn yell out sharply.

Seething, Skylan lowered his weapon. He could not attack. He could only defend.

Horg recovered his axe and walked back to his place on the cloth. Skylan investigated his shield. The blow had split two of the planks. The shield would fall apart at the next hit. Skylan walked over to Garn and flung the worthless shield onto the ground.

"That could have been your skull," Garn pointed out.

"Just give me another rutting shield!" Skylan muttered.

Garn handed it over. "Remember what we practiced."

Skylan nodded and went back to take his place on the cloth. Now Horg was on the defensive. His shield was swathed in leather, which would help protect it from splitting. A shield like that was more expensive than the wooden shields Skylan used, which had leather binding only around the rim. Such were the benefits of being Chief of Chiefs.

Horg was hoping for a quick end before he ran out of strength. Skylan hoped for a quick end before he ran out of shields. He walked forward swiftly, his eyes fixed on the shield, seeming to aim for it. At the last moment, still keeping his gaze fixed on the shield, he aimed his blade at Horg's unprotected right arm.

Horg was far too skilled to fall for the feint. His battle axe connected with Skylan's sword, nearly knocking it from his hand. Horg pivoted, slammed his shield into Skylan's, and shoved him backwards. Skylan's feet slipped, and he fell, landing on his rump.

Horg laughed uproariously, jarringly.

The blood rushed to Skylan's face. He had been made to look the fool in front of all the Clan Chiefs and the best warriors of the Vindrasi. Garn and his father were both yelling at him, but he paid no heed. Furious, he scrambled to his feet, raised his sword, and rushed at Horg.

"Stop!" the Kai Priestess called, adding sternly, "Return to your place, Warrior, or forfeit the contest!"

"Yeah, go back to your place, boy," Horg jeered.

Skylan skidded to a halt. He cast Horg a baleful glance, then turned and walked with what dignity he could muster back across the cloth.

Ordinarily, the crowd would have found the sight of a warrior falling on his backside hilarious. They would have laughed or groaned, depending on whom they favored. freely expressing their opinion of the fight and shouting out advice. On this occasion, though some men exclaimed and women caught their breaths, the Vindrasi mostly watched in silence. Children, not understanding, yet impressed by the awful solemnity, kept close to their parents and watched with wide eyes.

Skylan, breathing heavily, wiped sweat from his brow and once more took his place. Horg glowered at Skylan; then he suddenly threw down his shield. At first, Skylan couldn't understand what was happening. He thought for one wild moment that perhaps Horg was surrendering, conceding defeat.

Horg gave a smirk, then, grasping his battle axe with both hands, he ran headlong at Skylan. Horg's intent was obvious. He had just told all the world and the gods he had no need of a shield, not against such an inexperienced boy. His cronies in the crowd were jeering and chortling.

Skylan was outraged. Behind him, Garn was shouting himself hoarse. Norgaard was screaming at him. Skylan gripped his shield and braced himself for the shattering blow.

Disaster struck in a blur of motion. One moment Horg was thundering down on Skylan, axe raised to strike his shield. In a split second, Horg deftly shifted his axe from his right hand to his left and swept the blade low. The axe sliced through Skylan's boot and bit into the calf muscle of his right leg.

Skylan barely felt the wound. All he saw was that Horg had left himself wide open. Skylan started to lunge with his sword, only to feel strong fingers clamp over his arm.

"Skylan, stop!" Garn said. "It's over!"

Furious, Skylan tried to shake him loose. Garn's hands tightened their grip.

Skylan, red-faced, rounded on him. "Let go of me, Garn, or by Torval I'll—"

"It's over, Skylan," Garn repeated, giving him a shake. "You've lost."

He pointed. Skylan looked to see blood oozing from the wound, running down his foot, staining the white cloth.

Skylan could taste defeat in his mouth, and it was sickening. He flung down sword and shield. He could not look at anyone. He could not endure the disappointment in his father's eyes, the pity in Garn's. Head bowed, Skylan waited in bitter anguish for the Priestess to call out, "First blood! The gods have declared Horg the victor!"

The Kai Priestess said nothing.

Skylan wondered angrily what was taking her so long. Was she determined to prolong his shame? He glowered at her from beneath his lowered brows.

Draya stood outside the ring, her hands folded one atop the other, her gaze fixed on the gray rock of the cliffs behind him.

Horg, grinning, raised his axe, waiting expectantly for the Kai Priestess to make her judgment. When she was silent, Horg grew angry.

"I drew first blood!" he cried, and he gestured with his axe at the cloth beneath Skylan's feet. "I am the winner!"

The Kai Priestess regarded him with calm detachment.

"Return to your place, Horg Thekkson," she said, her voice cool, "or forfeit the contest."

Horg's jaw dropped. He stared at her and roared, "I drew first blood!"

"Skylan, pick up your sword!" Garn said urgently.

Skylan had no need to be told. He grabbed his sword and hefted his shield and stood ready for whatever came next.

In that moment Horg learned he was facing two foes in this ring, and the most dangerous was not the upstart young man wielding the sword.

The most dangerous was his wife.

His friends had warned Horg that Draya might try something treacherous. Horg had scoffed at them. Draya was a woman of blind, unreasoning faith. He should know. He'd been forced to put up with her pious bleatings for years. She might well cross him, but she would never cross her gods.

Now he realized she hated him enough to risk even being god-cursed. Looking back, he could see how she had brought him to this place, maneuvered and manipulated him every step of the way, in order to destroy him.

Well, he would see about that!

Horg turned to face the crowd.

"I drew first blood!" he shouted, appealing to them. "By the laws set down by the gods. I am the winner! The Kai Priestess is trying to thwart the will of Torval!"

No one spoke or called out in support. Then Draya said quietly, "It is late, Horg, for you to be calling on the gods."

Horg rounded on her. He walked closer, hulking over her, glaring down at her. "You scheming bitch! You had best pray I lose!"

He turned back to face the crowd. "If the Kai Priestess can break the rules, so can I! This will not be a fight between children. It will be a fight between men! A fight to the death!"

He looked over at Norgaard. "Do you agree to this, Chief of the Torgun?"

Norgaard opened his mouth, but it was Skylan who answered with a resounding and defiant, "I agree!"

Horg walked back to his place and was bending down to pick up his shield when a sharp pain jabbed him in the belly.

He grimaced and rubbed his stomach. Damn it, this was not the time for indigestion!

# CHAPTER 8

Ages hence, whenever famous battles between champions were mentioned, a Vindrasi elder would say with a smile and a nod, "Ah, you can talk about Thorgunnd and Krega all you want. But *I* was witness to the fight between Horg and Skylan!"

At which the youngsters would regard the old man with envy and clamor to hear the tale.

The fight was later celebrated in song by Balin, Talgogroth and bard, and it became his most famous work. Long, long years after his death, bards still sang it whenever Vindrasi warriors gathered.

The song began: "Skylan, the bright-haired, his bright blood flowing, his bright sword kissed by Aylis . . ." and went on to describe the fight against Horg, whom the poet deemed: "the god-cursed, a coward who was never more brave than when all bravery was futile." The song described every stroke and parry, every hit scored and thrust narrowly avoided. Indeed, the song was longer than the battle, which itself was relatively short.

And the song got the ending wrong. In this, one must not blame the bard. For Balin did not know the truth.

At that time, only two knew what really happened.

And one of them was dead.

Skylan advanced on Horg, watchful and wary. Too late, he had come to respect Horg—if not as a man, then at least as a warrior. Skylan had learned a bitter lesson. But for the judgment of Torval, Skylan would be back on board the dragonship at this very moment, sailing homeward in shame and humiliation. He meant to justify Torval's belief in him.

He watched Horg's every move, remembering belatedly to watch Horg's feet as well as his eyes, for Norgaard had taught his son that a man's eyes could lie, but his feet could not. Horg had to shift his weight in order to put force behind his strike, and by watching his feet, Skylan might be able to anticipate his move, create an opportunity.

Garn had bound up the wound on his leg. Skylan shoved the pain to the back of his mind. Such a wound was nothing. He had seen men fight in the shield-wall with far worse wounds, with eyeballs hanging out of their sockets or missing limbs.

"Time is on your side," said Norgaard. "Wear him out."

Larger and heavier, Horg would tire more quickly. Skylan was lighter, more agile, and younger. He did not do what he longed to do—rush to end this swiftly. He took his father's advice, prolonging the fight, drawing it out, waiting for Horg to tire.

Skylan dodged and lunged, jumped forward and fell back, striking with snakelike swiftness at Horg from all directions, keeping him confused and off balance, making him increasingly angry and frustrated. All the while Skylan waited and watched for his foe to make a mistake.

Horg landed his own hits, and they were devastating. His axe splintered Skylan's second shield with a blow so powerful that Skylan's arm went numb and he feared it was broken. He was forced to scramble backwards, retreat to his own side, not daring to take his eyes off Horg, who pursued him with his axe. That would have been the end of the song and of Skylan had not Garn risked his own life, jumping into the ring to hand Skylan his last shield.

Horg took a furious swipe at Garn, who was forced to dive to the ground, falling flat on his face to avoid being decapitated. At this, Horg's shield-bearer, Rulf, leaped into the ring, prepared to take on Garn. An angry reproof from the Kai Priestess sent both men back to their respective sides.

People lining the cliffs were now caught up in the excitement. All realized they were watching an epic battle, and forgetting the solemnity of the occasion, they began to shout and cheer, exclaiming, groaning, gasping, applauding.

Both warriors slowed. Horg was rapidly tiring. He dripped sweat, his face was the color of lead, and every so often, he would grimace, as though in pain. Skylan couldn't understand that; he had yet to do much damage. He had slashed Horg's arm, and that was about it.

Skylan himself was finding it more and more difficult to pretend he *wasn't* in pain. Sweat poured down his face and ran into his eyes. His sword was growing increasingly heavy. His knee ached; the cut on his leg burned and throbbed. He left bloody footprints on the trampled, mud-stained cloth.

His moment came. Horg was breathing hard, seemingly exhausted. He lowered his shield, provided a tempting opening. Skylan lunged forward to strike, put weight on his injured leg, and felt it give. He sagged to the ground. Horg ran at him, the blade of his axe flaring in the sun, and was on him in a flash. Skylan raised his shield, using it to deflect the deadly assault. Horg's axe blade glanced off the iron boss, sending up a shower of sparks. Skylan, struggling desperately to regain his footing, lashed out wildly with his sword. He had no hope he would hit Horg. He hoped only to buy himself time, and that hope was feeble. Horg would certainly close in for the kill. A sword swipe wouldn't stop him.

To Skylan's astonishment, Horg did not attack. Horg's face twisted in anguish. He doubled over, grabbing his gut. Skylan could only assume that he'd managed to strike Horg. Certainly the crowd thought he'd done so, for they gave a great roar.

Horg clasped his gut. Lifting his head, he stared, not at Skylan, but at Draya. His face twisted in pain and fury. He tried to speak. Foam bubbled on his mouth, and he choked. His jaw spasmed. His body shuddered. Horg moaned in agony and sank to his knees.

Skylan lowered his sword. He could have killed his foe, but he scorned to hit a man who was down. Horg was wounded, perhaps fatally. The Kai Priestess would call an end to the fight. Skylan, sweating and breathing heavily, waited for the end.

Draya said one word, speaking it coolly. "Continue."

Skylan wiped sweat from his eyes. The blood thrummed in his ears, and he wasn't certain he'd heard right. He glanced uncertainly at his father.

Norgaard gave a nod. "You have to finish it," he said harshly.

Skylan looked back at Horg, who was in wretched condition, shivering and puking. Skylan had no stomach for this, but he knew what he had to do, and he understood why. So long as Horg lived, he would be a threat. Every man who had earned Horg's ire would be forever looking over his shoulder, wondering where and when Horg would try to get his revenge. Still, it galled Skylan to win like this.

Skylan walked over to Horg and kicked him in the arm to draw his attention.

Horg turned pain-glazed eyes on him.

"Stand!" Skylan urged. "Pick up your axe."

A warrior would not be admitted to Torval's Hall unless he had died with his weapon in his hand.

Horg, gripping his gut, managed, with a great effort, to rise. He clamped his teeth over a groan and lifted his axe. He even tried to swing it.

Skylan drove his sword into the man's chest. He felt the metal scrape the bones of the rib cage and penetrate deep. Horg gasped. His eyes bulged. Blood spewed from his mouth. Skylan yanked out the sword. The blade, covered with gore, slid out of Horg's body. He pitched forward and lay on the ground in a crumpled heap.

Skylan bent over the corpse, intending to turn it over, make certain Horg was dead.

"Do not touch him! Go to your side!" Draya ordered Skylan sternly, almost angrily.

Skylan limped wearily back to where his father and Garn stood waiting for him. They thumped him on the back, congratulated him. Skylan slumped to the ground and sat there with his head between his knees. He was numb with fatigue. He did not feel triumphant. He felt only an overwhelming sense of relief that it was over.

The Kai Priestess felt for a pulse in Horg's neck, then rose to her feet.

"Torval has judged!" she cried out. "Skylan, son of Norgaard Ivorson, is the victor!"

There were a few murmurs, no cheers. No one mourned Horg's passing. The Heudjun knew Torval had judged fairly, but they did not rejoice in Horg's fall. His defeat was their defeat. Once Horg was buried, they could lift their heads, regain their pride. But this moment was bitter for them.

Draya understood their feelings. She grasped the muddy, bloodstained cloth and ripped it loose from its moorings. She covered the body with the cloth, wrapping it around Horg, hiding him from the sight of men and gods. Her face, as she did this, was cold, pale, expressionless. When she finished, her hands and her clothes were covered in blood and dirt. She walked over to the island's edge and washed her hands in the seawater. She even washed out the drinking horn, for Horg had been the last to drink from it. She filled the drinking horn with wine.

"Now is the time for celebration!" she called. She raised the drinking horn. "To Skylan Ivorson!"

A sigh rippled through the crowd. No one moved. And then one man, Sven Teinar, began to clap his hands. Soon, the rest of the crowd joined in. The clapping began halfheartedly, but then men began to stamp their feet on the ground. Women chanted his name.

"Rise, my son," said Norgaard proudly. "They honor you. You must acknowledge them."

Skylan rose unsteadily to his feet. He gazed up at the people assembled on the cliffs above him. Their applause reverberated through the earth, rising up from the ground, pulsing through his body, and seemed to carry him to heaven. He was giddy, dazed with happiness.

And there was Aylaen, clapping madly, looking down on him, her face radiant with pride.

Skylan raised his sword, and the crowd cheered wildly.

Hearing his name, he turned to find the Kai Priestess standing in front of him. She held out to him the drinking horn.

"Whoever drinks from this is the Chief of Chiefs," she said demurely. Her eyes met Skylan's.

He knew what he was supposed to do. He was supposed to take the drinking horn and hand it respectfully to his father, who was waiting to receive it.

Norgaard had thrown down his crutch. He stood tall and proud, this moment the crowning achievement of his life. The crowd went from chanting Skylan's name to chanting Norgaard's.

Skylan looked at his father, and he saw the old man who had slipped on the gangplank and gone sprawling on the ground.

I won the fight, Skylan said to himself. I defeated Horg.

He looked back at Aylaen.

If I were Chief of Chiefs, I would be a wealthy man. I could pay her bride-price three times over. Or perhaps I would not pay a bride-price at all! Perhaps I would tell Sigurd I intended to marry his daughter. He could not stop me, the Chief of Chiefs.

Skylan's gaze swept the crowd. He saw the young warriors, hundreds of them, a mighty army going to waste. He would lead them on raids, fill his ships with gold and silver and precious gems to take to the dragons. He would sail to the ogres' lands and take back the Vektan Torque and slaughter every ogre he could find. He would restore the Vindrasi to their former glory. Once again men would fear them, honor them, respect them.

Men would fear him, honor him, respect him.

Skylan Ivorson, Chief of Chiefs.

Skylan lifted the drinking horn, put it to his lips, and drank.

# CHAPTER 9

The chanting ceased. People watched in shock to see Skylan drink the wine, proclaiming himself Chief of Chiefs. No one could remember a time when a champion, fighting in the name of another, had taken it upon himself to claim the prize.

Skylan turned to his father. He found it hard to face him, and he avoided meeting his eyes. "I am sorry, Father. I think I will make a better Chief. You are old. I will take this burden from you."

Norgaard's lips were tightly clamped, his face dark. "What have you done, my son?" Norgaard said at last, more in sorrow than in anger. "What have you done?"

He picked up his crutch and, leaning on it heavily, he limped back to the dragonship.

Garn was far more harsh in his assessment. "You bloody fool!" Garn swore at him. "Of all the fool things you have done in your life, Skylan, this is the worst."

Skylan flushed angrily. "Why should I not be Chief of Chiefs? I fought the battle. I risked my life! I defeated Horg! Torval gave me the victory!"

"And Torval meant you to give it to your father," said Garn grimly. "You swore an oath, Skylan. Have you forgotten?"

Skylan stared at his friend, dismayed. He had, in truth, forgotten. His words to his father came back to him:

*Your honorable wounds, a testament to your skill and valor, give you the right to select a warrior to fight in your place. If the Heudjun agree to the Vutmana, give me the privilege. I will make you Chief of Chiefs! I vow to Torval!*

Skylan's hand touched the silver axe he wore around his neck. He had never in his life broken a vow to his god.

Torval understands. He is a warrior. He would not want a crippled old man to lead his people. Torval fought at my side. He made me the winner. He intends for me to be Chief of Chiefs. As for breaking my oath, the god will overlook it. If he meant to punish me, he would have done so by now.

At that moment, the Kai Priestess took hold of Skylan's hands.

"Skylan Ivorson, Torval has made you Chief of Chiefs of the Vindrasi," the Kai Priestess said, and she added, almost shyly, "Our wedding will be celebrated soon, so that all may attend and be witness to our joy."

Skylan stared at her, thunderstruck. "Our *what*?"

The *Venjekar* sailed away from the isle known popularly as Krega's Bane, bearing the new Chief of Chiefs of the Vindrasi. Skylan walked over to where Garn stood alone, leaning over the side of the ship, his arms resting on the timber.

"My friend, I need your help," Skylan said in a low voice.

Garn glanced at him. Brows lowering, he looked away.

"You must help me!" Skylan repeated urgently. "The Priestess says I have to marry her! Her—an old woman! How am I to get out of it?"

Garn remained silent. He did not look at Skylan or acknowledge his presence.

"Garn, I know you're mad at me," Skylan continued. "I know I broke my vow to Torval—"

"—*and* to your father," Garn inserted.

"Would you listen to me?" Skylan said, annoyed. "I'm trying to explain. It was Torval who put the idea in my head!"

Garn frowned.

"I swear it, Garn!" Skylan protested. "Torval knows my father would not make a good Chief of the Vindrasi. The Chief of Chiefs must lead men into battle, and Norgaard can't even walk!"

Garn shook his head. "A Chief of Chiefs is not a War Chief, Skylan. Every clan has its own War Chief. A Chief of Chiefs must be knowledgeable in the law and wise in his judgments—"

"And you're saying I'm not?" Skylan challenged.

"You didn't even know the law states that the Chief must marry the Kai Priestess," Garn pointed out.

Skylan was confounded, forced to admit Garn was right. Skylan didn't know anything about the law, but to his mind, laws didn't matter. That was why there were Talgogroths and Clan Councils and such. The Chief of Chiefs was the War Chief of the Vindrasi, despite what Garn said to the contrary. Skylan could already see himself leading the clans to glory, and he was convinced Torval agreed with him.

Torval had given him, Skylan, his victory over Horg. Unfortunately, Torval had also given Skylan a wife.

"Garn," said Skylan softly, "this is not what I'm trying to talk to you about. I'm talking to you about marrying the Kai Priestess! The woman is old enough to be my grandmother!"

"She's not that old, Skylan," said Garn, glancing sidelong at Draya. "A few years over thirty, maybe—"

"My own mother would have been that age if she'd lived, and she would be a grandmother by now," Skylan retorted. "Besides, I can't marry the woman. I'm going to marry Aylaen. And I *can* marry her now that I am Chief of Chiefs. I will have a house of my own and land and cattle. I can pay Sigurd the bride-price—"

Garn shifted away uncomfortably, his expression dark and troubled.

Skylan heaved a sigh, ran his hand through his hair, letting the sea breeze cool him. He couldn't understand what he'd done that was so wrong, and he was angry at Garn for making him feel miserable when this should have been the proudest, happiest day of his life. Skylan was of half a mind to walk off, let Garn sulk, but he was desperate for his friend's advice on how to avoid marrying Draya. He tried to make amends.

"Maybe some of what you say is right," Skylan admitted grudgingly. "And maybe I deserve some of your anger. But you can't abandon me now, my brother. I need you. Tell me what I am to do!"

Skylan gazed pleadingly at his friend, and as always when they quarreled, Garn sighed and gave in.

"First, Skylan, you must apologize to your father."

Skylan glanced over to where Norgaard sat on one of the bench seats, his leg propped out in front of him. His face was twisted in pain. Not from the old injury. Pain from his son's betrayal.

Skylan felt a pang of remorse. "You are right. I have done my father great wrong, and for that I am truly sorry."

"Second," said Garn, regarding Skylan intently, "you must make up your mind to the fact that you will wed the Kai Priestess. This is the law of the Vindrasi as laid down by the gods. You cannot get around it."

Skylan scowled. His fist clenched and he slammed it down on the timber rail. "I won't! I am Chief of Chiefs! I may do as I please—"

"No, you can't, Skylan!" Garn said sternly. "*Before* you were Chief of Chiefs, you could do what you please. Not anymore." He made an impatient gesture. "The very fact that you don't seem to understand this means you are not fit to be Chief!"

Skylan regarded Garn coldly. "I came to you for help. I thought you were my friend. I guess I was mistaken." Skylan started to walk off.

Garn caught hold of him. "Forgive me, Skylan. I should not have said that. But I am troubled for you. Deeply troubled. You have taken on an enormous burden. You don't seem to realize how enormous! The lives of our people are now in your care. You are Chief of Chiefs, Skylan. You are supposed to uphold the law, not break it!"

"Being forced to marry the Priestess is a stupid law," Skylan said. "And it should be changed."

Garn said softly, "Consider this, Skylan. If you refuse to marry the Kai Priestess, you will be back on Krega's Bane fighting for your life. The Chief of every clan in the Vindrasi will challenge you! I saw their faces when you were named Chief, Skylan. There were cheers, yes, but there were frowns, as well. Some are not happy that one they consider a mere boy was named Chief. They are probably already seeking an excuse to challenge you. Break the law of the Vindrasi that has stood inviolate for hundreds of years, and you give them a reason."

Skylan flared up at the use of the word *boy,* but he forced himself to calm down. Garn wasn't trying to insult him. Garn was saying what other men were thinking and maybe even daring to speak aloud. Men like Sven Teinar of the Heudjun. One of his sons was Skylan's own age. Skylan stared gloomily out to sea. Why had his life suddenly become so complicated? He'd won a great victory! Torval had rewarded him. It wasn't fair.

"Then what do I do about Aylaen?" Skylan asked.

"I don't know, Skylan," said Garn.

"I will ask her to wait for me," Skylan decided. "The Kai Priestess is over thirty. She can't live much longer—"

Garn shook his head in exasperation. "Think, Skylan! Aylaen would have to first be Kai Priestess in order to marry you! She's not even a Bone Priestess—"

"She must become one, then," said Skylan. "You must tell her, Garn. Tell her that she has to start studying to be a Bone Priestess."

"Skylan, you're not serious—"

Skylan ignored him. "I like this plan! Aylaen will move to Vindraholm. As Chief of Chiefs I must live in the lord city, as well. She will study with the Kai, and we can be together. What's wrong? Why do you look at me like that?"

But his friend had stalked off, going over to sit down beside Norgaard.

Skylan glared after Garn. He was about to pursue him; then he realized he didn't have the strength. He was worn out, not only from the battle and pain, but also from the excitement, the upheaval, the turmoil in his head and heart. Nothing had turned out like he had expected.

"I risked my life. I won a great victory," he told himself. "I deserve to be Chief of Chiefs! Yet now my father hates me. Garn won't speak to me. I have to marry an old hag. . . ."

He sagged down onto the deck and closed his eyes, trying to think things over.

"Forgive me, lord. . . ."

Skylan jerked his head up.

The Kai Priestess was back again, kneeling in front of him. "I am sorry. I should have attended to your wounds." She started to tug on his boot.

Skylan was about to tell the old woman impatiently that his wounds were nothing. He had no need of her fussing over him. Then he noticed Garn and his father both watching him, and he choked back the words. He forced himself to sit in silence, allowing Draya to pull off his boot and bathe his wound with a cloth she had dipped in seawater. The salt in the wound stung worse than the bite of the axe, and he clamped his teeth over the pain. Her fingers were cold; her thin hands were bony, like claws.

She is all bone, Skylan thought, no softness anywhere. He counted ten gray hairs on her head. Her breasts were barely visible beneath her dress, and he imagined them sagging down to her belly.

At least she is so old she will not expect me to bed her, Skylan thought, comforted. No matter that he was married, he would not break his vow to Aylaen, that he would love no other woman except her.

"I am sorry, lord, did I hurt you?" Draya asked in concern, feeling him flinch.

"No, Priestess," he said. "My leg is much better." He hurriedly pulled on his boot before she could offer to do it for him. "My throat is parched. If I could have a drink—"

"I will gladly fetch you something, lord," Draya said eagerly and hastened away.

He heard laughter. A group of Torgun warriors had come aboard the dragonship to do honor to their new Chief, and he saw them laughing—he thought—at him.

"Shut your mouths!" Skylan said angrily.

The warriors stared at him in puzzlement, and he realized they had been laughing because they were in good spirits. The Torgun had gone from being the clan at the bottom of the dung heap to the foremost clan of the Vindrasi, the clan of the Chief of Chiefs, and they were celebrating.

The Kai Priestess came to his rescue. "The Chief of Chiefs is right," Draya said reprovingly. She looked pointedly at the corpse wrapped in its bloody shroud. "The dead have not departed. Your mirth is not seemly."

The warriors spoke their respectful apologies. Horg had been this woman's husband, after all, and although the Priestess did not appear to be overcome with grief, she might be bravely covering her true feelings.

The Priestess handed Skylan a horn filled with ale. "I thought you would find this more refreshing than wine, lord," she said, and she gave him a tremulous smile.

Her eyes were large and brown and liquid, like a cow's.

"Thank you, Priestess," Skylan said. Her hand touched his as he handed back the empty drinking horn, and she blushed like a maiden.

"I will bring you more, lord," she offered.

"Not now," he said, adding, "I must apologize to my father."

The Kai Priestess glanced at Norgaard; then she looked back at Skylan. "You have nothing to apologize for, lord. You fought the Vutmana. The choice was rightly yours."

"I know that, but I made a vow to him and to Torval that my father would be Chief of Chiefs," Skylan said, sighing. "Will I be punished for breaking that vow, Priestess? Torval gave *me* the victory—"

"He did, lord," she murmured.

"Then how can he punish me?"

"None of us knows the minds of the gods," she said gravely. "But I believe that they are fair and practical and take many things into account, such as the need of the people in these troubled times for a strong Chief of Chiefs—"

"That is what I was trying to tell Garn!" exclaimed Skylan, pleased. "My father should understand that."

"I am certain he will. Come," Draya said, and she held out her hand to him. "We will speak to your father together."

Skylan drew back. The woman was already behaving like a wife!

"I made the vow," Skylan said gruffly. "I must make amends."

He limped off quickly, before she could insist on going with him. She made him feel uncomfortable, and he couldn't explain why.

Skylan walked over to where Norgaard sat on the deck, nursing his injured leg, massaging the scarred flesh.

"Father," Skylan began awkwardly.

Norgaard grimaced and glanced up at him. "You do not need to say anything, Skylan. I understand. Garn made me see that you were doing Torval's will."

Skylan glanced at his friend in astonishment.

"Torval spoke to you," Norgaard was continuing. "It was right for you to listen to the god. You will make a good Chief of Chiefs. Better than a cripple—"

"Don't say that, Father," Skylan protested, ashamed. He could not look at Garn, who was sitting some distance away, watching. "I will rely on you for advice, counsel—"

Norgaard smiled a brief, tight smile. "You fought well, my son. You made me proud." He continued rubbing his leg. He closed his eyes, pretending to rest. The conversation was over.

Skylan sat beside Garn. "Thank you."

"I didn't do it for you," Garn said. "I did it for your father, to spare him shame."

Skylan was silent a moment; then he said, "Now that my stepmother is dead and I am leaving, my father will be alone. He needs someone to look after him. Will you stay with him?"

"Of course," said Garn. "It will be my honor."

Skylan nodded. They made the rest of the short journey across the waves to Vindraholm in silence.

The dragonship arrived back at Vindraholm to cheers from the Heudjun people, all of them eager to welcome their new Chief of Chiefs, eager to put this shameful incident behind them. Torgun and Heudjun warriors splashed into the water together to help guide the ship ashore.

After the new Chief of Chiefs and the Kai Priestess and the others had disembarked, an uncomfortable silence fell on the crowd. Horg's corpse was still aboard, and no one knew what to do with it.

Horg would not be given the farewell ceremony due to a fallen hero. That was out of the question. He had distant relations in another clan, and he could have been buried on his family's land, in their traditional burial mound, but his cousins had disowned him, refused to claim him.

Several warriors, led by Sven, offered to carry the body off the dragonship. The Kai Priestess intervened.

"Leave him where he lies," Draya ordered. "The matter is out of our hands."

Draya stood on the beach and faced the dragon. She bowed low. The dragon's carved eyes flashed a fiery red, and the people watched in awe to see the dragonship sail away of its own accord. No crew manned it.

The *Venjekar,* bearing Horg's body wrapped in the bloody mantle of the god's judgment, sailed due east, heading into the vast waters of the open sea.

The people stood in silence, watching until the dragonship was lost to sight.

The *Venjekar* returned.

Horg was never seen again.

BOOK
3
THE GHOST SHIP

# CHAPTER 1

The wedding was an important ritual among the Vindrasi, for it marked the end of one portion of a person's life and the beginning of another. No matter what his age, a boy was not truly considered a man until he became head of his own household. A girl was not a woman until she was married. Thus the need for haste in marrying Skylan to the Kai Priestess. No matter how many battles he had fought and men he had slain, Skylan was not considered a man until he had taken a bride.

Weddings were customarily planned well in advance. Preparations for the ceremonies and the feasting to follow would often take weeks, if not months. For Skylan and Draya's wedding, such preparations had to be rushed, completed in less than a day and a night.

The people of the other clans who had come to Vindraholm for the Vutmana stayed for the wedding. They cheerfully pitched in to assist the Heudjun in the work. The mood was festive. Torval had made his choice, and though some privately had doubts as to the god's decision, none stated them openly. Everyone was determined to give the new young Chief of Chiefs a chance to prove himself.

The sacred grove of oak trees in which weddings were held was made ready. Children scoured the grounds, picking up fallen branches and twigs and sweeping away dead leaves and grass. In the Chief's Hall (a longhouse far larger than the hall in Luda), men assembled the long tables and benches that would be used for the feast. Other men went hunting, bringing back deer and elk, while older children were sent to round up the pigs that had been turned loose in the woods to graze. Women began baking numerous loaves of bread. They would rise early the next morning to roast the meat and prepare stews and fruits and vegetables.

Skylan and Norgaard were given a longhouse in which to change their clothes and rest and eat. Norgaard did not stay there long. He went to the Chief's Hall, where old friends were gathering. Skylan would have gone along, but his father insisted that he remain in the longhouse, rest, and see to his wounds. Norgaard sent Treia to tend to his son.

Weaker than he liked to admit, Skylan agreed.

Treia bathed the wounds, dressed them with poultices, and bandaged the cut on his leg. She was efficient in her ministrations, if not exactly gentle. She did not try to hide the fact that she found such work distasteful.

"Now you should rest," she told Skylan when she was finished. "You will need your strength."

"I want to see Aylaen," Skylan said to her as she was about to leave. "Would you tell her to come to me?"

"No, I will not," Treia answered dourly. "Tomorrow is your wedding. You must eschew the company of women until then."

"Aylaen is my betrothed," Skylan said, frowning. "She must be upset that I am marrying someone else. I need to explain things to her."

Treia gave him a strange look. "Aylaen wishes you joy, Skylan. We all do."

She left, again advising him to sleep, but Skylan had no intention of obeying. He had to find Aylaen. He was pulling on his boots, preparing to go in search of her, when she arrived, accompanied by Garn.

Skylan expected her to be grief-stricken, her eyes red with weeping at the thought that he must marry another woman. He was considerably taken aback when she seized hold of his hands and kissed him on the cheek.

"I am so proud, Skylan," she said warmly. "And so happy for you! I think Draya is a lovely woman."

Skylan regarded her in frowning astonishment. "I thought you would be upset and disappointed. I must break our betrothal—"

Aylaen immediately grew more somber.

"It is Torval's will, Skylan," she said, subdued. "We must accept the decision of the gods."

Skylan turned to Garn. "My brother, I am sure you have much to do in preparation for tomorrow. There is no need for you to stay. I want to talk to Aylaen alone."

Skylan wanted to tell her about his plan that she become a Bone Priestess and move here to Vindraholm to study with the Kai. He could see her every day. Be with her every night . . .

"I have work to do myself, Skylan," Aylaen said. "I am helping the other women with the baking. You are hurt and you must be exhausted. I will let you rest."

"But I don't want you to go, Aylaen," Skylan said bluntly. "Garn, you may leave."

"No, Garn, wait." Aylaen drew near Skylan and again pressed her lips against his cheek. "With all my heart, I wish you joy." She smiled at him, then hurried out the door. "Get some sleep!" she called over her shoulder.

Skylan seized hold of Garn. "You talk to her. Tell her she has to become a Bone Priestess."

"I don't think—" Garn hesitated. "It's just that Aylaen has never expressed any interest—"

"What does that matter?" Skylan demanded brusquely. "Tell her this is the only way we can be together."

"You cannot be together, Skylan. You will be married," Garn said, troubled.

"I have thought it all over," Skylan said. "We all know this marriage is only ceremonial in nature. Horg had concubines. All married men do—"

"I do not think Aylaen would be a concubine, Skylan," Garn said. "Even if she agreed, would you subject her to such dishonor?"

"It would only be until my wife dies—"

"I must go, Skylan," Garn said abruptly. "Norgaard is sending me back to Luda to fetch the bride-gift and the sword of your fathers. I will see you tomorrow morning."

Garn left. The longhouse was quiet. Skylan limped over to the sleeping platform and threw himself down on it. His wounds had not particularly bothered him, but once he lay down, they began to hurt. The salve Treia had used burned. He could not get comfortable.

The cure is worse than the sickness, he thought sourly.

He lay staring at the wooden timbers of the ceiling and thought about Aylaen and her reaction to him being married, a reaction he found puzzling. She was losing him to another woman, and yet she had wished him joy! He did not want Aylaen to be overcome with grief, of course, but he thought she should be a little miserable.

He thought back to her shining eyes and her sisterly kiss on the cheek.

"I know what she is doing!" Skylan said suddenly. "She is being strong for my sake. She fears that if she shows her sorrow, she will make me unhappy, and she does not want to spoil my triumph."

Pleased with this logic, Skylan quit thinking about Aylaen. He began to relive the day, his glorious victory over Horg. With the cheers of the crowd ringing in his ears, he sank luxuriously into well-earned sleep.

He slept the night through, so exhausted that he did not hear his father return.

Skylan woke early the next morning, rousting Norgaard out of his bed. Norgaard groaned. He had been up late visiting with friends and relatives from other clans. The ale had flowed freely, with the result that Norgaard was bleary-eyed and complained a good deal about the brightness of the sun.

Garn arrived soon after Skylan rose. Norgaard had sent Garn back to Luda to retrieve the bride-gift—a golden brooch formed in the shape of a dragon biting its own tail, adorned with two emerald eyes. Norgaard had won the valuable brooch in battle, and he had given it to Skylan's mother. Now Skylan would give it to his wife.

Garn also brought with him the ancient sword that had been in their family for generations. Norgaard had presented the sword to Skylan's mother on the day of their marriage to be held in trust for their son. Skylan would in turn give the sword to his wife, to be held in trust for their son. The absurdity of *that* happening made Skylan chuckle.

The *Venjekar* had sailed back to Vindraholm in triumph, accompanied by a flotilla of smaller boats. Every member of the Torgun Clan who could walk (and some who couldn't, but had to be carried on litters) came to see Skylan, Chief of Chiefs, wed the Kai Priestess. This was a proud day among the Torgun; their clan had never been so honored since the days of their founder, Thorgunnd. The people came dressed in their finest, bringing food and gifts.

The morning dawned clear and bright. The sun danced on the water, as though the Goddess Aylis was already looking forward to dancing at the wedding. The wedding day began with both bride and groom undergoing a ritual cleansing. Accompanied by his father and Garn and his best friends, Bjorn and Erdmun, Skylan entered the men's bathing house. Draya would be performing the same cleansing ritual in the women's bathing house, among her family and friends.

The house contained tubs of heated water. They would bathe, then enter a room filled with hot rocks. The men poured dippers onto the rocks to create clouds of steam, in which they relaxed, allowing the perspiration to flow from their bodies, taking with it all impurities.

As they sat in the steam, Norgaard imparted the wisdom fathers always shared with their sons on how best to live with a woman, ways to make her happy and keep her content. The young men added their own ribald comments and jests, causing much mirth and merriment. After the steaming, the men plunged into tubs of cold water to clear the pores, blowing and snorting and gasping at the shock.

Skylan returned to his dwelling and dressed in his finest clothes, including a new tunic given to him by Norgaard. Skylan was touched to learn that his late stepmother had sewn it just days before her death. Garn knelt before his friend to buckle the ancient sword around Skylan's waist. The sword was quite old, not fit for use in battle, but prized nonetheless. Skylan had sent the emerald brooch to his soon-to-be wife that morning, in care of Bjorn and Erdmun.

Due to the haste of the wedding, Skylan had not had time to commission the wedding ring. Norgaard, with considerable effort, removed his own ring from his gnarled finger and gave it to his son. Father and son embraced. Norgaard spoke a few words of love and pride that brought tears to Skylan's eyes.

Skylan clasped Garn in a bear hug.

"Did you talk to Aylaen?" he asked in a low tone.

Garn returned the hug. "Aylaen wishes you joy, Skylan. As do I, my brother. With all my heart."

Skylan was impatient. "I know that. But Garn, did you talk to her about coming to Vindraholm—?"

Garn pretended not to hear. "It is time for the ceremony. Look outside. Everyone is waiting to honor you."

Skylan could see that. The road in front of the dwelling was filled with friends, relations, comrades. Garn clapped Skylan on the shoulder and then led his friend forth. Skylan walked out of the shadowy dwelling, emerging, blinking, into the bright sunlight, to be greeted with rousing cheers. Skylan forgot about Aylaen, forgot everything except what he owed to the god.

He placed his hand on the silver amulet and whispered, "Thank you, Torval! I will try to be worthy of your faith in me. I swear on my life!"

The warriors would not permit Skylan to walk to the sacred grove. They hoisted him up on their shoulders and carried him through the streets. Women flung blossoms at him. Men sang the old songs that always accompanied the bridegroom to his wedding.

The grove was a sacred place of ancient lineage. Located well inland from the sea, the grove stood in a small valley surrounded by forests and grassy hills. Twelve enormous oaks formed an irregular circle at the bottom of the valley. Although these oaks were tall and straight and would have made excellent timber for the dragonships, no one even thought of cutting them. Every clan had its own sacred grove, but none were as old or honored as this one. Gogroth, God of the World Tree, was said to have planted the oaks in honor of the gods.

Early that morning, Bone Priestesses carried the statue of Vindrash to the grove and placed the statue in the center of a large sward of cut green grass. Acolytes decorated the statue with flowers, and the Bone Priestesses blessed the grove and invited the gods and goddesses to attend the wedding.

After the grove had been consecrated, the Heudjun and their guests from other clans crowded into the shadows beneath the enormous arms of the spreading oaks. Weddings were joyous affairs, this one especially, for it was the wedding of the two most important people in the lives of the Vindrasi.

Everyone was in a festive mood, able for a short time at least to put aside worries and problems. Those who had doubts about Skylan's youth and inexperience kept silent. Skylan was Torval's choice, and no one wanted to bring down the god's wrath by daring to question his judgment. The people clapped and cheered when Skylan arrived.

He took his place in front of the statue of Vindrash, together with his father, Garn, Bjorn, and Erdmun. Skylan scanned the crowd quickly, hoping to see Aylaen, but such was the press of people that he could not find her.

Strains of music came from the grove, the sound of a harp played by Balin, Togogroth and bard. The crowd hushed, for the music heralded the coming of the bride. Skylan toyed restlessly with the hilt of the sword. He hoped the ceremony would be soon over and he could move on to the feasting and merriment. In the Chief's Hall, he might have a chance to speak to Aylaen. Garn jabbed him with an elbow in the ribs, and Skylan ceased fidgeting.

The bard appeared from among the trees, and behind him came two lines of Bone Priestesses, singing a song of praise to Vindrash. They took their places around the statue. Among them was Treia, who stood cold and aloof and slightly apart from the others. Skylan smiled at her, but either she did not see him, which was possible, given her weak eyesight, or she chose to ignore him.

A hush fell over them. Customarily, Draya would have been escorted into the grove by her father or another male relative. She had no male relatives now living, however, and she had asked Sven to serve as her escort.

Sven walked ahead of Draya, carrying a sword that was the bride's traditional gift to the groom. Skylan had eyes more for the sword than for his future wife. Whereas the sword a groom gives his bride is ancestral, the sword a bride gives the groom is supposed to be newly forged.

Admittedly Draya had not had time to have one specially made for her husband, but she could have purchased or bartered a sword from a clansman. Skylan glanced at Draya as she walked behind her escort, and he was amazed to see she wore her hair unbound, as a maiden would do on her wedding day.

Draya's pale hair was long and fell about her shoulders. She wore the traditional crown woven of sweet-smelling grasses adorned with flowers. Her cheeks were flushed. She looked pleased and happy. Skylan trusted he and she would get on well together.

We will, he decided, so long as she leaves me alone and does not interfere with my plans.

Skylan studied the sword. Sven stood opposite Skylan. As Skylan eyed the weapon critically, he met Sven's gaze. Sven looked very stern and grave, as befitted his solemn duty as escort. He could see Skylan's interest in the sword, and the older warrior must have known what Skylan was thinking. Sven slightly altered his grip on the sword's hilt so that Skylan could get a good view of it.

Seeing Skylan's frown, Sven gave a half smile and a small shrug and said softly, "It will look well hanging on your wall, lord."

The sword, with its jeweled hilt, was a lovely thing, but swords weren't meant to be lovely. Skylan could tell from looking at it that it would not go two rounds with an enemy before breaking. He suppressed his disappointment, reminding himself that he was now wealthy enough to commission his own sword, have one made to his liking.

Draya came to stand at his side. A Bone Priestess came forth to conduct the ceremony. Skylan was startled and displeased to see it was Treia. Draya smiled meaningfully at him as Treia came to stand before them, and he realized that she had selected Treia as a compliment to him and his clan.

Treia conducted the joyous ceremony with a chill formality that left everyone gasping, as though they'd been doused with icy water. Usually the wedding would have begun with the formal conclusion of negotiations between the families for the dowry, the bride-price, and so forth. Since this was not an arranged marriage between families, none of that was necessary. Skylan obtained the lands and property in the lord city of Vindraholm that were designated for the Chief of Chiefs. Draya, as Kai Priestess, had her own wealth, though most of it was bound up in the Kai.

Treia began by calling the attention of the gods to the ceremony. She did this in a condescending tone that implied she would be astonished beyond measure if the gods actually responded. Taking a bundle of sage, she dipped it in mead and then splashed the mead on Draya, then on Skylan. She next splashed mead on the bride's party and then on the groom's. In ancient times, the liquid would have been blood from a sheep or some other animal that had been sacrificed to Torval. That practice was now considered barbaric and had been outlawed.

Skylan began to blink. Treia had flung the mead into his eyes, and it stung. Treia, having called upon the gods to be witness to the couple's union, now turned her unfocused gaze on Skylan. He knew a moment's panic. She was waiting for him to say or do something, but he couldn't remember what.

Garn bumped Skylan's hand so that it brushed against the hilt of his sword, and Skylan remembered. He drew the ancestral sword and, holding it by the blade, presented it hilt-first to his bride.

Draya took the sword, handling it clumsily, for it was old and heavy. "I will keep this in trust for our son," she said softly, her cheeks flushing.

Skylan almost laughed. An old woman of over thirty winters talking of having sons!

Draya took the sword from Sven and gave it to Skylan. He knew what was expected of him, and he pretended to admire it, all the while thinking Sven was right. It would look well upon a wall, which was where he intended to keep it.

He was in a good humor, and he smiled at Draya in thanks. She smiled back, her blush deepening. Were she ten years younger, she might almost have been pretty.

Treia called for the exchange of rings and the taking of the vows. Skylan placed the ring on the tip of the sword and extended the sword to Draya. She took the ring from the sword and, after some fumbling, placed her ring on the tip of his ancestral sword and held it out to him. He slid the ring that had been his mother's onto her finger. She pushed the ring onto his or tried to, for his hands were large and the ring did not fit. It would have to be remade. He clasped the ring in his hand and placed his hand upon the sword's hilt. Draya placed her hand over his. Her fingers trembled. Her hands were clammy.

The two of them knelt before the statue of Vindrash.

In accepting the bride's sword, Skylan accepted responsibility for her. He vowed to Torval to protect her and keep her. Draya vowed to Vindrash to be faithful to her husband and care for him, be his guide and advisor.

The ceremony ended with Treia summoning the gods to witness the couple's vows.

"I call upon all to join in celebrating the union of Draya Nerthusson, Kai Priestess, and Skylan Ivorson, Chief of Chiefs of the Vindrasi."

Skylan and Draya rose to their feet. Draya smiled tremulously. She seemed to want to keep hold of Skylan's hand, but he managed to disentangle himself from her grasp. This was the first time he had heard his title formally announced. The people were cheering him. His heart swelled, ready to burst with pride. He lifted his arms, with the sword in one hand, to acknowledge the cheers.

Under cover of clapping, Garn leaned over to whisper, "The wedding kiss."

Skylan had been hoping to avoid that. Draya was still standing beside him, looking at him expectantly. He leaned near, about to kiss her on the mouth, when he caught sight of Aylaen. She had managed to squirm her way through the crowd and now stood smiling happily beside Treia.

Skylan shifted his kiss from Draya's mouth to her cheek. Relieved that this was over, he turned back to Garn and the other men, who were shoving forward, eager to receive his notice. He grinned and rubbed his hands in satisfaction and to remove the feel of Draya's clammy touch.

"Now," announced Skylan, grinning, "we will have some fun."

The afternoon of the wedding was spent in games of skill. Men and boys showed off their prowess in various contests such as axe-throwing, wrestling, footraces, and battles with blunt-edged swords. There was even a mock shield-wall. Groups of Heudjun and Torgun warriors good-naturedly pushed and shoved, each clan trying to knock their opponents back across a line drawn in the dirt.

Skylan, as groom, was not permitted to join the games. He was supposed to be saving his strength for the wedding night—a jest he pretended not to hear. The men called upon him to judge the contests, a role he took seriously and enacted fairly, which pleased the men, who said among themselves that this boded well for his future leadership.

Unmarried women watched the games and cheered their favorites. Married women returned to the city to decorate the wedding bed with flowers and tease Draya about her handsome young husband. Then all the women and girls gathered together, laughing and gossiping, to prepare the feast.

When the Goddess Aylis's reddening rays shone through the treetops in the west, the men left their games and made ready for the feast. The groom's party entered the Chief's Hall first. Skylan barred the door with his new sword to prohibit the bride's entry until he could assist her to cross the threshold in safety. The door to the hall represented the entry into the bride's new life. A bride who stumbled over the threshold was considered to bring the worst possible luck to the marriage.

He took Draya's hand and led her over the threshold. She crossed without incident, and everyone applauded.

Skylan sat down in the chair of honor at the head of one of the long tables. Draya performed her first duty as wife by serving her new husband mead in a bowl with two handles formed of dragons in honor of Vindrash. Skylan raised the bowl into the air, offering the first sip symbolically to Torval, and then he drank from it. He handed the bowl to Draya, and she raised the bowl to Vindrash before she drank. Everyone took up their drinking horns and drank to the health and happiness of the couple. After that, the feasting and merriment began in earnest.

The hall was hot, noisy, and crowded. Once the ceremony of the loving cup was concluded, Skylan was free to enjoy himself. He searched the crowd and finally saw Aylaen sitting with her sister among a group of Bone Priestesses. Skylan caught Aylaen's eye. She smiled at him, then turned back to an animated conversation with her sister and another woman.

Skylan rose to his feet. Under cover of the laughter, he said in a low voice to Garn, "I'm going to go talk to Aylaen."

Garn seized hold of him by the sleeve. "No," he said, "you're not."

Skylan looked defiant, and Garn added emphatically, "A bridegroom does not leave his bride's side during the feasting, Skylan, especially to go talk to an unmarried woman. It would be unseemly."

Skylan realized Garn was right, and he slowly sat back down in his chair.

His new wife had seen him start to stand, and she turned to him, smiling. "Is everything to your liking, my husband? Do you want anything?"

Draya leaned closer to him. Her leg pressed against his thigh. Skylan squirmed in his chair, moving as far from her as possible. Her hand moved toward his hand, and he quickly grabbed his knife and speared a hunk of meat and began to eat as though he were starving. Shortly after that, Treia left the feast and Aylaen went with her.

The sun sank. The moon rose. The bard, Balin, sang of the joys of married life. Husbands and wives held hands and shared loving glances. The wedding day would end with the bedding of the happy couple.

In anticipation of that, Skylan got very drunk.

## CHAPTER 2

In a torchlit procession, men of the bride's party escorted Draya to the dwelling of the Chief of Chiefs, which was always in the lord city of Vindraholm. Horg's possessions had been hastily removed, and the longhouse had been thoroughly cleaned by Fria. She had burned all the bedding, replaced it with new. The mattress was scented with perfumed oil, and women had spread flowers over the blankets.

Draya's friends led her to the dwelling. Once there, they removed her shoes and stockings, her surcoat and her dress, leaving her linen shift. She left the fond embraces of her friends and slipped demurely under the blankets and waited in heart-throbbing anticipation for her new husband.

The groom's procession—considerably rowdier than the bride's—came next. Skylan had drunk a considerable amount of mead and ale, and he was unsteady on his feet. He draped his arms around his friends, and they lurched toward the longhouse, bawling out the bawdy songs that traditionally accompanied the bedding.

Draya was not so drunk as Skylan, but she had also been drinking. The honey mead was sweet on her lips, and she looked forward with thrills of desire to more sweetness still. She had been unable to take her eyes off her handsome young husband. Draya did not even mind that Skylan was drunk. Unlike Horg, who was mean and surly when he was drinking, Skylan was boisterous and cheerful, fond of boasting of his exploits in battle to her or anyone who would listen. He even acted these out, jumping to his feet at one point during the feast to demonstrate with an eating knife how he had decapitated the ogre godlord.

Draya's friends opened the door to allow the men into the dwelling. Skylan's friends removed his tunic and pulled off his boots, leaving him in his shirt and trousers. Then, lifting him up, they tossed him bodily onto the bed, where he lay roaring with laughter while his new wife lay blushing at his side. Men and women called out parting ribald jests and then left to return to the feast, which would last far into the night.

Skylan lay on the bed, laughing and singing to himself. Draya's blood burned. She drew near him. Sliding her hand beneath his shirt, she bent over to kiss him.

"My husband . . . ," she breathed.

The room was well lit, for the gods were meant to witness the consummation of the marriage. Skylan blinked at her blearily in the candlelight, as though only just now aware of her presence. He heard the husky note in Draya's voice, saw the glow in her eyes, and felt her body tremble as she pressed against him. Skylan realized suddenly that Draya was in love with him.

"I need a drink," he mumbled. Scrambling out of bed, he left the bedchamber and stumbled into the kitchen, where he found a drinking horn and filled it with ale. He drank it off at a gulp.

Skylan was shocked. A woman who had seen more than thirty winters had no business falling in love with any man! It was . . . unseemly. And she was a Priestess! She should be thinking of higher matters. He had not expected her to want to make love to him, and he was shaken. Hearing footfalls and the rustle of her gown, he poured himself more ale.

"My husband," said Draya, "my lord. Come back to our bed."

He turned to see her smiling at him, and then she lifted her hands and began to take off her shift, baring her breasts. Her breasts were small, the nipples covered with dark hair. She cupped her breasts with her hands, playfully offering them to him.

*I wish you joy!* Aylaen had said to him.

Skylan's stomach heaved. He had made love to many women since he had come to manhood, but not since he had pledged himself to Aylaen. He tried telling himself Draya was just one more, but he couldn't even look at her without disgust, much less touch her.

It wasn't just her age, though that was a factor. It wasn't that she wasn't Aylaen, though that was a major, major factor. Draya was Kai Priestess. He could still see her, pale and majestic, kneeling over Horg's bloody corpse.

"Go back to your bed," he told her harshly. "I will sleep on the floor."

"My lord, don't be silly," said Draya, laughter bubbling in her voice. She stole up behind him and slid her hands beneath his shirt. Her cold fingers caused his flesh to shrivel. "You need not be afraid of hurting me. I am not a maid. I know how to please a man."

And as though to prove it, she slid her hand into his trousers, reaching down to fondle his privates.

She smelled of sweat and perfumed oil, and her smell, combined with the mead and ale he'd been drinking, made him nauseated. He broke free of her embrace and angrily rounded on her.

"You should be ashamed of yourself," he told her. "A woman of your age behaving like a whore! I would as soon think of bedding my own grandmother!"

Draya's face went livid. Her dark eyes against the pale skin were enormous and seemed to swallow him.

"I am your *wife*!" she said.

"In name only!" Skylan shrugged, dismissive. "All know our marriage is cere . . . cere . . ceremonial." It took a couple of tries for his mead-numbed lips to form the word, but he managed. He gestured. "Besides, I am pledged to another. Go to your bed and do not trouble me."

"Another?" Draya flared with anger. "You are my husband. By law, you must lie with me!"

She was right. A husband was bound by law to consummate the marriage, as a wife was bound by law to submit to him. But this marriage wasn't a real marriage. It was ceremonial. She was an old woman. He didn't want to look at her. He certainly didn't want to make love to her. He just wanted her to go away and leave him alone to dream of Aylaen.

"Law?" Skylan drew himself up proudly. "I am the law, lady. I am Chief of Chiefs. You will do as I command!"

"You stupid boy!" Draya slapped him across the face. The blow was hard, stinging, and Skylan tasted blood on his lip. Her voice shook. Her dark eyes burned with soul-consuming fire. "If it were not for me, you would not be Chief of anything!"

Skylan laughed. "Torval gave me the victory. I killed Horg."

"No, you didn't," Draya cried. "I did! The wine Horg drank was poisoned. I poisoned him!"

Skylan stared at her in alcohol-fuddled bewilderment, unable to comprehend her words.

"The wine you both drank before the battle," Draya continued feverishly, hardly knowing what she was saying. "I gave you the drinking horn—then I wiped it with a cloth. In the cloth was a vial containing a slow-acting poison. I poured it into his wine."

"You lying bitch!" Skylan gasped. He could feel the hair rise on his arms in horror. His throat closed. He could scarcely breathe. "Stop lying to me. I killed Horg!"

Draya jeered derisively. "Horg was a man fighting a boy! He could have slain you three times over. He drew first blood, didn't he? I let the fight continue because I knew the poison would burn his gut and foul his senses. He would eventually make a mistake, and then you would be able to kill him."

Skylan remembered Horg grimacing and rubbing his gut. He remembered Horg's faltering steps and how he had doubled over, clasping his stomach and groaning, and Skylan knew with sickening certainty that Draya was telling the truth.

The woman had murdered her husband. She had stolen Skylan's victory. Worst of all, she had usurped Torval's judgment!

Draya suddenly realized what she had been saying. She moaned and covered her mouth with her hand. Then she hurried toward him, her hands outstretched. "My love, my lord, I did it for you!"

"Get away from me!" Skylan was cold and shaking, overcome with horror.

Draya pleaded with him. "I did it for our people!"

"Get away from me!" Skylan repeated, and he backed into a corner. He lowered his head, unable to look at her.

"Horg was an evil man," Draya said. "He was a coward and a bully. He offended the gods by giving the ogres the Vektan Torque. He cheated the day of the Vutmana. I saw him kick you. I knew that Torval wanted you to be Chief of Chiefs, but . . ."

Draya faltered, fell silent, stood gazing at Skylan with pleading eyes.

"But what?" Skylan yelled at her.

"I dared not take the chance that Torval might make a mistake." Draya faltered. "This was too important. This meant the survival of our people and of the gods! We need a strong, brave, courageous Chief of Chiefs. I had to make certain of the outcome. Don't you understand, my love?"

Skylan didn't understand. All he knew was that she had murdered Horg.

"Torval will curse you!" Skylan licked dry lips. He was trembling all over. "He will curse me!"

"Horg was a sacrifice," Draya said. "Torval understands. Vindrash understands. Don't you, Vindrash?"

Skylan stared at her. She was talking to someone else, and there was no one in the room. She was Kai Priestess. Perhaps the gods were here now! Skylan had faced death many times in the shield-wall. He'd known fear then, but he'd never known fear like this. He sank to his knees.

"Horg had to be sacrificed for our people to survive. For our gods to survive. And so I put the poison in his wine. . . ."

Skylan's glance went to the drinking horn he was still holding in his hand.

Draya was going on about the survival of the people, the survival of the gods. All he knew was that he'd been drinking her ale. He crawled toward the slop bucket and slumped over it and vomited, spewing up ale, spitting it out of his mouth. He kept vomiting until his stomach was empty and he brought up nothing, and then he heaved some more.

He sank back against the wall, wiping his lips.

"I have to tell my father," he said groggily. "I have to tell him what you did. . . ."

He rose unsteadily to his feet and staggered toward the door, but he didn't make it. He fell over a stool and landed flat on the floor. Kneeling beside him, Draya put her arms around his shoulders.

"You must not tell your father, Skylan," she said softly. "You must not tell anyone! Everyone will think we plotted this together. You will be stripped of your honors. We would be executed as murderers."

Skylan gave a moan and shook his head.

Draya grasped him tighter, whispering fiercely, "You are Torval's choice for Chief, Skylan. I know it in my heart, and I will prove it. Say nothing to anyone, keep my secret, and we will sail to the sacred Dragon Isles to seek the gods' forgiveness and their blessing."

Skylan pictured his shame and humiliation. He could never again look his father in the face. Aylaen would loathe him. He would never be able to marry her. Though he might be able to prove he was innocent of having poisoned Horg, in the eyes of the people, Skylan Ivorson would be the warrior who had tried to cheat the god. His reputation would be destroyed. Men would refuse to follow him into the craphouse, much less let him lead them into battle.

"Vindrash knew what I did," Draya said to him. "The Dragon Kahg knew what I did, for he is her servant. The Dragon Kahg honored you. He carried you in triumph back to Vindraholm. The dragon disposed of Horg's body, so that no one would find out."

Skylan looked at her uncertainly. "Vindrash knows you poisoned Horg?"

"Of course she did," Draya said eagerly. "Vindrash is my goddess. I tell her everything."

Skylan was still doubtful. There was something wrong with her words, but he couldn't think what. His brain was muddled. Garn would know what to do. If there was ever a time Skylan needed his friend's wise counsel, it was now. And this was the one time he could not seek it.

Skylan roughly shoved Draya away from him. "I will keep your secret," he said. He placed his hand on the amulet, started to vow to Torval, and then let his hand fall. "Now get out of my sight."

"We can still be husband and wife," Draya said in pleading tones.

"I would sooner bed a daemon!" Skylan said harshly.

Draya gave a little whimper. She looked every bit her age and more. Her skin was sallow, cheeks sagging. Her eyes were sunken, her lips bloodless.

"I will keep your secret," Skylan repeated, "but I will never sleep in your bed. And that will be my secret, one that *you* will keep."

Two tears spilled out of Draya's eyes, rolled down her face, and dropped unheeded onto her bare breasts.

"I want to give you a son," Draya moaned. She pressed her hand against her belly. "I can give you a son. I know it!"

Skylan regarded her with loathing. "As if I would want a son with your tainted blood in him! Now bring me a blanket, lady, and then go to your bed."

Draya rose shakily to her feet. She brought him blankets and bedding and arranged them on the floor. Skylan stood in a far corner and watched her. He had a horrible taste in his mouth, and he was parched with thirst, but his stomach recoiled at the thought of drinking or eating anything she had touched. After she made up his bed, Draya gave him a last pleading look. He averted his face and turned away. She went to her room and flung herself on the bridal bed. He could hear her weeping, great choking sobs. Skylan blew out the candles and lay down on the bedding and stared fearfully into the shadows.

Ghosts of murdered men did not rest quietly in their graves. They became walking corpses, known as draugrs, and they returned to haunt those who had been responsible for having cut short the thread of their wyrds. The Dragon Kahg had taken Horg's body far away, but perhaps he had not taken it far enough. Perhaps Horg would come back to accuse his treacherous wife? Perhaps he would come back to haunt Skylan. . . .

And then the terrible thought occurred to Skylan that perhaps he had more to fear from the living than from the dead. He knew Draya's guilty secret. He was a danger to her. She had killed one husband. She could easily kill another! How could he live with her, knowing that?

If he hadn't broken his vow to Torval, he would be back in the feast hall, drinking with his friends, celebrating with Aylaen. His father, Norgaard, would be the one living here. He would be married to this murderess. Skylan groaned aloud.

"You have punished me for my oath-breaking, Torval," he said. "I accept your punishment. I was wrong."

Skylan clasped his hand around the amulet and prayed more fervently than he had ever prayed in his life.

"Now you must help me, Torval! You must rid me of my wife!"

CHAPTER

# 3

Draya rose early on the morning after her wedding. She longed to go to the Great Hall of the Gods, to prostrate herself at the feet of Vindrash, and cleanse her soul by confessing everything to the goddess. Draya could not, however. The reason she gave herself was that people would think it very strange for her to be leaving the joys of the marriage bed the day after the wedding night. No one would say anything, of course, but there would be whispers and pitying looks.

The true reason Draya was not prepared to face Vindrash: Draya had lied to Skylan last night when she assured him Vindrash knew of her crime. Draya hoped she had acted with the goddess's knowledge and approval, but she didn't know for certain. Vindrash had not spoken to her since the night the goddess had said she must go into hiding to escape her enemies.

Torval had cursed her. Of that, Draya was sadly certain. She had usurped his judgment, taken it upon herself. He was furious with her, and he had vented his fury by causing her handsome young husband to hate her.

She must make the journey to the Dragon Isles, to the Hall of Vektia, to beg Torval's forgiveness. The gods would be there—if they were anywhere. Skylan would accompany her. It was traditional for a new Chief of Chiefs to travel to the Dragon Isles. Perhaps on that long sea voyage, alone together, they would be reconciled.

Draya splashed cold water on her face, trying to ease the burning of her eyes. She had been so happy yesterday. And she had spent her wedding night sobbing herself to sleep.

I brought it on myself, she realized miserably. I was wrong to lose my temper with him. I should have been patient, understanding. He is only eighteen. Of course he must think me old. I am one of the oldest women in the city! But in time, he would have come to see that age does not matter. In time, he would have come to love me.

She crept quietly into the living area, where Skylan lay asleep, tangled up in the blankets and the bedding. His hair was tousled and his face stern, as though even in sleep, he was still angry. She had heard him tossing and turning half the night before he settled down. She stood gazing on him and felt the hot tears sting her eyes again.

"I should never have told you the truth!" She spoke very softly. "I hoped you would understand, but I forgot how young you are. Youth sees everything either in the bright glare of the sun or hidden by impenetrable darkness. For the young, there is no twilight. You judged me harshly, as I deserve, but you cannot know the terrible burden of responsibility I bear!"

A part of her hoped he would hear her plaintive whisper and waken and smile at her and take her in his arms. Instead, he rolled onto his belly and pulled the fur blanket over his head. Draya sighed and went about her daily household tasks, moving silently so as not to waken him.

By midmorning, Draya was ready to leave the house. Her duties as Kai Priestess continued. She had arranged a Kai Moot, a meeting of the Bone Priestesses, some of whom had traveled a far distance to witness the Vutmana. This was a rare opportunity for the Priestesses from other clans to come together. They had much to discuss.

The Priestesses were upset over the failure of their prayers to Desiria, Goddess of Healing. Many had received other strange and ominous signs that all was not well in heaven. The worst of these were the destruction of the Torgun's ancient statue of Vindrash and Treia's report of her conversation with the Dragon Kahg that there had been a war in heaven and it had not gone well for the Gods of the Vindrasi.

Draya had to decide what to tell the Kai and what to conceal. She must tell them that Desiria was dead. Treia already knew that much from the Dragon Kahg, and she had spread the word. Treia seemed to relish spreading bad news. Draya had hoped that time spent working among her people would soften the woman. If anything, Treia was even more dour and angry than when she had first left Vindraholm.

Draya had never realized how deeply Treia resented her. Treia seemed to blame the Kai Priestess for the fact that her mother had essentially bartered her daughter to the gods. Draya had hoped to make amends by inviting Treia to perform the marriage ceremony. Strangely, the invitation seemed only to deepen Treia's resentment.

Draya retired to the sleeping chamber to put on clean clothing and the embroidered surcoat that marked her high office. She was braiding her hair when she heard Skylan moving around the living area.

Her hands shook; she had to quit her task. She must face him. There was no helping that. Her courage failed her. She could not remain hiding in the bedroom forever, however. She hastily finished the braid, winding it around her head, and put on the surcoat. She bravely attempted a smile and walked into the living area. She saw, with a start, that Skylan was dressing as though for a journey. He had on his tunic and helm, his silver armbands, and chain mail. Skylan's old sword (not the new one she had given him) bumped against his hip.

"Where are you going, lord?" Draya asked, startled.

Skylan continued to arm himself. Perhaps he was preparing to return to his own homeland! The Torgun were slated to leave today, and Skylan might well have decided to sail with them. Draya was panic-stricken. His sudden departure would look very, very bad.

She was about to press the issue, demand an answer, when he said abruptly, "I had a dream last night. Torval came to me. He ordered me to go to Hammerfall."

Skylan looked at her directly now, and his blue eyes were ice cold. "I have to seek the god's forgiveness."

Draya flushed in shame. A dream sent by the god must be acted upon, of course, but what would people think? She was about to tell Skylan he could not go, he could not possibly leave her now, but then she checked her words. Might not his departure be best for both of them?

Hammerfall was one of the most sacred sites of the Vindrasi. When Torval had finally won his battle over the Dragon Ilyrion, he had been so exhausted that his blood-covered war hammer had slipped from his hand. It had fallen an immense distance through the heavens until it struck the ground. The hammer's head gouged out a huge crater that was perfectly round with high walls and a smooth floor of black shining rock where nothing would grow. Warriors often traveled to Hammerfall to ask Torval's blessing before going to war or to dedicate a new sword or battle axe. Those who had told lies or done something else dishonorable went to Hammerfall to seek the god's forgiveness.

Hammerfall was located south of Vindraholm. The journey would take Skylan a fortnight, at least. Time spent alone, time to cool off, think things over. When the young man returned, he would feel better, and they could start over.

"I think that is an excellent idea, lord. Though, of course," Draya added in a low voice, "you must keep your reason for going a secret."

Skylan's lip curled. "If anyone asks, madam, I will say that I am traveling to Hammerfall to thank the god for the very great favor he has bestowed on me by giving you for my wife."

Draya flinched at his piercing sarcasm.

"I have a meeting with the Clan Chiefs this morning," Skylan continued, gathering his things. "Then I must bid farewell to my father and my clansmen. I will depart immediately after that."

Draya noticed Skylan was limping—his wound pained him. She knew better than to offer to help him. She could give him another kind of assistance, however.

"The journey is a long one. Too long for you to make on foot. If you go to the horse pen, lord, you will find another of my gifts to you: the black stallion with the white blaze. He is battle-trained and very fast. According to Sven, who bred him, he can run a hole in the wind. His name is Blade."

Skylan stopped in his work. A horse was a valuable and treasured gift. He frowned, as though considering whether or not to accept it. He obviously did not want to be beholden to her.

"As Chief of Chiefs," said Draya, seeing his dilemma, "it is right and proper that you have a fine mount."

Skylan thought this over and nodded. "I thank you," he said stiffly. "Your gift is . . . most generous."

"What will you and the Chiefs discuss?" Draya asked, trying to make conversation.

He seemed about to tell her it was none of her business. Then he shrugged. "What do you think, madam? We must make plans to recover the Vektan Torque from the ogres. While I am on my journey, the Chiefs will gather their warriors. On my return, they will be ready to sail—"

"—to the Hall of Vektia," said Draya. She dared not look at him. "You must have forgotten, Husband. First we sail to the Dragon Isles. You must present yourself as Chief of Chiefs to the gods—"

"The gods know me well enough already!" Skylan said angrily. "You are Kai Priestess! Do *you* want to leave the Vektan Torque in the hands of the ogres?"

"No, lord, of course I do not," said Draya. "But you have no idea where the ogres' lands are located!"

"I will find them," said Skylan.

"At the Hall of Vektia, we could ask Vindrash—"

"You can ask her now!" Skylan flared, glaring at Draya. "Why sail all the way to the Dragon Isles to speak to her?"

Skylan started to leave.

He is young and impatient, Draya counseled herself. He doesn't understand.

"My lord," she said, "we will first sail to the Dragon Isles. Together. While we are there, we will ask the gods' blessing for your voyage to the ogre lands."

Skylan didn't wait to hear the rest. Muttering something she was thankful she could not hear, he banged out the door, letting it slam shut after him.

Draya felt faint. She tried to reach a stool, but her legs gave way and she sank to the floor.

"Vindrash," she prayed, clasping her hands, "you know the reason I committed this terrible crime. You know I did not kill Horg out of hatred or revenge, though you also know no woman ever had better cause! What else could I do, Vindrash? He was threatening to destroy the Kai, and with it the faith, which is all that keeps our people alive! I did what I had to do!

You know that, Vindrash! I had no choice. Do not abandon me, Goddess! Do not!"

Draya listened tensely, waiting to hear the soothing, sibilant whisper of the goddess. She heard the fussing of robins, the sigh of the wind in the trees, the distant crashing of waves on the shore, but no sound of the goddess's voice.

Draya shuddered. Sighing deeply, she rose to her feet, gathered her robes around her, forced her lips to form a smile, and made her way to the Great Hall of the Gods.

Skylan left the house seething, half-blinded with rage. He was Chief of Chiefs! How dare she order him about? Now, instead of sailing off to battle and glory, he would have to endure a voyage with her! Skylan had considered defying her, but he knew that would never work. He was dependent on the Bone Priestesses. No dragon would sail without them. Draya had only to say the word, and his voyage to the ogre lands would end before it began.

Skylan could not bear to face the Clan Chiefs. He decided to go to the pen where the horses were kept. He was still of two minds whether to accept the horse or not. He disliked the thought of taking anything from his wife. Yet, Draya was right. As Chief of Chiefs, it was proper and fitting that he should have a fine mount.

He spotted Blade immediately. With his shining black coat, he stood out from the others in the community horse pen. The white mark on his forehead, shaped like a sword's blade, had inspired his name. Several young boys hanging about the horse pen were glad to help Skylan catch Blade and escort him out of the pen.

Blade was a proud animal who did not take kindly to being ridden, undoubtedly believing that having a man on his back was an affront to his dignity. When Skylan tried to put the saddle on him, Blade kicked and bucked, sending the small boys scrambling. Skylan laughed. He was glad the horse had spirit.

He was pleased with Draya's gift, though that did not mean he felt kindly toward the giver. Skylan had relived the battle over and over during the long night. Writhing in shame, he saw Horg collapse in agony, clasping his gut, and Skylan saw himself, triumphantly stabbing a dying man. Skylan hated Draya more now than he had when she'd first confessed, if that were possible.

I will take her gift, Skylan decided. Though not for love. She owes me reparation, and this will be part of her payment.

He offered Blade an apple, in token of friendship, and rubbed his nose and made much of him. Blade appeared inclined to think better of Skylan, and the horse deigned to allow him to mount, though he kept a wary eye on him.

Though Skylan did not own a horse, he knew how to ride. When he was young, his father had captured a horse in a raid, and he had taught his little son to ride. The horse had died a few winters ago, and Norgaard had not replaced it, much to his son's disappointment. Now Skylan himself owned a horse, a fine animal, one any man might envy.

Skylan rode Blade to the Chief's Hall, where the Clan Chiefs were already assembling. He was a bit late, for he and Blade had a dispute over which of them was going to be the master. Blade at first ignored Skylan's commands and took off at a gallop, heading straight for a low-hanging tree branch in an effort to dislodge him. Skylan flattened himself down over the horse's neck and hung on grimly. Blade tore over the fields and jumped a creek. Then, worn out, the horse came to a halt and stood blowing and puffing. He swiveled an eye around to Skylan, bowed his head, and shook his mane.

Skylan, who was thankful he hadn't broken his neck, patted the horse to show that all was forgiven. From then on, Blade did as Skylan commanded.

The Chiefs' Meeting went well, better than many of the Chiefs had expected. The men were skeptical about their new Chief of Chiefs, viewing him as an arrogant young pup, all swagger and bark, which is certainly how he'd appeared on his wedding day.

Skylan's guilty secret and his own inner turmoil served him well, forcing him to consider carefully every word before he spoke it. Skylan had never undergone anything so agonizing. He expected any moment that someone would stand up to accuse him. When no one did so, Skylan began to breathe easier. He still had to keep up his guard, with the result that he gave thought to what he said, and came across as far more mature and less reckless than he might have been. He saw Norgaard had been on edge, worried that Skylan might make a fool of himself. Norgaard relaxed and gave his son one of his rare smiles.

The Chiefs were keen to go to war against the ogres, and they were ready to give Skylan dragonships, warriors, silver—whatever he needed. Skylan said he had to postpone the war. He must first sail to the Dragon Isles. He secretly hoped the Chiefs would be upset by this. If the Chiefs showed a united front to the Kai Priestess, he could insist that they first go after the ogres. The Chiefs were content to wait until he had returned from this voyage, however, and Skylan could only fume silently at the delay.

The meeting was coming to a close when Skylan announced that he was traveling to Hammerfall and that he would be leaving this day.

That news caused considerable astonishment. Skylan told them that Torval had appeared to him in a dream, commanding him to go to Hammerfall, there to thank the god for his manifold blessings.

The Chiefs discussed this. All agreed that Skylan had much to be thankful for. Torval had made the young man Chief of Chiefs at the age of eighteen years, rewarding him with riches and a wife. The fact that Skylan was undertaking such a journey after having spent only a single night with his new bride was proof of his piety and devotion.

The meeting broke up soon after this discussion. Now that the Vutmana and the wedding celebrations were over, the Chiefs were eager to return to their clans. Several who were heading north said they would be honored to have Skylan accompany them. He thanked them, but told them he needed to perform his journey alone. Since this journey had been commanded by Torval, the Chiefs understood and wished him well.

Norgaard waited until the others had left; then he drew his son aside and regarded him shrewdly. "Torval appeared to you in a dream?" he said.

"Yes, Father," Skylan answered. He was pleased with himself. He had gained the Chiefs' admiration and respect.

Norgaard's brows came together. He fixed his son with a troubled gaze. "You never dream, Skylan. You always boast of that."

Skylan's tongue clove to the roof of his mouth. He did not know what to say. The truth was, he had dreamed no dream. Skylan had been wide awake when he concocted his plan to go to Hammerfall; he'd lied when he said the god had commanded him. He had been quite proud of his own cleverness. As a Priestess, Draya would have to honor the god's wishes and let Skylan go. And by traveling to Hammerfall, Skylan could escape his wife's loathsome presence. He'd forgotten all about the blasted voyage to the Dragon Isles. And he'd forgotten all about the fact that he always boasted of never dreaming.

"There is a first time for everything, Father," Skylan said at last.

Norgaard eyed him, then let the matter drop.

"You did well with the Chief's meeting, my son. I am proud of you."

"Thank you, Father," said Skylan, grimacing.

His lies gnawed at him, tearing at his insides like carrion crows feasting on a corpse.

"Is something wrong?" Norgaard asked, concerned.

"I did not get much sleep last night, that is all," said Skylan.

He abruptly changed the subject, calling upon his father to admire his new horse, and asking for advice on how best to care for the beast. Norgaard said he had never seen a finer animal, and their talk centered on horses all the way to the beach.

They arrived at the *Venjekar* to find the Torgun ready to sail. The warriors were already on board, their colorful shields lining the bulwarks. They grinned when Skylan came into view and shouted the customary crude remarks regarding his prowess and staying power that always greeted a new bridegroom the morning after.

Treia had not yet gone aboard. She was still onshore, the gods alone knew why. She looked dour and grim as always, and she said nothing to Skylan, though he greeted her politely. He wondered where Aylaen was, assumed she was on the ship. Just as well. Seeing her now would be too painful.

He cast a swift glance about for Garn and did not see him either. Skylan gave an inward sigh of relief. He could lie to all the world and get away with it, but he could never lie successfully to his friend and brother.

"You truly intend to go to Hammerfall?" Norgaard asked.

"Torval has given me so many blessings, I would be lacking in duty and respect if I disobeyed his command," Skylan answered glibly.

"What does Draya say to your leaving?"

"My wife"—Skylan had to work to speak without gagging—"supports me in my decision. Where is Garn?"

"He went into town hoping to meet you," Norgaard replied. "We must have missed him— Ah, look." Norgaard gestured. "Here he comes now."

Skylan turned to see both Garn and Aylaen hurrying across the beach.

"Here you are!" Aylaen called. "We went in search of you. Draya said we should find you here."

Skylan looked at her in dumb agony. Aylaen was radiant. Her hair glittered like red gold in the sun. Her emerald eyes danced and sparkled. Her creamy skin was sun-kissed, with a smattering of freckles across her nose. He thought of Draya, her flabby breasts and wrinkled skin, her hands stained with Horg's blood fondling his groin.

Skylan felt dirty, as though he had wallowed in muck. He did not like to think of Draya speaking to Aylaen, of being anywhere near her.

"What do you think of my new horse?" he asked.

Garn barely glanced at the animal. "I hear you are traveling to Hammerfall," he said in wonder.

"To thank the god for my great happiness," Skylan said tersely. He was sick and tired of everyone questioning him.

He rubbed Blade on the nose and praised the horse. "He has a warrior's heart. He jumped a creek as wide as the dragonship. You should see him."

"I would like to ride him," Aylaen said. "I am so proud of you, Skylan. I know you are married, but I claim a sister's privilege."

She pressed her lips to his. The touch of her lips was like a fiery brand, burning his flesh. He had the strange impression the kiss had left a mark, and he put his fingers to his lips to see if he could feel it. He loved her so much, his heart seemed to break with the pain.

"Aylaen," he said with quiet urgency, "I've been wanting to talk to you—"

Aylaen laughingly interrupted him. "We will talk, Skylan, only not now. I don't have time. I must say good-bye to Treia. She's staying for the Kai Moot."

And before Skylan could entreat her to stay, as well, Aylaen gave him a smile and hurried away.

Garn started to say something, but Skylan cut him off. He kept his gaze averted.

"You had better leave, as well, my friend, or the ship will miss the tide. Take care of my father." Skylan knew he was talking too fast, but he couldn't help it. "Let me know if there is anything he needs."

"Skylan, stop it," Garn said, catching hold of him. "Something's wrong. I know it. You can tell me. You know you can."

Skylan stood with his hand on the saddle. Part of him longed to spew out the awful truth. He longed to purge his soul, as last night he had purged his stomach.

Blade whinnied softly and pushed at Skylan with his nose, eager to be on the move. Skylan stroked the neck of his magnificent horse. He glanced back at his father, who was swelling with pride. He saw Aylaen, her hair shining in the sunlight, and felt the touch of her lips.

Norgaard would disown him. Aylaen would be lost to him forever.

"What could be wrong, my friend?" Skylan asked. "I am Chief of Chiefs."

He swung himself up on his horse and smiled down on his friend. Garn did not return the smile. He stood stubbornly at Skylan's stirrup, his hand holding on to the bridle.

Skylan felt a flash of irritation. He was not a child, to be badgered and questioned. Turning his horse's head, he dug in his heels and galloped off across the beach. He did not stop or look back until he had ridden over the windswept dunes. He climbed a ridge and pulled his horse to a halt and looked out to sea.

The *Venjekar* rose and dipped among the waves. He could see Garn on board, standing near the prow alongside Norgaard and Aylaen. There was Bjorn chatting with his brother, Erdmun. There was Alfric the One-Eyed, sharing a jest with Sigurd. He saw the others striding along the deck, gazing out to sea, talking together, probably talking of him and how proud they were. The young man who had slain Horg. The young man who had raised the Torgun to exalted heights. The young man who was Chief of Chiefs. His clansmen would return to Luda to take up their lives, leaving him behind.

This is the pain the dead feel, he thought. I stand on the cold and lonely shore, watching those I love sail away. They go on with life, while I remain alone.

His grief unmanned him, and he wept. Through the blur of tears, Skylan caught a flash of fire—the red eyes of the Dragon Kahg. The ship was just coming level with him. The eyes of the dragon sought him out, stared fixedly at him. He imagined he heard a voice speaking to him

*The spear is broken. The sword bent. The shield shattered. You cannot change what has happened. Will you fall to your knees and grovel at your enemy's boots in surrender, or will you keep fighting?*

There could be only one answer. Skylan drew his sword from its sheath and lifted it high in the air, so that the sunlight flared off the blade. The dragon's eyes flickered in response.

Sheathing his sword, Skylan turned his horse's head south, toward Hammerfall.

## CHAPTER 4

Skylan was on the road for more than two weeks, riding through dark forests and over sunny grasslands. He had never traveled this extensively, and he enjoyed the journey. He dawdled, took his time, loathe to return home. Each day brought new sights, and along with that, the somber realization that the Vindrasi were in trouble. He rode past crops withering in the cracked, dry earth. He saw too many cattle herds whose numbers were small, the beasts pitifully thin. Rivers were sluggish and shrunken. Creeks had dried up. And still, the Sun Goddess Aylis blazed in the heavens, her eye glaring down on the land. He could not remember the last time it had rained.

Skylan knew the reason. Treia had explained it to him: Aylis was furious about the death of her daughter, the Goddess Desiria, and she was taking out her fury and her grief on the Vindrasi. Skylan had stated that he considered this unreasonable on the part of the goddess. She should take out her anger on the evil gods who were responsible for slaying Desiria, not punish her loyal followers.

Treia had asked him snidely if he considered himself wiser than the gods. Skylan said no, of course not, but privately he thought that in this instance he was. He recalled the ill-fated dinner with the ogre godlords. They had looked well-fed, their bellies huge, even after a prolonged sea journey during which they'd been forced to cut back on rations. They had bragged that their harvests were large, their people prosperous. The shaman had been loud in his praise of the Gods of Raj, who lavished blessings upon their people. "The Vindrasi should be glad to worship them," he'd said.

Our people need to go raiding, Skylan resolved. Our warriors need to feel good about themselves. They need to win silver and gold and jewels for the dragons. They need to bring back fat cattle to feed their hungry children. The ogres bragged that their land was wealthy. Then we will raid the ogres.

Skylan had no idea where the ogres' lands were located. He doubted any of the Vindrasi still living did. But the ogres would have left evidence of their route along the way. Skylan could follow the trail of plundered villages and burned-out houses to trace his route to their lands.

He longed more than ever to undertake this epic voyage. He could picture himself sailing back to Vindraholm in triumph, the sacred torque gleaming on his neck, his dragonship filled with ogre silver, gold, and jewels.

Instead, he would be sailing with his wife to the Dragon Isles.

On the seventh day of his journey, Skylan stopped at a farmhouse to ask directions. He had to be getting close to his destination. The farmer told him that, yes, he was within a day's ride of Hammerfall. He had only to follow the road until he came to a trail, which was not marked, but which he could not fail to recognize, for it had been made by many warriors before him.

Skylan followed the road and came across the trail, just as the farmer had said. He turned Blade's head and rode along the trail a short distance. Reaching the summit of a hill, he reined in the horse. The steep rock walls of the crater jutted up from the grassland, like sharp teeth eager to take a bite out of the blue sky.

The trail on which he was riding cut through the grasslands, led straight to those gray walls. He looked down on the trail with a feeling of awe. Warriors had walked this trail since time's beginning. Perhaps the great Thorgunnd had walked this path. Devout warriors all, going to honor Torval with noble hearts and unstained souls.

Whereas Skylan was an oath-breaker and a murderer—or as near to being a murderer as did not matter. He was a cheat and a liar, and he had invoked Torval's name in his lies.

I try to do right. It's just that things keep going wrong. Torval understands. Skylan tried to reassure himself. The god sees into my heart.

He guided his horse to the top of the ridge and was about to ride down the hill, when he heard a raucous caw. A shadow swept over him, causing him to duck involuntarily. An unusually large raven landed with a flurry of black wings on the trail directly in front of Skylan, spooking Blade, who snorted nervously and did a little sideways dance. Skylan pulled on the reins, dragging his startled horse to a halt.

A dead hare lay on the trail. The raven glared at Skylan, warning him away from the prize. Calmly, unafraid, the raven hopped onto the carcass, dug its claws into the brown fur, and just as calmly began to peck out the rabbit's eyes.

Skylan shuddered. The raven was sacred to Hevis, God of Fire, Deceit, Hidden Acts, and Treachery. No omen could be clearer or more terrible.

Skylan shouted, hoping the bird would take fright and fly away. The raven continued to feast on the rabbit. Skylan urged Blade forward. The raven glanced at him and then, to his horror, the bird spread enormous black wings, leaped off the corpse, and flew straight at Skylan's head.

Skylan ducked, yanking on the reins so hard that Blade spun around and nearly lost his footing. Terrified, Skylan rode at a gallop back down the trail, retracing his steps.

Behind him, the raven gave a raucous, cawing laugh.

Skylan rode for days with no clear notion of where he was or where he was going. He wanted only to put as much distance between himself and Hammerfall as possible. When Blade grew tired, Skylan dismounted and continued on foot, leading the horse. He fell asleep on his feet, only to wake with a start from dreams that ravens were pecking out his eyes.

Skylan, who never dreamed, now dreamed all the time.

Torval was clearly furious with Skylan. The god had turned his back on him. Not content with that, Torval had sent the treacherous Hevis to bar Skylan from the sacred site. Skylan had to find a way to propitiate Torval, appease the angry god. He had no idea how to go about this. As a child, whenever Skylan had made Norgaard angry, the boy had simply kept out of his father's way until Norgaard cooled off. Skylan had hoped such a tactic would work with the god, but obviously it did not. He did not know what more he could do. He needed advice, and Garn was not around.

The road on which Skylan traveled led inland for a long distance. Stopped by the foothills of the Kairnholm Mountains, the road turned toward the coast, dipped down to the Hesvolm Sea.

Days had passed since he'd fled Hammerfall. The afternoon was waning. Skylan had to start thinking wearily about finding somewhere to make camp. He stood gazing at the vast expanse of water that spread gleaming before him and noted several boats drawn up along a barren strandline.

Skylan first thought this was a raiding party, but then he realized that didn't make much sense. There were no villages anywhere near. The boats were only five in number, and they were not swift-sailing, sleek warships. They were short, squat merchant vessels, designed to carry goods, not warriors.

The boats were far from any town, and he wondered if they were lost. Moving closer, he could see that one boat had been turned upside down. Men swarmed over it. That was the explanation. A boat had been damaged, and the traders had put ashore to repair it.

Skylan longed to hear a human voice after listening so long to his own confused, dark thoughts, and he urged his horse to a gallop. Traders went everywhere, saw everything. They tended to remain neutral, and even if their countries were at war, they still plied their routes, selling goods to friend and foe alike. Anything to make a living.

Traders traveled far, as well. The thought was in Skylan's mind that they might know how to find the ogres' lands.

One of the traders caught sight of Skylan, as he came galloping across the sands, and he gave a warning shout. Seeing a warrior clad in armor, armed, and bearing a shield, the men left the work on the damaged boat to form a line across the road. They were armed with swords and axes and looked like they knew what they were about. Skylan removed his helm and kept his sword sheathed, showing he had no hostile intent.

The men had the black hair and beards and swarthy complexions of those who lived in lands far, far to the south. All except one. This man had blond hair and a bushy blond beard. He was taller than the others, broad-shouldered, and big-boned. Skylan regarded this man with interest. He had to be Vindrasi.

Skylan's first thought was that he was a guide hired by the Southlanders. Then he saw that the blond man was dressed in the same type of clothing as the Southlanders—long, flowing robes belted at the waist with loose-fitting sleeves. He gestured at Skylan, then shouted something at his companions. The men put away their weapons and returned to their work—or rather, to supervising the work. Skylan saw now that the men repairing the ship were slaves, wearing leg irons and shackles.

Skylan noted that there were women among the group; short, dark women with long black curling hair, black eyes, and smooth brown skin. He saw the women eyeing him, and he regretted the fact that he had not shaved in several days or combed his hair or bathed.

"I am Skylan Ivorson," Skylan called out when he was within hailing distance. He was the stranger, and it was up to him to proclaim himself. "I am the son of Norgaard of the Torgun."

He almost added proudly, "Chief of Chiefs of the Vindrasi," but at the last moment, he thought better of it. He did not know these men or why they were here. A Chief of Chiefs would be worth his weight in ransom.

The blond man stared at Skylan in amazement, and then he gave a great roar. "I do not believe it! It is little Skylan!"

Now it was Skylan's turn to stare. Who was this man?

The blond-bearded face split in a wide grin. "The last time I saw you was thirteen winters ago," the man proclaimed. "You were five then, and nearly sliced off my thumb with your father's sword. I have the scar to prove it!"

Skylan swung himself down off his horse. He looked with curious puzzlement at the man, who did seem vaguely familiar.

"Don't you know me? Have I changed so much? Ah, I suppose I have. It is Raegar Gustafson!" The blond man thumped himself on the chest. "I am the son of your mother's brother. We are cousins, little Skylan!"

Raegar shook his head. "Imagine us meeting like this in the middle of nowhere. Some god must have arranged it!"

# CHAPTER 5

Skylan gaped at his cousin in astonishment.

"Raegar! We mourned you for dead!"

Skylan had been only five, but he still remembered that sad time, for it had been his first true awareness of death. As a small boy, Skylan had worshipped his cousin Raegar. A bold warrior—big, jovial, handsome, liked by everyone—Raegar had been lost in a raid. The last anyone saw of him, he had gone down while battling three warriors. They searched for his body the next day, but the men had not been able to find him, and they assumed the corpse had been devoured by wolves. Raegar had been around twenty then, Skylan reckoned, which would make him about thirty-three now.

Skylan had grieved his favorite cousin's loss to such an extent that Norgaard had smacked him, saying sternly that Skylan dishonored his cousin's memory by sniveling over him.

"What happened to you?" Skylan asked. "Obviously you did not die."

Raegar grimaced and shook his head. "I should have died, Cousin. There were times—many times—I wished I had died. I was badly wounded, and when I could not fight, I pleaded with the sons of whores to kill me, to send me to Torval with honor. They said I was too valuable to waste—a big strong man like myself. They took me captive, nursed me back to health, and carried me to Oran in shackles."

Raegar jerked a thumb over his shoulder. "See those poor bastards? Like them, I was a slave. I was sold in the slave market, and I might well have been sent to the iron mines, which means I would have been dead in a year, but a god was watching over me. A man of wealth and influence purchased me, and he put me to work in his household. His secretary taught me to read and write the language of the Southland. He had to teach me in secret, for it is forbidden that slaves should be educated.

"My master found out, and I feared I would be whipped or perhaps even killed. Instead, he furthered my education. Eventually I became head of his household. I earned enough to buy my freedom, and now I am a merchant trader. These men"—Raegar gestured to those who were supervising the work of the slaves on the boat—"are my partners."

Skylan regarded his cousin in bafflement. "I don't understand, Cousin. If you were a free man, why didn't you return to us, to your homeland? First avenging yourself on those who had enslaved you, of course."

Raegar scratched his bearded chin. "I considered coming back to Luda. But a man finds his happiness where he can, Cousin. I had a good life. I owned my own house. I had a wife, children. All gone now, sadly." Raegar looked downcast. "They perished in a fire."

"Freilis give them peace," said Skylan, naming the Goddess of the Dead, who took care of women and children.

Raegar nodded; then he shrugged and smiled again. "I like Oran, Cousin. I like the people, I like the climate." He grinned expansively. "Always plenty to eat and no more freezing off your balls in the winter. And the women are beautiful. As you can see."

Skylan had been looking at the women. They were much different from Vindrasi women, who were mostly blond and blue-eyed. One of the prettiest smiled at him. Skylan smiled back.

"I had a longing to see my homeland," Raegar was saying, "and when my partners proposed this voyage, I decided to go with them. We have been visiting the clans in the south. It was there that I heard the remarkable news that my cousin, little Skylan, was now Chief of Chiefs! I was on my way to wish you joy when this motherless boat struck a rock and started taking on water."

Skylan did not understand how a man could turn his back upon his kin and make a new life in a strange land, especially a land whose people had made him a slave.

"Torval must have wrecked our boat on purpose, for here you are. The god has dropped you into my arms, so to speak."

Skylan shifted uncomfortably at the naming of the god, though, on second thought, it was a good sign that Torval had relented toward him enough to give him back his favorite cousin, return him from the dead.

Raegar stood regarding Skylan with undisguised admiration. "Chief of Chiefs. I am not surprised. The day you were born, an eagle fought an adder outside your house. The eagle won, slaying the snake. An omen of greatness, for all know the eagle is favored of Torval."

"I never knew that," Skylan said.

"Norgaard never told you? Ah, well, that is like him. He probably feared it would give you a swelled head. How is your father? I hear he was badly wounded and he finds it difficult to get around, yet he is still Chief of the Clan."

Skylan was about to answer when Raegar suddenly struck himself on the forehead. "Where are my manners? You have ridden far. You must be thirsty and hungry. Come, I will introduce you to my partners, and you will share our evening meal. The wine of Oran is excellent. And"—Raegar smiled—"I have a gift for you. I will show you after dinner. When I knew I was sailing north, I had this present made especially for my favorite cousin. I had no idea then that I would find little Skylan Chief of Chiefs and married to the Kai Priestess!"

Skylan frowned, not liking the reminder.

"Speaking of which," Raegar added teasingly, "what are you doing riding around the countryside when you should be enjoying the pleasures of the marriage bed?"

Skylan's frown deepened to a scowl.

"Have I said something wrong, Cousin?" Raegar asked in some confusion.

"It is nothing," said Skylan. "I will explain later." He glanced again at the pretty girl who had smiled at him. She was still keeping her eyes on him. "First I would like to bathe and make myself presentable."

Raegar grinned. "Go ahead. I will take care of this fine beast for you."

Skylan walked back down the beach to a sheltered cove. Stripping off his clothes, he plunged into the water and swam for a long time. He emerged from the water and let the sun warm and dry his wet skin. He combed his hair and was shaving off the stubble on his chin when he was aware that he was not alone. The pretty girl had come up on him silently. She was regarding him with unabashed admiration. Pointing at his clothes that he'd left in a heap on the sand, she made a motion as of washing and then wringing.

"Ah, yes, thank you," Skylan said, wondering if she understood him.

The girl gathered his clothes in her arms and, with a smile, carried them away.

Skylan had brought a change of clothes with him. He dressed himself and felt better, much better. He made certain that Blade had been cared for, and found the animal contentedly munching on grain.

Raegar led Skylan to the group of men gathered around the damaged boat.

"Gentlemen, let me introduce my cousin Skylan Ivorson, Chief of Chiefs of the Vindrasi," Raegar said. He explained the relationship and then glanced at Skylan. "Did you understand what I said?"

"It was all so fast," said Skylan.

"The language is similar to ours, except that the words flow more rapidly, like a babbling brook. It is hard at first to tell where one word ends and another begins. You will get the hang of it eventually."

The men greeted Skylan with respect, which pleased him.

"Who are the women?" Skylan asked. "Are they your wives?"

Raegar laughed. "They are slaves. They do the cooking and washing and keep us warm at night. I see one has caught your fancy."

Skylan was watching the pretty girl, who had gone off to do his laundry. She had scrubbed his shirt in seawater and was now spreading it out on a boulder to dry. It had been two years since he'd lain with a woman. He had pledged himself to Aylaen, but then had come Draya. He could still feel her horrid hands groping him. He thought of that, and he watched the pretty girl.

The men sat down to a meal of fish stew, bread, and cheese, washed down by a truly remarkable wine. At a word from Raegar, who was clearly their leader, the Southlanders left him and his cousin to themselves. The two sat together on the beach before a fire of driftwood, watching the flames change color and drinking wine from cups made of polished wood.

"This wood comes from the olive tree," Raegar said. "Here, try some of the fruit." He held out a bowl filled with green and black olives.

"You're supposed to spit out the seed," he advised Skylan, who had swallowed the pit and nearly choked.

Skylan found the olives delicious. The wine warmed his blood, made his cares and worries seem small and insignificant, meant to be spit out, like the pits of the olives. Raegar told stories of his life in Oran. As Skylan listened, fascinated, his boyish admiration and affection for his cousin came back to him. He enjoyed Raegar's outlandish tales, though he privately suspected his cousin had made most of them up.

He told about huge ships with three banks of oars that could each carry two hundred warriors and a single city whose population was larger than that of the entire Vindrasi nation. He spoke of a thousand or more warriors who did not fight in shield-walls, but marched about the field of battle, wheeling and turning in complex formations.

"Come, Cousin, what do you take me for—a yokel?" Skylan said, laughing. "Warriors who do not fight in a shield-wall? A child would believe such a thing!"

"It is the truth, I swear by Torval," Raegar stated. "Ah, but that reminds me! Your gift!"

He summoned the pretty girl and sent her running to one of the boats. She rummaged around in it for a short time, then returned bearing a large bundle wrapped in coarse cloth. She handed the bundle to Raegar, who dismissed her, sent her scurrying away.

"I wish you joy of your bride, Cousin," said Raegar, and he presented his gift.

Skylan unwrapped the layers of cloth to find a sword in a leather sheath. He grasped the hilt, drew out the blade, and gave an audible gasp.

The sword was pattern-welded, which meant that the blade was made of different types of iron twisted together while the metal was hot, forming intricate patterns that seemed to shimmer and change color in the firelight. The blade's edge gleamed; it was made of hard steel. The center groove, made of softer steel, was decorated with whorls and swirls, all twining together in an intricate dance.

"And that is what I will name it," said Skylan softly, turning the blade to catch the light. "Blood Dancer."

"Hard yet flexible," said Raegar. "Do you like it?"

Skylan could only nod. The clans in the north forged pattern-welded swords, but nothing of this quality. And their swords were dear.

He regarded Raegar in wonder. "This must have cost you a fortune, Cousin."

"The smith is a friend of mine. He owed me a favor," Raegar said lightly, passing it off. "There is no finer sword in all Oran. Except my own," he added with a laugh.

Skylan had never held such a weapon. The wine made him a little unsteady on his feet, but he had to test the blade. The weight, the balance, was perfect.

"I thank you, Cousin," Skylan said.

He removed his old sword from its sheath and replaced it with the new. He would honor the old sword, which had been his father's, keep it with him always. But Blood Dancer would never leave his side.

Raegar lifted the leather skin containing the wine.

"Let us drink to your wedding," he said, starting to pour.

Skylan placed his hand over the cup. Wine sloshed onto his fingers before Raegar could stop.

"I would rather drink to something else," Skylan said.

Raegar hesitated, uncertain how to react. "Well, then, we will drink to the memory of your mother, my aunt."

Skylan conceded that they could drink to this, and he allowed Raegar to pour a generous portion into the olive-wood cup. They drank to Skylan's mother and spoke of her spirit being safe with Freilis.

"I fear you are unhappy, Cousin," said Raegar quietly. "Would you like to talk about it?"

Skylan was silent, did not answer.

"Do you mind if I talk about it, then?" Raegar said. "I have heard rumors—"

Skylan cast him a sharp glance. "What? What have you heard?"

"Your wife is the Kai Priestess," Raegar said. "Her name is Draya."

Skylan gave a brooding nod.

Raegar looked grave. He sighed deeply and leaned forward to poke at the fire with a stick, sending a shower of sparks into the night.

Skylan eyed his cousin intently. "What is it? What is wrong?"

"I know Draya, Cousin," Raegar said. "I knew Horg, as well. Horg was a brave man before he married her. He was a bold warrior. No man better."

Skylan snorted in disgust. "Horg was a coward. You heard what he did? He bartered away the sacred Vektan Torque to the ogres to save his own skin! He admitted to it before the people. I myself killed the ogre godlord who wore the torque around his neck."

"I heard all that," Raegar said. He cast Skylan a troubled glance. "You must be careful of her, Cousin. The Horg I knew would never have done such a thing. When he married her, he changed. But I am not surprised. As I said, I knew Draya. I almost married her." Raegar seemed vexed with himself. "What am I doing? It is the wine making me talk like this. Forgive me, Cousin. Draya is your wife. I should say nothing against her."

"Except that I should be careful!" Skylan exclaimed. "You have already said too much, Cousin. You cannot put the spilled ale back in the pitcher. Why didn't you marry her?"

Raegar shook his head. "I wish you wouldn't ask me."

"And I wish you would speak plainly," said Skylan.

Raegar was silent for a long moment. When he finally spoke, it was in a low tone. "I caught Draya trying to bewitch me."

Skylan regarded him skeptically. "Bewitch you? How can that be? She is Kai Priestess! Dedicated to Vindrash."

"So she claims. I see I must tell you the whole story. This happened back before she was made Kai Priestess. Our families had arranged our marriage when we were little. The Heudjun and the Torgun were at war, and they thought it would establish peace between the clans. But when we came of age, her parents were dead and so were mine. The clans were no longer at war. We could choose for ourselves whether or not we wanted to wed. She was eager, but I was beginning to have doubts. I had heard strange whispers about her. How she consorted with that crone known as Owl Mother—"

"Owl Mother!" Skylan repeated, astonished. "I know her."

"The old woman's still alive?" Raegar asked in wonder.

"She is," said Skylan. "She healed my wounds when I was attacked by a boar."

"And you let her touch you?" Raegar was horrified.

"I didn't have much choice," Skylan said. "The ogres had invaded our village, demanding hostages and cattle and silver. I was War Chief. I had to lead the men in battle. And I could barely stand, let alone walk."

"The Torgun Bone Priestess—"

"—refused to heal me. She hates me," said Skylan, shrugging. "Though that was not the reason she wouldn't heal me. As it turned out—"

He stopped. He had been going to tell his cousin about the death of the Goddess of Healing, but he was afraid that the dire news might get back to the Southlanders, who worshipped their own gods. Perhaps evil gods, like the Gods of Raj.

"Tell me about Draya. What did she do to you?"

"She accused me of loving someone else, a charge I denied. She didn't believe me. One night when I was alone in my dwelling, I drank some mead with my meal, as was my usual custom. I noticed the mead had a strange taste, but I thought nothing of it. And then my head began to swim. My vision blurred. I tried to stand, but my legs would not work. The next thing I knew, I woke to find myself lying in my bed. I had been stripped naked. Draya was beside me. She was naked, too. She was drawing runes on my bare breast in blood, and singing strange words.

"She was startled to see me wake up. The potion she fed me wore off too quickly, I guess. She tried to make love to me, but I ordered her to dress herself, and then I threw her out of my dwelling. I should have publicly proclaimed her a witch, but she begged and pleaded with me to spare her."

Raegar sighed deeply. "I said I would, if she would swear to cease practicing her foul magic. She promised she would. Obviously she lied. Horg was her next victim."

"What do you mean by that?" Skylan asked, alarmed. He thought Raegar was referring to the poisoning.

"Only that Draya wanted to be the ruler of the Vindrasi," said Raegar. "When Horg refused to give in to her demands, she used her spells to steal his manhood. Rumor has it that after he lay with her, Horg never fathered a child. Not with Draya or with any woman."

Skylan sat staring gloomily into the fire. It all made perfect sense.

Raegar eyed him. "I fear my warning comes too late. Has she cast a spell on you?"

"Not on me," said Skylan, shaken.

"I have upset you. I am sorry," Raegar said. "I should have kept my mouth shut. Here, this will settle your nerves."

He poured more wine. Skylan stared into the red liquid, then downed it at a gulp.

Images swam in his head: the raven with its black eyes and Draya pulling off her gown and Horg doubled over, clutching his gut . . .

Skylan groaned and let his swimming head sink into his hands. His cousin put his arm around his shoulders.

"One of the female slaves knows something of love charms," said Raegar softly. "Tell me what Draya did to you, and perhaps she can remove the charm—"

"She didn't do anything to me," Skylan said.

Raegar frowned. "Perhaps she did and you didn't know it. If you lay with her—"

"I didn't!" Skylan cried vehemently. "Something warned me against her. I left her bed."

"On her wedding night? Draya must have been furious. You are lucky you are still alive!" Raegar said.

"You do not know *how* lucky!" Skylan said in a shuddering whisper. "She poisoned Horg!"

Raegar drew in a hissing breath; then he cast a swift glance around the camp. "Keep your voice down, Skylan!"

Skylan picked up his cup to take another drink, only to find it was empty.

"You fill me with horror, Cousin," Raegar added, pouring more wine. "I won't press you, but if you want to talk about it, I swear by Torval's beard that anything you say to me I will hold in strictest confidence."

Skylan wanted to talk. He had to talk. He told his cousin everything. Like lancing a boil, the ugly pus flowed out. He talked about the battle with Horg, Draya's confession, his own horror and his determination to travel to Hammerfall and beg Torval's forgiveness. He talked about the raven who had blocked his path.

"And now I don't know what to do," Skylan said miserably. "If I accuse Draya, I accuse myself. I could be sent into exile or even hanged! Torval has cursed me!"

"You must do something to seek his forgiveness," said Raegar.

"I could bring back the Vektan Torque," said Skylan. "That is what I believe he wants me to do. But Draya insists that I must waste time sailing to the Dragon Isles."

"You dare not oppose her," said Raegar. "She might do something terrible to you."

Skylan shuddered at the thought.

"I have an idea," Raegar said after a moment. "But I want to sleep on it. We will speak of this again in the morning. You should go to your rest now, my cousin. The girl will take you to where she has prepared your bed."

The pretty girl came gliding out of the shadows. She smiled at him.

Skylan lurched to his feet and nearly fell headlong into the fire. Raegar, laughing, caught hold of him. Skylan was not so drunk that he forgot the precious sword. He grabbed it, held it fast. The girl put her arms around Skylan and led him some distance down the beach and into the tall grass. Here, far from the others, she had spread out a blanket.

Skylan stripped off his shirt and pants, then threw himself onto the blanket. The girl started to lie down beside him. Skylan was about to tell her to leave, and then he remembered that Draya had stolen Horg's manhood. Perhaps she had done the same to him and, as Raegar had said, Skylan did not know it.

He pulled the giggling girl close to him. She kissed his bare chest. Their arms and legs entwined. He fondled her breasts as she pressed against him. Closing his eyes, he pretended she was Aylaen. He groaned with pleasure, then collapsed on top of the girl.

Skylan fell into a drunken stupor so deep that he did not move. The girl had to wriggle out from underneath him.

# CHAPTER 6

Skylan remained in his bed till late the next morning. Even through closed eyelids, he felt the sunlight piercing his brain with the force of a thrown spear, and he was loath to rise. Unlike some who imbibed too much, he had a relatively clear memory of everything he'd said and done the night before. He was vaguely disappointed to find the girl had gone, but he supposed she had chores to do.

His brain throbbed, seemed about to crack his skull. Aside from that, he felt better than he had in many days. He was glad he had unburdened himself. His only concern was that Raegar would tell what he knew, and that concern was small, almost nonexistent. Raegar was Skylan's cousin. He had sworn by Torval to keep Skylan's secret, and he had brought Skylan a valuable gift. Skylan fumbled about the blankets until he found his sword. Placing his hand reassuringly on the hilt, he shut his eyes against the sun and lay in his bed until the smell of food and the pressing need to relieve himself roused him.

Skylan went for a swim to clear his head, then put on the clean clothes the girl had washed for him. He walked across the beach to where the slave women were roasting fish. The pretty girl served him.

He did not see Raegar, and he asked the girl where he was, for he was eager to hear his cousin's plan. He spoke his words slowly and loudly, repeating Raegar's name, so that she would understand him. The girl stared at him blankly, and finally Skylan gave up and ate his meal.

At last Raegar appeared, yawning and scratching himself, from a tent some distance down the beach. Like Skylan, Raegar went for a swim and then came over to sit by the fire, shaking the water from his hair and beard like a dog.

Skylan squatted by the fire and helped himself to fish and bread. His stomach was ready to rebel at the smell of food, but Skylan would need his strength, for he had a long ride ahead of him, and he forced himself to eat.

"I see one of the boats is gone," Skylan noted. "Along with two of your partners."

"There is a fishing village not far from here. They went to peddle our wares. I have to join them there, but I wanted to talk to you first."

Raegar regarded Skylan in wry concern. "You drank a lot of wine, Cousin. Do you remember what we spoke about last night? The trouble you are in?"

"There is not wine enough in the world to drown my trouble," said Skylan harshly. "I only wish there were."

Raegar sighed deeply; then, slapping his knees, he rose to his feet. "If you are finished eating, come with me."

The two strolled along the beach. Above them, seabirds wheeled over the waves. On the shore, two gulls screamed at each other, fighting over a dead fish.

"I lay awake a long time last night, Cousin, thinking about your problem. First," said Raegar, "you are in grave danger. You know Draya's secret. You are lucky in one regard, however. She is in love with you, and so long as she believes there is a chance you will love her—"

Skylan gave a snort. "Never!"

"Hear me out, Cousin," said Raegar. "So long as Draya thinks she has a chance to win you, she will not harm you. If she comes to believe that you hate her . . ." Raegar shrugged. "There is no telling what she might do to you. She has killed one husband already."

"Don't you think I know that?" Skylan said bitterly. "But what can I do?"

"First, you must seek Torval's forgiveness," said Raegar. "Not for the murder of Horg. Draya did that. Torval knows you are innocent. But you broke your oath to your father, and that is a serious thing. A warrior's honor is the banner that flies above his head to which all men are witness."

"I know," said Skylan. "I am sorry for that. Yet it was Torval who put the idea into my head! How can the god punish me for doing his bidding?"

"Who can understand the mind of a god?" Raegar said. "Who would want to! Take me, for instance. I begged Torval to let me die, and I cursed him when he let me be sold into slavery. Yet, the god knew what he was about. Torval kept me alive and brought me here for a reason—to bring us together. He wanted me to be able to offer you my help."

Raegar drew near, said emphatically, "Rest assured, Skylan, Torval wants you to be Chief of Chiefs! He wants you to recover the Vektan Torque, take it from the ogres. He is testing you, judging your resolve. When you have the torque, you must take it to Hammerfall, offer it to Torval, and ask his forgiveness. He will not only grant it, he will reward you handsomely! Of that I am certain."

"I would do all that!" Skylan said fervently. "I would sail tomorrow if I could. But I told you last night, Draya forbids it. She will make me go on this honeymoon journey of hers to the Dragon Isles."

"I have a solution to all your problems. First, tell me what you know of the Vektan Torque. Why is it so valuable?"

Skylan thought back. "I don't know much about the torque," he admitted.

"It is a mystery kept by the Kai. It is ancient, I know that. And it is said that the spiritbone belongs to one of the Five Vektia dragons, a dragon so powerful that both men and gods are prohibited from summoning it unless Vindrash herself commands."

"So what would happen if the ogres tried to summon this dragon?" Raegar asked.

"They can't," Skylan pointed out. "They have no Bone Priestesses."

"That is true. But say they did," Raegar argued. "Say they captured a Bone Priestess. What then? Could they force her to summon the dragon?"

"If she did, I assume the first thing she would do would be to order the dragon to slay the ogres," Skylan said with a smile.

Raegar stared at him a moment, then roared out a booming laugh. "Hah! Hah! Of course she would. I had not thought of that." He slapped Skylan on the back. "Such wisdom is why Torval made you Chief of Chiefs. Still, the ogres might find a way to persuade the Bone Priestess to work for them."

"Bah! They are ogres," said Skylan scornfully. "They couldn't persuade a cat to drink milk. But what does all this matter, Cousin?" he added impatiently. "Tell me your plan."

"Very well," said Raegar. "My plan is this: You and Draya go on your honeymoon— No, wait! Hear me out! You sail the *Venjekar* to the Dragon Isles. On the way, there is a large settlement of humans who live on an island known as the Isle of Apensia. The settlement is very rich. I was there not long ago. They have herds of fat cattle, hoards of silver and jewels. On your way to the Dragon Isles, you stop to raid this settlement—"

"Wait a moment," Skylan interrupted. "I have heard of the Isle of Apensia. All men avoid it. The isle is ruled by druids who guard it with powerful magicks."

Raegar laughed loudly. "So the druids would have you believe! Who do you think spread the tales of this fearsome magic? I myself have traded there. I have met these fearsome druids. They are nothing but a bunch of old graybeards who do not carry weapons. They do not permit their people to carry weapons. They have no warriors, no defenses. What they do have is hoards of silver and gold and jewels."

Skylan was skeptical. "If that is true, how have they survived all these years without being raided?"

"By spreading false tales about their vaunted magical powers," explained Raegar. "Lies, all lies, I assure you, Cousin. All you have to do is tell your warriors about the rich treasure they will acquire, and Draya will be powerless to stop your men from going to Apensia."

"What you say may be true," said Skylan. "But I must still travel to the Dragon Isles—"

"Not if something happens to Draya on Apensia," said Raegar.

Skylan glanced sharply at his cousin. "What do you mean?"

Raegar shrugged. "Let us suppose that during the raid, Draya vanishes and cannot be found. You would have no Bone Priestess to summon the dragon. You would have to sail back to Vindraholm and once there—"

"—the Kai would have to choose a new Kai Priestess—"

"—which could be the lovely Aylaen," inserted Raegar slyly. Skylan had told Raegar about her last night, as well. He didn't like hearing his cousin speak of her in that familiar tone, however.

"While the Kai are meeting, I could set off in pursuit of the ogres!" Skylan eyed Raegar. "So how is Draya to 'disappear'?"

"Leave that to me and my partners, Cousin," said Raegar quietly.

Skylan was alarmed. "No killing! She is not to be harmed. I don't want her draugr chasing after me the rest of my life."

"No, no, of course not," Raegar assured him. "I swear by Torval her life will be as sacred to me as my own. My partners and I will meet you on Apensia. While you are off raiding, I will sneak aboard the dragonship and carry off Draya. We will take her into exile in Djekar. That is the city where I live in Oran. She will not be able to hurt anyone ever again."

"If she is, as you say, a witch," Skylan said after a moment's thought, "she might be able to work her foul magicks and escape."

Raegar shook his head. "I will tell her that if she returns, you will expose her crimes. She can either live in exile or die in Vindraholm."

Skylan stared out moodily to sea. "You are undertaking a lot on my account. . . ."

"We are cousins!" said Raegar, grinning broadly.

"I can understand that, but your partners are not my cousins." Skylan cast Raegar a sharp glance. "What do they get out of this?"

"As I said, the settlement on Apensia is a fat one. You and I will divide the spoils between our men. Now, are we agreed?"

Skylan mulled it over. The plan was a good one. He could find no fault. He would rid himself of Draya without anyone having the least suspicion that he was involved. No one would think to question her abduction. Bone Priestesses were accustomed to facing such danger when the dragonships went raiding.

Still Skylan hesitated. A starving man would eat whatever rancid meat he found, and a thirsty man would drink swamp water. Skylan knew that if he looked at this plan too closely, he would see things crawling in it.

"Draya is a murderess, Cousin," Raegar reminded him. "She is accursed in the eyes of men and gods. If you told the people she poisoned her husband, she would be hanged." Raegar's voice softened. "Think of Draya,

Skylan, if you have no thought for yourself. You are arranging for her to live a comfortable life in exile. You are being far more merciful to her than she deserves. As Chief of Chiefs, you have a right to judge her and to pass sentence on her."

"What you say is true," Skylan conceded.

"Then we are agreed?"

"We are," said Skylan, and he gave his cousin his hand. The two shook on it, sealing the deal.

Yet, even as Skylan took his cousin's hand, the thought came to him that this was yet another secret he could not tell Garn, for Skylan knew as sure as the Norn spun a man's life thread that his friend would be appalled at the very idea.

The two men finalized their plans. Raegar gave Skylan directions on how to find the settlement. They estimated the length of time required for Skylan to return to Vindraholm and prepare for the voyage to the Dragon Isles and calculated that the *Venjekar* would arrive on Apensia sometime during the next fullness of the moon. Raegar said this would suit him and his partners. They would be waiting for Skylan at Apensia. He ended by cautioning Skylan that no one must suspect anything was amiss. He hinted that if Skylan could bring himself to make love to his wife, so much the better.

"After all, in the dark, all cats are black," Raegar added, chuckling.

Skylan did not consider this a laughing matter. He was already feeling a little guilty over having broken his vow to Aylaen by making love to the slave girl last night. He couldn't bear the thought of bedding Draya. He said nothing, however, for fear Raegar would start to question his manhood.

"I must tell people how I came by such a fine sword," Skylan said.

"Say it was a gift from Torval," Raegar suggested. "In a way, it is. The god brought us together by forcing you to change your route."

That was true as far as it went. There might be some question as to which god—Torval or Hevis—had dropped Skylan into his cousin's arms. Skylan didn't like to think about that, however.

"And now," said Raegar, "I have to leave to meet my partners."

"You must come visit us," said Skylan, embracing his cousin, and he added impulsively, "Why don't you come back with me now? My father is not in good health. I fear he will soon go to join Torval. You should see him before he dies, see your other kinsmen—"

"I will come, I promise. But it would never do for Draya to know I am alive, would it?"

"No, I suppose not," Skylan said.

"You must not tell her you have seen me," Raegar cautioned, eyeing him. "You must tell no one, not even your father, lest word get back to her."

Skylan agreed.

"Thank you for everything, Cousin," Skylan said in parting. "Especially for Blood Dancer."

"May she bring you honor and glory, Cousin," said Raegar heartily.

The two parted, Raegar going to his boats and Skylan to his horse. He had dawdled on his way to Hammerfall, hoping to put off going back for as long as possible.

He now had to make up for lost time.

Draya was pleased and astonished to return to the longhouse one evening to find Skylan's shield hanging on the wall. She took this as a happy sign. He had thought things over, and all would be well between them. She could make plans for their honeymoon journey to the Dragon Isles.

She prepared food for him and waited eagerly for him to return. He arrived home at the supper hour. His greeting to her was cool and thus not propitious, but at least he was home. He ate his meal with a good appetite. After he was finished, he sat down and began to clean and polish a sword.

"That is new, lord, isn't it?" she asked, gazing down at the weapon and marveling. "Where did you get it?" She bent near to examine it. "I've never seen anything like it!"

"It was a gift," said Skylan, intent upon his work. "From Torval."

Draya drew in an awed breath. "Tell me," she said, taking a seat beside him. "Tell me of your experience in Hammerfall!"

"What happened is between myself and the god," said Skylan. "I may not speak of it."

Draya was disappointed, but he was right not to reveal the god's mysteries. She herself never told anyone about her meetings with Vindrash. Not that there had been anything to tell lately. The goddess remained silent.

Skylan continued to polish his sword, rubbing the rainbow metal lovingly with a cloth. She watched his hands, strong and capable at their work. She thought of his hands taking hold of her, and she burned with desire. She found it hard to concentrate on what he was saying.

"I want to leave immediately" were the first words she caught.

"For the Dragon Isles?" she asked.

"Of course," Skylan returned, slightly frowning. "Where else? We will sail on the Torgun dragonship, the *Venjekar*."

"We will send a messenger to your father—," Draya began.

"No, I will go myself," said Skylan, sliding the cloth up and down the shining blade. "I want to talk to my father, make arrangements. That will mean I must leave you again, I fear."

"But you have only just returned, lord. Let me send a messenger—"

"I said I will go myself," said Skylan. "My father would take it ill otherwise."

Draya did not think Norgaard would care. She was certain that this was simply another of Skylan's excuses to avoid being alone with her, and her heart sank. She tried to smile, however, to make herself as agreeable as possible. She had lost her temper with him once before, and the consequences had been disastrous.

"Just as you say, lord. You will, of course, want to bring your father and your friends to the Dragon Isles with us. And Treia will come as Bone Priestess—"

"No!" Skylan said sharply.

He ceased his work and lifted his gaze to meet hers. His blue eyes glinted in the firelight.

She stared at him in wonder. He stood up abruptly and slid the sword into its leather sheath. He turned to face her, speaking in gentler tones.

"I want Heudjun warriors to man the dragonship. And you will serve as Bone Priestess." He gave a stiff smile. "Now you see why I must explain matters to my father. He might be offended otherwise."

"The Heudjun will be honored to be chosen, of course," said Draya, "but your friends could come, as well."

"There might be trouble between the men," said Skylan. "And nothing must go wrong on this journey."

"Very well," said Draya, though she remained puzzled. "When will you leave?"

"Tomorrow morning. This must be done without delay. Thank you for supper," he added politely. "It was delicious. Do not wait up for me."

He walked to the door.

"Husband," said Draya, "where are you going?"

"To the stables," he replied. "Blade was not acting right. I fear he may have colic. I'm going to sit up with him tonight."

Draya sighed. Colic in horses was extremely serious and could be fatal. Skylan was right to be concerned, and yet one of the stable boys could sit up with the horse. She bit her tongue, said nothing. Skylan made her a slight bow and then left.

Draya remained at home, fussing about the dwelling, and then she could stand it no longer. She put on a dark cloak, pulled the hood up over her head, and went out into the night.

Perhaps the horse was truly ill. If so, she might be able to help. Certain poultices were said to ease colic. She would have to give some excuse to explain her presence. She couldn't let Skylan know she didn't trust him. She drew near the stable door, and then she heard laughter, raucous laughter, the laughter of young men handing around the ale pitcher.

Skylan's voice rose above the laughter. He was telling some tale about some battle or other. He sounded very drunk.

Tears filled Draya's eyes. She listened to him and thought of how greatly she loved him.

And how greatly she had wronged him.

# CHAPTER 7

Guided by the spirit of the Dragon Kahg, the *Venjekar* bounded over the waves. Skylan leaned on the rail, enjoying the exhilarating ride. He was in good spirits, and he grinned as a wave broke over the keel, completely soaking him. Skylan shook back his wet hair and cast a smiling glance over his shoulder at the young Heudjun warriors, who laughed at the sight of their Chief of Chiefs being drenched. The young men were in an excellent mood, proud of having been chosen to serve as bodyguards, excited to be traveling to the Dragon Isles in company with their Kai Priestess and their Chief of Chiefs.

Skylan looked back out to sea. He had brought along a guide, a man familiar with the territory, and Skylan could have left the navigation up to him. Skylan liked to know where he was, however, and he had the guide point out to him the various landmarks as they sailed along the coastline.

Everything had gone well thus far—so well that Skylan began to think Torval had relented and was once again smiling down on him with favor. True, the Torgun warriors had been furious when he had not chosen them to sail with him to the Dragon Isles, but Norgaard had taken Skylan's part, approving his son's decision to bring Heudjun warriors as a guard of honor. Tensions still ran high between the clans, and this would help ease them. The real reason Skylan had chosen not to take Torgun warriors was that he would have been forced to take Garn, and Skylan knew he could not be around his friend for any length of time without blurting out all his secrets.

He found it difficult enough to be around Garn only for the short time he was in Luda. Skylan made certain the two of them were never alone, and he'd left Luda as soon as the *Venjekar* could be stocked with supplies and ready to sail.

The only disappointment in his visit to his clan was that he didn't have a chance to talk privately with Aylaen. She was always with her sister, Treia. Whenever Skylan was with the sisters, he would hint more than once that Treia might want to take a walk. Treia would have happily complied, for she made her dislike of Skylan obvious. But whenever Treia started to leave, Aylaen would seize her sister's hand and detain her with some excuse. If it had not been too absurd, Skylan would have thought Aylaen was avoiding being alone with him, just as he was avoiding being alone with Garn.

Skylan asked his father about Raegar, using an excuse that he'd heard gossip among the Heudjun that once, long ago, his uncle Raegar had been betrothed to Draya.

Norgaard had some vague recollection that this was true, but he could not remember details. Skylan brought up the tale of the eagle killing the adder outside his dwelling on the day of his birth. Norgaard said that might have happened, but he had been distraught over the death of Skylan's mother and had paid little heed to anything else.

Treia acted as Bone Priestess when the Dragon Kahg took the *Venjekar* back to Vindraholm. She was silent on the journey, would not talk to him, not even about Aylaen. When he brought up the subject of Aylaen becoming a Bone Priestess, Treia cast him a scornful glance and walked away.

In Vindraholm, Draya and the Heudjun warriors came on board. Draya took over the private cabin belowdeck, which was where the Bone Priestess stayed during the voyage. The cabin was small and cramped, for most of the area below the deck was used for storing the loot seized during raids. Draya spread out fur blankets, making a comfortable sleeping area for herself and Skylan.

He had been cudgeling his brain for days, trying to think of how he was going to avoid having to lie with her, and thus far he had not been able to manufacture an adequate excuse, one that would satisfy her and the Heudjun warriors, who would expect the married couple to behave like a married couple.

Fortunately, the Sea Goddess Akaria came to Skylan's rescue. She and Svanses, Goddess of the Wind, were waging one of their endless battles. The wind blew strong and, in retaliation, Akaria caused the sea to rise to challenge her. The waves fought the wind, and the *Venjekar* swooped up and plunged down, swooped up and plunged down. Draya became so ill, she was forced to seek refuge below.

The war between the goddesses continued for days. Draya could do nothing except groan on her bed and puke into a bucket. Skylan promised Akaria a silver ring if she would keep the seas rough for the duration of the journey.

For him, the voyage was a pleasant one. Skylan had selected twenty young warriors to accompany him. He chose young men over veterans, such as Draya's friend, Sven. The voyage was going to be peaceful, he said, and this would give the young men good experience. In truth, Skylan did not want the older men, who would be more likely to oppose a raid on the druid settlement. Here was yet another lie.

Skylan was troubled by his lies: lies to Draya, lies to his father, lies to his clansmen, lies mounting on top of lies like corpses piled atop one another when a shield-wall crumbled. Torval was a god of honor. He despised liars. Once Skylan had the Vektan Torque, he could stop lying. He would give the torque to the god, and all would be forgiven. Skylan fixed his gaze on that bright horizon and took care not to look too closely at the stinking, murky water through which he had to wade in order to reach it.

They passed the landmark—One Tree Rock—that denoted the end of Vindrasi lands, and the *Venjekar* sailed out into the open seas. The Isle of Apensia did not lie on the route normally taken by the dragonships when they sailed to the Dragon Isles. It lay farther to the south. Once they were out to sea, Skylan told the steersman to head the ship that direction. Draya's illness gave him an excuse. He claimed he was trying to find calmer seas to ease her sickness.

The moon had been full last night and the night before. He had promised Raegar to meet at the time of the full moon. Skylan wandered the deck daily, eyes on the horizon, waiting tensely for the shout that meant the lookout had sighted land. He was eager to reach the place where he would rid himself of an unwanted wife and gain fabulous wealth in return, wealth he would use to fund the venture to the ogres' lands.

Three days had passed since they left behind One Tree Rock, and Draya appeared on deck. She looked exceedingly pale, thin and haggard, but she was no longer puking. She gave Skylan a wan smile and said in a low voice she was sorry he'd been forced to sleep on deck with the other warriors.

Skylan answered politely that he was very glad to see her in better health.

She said softly she hoped he would come to their bed this night.

He answered gravely he would not think of imposing himself upon her while she was still so weak.

Draya cast him a despairing glance. Tears shimmered in her eyes.

He realized that the young Heudjun warriors were watching this exchange between him and his wife. Had they overheard? He glanced about and didn't think so. He and Draya had kept their voices down, and the warriors had all politely moved out of earshot when she came on deck to speak to her husband. They could not help but see her turn away from him and put her hand to her eyes. Several were regarding them both with lowered brows, worried looks.

Damn it all, anyway! Skylan thought angrily, glaring at them. Haven't any of you ever seen a husband and wife quarrel before?

He was about to order the men to keep their eyeballs in their heads, when he remembered Raegar's warning: He must not arouse suspicion.

Lies, suspicions, guilt. Skylan's wyrd had once been a single thread of sunshine and blue sky and a freshening sea breeze. Now it was twisted strands of darkness and slime and stinking swamp water.

Skylan forged a smile for his lips and walked over to stand beside Draya. She looked so pale and wan, he could not help but feel sorry for her and more than a little guilty about his plan.

"Sit down, madam," he said. "You are newly risen from your sickbed. You must take care of yourself."

Draya looked at him, startled at his unusually respectful tone, and she gave him a pallid smile.

"Take your ease," he continued, assisting her to sit on one of the chests the men had brought on board. They not only stored belongings in the chests, they also used them as benches. "I will bring you something to eat and drink, food your weak stomach can tolerate."

He brought her bread soaked in ale, and he sat down beside her while she ate, talking of the Dragon Isles. He had not traveled there in some time. He asked her questions and tried to listen to her answers, but his mind kept wandering, as did his gaze—to the horizon.

We should already be at Apensia! Perhaps I miscalculated the route. Perhaps the lookout is asleep at his post. I will go check on him. No, that would look odd.

He made himself sit beside Draya, made himself attend to her. She was touchingly pleased by his attention and returned his smile with a loving smile of her own. He felt wretched and didn't know how much more of this play-acting he could tolerate, and he was thinking he would excuse himself to go take a piss when a voice cried out, "Land!"

Skylan leaped to his feet, as did everyone else on board ship. The warriors crowded the rail, peering out at the smudge on the horizon and speculating what place this might be. It was not the Dragon Isles, with their cloud-topped mountain peaks.

The *Venjekar* drew nearer, and soon they could see a rocky shoreline covered with trees, and here and there a few stone dwellings. The dwellings became more numerous, revealing a settlement, nestled in a cove.

Smoke from cook fires rose into the air and drifted out to sea. A number of boats bobbed in the calm waters of the cove. Fishing boats, by the looks of them. Skylan's spirits rose. He thought he recognized Raegar's boats among the others.

"Sail closer," Skylan ordered.

"No, don't!" Draya cried.

Skylan turned to glare at her in displeasure. On board the *Venjekar,* he was master. No one, not even the Kai Priestess, had the right to countermand his orders.

Draya realized she had broken an unwritten law, and she hastened to provide an explanation. "That is the Isle of Apensia, an isle ruled by druids. As we value our lives, we should not venture anywhere near there!"

Skylan gave a laugh. "I have heard about these druids. I hear they love peace so much that they do not carry weapons or even allow weapons to be forged on their island."

Skylan spread his legs to maintain his balance on the rocking deck. He put his hands on his hips and gazed out at the island. "I have also heard that their storehouses are stuffed with silver and gold and jewels."

The young warriors broke into excited talk, each eager to tell the stories he'd heard about druids. No one could lay claim to any facts. No Vindrasi had set foot on the Isle of Apensia for as long as anyone could remember. The Bone Priestesses had always forbidden it.

"Lord Skylan!" Draya called from where she sat clutching the bench with both hands. "I would speak with you."

Skylan pretended he didn't hear her.

"What if the Kai are wrong?" he asked several of the young men who stood near him. "What if year after year we have sailed past a fortune that is ours for the taking? I say we raid it and find out!"

"Husband! Please come to me," Draya called.

Skylan continued ignoring her. Some of the men were opposed to the notion of raiding the settlement, but the majority were in favor. They were young and thirsting for battle. Most had yet to win their first silver armbands. The stories they had heard about druids were firelight tales, insubstantial as smoke, and their longing for glory and wealth was very real.

Draya listened to the talk of raiding, and her face grew increasingly grave. Skylan wished she would give up and go below.

That didn't happen. Rising to her feet, Draya tottered unsteadily across the deck. The ship rolled, and she fetched up against Skylan, seizing hold of his arm to keep from falling.

He steadied her and said, "Well, madam, what do you want of me?"

Draya flushed at his cold tone. "I want you to turn this ship around! Think, lord! There is a reason druids do not forge weapons. They do not need them! They have weapons of their own, and they are formidable!"

"How do you know this, madam?" Skylan asked. "Have *you* visited this island? Has *any* Kai Priestess visited this island?" He shook off her clutching hand.

She staggered again as the ship rocked, and grabbed hold of the rail. "Not for many, many years," Draya admitted. "But that is because we were warned against it by Vindrash. A warning you should heed!"

Some of the warriors were now starting to look doubtful, casting uncertain glances at the shoreline. Skylan could order his men to land on Apensia, and they would have to obey him, but he knew that men who fought reluctantly did not put their hearts into their blades, as the saying went. Skylan glanced up at the dragon's carved head, and he thought he saw a flicker of red in the wooden eyes. That gave him an idea.

"If Vindrash does not want us to go to Apensia," said Skylan, "then I presume she would order the Dragon Kahg to refuse to take us."

Skylan was taking a risk, bringing the dragon into the dispute. Yet the risk was calculated. The Dragon Kahg was as greedy for jewels as any of the warriors on board. He had been sulking for months over the fact that Vindrasi raids had been fruitless. The eyes of the carved figurehead gazed upon the island. Perhaps the Dragon Kahg could see the glitter of rubies and sapphires and emeralds.

Or perhaps not. The *Venjekar* slowed its forward progress. The waves that had once broken over the bows now stirred beneath the hull in a creamy froth. Skylan's heart sank.

Vindrash will not allow it, he thought. The Dragon Kahg will refuse to sail to Apensia. Draya will insist that we go to the Dragon Isles, and I will be stuck with her for the rest of my life! Unless she poisons me first.

Their progress slowed even more. Skylan cast a bitter glance at his wife, expecting to see Draya smug and triumphant.

The wind whipped her straggling hair into her face. She was having trouble standing and was forced to cling to the rail with both hands. She did not look up at the dragon. She stared straight out toward the sea. Her face was pale, taut, strained.

The *Venjekar* had slowed, but was still maintaining forward progress. The lookout called out a warning, sandbars ahead, and Skylan sighed in relief. The Dragon Kahg had slowed the ship because the water was growing more shallow, not because he had been commanded by the goddess to sail away.

"It appears Vindrash favors our going, madam," said Skylan.

The young warriors were cheered by the dragon's response, and they hastened to remove their shields from the rack, put on their armor and helms, and pick up their weapons. They watched the shore approach and spoke excitedly of the valiant deeds they would do. Guided by the lookout, the dragon steered the ship around the sandbars and headed straight for the island.

People who lived along the shoreline had seen the dragonship by now. They raced over the sand, fleeing inland. Skylan stared intently at the boats belonging to Raegar and his partners. No one was around, no slaves guarding them. Skylan thought this odd, for he could see that the boats were loaded with trade goods.

Perhaps Raegar has no need for guards. Maybe these druids are trustworthy, not given to thievery, he said to himself with a shrug.

Skylan put on the chain mail and a shining new helm he'd had made while he was in Vindraholm. He buckled his sword belt around his waist. He had purchased a fine new fleece-lined sheath made for Blood Dancer. The sword garnered the universal admiration of all who saw it. Skylan never tired of showing it off. He had told the story of how Torval had given him the sword so often that he had almost come to believe it himself. He added a new short sword to his belt, then draped over his shoulders a fine new woolen cloak, blue as the sky in raiding season. Before he sailed to the ogres' lands, he would have the cloak embroidered with the image of an eagle killing an adder.

The *Venjekar* sailed into the cove. Skylan, standing on deck, went over the plan in his mind. He and his warriors would go ashore. Draya and the two warriors who would serve as her guards would remain on board the dragonship. Skylan would demand to be taken to the druids, the leaders of the settlement. Raegar had described them as a group of stoop-shouldered old men and women. Skylan would rattle his sword at them, point to his fierce, heavily armed warriors, and threaten to butcher the men, carry off the women, and enslave the children unless the druids paid him to leave them in peace.

The druids would want to negotiate. While this was happening, Raegar and his men, disguised as druids, wearing long, gray hooded robes, would board the dragonship. They would greet Draya as an honored guest and invite her to leave the ship, to take some refreshment.

Draya would probably be suspicious. People of a settlement about to be plundered rarely invited the enemy to dinner. If she refused, Raegar would tell her that the negotiations were going well and that her husband, Skylan, wanted to present her to the leaders. The use of Skylan's name would disarm her, and she would go ashore.

Skylan was worried that Draya might recognize Raegar. The two had been affianced, after all. Raegar had assured Skylan that he would keep his face concealed by the hood. And he reminded Skylan that when Draya had known him, he had been clean-shaven, as was the custom among Vindrasi warriors. She would never recognize him with a long flowing blond beard.

The *Venjekar* glided into the calm, shallow waters of the cove. Warriors leaped over the side to haul the dragonship up onto the beach. Skylan made ready to join them.

Draya stood on deck, her hands clasping and unclasping, her fingers twisting. She was pale, her gaze roving the empty shore or glancing up at the dragon. Skylan walked over to bid her farewell. Farewell forever. This would be the last time he saw her. He should have been elated. He was surprised to find that he felt tense, uneasy.

"I will send you word of how our negotiations proceed, madam," Skylan said, trying to make his voice sound natural—and failing. He coughed and continued. "With Torval's blessing, we will be on our way to the Dragon Isles by nightfall, our hold filled with jewels as an offering to the dragons."

Draya shook her head, made no reply.

Skylan tried again. "I know you disapprove, madam, but I am Chief of Chiefs, and this is my decision."

She gave him a bleak look and then lowered her eyes.

Skylan could think of nothing more to say, and he made ready to vault over the ship's side when he was stopped by the touch of Draya's hand on his. Her fingers were cold as those of a day-old corpse.

The unexpected chill made him flinch, and he turned to her and asked irritably, "Well, what is it?"

"I wronged you, Skylan," Draya said. "I see that now. I am sorry for that. Deeply sorry. I hope someday you can find it in your heart to forgive me."

She released his hand and moved to the prow, to the curved neck of the carven dragon's head. She took down the spiritbone from the nail on which it hung. Skylan thought at first she meant to summon the Dragon Kahg, and that would not fit into his plans. He was about to tell her angrily to put it back.

Draya lifted the spiritbone to her lips and kissed it, then hung the bone back in its place. She remained standing there, leaning her cheek against the dragon's neck, her hand resting on the spiritbone.

Her words made him uneasy. He looked at the shore and was assailed by doubts. What if she is right? What if our doom awaits us on that isle? Maybe I should leave. . . .

Stop it! Skylan told himself, realizing what he'd been thinking. Raegar is right. Draya is stealing my manhood! I will soon be a cider-swilling coward like Horg if I don't get rid of her.

Skylan jumped over the side and landed with a splash in water that came to his knees. He and the other warriors seized hold of the *Venjekar*'s hull and with triumphant yells, hauled the dragonship up onto the sandy beach.

The Vindrasi were at last doing what they had been born to do. With a bold chief to lead them, the Vindrasi were going to war.

# CHAPTER 8

Skylan and eighteen eager young Heudjun warriors came across a dirt trail that led from the shore through waist-high grass to a long wooden bridge. Built across a large stretch of freshwater marshland filled with murky brown water, the bridge was made of planks held together with wooden pegs. Cattails, taller than a man, rustled in the breeze. The marsh was thick with plant life, and Skylan could guess that the bottom was sticky, oozing mud.

Skylan approved the defenses, even as he saw his danger. If the druids sighted a foe approaching from the sea, they would set fire to the bridge, forcing their enemies to wade through this miasma of plants and water. Dressed in chain mail and lugging axes, swords, shields, and spears, an enemy would soon find himself in trouble—quite literally bogged down. Skylan could imagine the druids lighting their torches at this moment.

He ordered his men to run.

As they pounded over the wooden bridge, he kept waiting to see tongues of orange flame and the first tendrils of smoke. He saw only the plants, waving in the wind, and small black birds with red patches on their wings clinging to the reeds, guarding their nests with throaty warbles.

The warriors reached the end of the bridge in safety and found themselves in a thick forest. At first glance, Skylan couldn't see any signs of life, and he wondered if he'd followed a bridge to nowhere. Staring into the shadows, he saw that the dwellings had been built in such a manner that they were part of the forest. Made of logs, the dwellings huddled beneath the large trunks of ancient oak trees. The dwellings were small with shuttered windows and thatched roofs. Narrow dirt lanes wound mazelike among the tree trunks. Rays of sun slanted through the canopy of the leaves whose dappled shadows cooled the air.

Off in the distance, Skylan could see hills of lush green grass dotted with grazing sheep and cattle. Fields of tall grain lay golden in the sunlight. He contrasted this land of plenty with his own land of parched grass, starving cattle, withered crops—and his resolve hardened. He was glad he'd come.

"Where is everyone? Aren't they going to challenge us?" asked Tubbi. He was a young man of sixteen, on his first raid. Short and barrel-chested, Tubbi had become one of Skylan's favorites.

His question was a good one. Smoke from cook fires rose from the dwellings and drifted among the branches. Chickens and ducks roamed about, pecking at scattered grain. Dogs came out to sniff in friendly fashion at the strangers. But there were no people.

Skylan was baffled. He had not really believed Raegar's tales of a peace-loving people. He had expected armed men prepared to die to defend their homes. Instead, a mongrel dog thrust its nose into Skylan's crotch. He stood alongside his warriors, every man armed to the teeth, and no one to fight.

"I am Chief of Chiefs of the Vindrasi," he called out loudly. "If the men of Apensia are such cowards that they will not fight us, we will take what we want!"

He waited for a response, and when none came, he was about to order his men to ransack the houses, but then one of his warriors nudged him. A tall spare man in the gray robes of a druid walked with unhurried pace beneath the shadows of the trees. The man had a long beard, black streaked with white. His beard was plaited, as was his white hair. His skin was brown and heavily wrinkled and creased. His gray robes were plain and unadorned. His hazel eyes were mild. He did not appear afraid, or even particularly concerned, at the sight of Skylan's eighteen armed warriors.

"Greetings, Skylan Ivorson," said the man. "You are welcome to Apensia. It has been many years since our Vindrasi neighbors have honored us with a visit."

Skylan was startled. How did the man know his name? The only answer was that Raegar must have mentioned it, and why in the name of Hevis would Raegar do such a thing? He could feel the eyes of his warriors boring into his back. They were growing jittery. Draya's tales of druidic magicks came back to them. They would not have feared an army. This strange old man, who seemed to have stepped out of a twilight tale, unnerved them.

Skylan had to give them back their courage.

"We are not your neighbors," he said, his voice grating. "We are your enemies. Our children starve, while even your dogs are fat! We do not want to make war on you. Fill our ship with gold and silver and jewels, and we will leave you in peace."

The warriors behind him felt better. They growled their agreement and struck their blades on their shields or thumped the butts of their spears on the ground.

"I am sorry to hear the Vindrasi people are suffering," said the druid gently. "It is true that the land has been good to us. We will be glad to share our bounty with you. We can fill your ship with grain and cattle, though not, I fear, with precious metals or gems. Of these we have none."

The warriors jeered. Skylan laughed and said, "You are an old man, sir, and old men are prone to confusion. You have gold and silver and jewels. You have just forgotten that you have them. You will forgive me if I look for myself. You men"—he gestured—"go search those houses."

The druid said nothing. He made no move to stop them. He stood calmly watching, his hands folded in his long sleeves.

Tubbi led the warriors to several houses. They kicked in the doors and, weapons drawn, barged inside. Skylan heard sounds of breaking furniture. The men tore up beds. They tossed blankets and linens out the doors and flung clay pots and dishes out the windows. They emerged, shaking their heads.

"No silver or gold, lord," called Tubbi in disgust. "Nothing. Not so much as an iron stewpot!"

"You will find no metal of any kind on Apensia, lord. Precious or otherwise," said the druid. "We have no use for it."

Skylan had never heard anything so ridiculous. Raegar had said there was wealth in abundance. The druid was lying.

"They must have buried their gold and silver somewhere, lord," said Tubbi, coming up to him. "Or maybe it's hidden in a storehouse."

Skylan seemed to remember Raegar mentioning a storehouse. He was determined to find it.

"I think you lie," Skylan said harshly. "Tubbi, you and the men, set fire to the houses."

"No, wait!" cried the druid, his mild and gentle demeanor shaken. "We can discuss this, lord. Perhaps we can come to some arrangement."

"Perhaps we can," said Skylan, grinning. He winked at his men. "We are hungry. Give us food and drink. The best you have to offer."

"Of course, lord. You will be our honored guests," the druid said humbly.

"Tell them we want to see their women," said Tubbi in a low voice.

Skylan laughed. "And bring your young women out of hiding to serve us," he added. "We want to feast our eyes as well as our bellies."

The young men laughed, well pleased. They liked Skylan, who was proving himself a worthy Chief, and they crowded around him, vying for places of honor at his side.

Skylan was pleased with himself. There were riches to be had here. He did not expect any resistance. These druids were, as Raegar had assured him, a cowardly lot.

Speaking of Raegar, Skylan wondered if his cousin had abducted Draya yet and, if so, how long it would take him to smuggle her off the island. Skylan would wait for evening before he went back to the ship, he decided. When he discovered Draya missing, he would have to institute a search, and he did not want to take the chance of accidentally finding her.

Skylan made no complaint, therefore, when the druid said apologetically that the grove where the feast would be held was some distance away. The walk would be a long one.

The druid led Skylan and his men deep into the forest. The journey through the dark and gloom-ridden forest was not only long, it was also hot and tiresome. The air was damp, hard to breathe, the ground muddy and squishy underfoot. Tree branches creaked; leaves whispered. The path was narrow, forcing the warriors to walk single-file. Insects bit them, raising itchy bumps on their flesh. Their laughter and talk ceased. They could see things moving in the shadows. They were a long way from their dragonship.

Skylan was starting to grow uneasy, and he was about to tell the druid sharply that he should hand over the silver and gold now or find a hole in his belly.

The druid, seeming to read his thoughts, smiled at him. "The walk has been long, as I said, but it has ended now. The festive grove." He made a sweeping gesture.

The grove was the strangest Skylan had ever seen. At first he thought it was formed of a great many trees. Then he realized to his astonishment that it was only a single tree with an enormous trunk and long, branching limbs. The limbs were so long, extended so far out from the main trunk, that they needed smaller trunks to support them. The leaves were broad and green. It seemed to Skylan that he had entered a vast hall with living support beams holding a green, leafy roof. He stood and gawked at the astounding tree, and the young men with him did the same.

"The tree is called a strangler fig," said the druid. "The fruit is quite delicious."

"What magic is at work here?" Skylan demanded, frowning. "Such a tree is not natural."

He touched the amulet of Torval to keep himself safe.

The druid chuckled. "The tree is as natural as the oak or the walnut, though the strangler fig is not, I admit, native to this part of the world. Strangler figs grow only in those lands where summer is endless. Many hundreds of years ago, however, some of our brethren happened to be visiting those lands. They took a fancy to the strangler figs and brought back a sapling."

The druid sighed, then smiled. "We have to work very hard to maintain the warm climate to which the tree is accustomed, particularly in the winter. But we find it is worth it."

Skylan had noticed that the air in the grove was even hotter and more humid than back in the forest. Sweat rolled down his face and neck. His linen shirt stuck to his skin, and he regretted wearing the sky-blue woolen cape. He scoffed at the notion that the druids ruled the weather. All knew the gods commanded the wind and the sun, sent the rain or withheld it, shook the snow out of the clouds, and kept the temperature of a cave the same year-round.

The druid gestured to the inner portion of the grove, where people—the first Skylan had seen since landing, other than the druid—were setting up plank tables. "If you and your men will seat yourselves, lord . . ."

"I will not go anywhere near that fae tree," Skylan said, and behind him his young warriors were loud in agreement.

The druid raised his eyebrows. A smile played about his lips, but he swiftly hid it by stroking his long mustache. Bowing in acquiescence, he left to instruct the men to move the tables.

The warriors seated themselves. Young women came out from the shadows, bearing platters of roasted meat, bowls of stew, bread, large wheels of cheese, and pitchers of foaming ale. The bowls and plates and cups were carved out of wood, the knives made of deer horn. Skylan drank and ate and eyed the young women, especially one who had red hair and green eyes and reminded him of Aylaen.

The people of Apersia dressed quite plainly. Their clothes were simple, drab in color, yet well made. The people appeared healthy and content and not at all afraid of the fearsome warriors who had come to kill them and steal their wealth. Skylan began to wonder if this was a settlement of simpletons.

He looked hard at the women who waited on him. None of them wore jewelry. No silver bracelets or golden brooches, no jeweled hair combs. Some did wear rings, but they were carved of wood. These people had certainly gone to a lot of trouble to conceal their wealth, which meant it must be vast indeed!

"More ale!" Skylan demanded, motioning to the red-haired girl and holding out his wooden mug.

The ale was the best he'd ever tasted: dark and earthy. He did not drink to excess, thinking that since they were in a "hostile" land, he should remain sober. His young warriors felt no such compunction, however, and were refilling their mugs at regular intervals.

Their faces flushed red, they pounded their fists on the table and boasted and laughed. Skylan joined in the merriment, telling tales of his past triumphs. The young men gazed at him, their eyes warm with admiration and strong drink. Raising their mugs to him, they bawled out their undying devotion.

Tubbi called for yet more ale. As one of the young women started to pour, he jostled her arm, causing her to slosh the ale over his hand. Tubbi cursed in mock anger and, in "punishment," seized the woman around the waist, dragged her onto his lap, and began to nuzzle her neck. His hand pawed at her breasts.

One of the men who had helped set up the table started to go to the girl's aid. Skylan saw the druid give a barely perceivable shake of his head. The man watched a moment more, then turned and walked off.

Tubbi found this hilarious. "Come back! I'll fight you for her!" he shouted, fumbling for his weapon as he tried at the same time to hold on to the girl.

"Stop squirming!" he ordered her, giving her a kiss on the neck. "Be good to me, and I'll show you the love of a real man, not the cowards you grow around here! If you are lucky, I might even get you pregnant with a warrior son!"

Tubbi flung the young woman onto the table, and ignoring her pleas, he began to pull down his trousers. The warriors roared in approval. The other women were now trying to flee into the forest. The young men leaped to their feet and dragged them back.

"Your men are out of control," observed the druid mildly. "You should put a stop to this."

"My men are my men," Skylan returned sternly. "We are the masters here! We will take your women and anything else we want unless you meet our demands."

He slammed down his mug and rose to face the druid. "What will you give me to leave you and your people in peace?"

"Kill him, Skylan! It's a trap!"

Startled, Skylan turned to see who had yelled. He stared, stupefied. His cousin's face was half covered with blood, but Skylan knew Raegar by his blond beard and hair. He was tied to one of the smaller trunks of the strange tree. Green vines wound about his body.

"It's a trap!" Raegar shouted. He flung himself against the vines. "Kill the old man!"

Raegar's shout jolted Skylan into action. He drew his sword and fell back.

"Form the shield-wall!" he roared.

He turned to rally his men and found he had no men.

"I warned you," the druid said, sighing.

Their armor was there, leather and chain mail, lying on the grass. Their helms and swords and axes, shields and spears were there. Their boots and belts and tunics were there. His warriors had vanished.

"What have you done with my men?" Skylan shouted hoarsely.

The druid shook his head. "I have done nothing," he said sadly. "It is the forest. It believed they were a threat to me and my people."

He pointed. Near each pile of armor and clothing crouched a rabbit, small body trembling, nose twitching, eyes round with terror.

"Your men have been changed into hares. I'm sorry," said the druid, and he truly sounded upset. "I tried to warn you."

Skylan staggered and nearly fell. He stared at the eighteen rabbits, and his mind revolted. "I don't believe it. This is some sort of trick!"

The druid shook his head. The rabbits twitched and stared at him. Skylan searched the shadows. He yelled and shouted, calling each man by name. No one answered. There was no sign of his warriors. The rabbits hopped aimlessly about, looking miserable. Skylan felt a shiver crawl up his spine.

"Bring them back," he ordered, his voice shaking. "Bring them back—or by Torval, I will rip you from gut to groin!"

He started to swing his sword, only to feel the weapon plucked out of his hand. Skylan looked up. His sword hung from the branch of the tree. Blood Dancer dangled above his head, just out of reach.

He grabbed hold of the hilt of his short sword, only to feel the hilt grab back. The sword was gone. A green-and-black snake coiled around his hand. Skylan let out a terrified cry and shook his hand until the snake fell to the ground.

"You asked what I would give you to depart in peace, Skylan Ivorson," said the druid with a gentle smile. "My answer is this: I will give you your life."

# CHAPTER 9

Draya stood with her cheek resting against the neck of the carved figurehead of the dragon, her hand resting on the spiritbone. She seemed to feel the dragon quiver. Looking up, she saw the red eyes fixed, staring straight ahead.

"Priestess," said one of the two men Skylan had left behind to guard her and the dragonship, "someone is coming."

Draya looked out to the shore to see four druids in gray robes walking over the sand.

"Should we kill them, Priestess?" asked one of the young men eagerly, lifting his spear.

"No," said Draya quietly. "They mean me no harm."

The druids waded out into the water. They stood beneath the dragonship. Draya gazed down on them, her hand on the spiritbone.

The four druids bowed low.

"We come in the name of Vindrash," said one. "We ask you to accompany us."

Draya clung to the dragon's neck, her courage failing her. And then she heard another voice, one that had not spoken to her in many long days. Draya listened to the blessed voice, and her eyes filled with tears. She gave the dragon's neck a caress and walked to the ship's side.

"Lower the gangplank," she said.

"You shouldn't go with these druids, Priestess," said one of the warriors sternly. "The Chief said you were to remain on the ship!"

Draya managed a smile. "I do not want to offend them. I will go with them. The Chief . . ." She hesitated, then, giving a little sigh, she said, "He will understand."

The warriors did as she commanded and lowered the gangplank. Draya descended. The druids received her with every mark of honor and respect. One gave her his hand. She clasped it and, with firm step, walked alongside him through the water and onto the beach.

The warriors watched Draya and her gray-robed escort vanish among the trees. The two conferred quickly.

"The Chief of Chiefs must know about this," said one, and the other agreed.

They leaped over the side and went running across the beach toward the footbridge. They never reached Skylan. The forest dealt with them as it had dealt with the others.

Draya paid no heed to her surroundings. Her vision had turned inward; she did not see the physical path she walked, did not feel it beneath her feet. Several times her escorts were forced to steady her stumbling steps or guide her around a fallen branch or prevent her from wandering into a bog.

Her body weakened by sickness, she left it behind. Her restless, fomenting mind was calm, quiet, becoming like a pool of still, clear water in which she could see her own reflection. What she saw horrified her. She made herself confront the wretched, tortured being she had become. She looked steadfastly into the dark and sorrow-filled eyes. She listened to the silent, desperate wail of despair.

She stopped walking only when the druid told her she had arrived.

"Your journey has been a long and unhappy one," the druid said in soft compassion. "We hope you find rest."

The druids departed, leaving her alone.

For long moments she remained standing where they'd left her, coming to herself only when prodded by her body. She had to either sit down or fall down. She looked about and saw where she was. She gazed in wonder and awe.

Loving care had transformed a small forest glade into a living shrine. Bay laurel trees, each standing taller than a man, filled the air with fragrance. The smooth ground was covered with green moss soft to the touch as the finest lamb's-wool blanket. A fallen log covered with the same moss lay at the foot of an ancient oak tree and appeared to be a kind of throne. Violets bloomed amid the moss. White lilies and purple irises flanked the throne; red poppies flamed. The Sun Goddess filled the glade with light.

The holiness, the sanctity of this blessed place soothed Draya's spirit. She sank to her knees in the soft moss before the throne and closed her eyes and whispered brokenly, "Vindrash, forgive your wretched servant."

"My daughter," said a voice, "I have waited long to hear those words."

Draya lifted her head. The Dragon Goddess shimmered into being before her. Clawed feet dug into the moss. Translucent wings were folded against her body. The long graceful tail trailed sinuously among the irises and the lilies. The gilded mane quivered and stirred. Scales the colors of ruby and sapphire, emerald and diamond sparkled in the sunshine, half-blinding in their radiance. The dragon's head, balanced gracefully upon the long curving neck, was massive yet delicately formed. The eyes were large, and though they could flare fiery red orange with righteous anger, they were now soft pale yellow, incandescent with understanding and compassion.

Draya had served the goddess all her life, and she had never seen her in her awful majesty and splendor. She realized that few mortals saw Vindrash like this. Draya was being honored, and that made her feel even worse.

"I lost my faith in you, Vindrash," said Draya. Her confession poured forth in a cleansing wave. "I did not trust you to know what was good for our people. I did not trust Torval to judge Horg in the Vutmana. I poisoned Horg and then hid my crime by making it appear as if Skylan had slain him."

Draya clenched her fists in her lap. "And I fear, Vindrash, that I did not kill Horg out of care for our people. I killed him because I hated and loathed him."

The dragon's nostrils flared slightly. The jaws barely moved, the voice came as breath gliding through the sharp curved front fangs. The slit tongue flickered.

"Do not judge yourself too harshly, Daughter," Vindrash said morosely. "By judging yourself, you also judge us. And we are all found lacking."

"I would never judge you, Blessed One!" said Draya, shocked.

"Yet you might be right to do so," said Vindrash.

The dragon fell into a brooding silence. Her wings spread and fanned the air, stirring the perfume of the bay leaves and the flowers. The breeze cooled Draya's skin and dried the tears she did not know she had cried until she felt them on her cheeks. She felt calm, at peace.

I could sleep, she thought. Sleep for a long time. Sleep and forget . . .

"You vowed, Daughter, that you would do anything for me," said Vindrash at last.

"I did make that vow, Blessed Goddess," Draya said. "And I make that vow again."

"Would you sacrifice your life?"

"I would, Vindrash," Draya said. She hesitated a moment, then, lowering her head, she asked in a grave voice, "Is death to be my punishment, then?"

"There is no talk of punishment, Daughter. If we punish you, we must also punish ourselves. And we are far too wise and puissant for that!" Vindrash added with bitter irony.

The dragon's tail switched moodily, back and forth.

A druidess entered the grove. She held in her hands a wooden bowl, and she stood waiting in respectful silence for the goddess to acknowledge her presence.

Vindrash gazed into Draya's eyes, delving deep. "I need a place to hide," said the goddess. "A body. Your body."

Draya looked at the druidess's bowl, and her mouth went dry. Her heart constricted, her hands trembled, her stomach clenched. Her terror was reflexive—her body's desperate need to survive. Her soul was strong and unafraid.

"The sacrifice must be made willingly," said Vindrash.

"I am willing," Draya replied.

The druidess brought forth the bowl. Draya's hands as they grasped hold of the bowl were steady and did not tremble.

"I ask one favor, Blessed Vindrash," Draya said. "Skylan is young and foolish. He has much to learn. But he is brave, with a warrior's spirit and a noble heart. He will make a good leader. Be merciful to him. Our people need him."

"We fight for our very survival," Vindrash returned sternly. "We do not have the luxury of mercy. Now that he is Chief of Chiefs, Skylan Ivorson must prove himself to be worthy of our trust or he will be swept aside to make room for another."

Draya gazed into the clear liquid. She saw reflected back to her a young girl, newly made Kai Priestess, facing the unknown, her eyes alight with joy and hope and faith.

"Will you answer one question for me?" Draya asked.

"If I can, Daughter," said Vindrash.

"Did Torval choose Skylan?"

Vindrash was silent for long moments. Then she said quietly, "It doesn't matter, Daughter. The wheel has turned. The thread is spun."

"Thank you, Vindrash," said Draya. "For this and all your blessings."

She brought the bowl to her lips and drank long and deep.

# CHAPTER 10

Skylan gazed at his sword, wrenched from his hand by the branch of a tree. He looked down at his short sword, now a snake slithering off beneath the tree roots. He saw eighteen rabbits hopping about in a confused and desultory manner, sniffing pitifully at their weapons and armor. His mind overwhelmed with horror, Skylan surrendered without a fight.

The druids tied him to the same tree trunk as Raegar. Vines sprang from the ground and wound around Skylan's ankles and legs, twined over his chest and across his arms. He managed, by twisting his body, to keep his men in sight.

They had been his care, his responsibility. He thought of their families, of their fathers and mothers, of young mothers and children. He thought of them dying ignominiously, in the claws of a hawk or the teeth of a fox. Their souls would not be admitted into Torval's Hall. The god would roar with laughter at the sight: rabbits hopping on the threshold.

Skylan had brought them to this. He was their commander.

"Forgive me, Father of Trees," Skylan said humbly to the druid as the vines tightened around him. "I should not have come to Apensia, and if you will free my men from whatever dread enchantment you have cast upon them, we will leave and never return! I swear by Torval!"

"We offered to share all we have with you, Skylan Ivorson. You spurned our offer and returned it with violence." The druid sighed deeply. "Steel and blood rule the world. We cannot change that. But we can make certain war does not come to Apensia."

"You pagans will regret your defiance," Raegar snarled, clenching his fists, a gesture that lost much of its effect due to the fact that his hands were bound to his thighs by vines. "I will see to that!"

"We would regret far more losing our way of life," the druid replied.

Folding his hands in the capacious sleeves of his gray robes, he walked away.

"What do you mean to do to us?" Skylan shouted after him.

The druid did not respond. He kept walking and was soon lost among the trunks of the tree known as the strangler fig.

Skylan understood how it came by its name. He strained against his bonds, bunching his arm and shoulder muscles in an effort to break the vines. Tough and sinewy, the vines grew tighter the more he struggled. When they drove the links of his chain mail shirt painfully into his flesh and started to constrict his breathing, Skylan sagged in defeat. He could only watch in heart-wrenching agony as one by one, the rabbits took fright and scampered off into the shelter of the woods.

"Where are your men?" he asked. "Are they close by?"

Raegar glowered and shook his head. "Do *you* have any more men?"

"Only the two I left to guard Draya— *Draya!*" Skylan gasped in excitement. He wriggled as close to his cousin as possible and said in a loud whisper, "What about Draya? Did you—?"

"No," returned Raegar. "I never had the chance."

"But that is good! When I do not return, she will come looking for me," said Skylan. "She will find that we have been taken prisoner, and she will summon the dragon and he will lay waste to this— Why do you shake your head?"

"Because I have no doubt that Draya is a prisoner, just as we are," Raegar remarked gloomily.

"How do you know?" Skylan demanded.

"I will tell you. We arrived three days ago, presenting ourselves as peaceful traders. We entered the settlement to offer our wares in trade. The pagans would not let us. They stated that they did not approve of slavery and they would trade with us only after we had freed our slaves. That was nonsense, of course, and we said so, and returned to our camp. The next morning we woke to find our slaves gone. They had been set free during the night."

"You saw nothing, heard nothing?" Skylan asked, amazed.

"Not a sound," Raegar growled. "My slave woman, who was sleeping right next to me, vanished from my bed! As for the men, we found their shackles and leg irons locked to the post, but they were gone. I assumed the pagans had helped the slaves escape. I demanded that they either return my slaves or give me what they were worth. The pagans said neither yea nor nay. I made myself clear about what would happen to them if they defied me.

"That was yesterday afternoon. This morning," Raegar continued, his face darkening, "I woke to find myself alone. My partners had vanished in the night, just like the slaves. Again, I heard nothing."

Skylan caught sight of a rabbit hopping about among the trees, and he shuddered.

"When I saw your dragonship sailing toward the island, I was going to warn you to sail away from this accursed place as fast as possible. I was starting to shout when the next thing I knew, I woke with a pounding head and blood on my face, tied to this tree. So, you see, you can't count on Draya saving us."

Skylan mulled this over. "What do you think the druids mean to do to us? They left us alive, after all."

"Nothing good," Raegar muttered.

"Perhaps they're going to hold us for ransom."

"The pagans don't hold people for ransom. They put no store in gold or silver or jewels—"

"You told me they had storehouses filled with jewels," Skylan said, frowning. He stopped talking to stare at Raegar, who was wriggling and squirming about in his bonds. "What are you doing?"

"I have a knife in my boot," said Raegar. "If I can loosen these vines, I think I can reach it. Keep watch. Let me know if anyone's coming."

Skylan fixed his gaze on the shadows. He heard Raegar grunting and muttering, and he glanced over his shoulder to see that Raegar had managed to wriggle his body down the trunk. He was reaching for his boot, wiggling his fingers.

"I can't see the knife!" Raegar gasped. "How close am I?"

The bone hilt protruded from the top of the boot. The knife was small, of the sort used to cut fishing line.

"The breadth of three fingers," Skylan reported. He caught a movement out of the corner of his eye. "Hold still! Someone's out there!"

Raegar froze.

Skylan stared hard into the shadows. "I guess it was nothing. It's not there now."

Raegar started squirming again. Sweat rolled down his face. His back scraped against the tree trunk.

"You've almost got it," Skylan said excitedly.

With a desperate effort, Raegar lunged and managed to touch the knife with his fingertips. Scrunching down a little more, he took hold of the tip with two fingers and his thumb.

"Don't drop it!" Skylan breathed.

"Shut up!" Raegar hissed. "Keep watch!"

Skylan looked back into the shadows. This time, there was no doubt. "Someone's coming. That old graybeard!"

"Got it!" Raegar gasped. He palmed the knife and tried hurriedly to wriggle his body back into place.

"What are you going to do to us, Graybeard?" Skylan cried, hoping to distract the druid's attention away from Raegar.

The druid took his time, approaching them at a leisurely pace. He regarded them mildly. "This night, we will make an offering to appease the spirits who have been angered by your presence," he said. "You will join us."

"Not me!" Skylan cried, lunging against his bonds. "Set me free! I'll fight you and your spirits—"

The druid smiled slightly. "There will be no fighting. As I was about to say, you both will be present to offer your apologies to the spirits for bringing violence to our land."

"And then what?" Raegar sneered. "You'll slit our throats?"

"You will be released," said the druid.

"And what about my men? What about my wife, Draya, the woman who was aboard the dragonship?" Skylan demanded. "What have you done with her?"

"And what about my men and my slaves?" Raegar added angrily. "What have you done with them?"

"*I* did nothing to anyone. You angered the blessed spirits who guard us. They perceived you as a danger, and they acted to put an end to the threat. I cannot undo what they have done. I will return for you when the moon rises from the sea."

After the druid had departed, Skylan glanced uneasily about the woods. "The druid said we angered the spirits. Is he saying that these spirits cast the enchantment on my men?"

"Spirits my ass!" Raegar snorted. "He's lying. It's that pagan sorcerer who worked foul magicks on your men, and he's going to do it to us, as well."

"I'll fight them all with my bare hands first," Skylan said grimly.

"If I can free myself, you will have a better weapon than your hands," Raegar stated, and he began to saw at the vines with his knife.

The going was slow. The vines were sinewy, and there were a great many of them, and Raegar was further hampered by his bonds. He persevered, however, cutting his way through the tangle.

Skylan watched the rays of the Sun Goddess dwindle among the trees. "Moonrise will be early tonight," he said. "I've been thinking. Once we are free, how will we find our way out of this forest? Trails and paths lead everywhere."

"We'll wait until one of the pagans comes to fetch us, and then we'll jump him, take him hostage, and threaten to slit his throat if he doesn't show us the way," Raegar replied.

"What if the druid casts one of his enchantments on us?" Skylan asked.

He could face with equanimity the thought of a sword thrust through the gut in battle. The idea of being spellbound again, as the ogre shaman had done to him, sent a sliver of fear lancing through him.

"If you tie a sorcerer's hands and gag him, he can't cast a spell," said Raegar.

He spoke with confidence, as though he knew what he was talking about, but Skylan had doubts. He couldn't recall the druid doing or saying anything, and yet his men were now hopping through the woods nibbling dandelions. Still, Raegar's plan sounded as good as any. They didn't have much choice.

"Keep watch," Raegar ordered, and Skylan stared intently into the shadows that grew deeper with every passing moment.

By the time night had fallen, Raegar had managed to cut loose his own arms and legs and Skylan's arms, as well. An especially strong, tough vine clung stubbornly to Skylan's ankles.

"These damn vines have dulled the blade," Raegar complained.

"Then fetch my sword," Skylan urged. "It is hanging there in that tree. You are tall enough—you can reach it."

"Good thought!" said Raegar. He left off sawing at the vines. Wiping sweat from his brow, he walked over and stood beneath the blade that dangled from the tree limb.

"Mind you come back for me," Skylan said. "Don't take my sword and run off."

Raegar eyed Skylan darkly. "Don't you trust me, Cousin?"

"I was kidding," said Skylan.

Raegar grunted. "I'm not in the mood for jests."

Skylan wondered suddenly if he did trust Raegar. His cousin had claimed to have been on Apensia; he'd claimed the druids possessed hoards of gold and silver and jewels. Skylan had the feeling Raegar had never been on Apensia before and that he'd made up the tale of wealth, all to convince Skylan to come here. Skylan didn't have any idea why Raegar would lie, but the fact was, no, he didn't trust his cousin.

"Make haste!" Skylan called, tugging ineffectually at the vine that bound his ankles. "I think I see the moon shining through those trees."

Raegar looked over his shoulder. "That's not the moon. It's torchlight! Men, coming this way."

"Get back!" Skylan urged. Grabbing hold of the severed vines, he strung them across his chest. "Make it look as though you're tied up."

Raegar was already flattening himself against the tree trunk, draping the vines across his arms and shoulders.

"The druid will see the vines are cut," said Skylan.

"By the time he does, it will be too late. I'll have my knife at his throat. I'll make the bastard loosen your bonds," said Raegar in a low voice. "Once you're free, run for the tree, grab your sword, and we'll head out."

"What about Draya?" Skylan asked. "I need to find her."

"What do you care what happens to your wife?" Raegar said. "I thought you wanted to be rid of her."

"I did. It's just . . ." Skylan hesitated. "I forced her to come here. She didn't want to. She warned me against the druids."

"Feeling guilty?" Raegar grunted.

"No," Skylan said. "I should have listened to her, that's all."

"Since you're so concerned about her, we'll make the druid tell us where she is," said Raegar. "If she's alive, we'll find her. Do you want her back? Or do you want me to take her?"

Skylan thought this over. True, Draya had warned him against coming, and he should have paid heed to her warning. He remembered her odd words to him, how she had wronged him. She had—there was no doubt of that. But he'd heard whispered talk among the young Heudjun about how Horg had beaten her, abused her. Women were weak; they could not challenge a man who had wronged them to battle. Perhaps Draya had fought Horg the only way she knew how.

"She should return to her people," Skylan said at last.

"You're a fool," said Raegar. "Still, I don't suppose it matters. She's probably dead now anyway."

Torches flickered in the darkness, hundreds of them, winding through the far-flung limbs of the strangler fig, heading in their direction. The people sang as they came. The song was beautiful, sad, haunting. A song of praise, a song of mourning—or so Skylan guessed. He could not understand the words.

Several druids appeared, coming from different directions, meeting beneath the tree. The druids paid no attention to their captives. They met for a brief discussion, then began to make preparations to do whatever it was they did to appease the spirits. Skylan watched, flexing his muscles, stiff from disuse.

"Do you know what they are doing?" he asked softly.

"I have no idea what the pagans are up to," said Raegar in disgust.

Several men bore between them a large stake. Under the druid's directions, they carried the stake to a place where the moonlight slanted down between the leafy branches, forming a moon glade. Here they upended the stake, which was taller than Raegar, and dropped it into a hole in the ground. Once the stake was settled in position, the druid entered the moon glade. He studied the stake, pushed and shoved on it to make certain it was stable.

"We are ready for the sacrifice," the druid said.

He turned to look at Skylan and Raegar and gave a command to the men. "Fetch the Vindrasi."

# CHAPTER 11

The wooden stake gleamed silver in the moonlight. The men carried heavy ropes to the site and laid them in coils at the base of the stake. The druid stood with his hands folded, patiently waiting. Two men headed for Skylan and Raegar.

"Cut these damn vines!" Skylan hissed, trying to kick loose the vine that wrapped around his boots.

"Shut up!" Raegar hissed back. "You'll make the bastards suspicious."

"Then give me the knife!" Skylan said. "I will fight them! I won't die like a cow!"

"Be patient," Raegar returned. "Stick to the plan. When the men start to untie us, I'll grab one of them and hold my knife at his throat. The other will do what I tell him."

Skylan didn't like having to trust Raegar or anyone to save his life. He continued to struggle to free himself, with the result that the vines slipped down from around his arms. The two men had drawn near enough to see clearly in the moonlight. Their eyes widened; they slowed their pace. One of them started to turn to shout a warning.

Raegar gave a leap and flung himself on the man. Grabbing him by the shoulders, he put the knife's blade to his throat.

"Free my friend," Raegar ordered the other man savagely. "Or I swear by Torval, I will slit *your* friend's throat from ear to ear!"

The man did not move. He seemed paralyzed by fear.

"You! Pagan!" Raegar shouted to the druid. "Tell him to obey me or this bastard will be tonight's sacrifice!"

"Do as he says," the druid ordered.

The man drew a bone knife from his belt and, bending down, sliced through the vines that held Skylan.

"Grab your sword!" Raegar told him, still holding on to his hostage. He'd nicked the man's flesh with his knife. A trickle of blood ran down the neck. The man's eyes were wide with fright.

Hundreds of people, all bearing torches, had assembled to witness the sacrifice. They stood watching in silence, making no outcry, as Skylan dashed over to the tree that held his sword. The orange light of the fire and the silver light of the moon gilded the sword's blade, which hung suspended from the tree limb, hilt facing downward.

Skylan gazed up at his sword. At first he thought the druid had somehow caused it to magically fly up into the tree. Now, he was not so certain. He had the uneasy feeling the tree itself had seized his sword. Skylan eyed the tree warily.

"Hurry up!" Raegar shouted.

The sword dangled just out of reach. Skylan jumped, trying desperately to grab it. His fingers brushed the hilt, but he couldn't catch hold of it, and he fell back down. The sword swung back and forth, as though the tree were taunting him.

Skylan was about to leap again when he heard a frantic cry. "Skylan! Help me! Skylan! Please!"

He turned to see Draya, struggling in the grip of her captors, being tied to the stake.

He was not to be the sacrifice.

She was.

"Skylan!" Draya pleaded. "They mean to murder me! Help me!"

Skylan stared, horrified. The men shoved Draya against the stake and began to tie the ropes around her body, binding her fast.

"Let her go!" Skylan bellowed. He pointed at Raegar's captive. "Or we will slay this man!"

"You must do what you have to do," said the druid sadly. "As do we."

The druid gestured. A man with white hair, clothed all in white, emerged from the crowd. He held in one hand a large wooden hammer and in the other a branch cut to a sharp point.

Raegar flung the hostage into his fellow, knocking both men to the ground, then dashed toward Skylan. "Run for it, fool!" he shouted. "Run!"

Skylan was tempted. He longed to run and never look back. He heard Draya's terrified cries. He saw rabbits watching from the shadows. He heard a raven jeering at him.

Draya was his wife. He had vowed to Torval to protect her.

"I have broken so many vows," Skylan muttered. "At least I will not break this one."

He looked up at the sword. "Torval, grant me the strength to reach it!" He crouched and then hurled himself into the air, his arm extended as far as it would reach. He struck the hilt with his hand, knocking the sword loose. The blade twisted in the air as it fell, flashing orange and silver, and landed on the grass at Skylan's feet. He picked it up.

"Are you coming?" Raegar cried from the shadows.

"After I have rescued Draya," said Skylan.

"Then I'll see you in the Hall of Heroes," Raegar cried. He vanished among the trees.

The man in white was handing the wooden spike to the druid, who placed it against Draya's midriff. The man in white lifted the hammer.

Skylan roared a challenge, brandishing his sword, and broke into a run. Again he shouted for them to stop, and he told them what he would do to them if they harmed her, how he would cut off their heads and slice open their guts and feast on their livers. He raved and yelled as he ran.

No one even looked at him. They were all watching the sacrifice.

The man in white swung the mallet back and forth, testing his aim, preparing to hit the spike a blow that would drive it through Draya's body. Skylan, howling like one of Freilis's daemons, leaped at the man, who was rearing back, prepared to make the killing strike.

One of the trunks from the strangler fig suddenly shifted, moved to block Skylan's way. He dodged around it, only to find himself blocked by another. The strangler fig tree vented its rage on him. The trunks danced around him, snaking down from the limbs of the tree, plunging into the ground, surrounding him. Skylan swore in fury and slashed at a slender trunk with his sword. The trunk recoiled like a whip and lashed him across the face.

He staggered, half-stunned, tasting blood. The hammer, illuminated in the moonlight, was swinging slowly, slowly through the air. Just two steps and he could stop it.

The tree flung down another trunk, right in front of him. Skylan struck the tree with his sword, and the trunk struck him back, slamming into his head. Pain burst in Skylan's skull. He stumbled, almost fell. Force of will and Draya's pleas for him to save her kept him on his feet. He tried to go around the trunk, and it bashed him across the throat.

Skylan went down. Landing heavily on his back, he struck his head on a rock. He was slipping into a pain-filled darkness when a scream, a terrible scream, a scream he knew he would hear until merciful death stopped his ears, roused him. He raised his throbbing head to see the hammer drive the stake deep into Draya's body. Blood blossomed, a horrible flower, drenching her robes. Draya moaned and writhed in agony.

Skylan tried to stand. Pain cleaved his skull. Lights burst behind his eyes. The tree bashed him and he fell forward, landing on his stomach. He had to reach her, his wife. Cursing in pain and in rage, he crawled on his knees. His hands slipped on the blood-soaked ground beneath the stake. He looked up at her. Her face was white with the death that was coming, and it contorted in agony.

"Forgive me, Draya!" he begged. "I never meant for this to happen!"

She gave a shuddering gasp, and he hoped she was going to speak words of forgiveness that would free him from the guilt of her death.

She opened her mouth, but no words came out. Black blood, warm from her body, spewed from her mouth and splashed into Skylan's upturned face.

Horror overcame him, and choking on the blood of his murdered wife, Skylan collapsed.

# CHAPTER 12

From his vantage point in the woods, the boy had witnessed everything. In the morning there had been the landing of the wondrous dragonship. Then the riotous departure of the band of warriors, and after that, the frightening arrival of the druids. (The boy had been afraid his teachers had come looking for him. He'd been vastly relieved to see the druids had instead come for the woman.)

The druids had gone off without taking any notice of him, which was not surprising. The boy was adept at blending in with his surroundings.

He remained in the woods all that day, unable to take his gaze off the beautiful ship, which was now empty, resting on the sandy bottom, with waves rolling in around it. The boy longed to move closer to the ship, but he was afraid the druids might come back, and so he remained in hiding, trying to work up his courage.

The boy was eleven years old, and he was odd-looking, with his yellow lupine eyes and shaggy, unkempt, gray-brown hair. He was thin and wiry, and he wore the green robes of an ovate—one who studies to become a druidic priest.

The sun sank. Night came. And still the boy crouched in the woods. He'd made a couple of forays in the direction of the ship, but he'd always taken fright and returned to his hiding place.

"They're not coming back, Wulfe," she said.

"How do you know?" he asked.

"My sisters told me."

A graceful young woman, naked except for a smattering of leaves that twined around her lithe body, slipped out of the tree under which Wulfe was hiding. "You can hear the limbs creak with their news."

Wulfe nodded. He was familiar with the way dryads communicated. Each dryad lived within the tree she guarded and could not leave it. Intensely curious—particularly in regard to the affairs of the Ugly Ones—each dryad avidly watched everything happening around her and gleefully communicated it to her sisters.

"What do they say?" Wulfe asked.

The dryad happily related the news. "My sisters of the sacred grove tell that the priestess drank poison and fell down dead and then the Dragon

Goddess entered her body. And my sisters of the strangler fig tree turned bad men into rabbits."

The dryad giggled at this, and so did Wulfe.

"I wish I had seen that," he said.

"So do I," said the dryad. "But you and me—we have seen the great dragonship. Go ahead, Wulfe! You can sneak aboard it while everyone's gone."

Wulfe looked longingly at the ship. "I will get into trouble with the elders. . . ."

"Not if they don't find out," said the dryad. She had bright green eyes and a pert, sly face with a pointed chin, an upturned nose, and wild russet curls that fell into her eyes. "You don't have to stay long. Just go on board, look around, and then come back to tell me what it is like. Please! My sisters will be wild with envy!"

"I don't know. . . ." Wulfe continued to hesitate.

"The elders won't be back until dawn," urged the dryad. Her voice was high-pitched and piping, but she could make it soft and wheedling when she wanted. "They are performing some sort of ceremony. You have time."

Wulfe knew perfectly well he should not trust the dryad. She would do or say anything to satisfy her curiosity. But he had never seen anything so wonderful as this dragonship, and so he let the dryad's argument persuade him. He crept out of hiding and then halted, not because he was afraid, but to wrestle with his inner daemons, a battle he'd been fighting since the druids had found the four-year-old child running wild in the woods and taken him to live among them.

Wulfe's inner daemons were continually making the boy do things that landed him in trouble. His battles against them were hard-fought, especially when the daemons urged the boy to do things he didn't want to do.

This wasn't so bad. His daemons were urging him to board the dragonship even though he knew he should not. The druids would be angry with him. Well, not angry. The druids were never angry. But they would be disappointed. The druid elder who had raised the boy would look at him sadly and shake his head in sorrow. And that was worse than anger, for Wulfe truly loved the druid, who had been a father to him for seven years now.

The boy was always striving to please the elder, to do things that brought a look of pride and pleasure to the aged face instead of the look of sorrow. Wulfe tried to learn to read, though that was proving impossible. The words seemed to crawl around like bugs and made no sense. He tried to sit still with the other ovates in their classroom among the trees, but unlike the other ovates, who could hear only the voice of the teacher, the boy could hear nymphs dancing in the woods, calling to him to come join them, or the giggling gossip of the dryads, or the lewd jokes of a satyr. Small wonder he couldn't pay attention.

The worst were the nights, when the daemons sometimes made the boy do terrible things. Horrible things. Things he didn't like to think about, and so he didn't. Ever.

The druids thought they understood the boy's struggles. They had once been confident they could teach him to find the strength to turn a deaf ear to the songs of the nymphs and the whispers of the daemons. The druids still hoped he would outgrow it, for they took an optimistic view of life. But Wulfe was eleven now, and their hopes were growing a little ragged.

In the end, the daemons won as they almost always did. Wulfe bolted out of the woods. Running across the narrow strip of sand, he came to a halt before the dragonship. He gazed up in awe at the carved figurehead, which was not, in his eyes, a thing made of wood. He saw scales glittering in the moonlight and a gilded mane and fiery red eyes.

"Please, Mighty Dragon, may I come aboard your ship?" Wulfe asked politely.

He had been taught that when speaking to great personages, such as dragons, it was important to be polite.

The Dragon Kahg stared down at the boy in astonishment. The dragon didn't know how to respond, for such a thing had never happened in all the years of his existence. The boy had done what no mortal could do. He could apparently see the dragon's spirit. That was impossible, and therefore the Dragon Kahg decided it wasn't happening. The child must be playing a game of make-believe.

The Dragon Kahg chose to ignore the boy.

The boy chose to take the dragon's silence for approval.

Wulfe happily splashed out into the moonlit water and ran up the gangplank and boarded the dragonship. He wandered around the deck, standing on the chests and investigating the single large rudder that steered the ship. He climbed down the ladder to discover that someone had built a house inside the ship, or so it seemed to the delighted boy.

The hold was dark, but he could see well in darkness, and he gazed around at the furs that made a bed, plates and bowls for eating, and a lovely carved wooden chest. He would have opened the chest to see what was inside, but it was locked with an iron lock, and the boy hated iron. He hated the feel of it. He couldn't even stand the smell.

Wulfe wandered back up on deck and walked over to the prow with the dragon's curved neck and fierce head and the spiritbone, hanging from the nail. Wulfe could sense the spiritbone's powerful magic, and though his inner daemons urged him to touch it, he was daunted by the majesty of the dragon, and for once he was able to ignore the daemons. He gazed at the spiritbone from a respectful distance and left it alone.

Wulfe climbed up the dragon's neck, his bare, nimble feet finding easy purchase, and, clinging to the head, he stared out at the beauty of the vast moonlit sea, marveling that it looked so different from this vantage point than it did from the shore.

He wondered what it would be like to sail over the shining waves, and when he returned to the deck again, he sat on one of the chests, enjoying the feel of the ship sliding up and down gently with the waves. He was afraid the druids would be coming any moment, and he told himself he should leave. But the sight of the moon forming a silver path over the dark waves was so entrancing, the boy could only sit and gaze in silent enjoyment.

The moon rose higher, and still Wulfe lingered on the ship. Then he saw the lights—torchlights, coming across the bridge over the marshland. He froze like a rabbit did when it saw the fox. He could make a run for the woods, but the moonlight was bright on the white sand beach, and the druids had very good eyesight. They would spot him instantly, and they would know it was him, for all *good* children were in their beds.

Wulfe couldn't bear the thought of disappointing the elder. He'd done something very wrong, and this time the punishment might be more severe than usual. He decided he would wait until the druids did whatever it was they had come to the beach to do, and then he would sneak off the ship and race back to his dwelling. He would climb in through the window while the elder slept. Wulfe hunkered down on the deck among the sea chests.

He couldn't see from his vantage point, but he could hear, and he sucked in a dismayed breath when he heard water splashing.

The druids were boarding the ship!

He looked about frantically for a better place to hide, and there was the ladder that led to the dwelling place below. He scrambled across the deck, tumbled down the ladder, and dived into the pile of furs, pulling them over his head.

He heard footsteps on the deck above him. He could hear people talking, and he recognized the voices of the elder and some of the men of the settlement.

"Carry the young man belowdeck," said the elder. "He is badly injured. I will tend his wounds."

Wulfe heard another voice, one he did not recognize, a woman's voice, low and rich.

"Bah! Let him bleed a little," said the woman. "He deserves to suffer. Pain will do him good."

"Death, on the other hand, will not," the druid said mildly.

Wulfe heard feet coming his way, and he snuggled deep among the furs. The young man they were carrying must have been heavy, for they had difficulty negotiating the ladder. They managed, or so he assumed, for he could hear them deposit their burden on the deck. Then they clomped back up the ladder and reported to the druid that they had laid the young man on his bed.

The boy peeped out cautiously from the furs.

"Skylan did show courage. He tried to rescue her," the elder remarked. "The older man basely fled."

"That is true," the woman said. "Skylan did try to save Draya, at the risk of his own life. I must admit I did not expect him to do that."

"He is lucky," the druid said, sighing. "The spirits of the woods were extremely angry."

"Skylan has Torval to thank for his survival," the woman replied. "Though I doubt he will find much cause to be grateful."

"You have entered the body of Draya in order to hide from your enemies, Vindrash," the elder remarked. "Do you also plan to torment this young man with guilt?" He sounded disapproving.

"Skylan is a weapon in Torval's hand. The god demands the finest steel, and this young Skylan is of poor quality, brittle and liable to break. He must prove himself or Torval will throw him on the scrap heap."

Feet walked across the deck. Wulfe heard splashes in the water. The men were leaving the ship. He was about to slip out of his hiding place, when he heard the woman's voice and he realized she and the elder were still on board.

"We will honor Draya's memory," the druid was saying. "Her spirit now dwells in peace with her gods. She will hear our hymns of praise, and when you have no more need of her mortal form, Blessed Vindrash, we will return her body to her people."

"I thank you for everything you have done, Elder." The woman's voice was soft, no longer grim and harsh. "I know acting out the sacrifice was not an easy thing for you or your people."

"We do not believe in human sacrifice," the druid said severely. "I had to keep reminding myself that we were slaying a goddess, one who could not be slain. Even then I found it horrible to witness. I fear the dreadful sight will scar my people."

"Your people saw the moonlight shining down on a glade and a foolish young man battling a tree," said Vindrash. "Nothing more."

"Yet I see you," the druid returned doubtfully. "I see you now as the Kai Priestess, Draya."

"That is because I permit you to see me in the human form. The evil Gods of Raj and Aelon, Lord of the New Dawn, look at me, and they see only a human, one ant in the anthill of humanity. Mortal minds see a goddess, and they cannot bear the sight and so they blot it out. Only Skylan will be able to see me. I will be his worst nightmare."

"Poor young man," murmured the druid. "He believes he saw his wife murdered before his eyes and that it was his fault. He will live with that forever."

"Guilt is a powerful force," said Vindrash. "As any mother will tell you."

"And what of the dragon?" the druid asked.

"The Dragon Kahg is my loyal servant. He has sworn an oath that he will tell no one where I am hiding, not even the others of his own kind. I trust him as I trust you, my dear friend."

"Our enemies are strong, and they grow stronger with every passing day," the druid said. "I look into the future and I see flames and bitter smoke and a city built on the bones of our dead."

"That is why we fight," said Vindrash. "And why we keep on fighting when it would be far easier to sink into oblivion."

Wulfe had no idea what the two were talking about. He generally found most of what adults said to each other either boring or confusing or both, and he quit paying attention. He was more concerned over what his stomach was saying, which was that it was past time to eat. Wulfe was relieved when the druid and the woman finally quit talking. He heard them walking across the deck and the sound of their feet going down the gangplank.

Wulfe didn't stir. Not yet. He would give the druid and the woman plenty of time to return to the settlement so he wouldn't meet them on the trail. The elder had an uncanny way of knowing just by looking at the boy that Wulfe had been up to mischief. To while away the time, Wulfe crept over to stare curiously at the young man.

He smelled disgustingly of iron.

At first Wulfe thought the young man was a corpse, for he was covered in blood. The boy studied the young man's battered and bloodied face. "Ugly Ones" was his mother's term for humans. Wulfe thought it fitting. He had watched this Ugly One strutting about in his iron shirt, brandishing the horrible sword, which now lay on the deck at his side. Wulfe eyed the weapon with disgust and gave it a wide berth as he hurried to the ladder. Unless some god loved him, the young man would likely die.

One less Ugly One in the world, his mother would have said.

Wulfe walked across the deck and then stopped to stare in blank dismay at the island on which he lived.

The island that was nothing but a black blotch on a starlit horizon. The moonlit ocean lay between Wulfe and his home.

The dragonship had sailed and taken the boy with it.

# CHAPTER 13

Wulfe stared across the silvered sea in dismay. His home was gone, vanishing beyond sight.

"Stop!" Wulfe cried frantically, turning to the dragon. "You have to take me back. I'm not supposed to be here! I— Ulp!"

The words caught in his throat. He ducked behind one of the sea chests and crouched there, quaking. He was not alone. A woman stood beside the rudder, guiding the ship into the gentle wind.

This had to be the woman who boarded the ship with the druids, the woman Wulfe had overheard speaking to the elder. He had thought she left with the elder, but apparently not.

She looked like she sounded—stern and cold and severe. Wulfe was reminded of the time his mother had taken him to meet his grandmamma. He had been only three, yet he remembered his grandmamma vividly. She was radiant and beautiful and terrible. She had made his mother cry. She had made him cry. There was the same sort of something about this woman—something beautiful and terrible. She frightened the boy more than did the Ugly One who lay dying below.

Wulfe was in agony. He was afraid to stay where he was, and he was afraid to move. The woman seemed absorbed in either her task or her thoughts. Her gaze was fixed, abstracted. Wulfe decided to chance it. Crawling on all fours (he could move exceptionally quickly that way), he scampered across the deck and once more dived down into the hold. Landing soft-footed at the bottom, he kept very still, his ears stretched, listening for some sound that the woman was in pursuit.

Hearing only the sighing of the wind, he looked upward. A sliding trapdoor could be drawn across the hatch's opening, closing it. Wulfe wondered if he dared. The woman might hear him. He decided to risk it. He stood precariously balanced on a rung of the ladder, reached up, and carefully and cautiously, using the tip ends of his fingers, slid the trapdoor shut.

The hold was now dark and snug, giving Wulfe the comforting impression of being in a den. He crept over to check on the Ugly One. Wulfe squatted on his haunches, his chin on his knees, and regarded the young man in frowning consternation. Wulfe had often accompanied the druids when they tended the sick, for he had some skills in the art of healing. Since he was skilled in nothing else, the druids had encouraged him in this pursuit.

Wulfe had seen death before, and this Ugly One was dying. He burned with fever; his wounds were festering. His body twitched and jerked. He moaned in pain, and once, to Wulfe's alarm, he gave a great shout. Wulfe tried to hush him, for he feared the woman would hear and come to investigate. She did not come—either she didn't hear or she didn't care. Night deepened; the Ugly One grew steadily worse.

Wulfe pondered. He had the power to save the young man. His skills in magic were considerable. They were also, unfortunately, erratic, sometimes ending in disaster. There was another problem. The druids had forbidden him to use his magic.

"Just because you *can* do a thing does not mean you *should,*" the elder had told him. "You do not understand these skills you possess, Wulfe. Are they a gift or a curse? You can do good, that is true. Sadly, you have also done great harm. Thus, until you understand how to exert control over this wayward power you possess, it is better that you do not use it."

Wulfe was in a quandary. He was afraid of the Ugly One, who carried iron and stank of death. Yet Wulfe felt a strange sort of kinship for him. Like Wulfe, the young man appeared to be beset by his own inner daemons.

The druids taught that the soul leads an existence separate from the body. When the body sleeps, the soul travels to a twilight realm where it lives and loves and does all sorts of strange and wonderful things. But while beautiful, this realm was also dangerous. Souls were sometimes lost in the twilight realm. Unable to find their way out, they never returned and the body died. That was why one must never wake a person who was dreaming or sleepwalking, for fear the soul would not find its way back.

Daemons populated this twilight realm, taking the form of people known in life. Wulfe knew that for a fact. He often saw his father in the twilight realm, when his father had died long ago. These daemons were now besetting the Ugly One.

The young man begged someone called Draya to forgive him. He fought a daemon named Horg, and he groped about for his sword. This terrified Wulfe. He would have tossed the hideous weapon overboard, only he could not bear to touch it. Fearing the Ugly One would find the sword, which lay on the deck near him, Wulfe threw a blanket over it. Then he crept into a corner of the hold and stayed there until the Ugly One's battle with the daemons ended.

The Ugly One sank into a stupor. Wulfe was torn. He was afraid of the young man, afraid of the sword. At the same time, he pitied him. He was in such terrible pain. It occurred to Wulfe that if the Ugly One died, the dragonship might sail on and on forever, and Wulfe would never see his home again. He couldn't decide what to do, and while he argued with himself this way and that, he fell asleep.

Wulfe woke to find the sun peeking in through chinks in the planks. To his astonishment, the Ugly One was still alive. Wulfe cautiously slid open the trapdoor a crack and peeked out. If the woman was still there, he would gather his courage and tell her the young man was dying and that the druids could help him and would she please ask the dragon to take him home.

The woman was gone. The rudder had been lashed in place, keeping the ship on a steady course. Wulfe searched the deck as best he could from his vantage point and did not see her. He was about to climb onto the deck, when he caught sight of the dragon's angry eye swiveling in his direction. Wulfe hurriedly ducked back down into the hold. He did not go up on deck again.

He found food and water, and he ate and drank and tended to the Ugly One as best he could, bathing his hot flesh and forcing water down his throat and spreading a potion he found on the wounds.

None of that helped. The Ugly One grew steadily worse. He no longer sat up or cried out. His breathing was labored; his heartbeat was weak. Wulfe could barely feel a pulse. The young man's soul was far from his body and roving farther still.

The only way to save him was for Wulfe to use his magic. The cure might kill him, but the young man was dying anyway. Wulfe was more afraid of the druids finding out that he'd broken their rules.

Wulfe decided to risk it. Hoping he didn't do anything terrible, such as turn the young man inside out (Wulfe had mistakenly done this to a girl's pet cat once—a horrible experience for all concerned), Wulfe put his hand over the young man's heart and began to sing to him.

The song Wulfe sang in a thin and wavering voice was a song his mother had sung to him.

He had only vague memories of his mother. A woman lovelier than the dawn, she had smelled of laurel and rosemary and violet. She was clothed in gossamer and moonlight Her long golden hair, which went to her feet, was spangled with dewdrops. He had never seen her by day, only by night, when she came to dance with him and laugh with him, hold him and weep over him. At such times, the wolves who were his guardians would throw back their heads and wail in sorrow.

His mother sang songs to him, over and over until the songs became a part of him, like his blood and his bones and his skin.

"The Ugly Ones will seek to harm you, because you are not one of them," his mother had whispered to him again and again. "I cannot be there to protect you, but so long as you remember the songs of your people, the Ugly Ones cannot hurt you."

Wulfe had told the elder what his mother had said. The elder had looked very sad and said that, although his mother meant well, she should not have given him such a dangerous gift. At that time, Wulfe didn't understand what the druid meant by the songs being dangerous. He had come to understand a little when he'd sung his songs to the poor sick cat.

Wulfe sang one of his mother's songs to the dying young man. His mother would not have approved, for the young man was one of those very Ugly Ones who would try to harm him. The druid would not approve, for such magic was dangerous, and Wulfe couldn't control it.

It seemed Wulfe could never make anyone happy.

The song dated back to the time when his mother's people dwelt happily in a darkness lit only by the light of distant stars. A time before the first gods came to banish the starlight with bright, fierce fire and give the rulership of nature to fleshy, hairy creatures who had crawled out of the swamps and now walked upright on two legs. These creatures termed themselves "men," and they were big and gross and ugly, and they used fire to make iron and used iron to kill.

Wulfe knew the meaning of the words in his heart, though not his head. Sometimes the words were joyous and sometimes cruel. They were funny and hideous and beautiful and shining. They were not afraid, for when the songs were first sung, there had been nothing to fear. The fear had come later.

Wulfe sang and pressed his hand over the Ugly One's heart and hoped fervently that he would not turn the young man inside out. He breathed a sigh of relief to see the flesh remaining on the outside of the bones, where it belonged. The song seemed to work. The Ugly One drew a deep and easeful breath. His life's blood tinged his face. The lines of pain smoothed away. His skin grew cool to the touch and beaded with sweat. The fever had broken.

The Ugly One flung his arm over his forehead and slept deeply. His soul was still in the twilight realm, but he was no longer doing battle. Wulfe pictured his soul walking through pleasant meadows filled with flowers.

Wulfe was pleased with himself. The Ugly One would sleep a long time, and that would be good for him. Wulfe huddled down in the nest he'd made for himself among the blankets and whispered a thank-you to his mother. Thinking of her, he wondered sadly why she never came to sing to him anymore.

The boy missed her. He missed the elder. He missed his home. He felt so lost and alone that he began to cry, something he had not done since he was four years old and the druids had taken him from his father and the wolves who had been his family.

When Skylan woke, he was content to simply lie drowsily among the blankets, reveling in the warmth of the bed. He recognized his surroundings. He was in the hold of his *Venjekar.*

His contentment did not last long.

Memory returned, crashing into him like ogres crashing into the shield-wall. Memory, like ogres, stabbed him with sharp swords.

Warriors who suffered cracked skulls almost never remembered the blow or even the battle. Unfortunately, Skylan remembered everything. He saw his young warriors transformed into rabbits. He saw Draya's gruesome death.

Skylan wished his eyes might have been gouged out before he saw that horrible sight, one he knew he would keep on seeing for as long as he lived.

He felt the ship's motion and realized they had set sail. He wondered who was sailing the ship. The Dragon Kahg would never permit an enemy to seize the ship. Perhaps druids had released Skylan's men from their enchantment. His men were taking him home.

Weak in mind and body, Skylan accepted this notion and drifted back to sleep. When he woke again, he saw the boy.

He was a strange-looking boy, thin and sinewy, with a thatch of shaggy hair. The boy was pouring water from a jug into a drinking horn, and he had his back to Skylan. Propping himself up on his elbows, Skylan stared at him.

"Who in the name of Freilis are you?" Skylan demanded.

The boy sucked in a hissing breath. Whipping around, he flung the drinking horn at Skylan's head and fled, scampering up the ladder and disappearing.

Skylan wiped water from his face and licked it from his parched lips. He gazed up the ladder, trying to catch a glimpse of the strange boy. When the boy did not return, Skylan called out to him.

"No need to be afraid. I'm not going to hurt you."

Skylan heard the lapping of the waves against the hull and nothing more, and he realized something was not right. He should have heard his men tramping about the deck. The silence made him uneasy. Who was sailing the ship? He coughed, cleared his throat, and tried again.

"I *can't* hurt you, if it comes to that," he told the boy ruefully. "I am weak as watered ale."

The boy returned, hovering in the hatchway. He had yellow eyes the likes of which Skylan had never seen in a human, and he stared at Skylan distrustfully from beneath crudely cut bangs. He did not speak.

"What is your name?" Skylan asked.

"Names are powerful," the boy countered. "Tell me yours first."

He cautiously descended to the topmost rung of the ladder, but would come no farther.

"Skylan Ivorson," Skylan answered. He was about to add proudly, "Chief of Chiefs of the Vindrasi," but that wouldn't sound well coming from a man lying naked in his own filth on sweat-soaked blankets. A man too weak to pour himself a cup of water.

The boy hesitated, then mumbled something.

"I couldn't hear. Did you say 'wolf'?" Skylan asked.

"Wulfe," the boy repeated loudly, annoyed.

"Wulfe," Skylan said, pronouncing the name as the boy did. "Would you tell one of my men to come down here?"

Wulfe shrugged. "There aren't any men. Only the dragon. And maybe the woman."

"This is no time for jests," Skylan said sharply. "Someone is sailing this ship. I don't know how you came to be aboard, but now that you're here, send my men down to me at once!"

Wulfe shrugged again. He was dressed in robes like the druids wore, too large for his small frame, and when he shrugged, the opening for his neck slid down around his shoulder.

"I told you. There are no men. The druids brought you on board and left. The dragon made the ship sail away, taking me with it. I didn't want to go," Wulfe added in aggrieved tones.

"Then who is sailing the ship?" Skylan demanded.

"The dragon!" Wulfe cried. "I keep telling you that! Please ask him to take me home."

"Why don't *you* ask him?" said Skylan, annoyed. He thought the boy was making all this up.

"I don't think the dragon likes me," Wulfe said sulkily. "I asked him if I could come on board, and he didn't say I couldn't. But now he glares at me whenever I go up on deck."

"You're telling me you can see the dragon, speak to him?" Skylan frowned in disbelief.

Wulfe's eyes widened in fright, and he edged back toward the ladder. "I didn't know that was wrong! Are you going to kill me?"

"No, of course not," Skylan said. "It's not wrong, exactly. It's just . . . odd. The only person who can speak to the dragon is a Bone Priestess. And even she cannot see the dragon until he answers the summons."

Skylan still thought the boy was pretending, playing make-believe.

"Tell me, Wulfe, what does the dragon look like?"

"He looks like a dragon," said Wulfe.

"Describe him," said Skylan, thinking he would hear some outlandish tale.

"He has blue scales, and his mane is the color of sea foam and his crest is like the moon glade on the water I saw the other night. And his eyes are red and horrid."

Skylan was astonished. Wulfe had accurately described the Dragon Kahg in his water form, down to the last scale. Here was a mystery.

The boy had to be telling the truth, incredible as it seemed. The Dragon Kahg had the power to sail the ship on his own if he chose. Skylan remembered watching the ship sail off with Horg's corpse, and he shuddered. Perhaps the Dragon Kahg was carrying Skylan to his grave! Planning to dump his body where neither man nor gods could find it.

"Do you hurt somewhere?" Wulfe crept down another rung.

Skylan shook his head. Weak in mind and body, he turned his head into the pillow to hide his grief.

He heard bare feet patter down the rungs of the ladder and felt a hand timidly touch his shoulder. Skylan lifted his head, and Wulfe sprang back.

"You should drink." The boy held the horn at arm's length.

Skylan took the drinking horn and gulped the water thirstily and handed it back. He lay quiet a moment, wondering if he had the strength to rise. He didn't have a choice. He had to find out what was going on.

"I need to go up on deck."

Wulfe clutched the empty drinking horn to his chest. "Will you ask the dragon to take me home?"

Skylan gave a bleak smile. "I must first ask the dragon where he is taking *me*. You said the druids brought me on board. They must have brought you, as well. Why did they leave you here?"

Wulfe flushed and shook his head. "The elder didn't know I was on the ship. I sneaked on. I know it was wrong, but I couldn't help it. The dragonship was the most wonderful thing I'd ever seen. Now I hate it," he added sullenly.

"Can you help me up the ladder to the deck?"

Wulfe eyed him suspiciously. "What are you going to do?"

"I'm going to try to find out where we are—"

"I can tell you that. We're on the ocean."

"If I can see landmarks and the position of the sun, I'll know where we are on the ocean," said Skylan.

Wulfe seemed to think this over and decide it made sense. He gingerly slid his arm beneath Skylan's shoulder. The boy was surprisingly strong. He helped Skylan stand.

Everything tilted and wobbled. Skylan shut his eyes and clung to Wulfe and waited for the dizziness to pass.

"Where are my clothes?" Skylan asked.

The boy gestured to a corner where he'd dumped the bloodstained trousers and shirt and boots in a heap.

"And my sword?"

Wulfe let Skylan loose and darted off into a corner. Bereft of his support, Skylan had to grab hold of a beam to keep from falling. The sudden movement sent pain stabbing through his head, but he was more worried about his sword.

"The weapon is valuable. Did the druids keep it? Tell me, what happened to it?" He was almost frantic with worry.

Wulfe pointed a jabbing finger at something. Skylan saw a blanket and the faint outline of a sword beneath it. He gave a huge sigh of relief. Clasping the amulet at his neck, he thanked Torval.

"I will leave the sword where it is," he told the boy. "You do not need to be afraid."

Keeping a wary eye on the blanket, as though fearful the sword might somehow wriggle out, Wulfe helped Skylan to climb the ladder.

Once on deck, Skylan was disappointed to find that the ship had sailed into a fog bank. He could not see the top of the mast, much less the sun. He could barely tell fore from aft.

Skylan drew in a deep breath. The air was thick and moist, but it was a welcome change from the stinking, fetid air below. He sat down on a sea chest. He could feel the dragon's eye on him, but he didn't look up.

"I want to bathe," said Skylan. "Will you fetch me water and my clothes? You will find clean ones in my sea chest."

Wulfe wrinkled his nose, indicating he agreed, and ran below. Skylan sat resting, a lone figure on the empty deck. The dragonship moved slowly, sluggishly through the fog. The sail was furled. Skylan saw that the rudder had been lashed in place. He was puzzled by this, wondered if the boy had done it.

Skylan's sea chest had no lock on it. Wulfe returned with Skylan's clothes and boots. He lowered a bucket attached to a rope into the sea and hauled it back up, sloshing much of it over his bare feet. Skylan rinsed off the dried blood and filth, gasping at the cold water and wincing at the sting of the salt on his fresh wounds. He finished by dumping a second bucket of water over his head, washing his hair and new growth of beard.

Bathed and dressed, Skylan felt better. Wulfe brought dried meat and fruit and the rock-hard brown bread that kept a long time before going moldy. As he and Wulfe shared the meal, Skylan eyed the Dragon Kahg, barely able to see the dragon's head through the thick mists.

Skylan needed to know where he stood. He had to find out what the dragon knew and if Kahg blamed him for Draya's death and, if so, what the dragon intended to do about it. Skylan took some comfort from the fact that he was still alive.

Torval had again healed him, spared his life. The god had forgiven him. Hopefully the dragon would, too.

Skylan walked over to where the spiritbone hung suspended on the leather thong. The bone swayed gently back and forth with the motion of the ship. Skylan had never before spoken with the dragon. He was not even certain if he could. As he had told Wulfe, communicating with the dragons was the province of the Bone Priestess.

The thought brought Draya to mind, and guilt and remorse twisted inside him like a sword in his gut. He had brought her to that horrible place. He had brought her to her terrible death. He remembered Draya leaning against the dragon's carved neck, and he remembered her final words to him. She was sorry she had wronged him.

Skylan placed his hand on the spiritbone and said in a low, harsh voice, not looking at the dragon, "Where are you taking me?"

It was Wulfe who spoke.

"The dragon says he is taking you to Luda."

"This is serious," Skylan snapped. He stopped, glanced back at the boy. "How did you know about Luda?"

"I don't know anything about Luda," said Wulfe. "What is Luda anyway?"

"Luda is my home," said Skylan.

"Then that's where we're going. The woman told the dragon to take you there."

"Who is this woman you keep talking about?"

"That woman," said Wulfe, and he pointed.

Startled, Skylan swiftly turned.

A draugr stood behind him.

Most dead slept peacefully in their graves, but there were those who sometimes left their tombs to walk among the living. These walking corpses were known as draugrs, and the Vindrasi feared them, for draugrs hated the living and often went on murderous rampages.

Skylan recognized the draugr. It was Draya. She had come back to claim her revenge on him.

Skylan had never known such terror. His heart lurched and thudded erratically in his breast. His bowels gripped, and his stomach shriveled. He could not breathe. He could not speak. He had no thought of fighting the draugr. He stood staring at it, paralyzed with fear.

The draugr's face—Draya's face—was corpse-white, her eyes fixed and staring. Blood stained her gown and dripped from her hands. Her hair was unbound and fell about her shoulders. She walked toward him, her hand outstretched.

Skylan fell to his knees, babbling incoherently, begging for mercy. The cold fingers touched him on the shoulder. Skylan shuddered and closed his eyes, waiting to die.

The hand patted him timidly.

"You're safe," said Wulfe. "The draugr's gone."

Skylan opened his eyes and looked wildly about. The deck was empty except for the boy. Skylan seized hold of him, and was thankful to feel warm flesh.

"You saw her? The draugr?" Skylan gasped, and he shuddered again at the thought.

Wulfe nodded. "She is the woman I saw steering the ship. I didn't know then she was a draugr. Who is she? Do you know her?"

Skylan sank back onto the deck with a groan. "She is . . . or was . . . my wife."

# CHAPTER 14

Skylan sat hunched miserably on a sea chest, his head in his hands. He had no idea what was happening to him. He could not see the sun for the thick wall of fog. He could not see the land, though he knew it must be near, for he would sometimes sight a broken branch or leaves floating on the water. The sea was flat, sullen, an oily gray. Fog shrouded the ship, hanging from the mast like a tattered sail, and it dripped like saliva from the dragon's fangs. The fog transformed the *Venjekar* into a thing he did not know.

Skylan, who had crawled the decks of this ship before he could walk, could not distinguish starboard from port, aft from stern. He stared into the mists, trying to pierce them, but the fog made his eyes swim, and he grew dizzy. The air was smothering, clogging his lungs. And out of the fog had come the apparition of his dead wife. Skylan wondered, with a feeling of dread, if he was trapped in the Nethervoid.

The boy was no comfort, for though he was made of flesh and bone and warm to the touch, there was something strange about Wulfe, something not of this world. He could see the dragon in his spirit form, and that was not possible.

"Did you murder your wife?"

The boy had been quiet such a long time that Skylan was startled by the question. "Is that why the draugr came for you?"

"I did not!" Skylan cried, and he grasped hold of the amulet and raised his face to the sky he could not see. "I swear by Torval, I meant no harm to come to Draya!"

"Then why does she haunt you?" Wulfe asked.

Skylan could think of many reasons, but he chose not to. "You are awfully calm about it," he said, somewhat resentfully. His heartbeat was just starting to return to normal

"The draugr didn't come for me," Wulfe pointed out. "She came for you."

"Do you . . ." Skylan licked dry lips. "Do you know why?"

"Sometimes draugrs come only to kill, because they hate the living. Sometimes they come back for a reason. There was a draugr in our village who came back to be with his wife. The draugr was a real nuisance, scaring away all the men who wanted to marry her. The elder tried to talk to the draugr, but he wouldn't listen, and finally his family had to dig up the corpse and burn it. Since the draugr didn't kill you," Wulfe concluded, "she must want something from you."

"You mean she'll come back?" Skylan asked, horrified.

"Oh yes. They always do."

Skylan groaned. "I can't bear this!"

Groping his way through the thick fog, he crossed the deck to the rudder. He had decided to remove the lashing and steer the ship toward where he thought he would find land. He could feel the dragon's baleful gaze on him, but Skylan didn't care. If he didn't escape this ship, he would go mad. Skylan tugged desperately at the knots of the rope that held the rudder in place. The knots had been tied tight. The rope was wet. His fingers slipped and fumbled, and at last, in despair, he gave up.

Probably just as well, Skylan reflected bitterly. He might have steered the ship away from land, not toward it, sailed out into unknown waters and been lost forever.

If he wasn't lost now.

Wulfe had said the dragonship was taking him home. Skylan hoped the boy was right, although returning home presented him with new problems. He would have to explain what had happened to Draya and what had become of his men.

I cannot tell the truth. Not for my sake, but for Draya's. I would have to reveal that she was a murderer. She would be forever reviled among our people, and I won't do that to her. I have caused her grief enough already. And then there are the warriors. If their families discovered they have fallen victim to enchantment, the news would kill them. I cannot do that to them. I will have to lie.

Torval despises lies and liars, but he will forgive this. I lie to spare others pain. Torval understands that.

The story would have to be a good one. Skylan would have to give it considerable thought. He turned from the rudder, walked back across the deck. His eye fell on Wulfe. The boy knew the truth. How could he prevent him from blabbing?

To be truly safe, Skylan should ensure the boy's silence by killing him and disposing of the body. No one would ever know about the murder. Skylan shook his head at the thought. Whatever wrongs he had done, he would not stoop to murdering children.

The boy probably doesn't know all that much, Skylan reflected. I'll find out what he does know and work around it.

"Let's play a game," said Skylan, thinking this would be a good way to help the boy relax, start him talking.

"I don't like games," Wulfe said.

"You'll like this one. It's called dragonbone."

The game being a favorite of the Vindrasi people, men often brought their boards and gamepieces aboard ship to while away the long hours at sea. Skylan had his own board and pieces he had carved himself.

Skylan set up the game board on an overturned water barrel down in the hold and arranged the pieces, explaining the game as he did so.

"Why is it called dragonbone?" Wulfe asked, regarding the pieces with distrust. "Are those the bones of dragons?"

"No, of course not," Skylan scoffed. "The dragonbones are sacred to us. Real dragonbones would never be used in a game. The pieces represent dragonbones, that's all."

Wulfe found this puzzling. "Why call them bones, then?"

"Because it wouldn't be a dragonbone game otherwise," Skylan said. His cup of patience, never very full to begin with, was fast draining. "Now be quiet, and I'll teach you the rules."

Skylan set up the game board, which was made of oak, and painted with colored pictures, and began to explain the game, much to Wulfe's mystification. There were lines that Skylan termed "paths," though these paths didn't appear to lead anywhere except straight into each other. The paths were marked with runes, which Wulfe could not read, and outside the paths were portrayals of sun and moon and stars, dragons and dragonships, swords and shields, trees and mountains and seas all entwined. The paintings were very beautiful, and Wulfe wanted to ask about them, but apparently that wasn't part of the game.

Skylan laid down what he termed the "bones," which didn't look like bones at all, at least any bones that Wulfe had ever seen. The bones were of different shapes and different colors, and all of them were marked with runes. Skylan said some of the bones belonged to Wulfe and some to him. Wulfe was supposed to throw a bone on the table, and then he was to march the bones along the path, though to what end Wulfe could not see, since the paths went nowhere. Sometimes a bone could fly over another bone. Sometimes a bone landed on another bone. Sometimes bones "died" and were taken off the board.

Wulfe found the entire concept baffling. The idea of playing a game was foreign to him. He didn't understand why he should want to move the bones that weren't bones around in the first place, and then to be told that some bones could move one way and some another depending on where they were in relationship to each other confounded him.

Skylan could see that the boy was floundering, but carried on anyway. The game play distracted him, took his mind off his troubles. In order to teach Wulfe, Skylan played both sides, showing the boy as the game progressed what piece to play and explaining why he was playing it.

Wulfe had no idea what he was doing or why he was doing it. He moved the pieces at random, sometimes picking up Skylan's piece instead of his own, for the boy truly couldn't understand the difference. He wasn't enjoying this at all, but he continued to play because he could see the game brought pleasure to the downcast, brooding, and unhappy young man.

Wulfe was starting to like Skylan. He didn't think of him as an Ugly One anymore. Skylan was different from the druids who had raised Wulfe. Studied, scholarly, soft-spoken, self-possessed, the druids eschewed all strong emotions. This was partly necessitated by the fact that the fae who inhabited and loved the forest also loved the druids for the care they took of the trees and plants. If anyone sought to harm the druids, the fae would take it upon themselves to remove the threat, never mind that the druids might not want them to do so. The druids had not turned Skylan's men into rabbits or ordered the strangler fig to attack. The dryads and hamadryads, sprites and wood nymphs and tree nymphs, undine and sylphids and all the rest of the fae had been roused to anger by the aggressive actions of the warriors, and the results had been disastrous.

The druids were oftentimes shocked and horrified by the actions of the faeries, who could be incredibly thoughtless and cruel. Unable to forgive or forget the terrible war that had brought death to so many and destroyed their world, the fae were always glad for a chance to lash out at the Ugly Ones. The fae lived in the moment, from moment to moment. They did not worry about the consequences of their actions because, for them, actions had no consequences. The druids had learned that the only way to exert a modicum of control over the fae was to maintain control over themselves. Strong emotions such as fear and anger could precipitate a calamity.

Thus, in his eleven years among the druids, Wulfe had never heard a raised voice. People had learned not to quarrel (or to keep their quarrels private), for the fae might take sides. Life proceeded at a calm, placid, and easy pace. Skylan, by contrast, crackled with emotions, all shooting off in different directions like jagged streaks of lightning. Wulfe found this exciting, if a little dangerous, and while it took some getting used to, Wulfe liked it. He was dangerous, too, in his own way.

Still, Wulfe hadn't counted on quite so much danger.

He was reaching for one of the pieces, about to pick it up, when his hand froze in midair.

"What's the matter?" Skylan asked, seeing the boy's face pale and eyes widen.

"The draugr!" Wulfe said in a low voice. "She's standing right behind you. No! Don't turn around!"

Skylan stiffened. His hand tightened over the piece he was holding. Sweat broke out on his forehead.

"What is she doing?" Skylan asked, shuddering.

"I . . . I think she wants to play the game with you," Wulfe said. He stood up and edged away from the stool.

The draugr took the boy's place, seating herself across the board from Skylan. He stared at the corpse-face, with its dead, sunken eyes and bluish lips, and he had to fight the urge to flee.

The draugr silently moved a piece, then pointed to him, indicating it was his move.

"I'm not going to play with a draugr," Skylan said, his throat constricting.

"I don't think you have a choice," Wulfe told him.

"Where are you going? Don't leave!"

Wulfe scampered up the ladder, out the open hatchway, and disappeared.

Skylan stood up from the stool. His sword lay on the deck, covered by the blanket.

"I'm not playing," he said defiantly.

The draugr pointed at the dragonbones. Skylan snatched off the blanket, picked up the sword, and swung it in a slashing arc meant to decapitate the draugr.

The sword glowed red, as hot as if it had come from the forge fire. Skylan dropped it with a cry. The smell of hot steel mingled with the stench of burning flesh.

Skylan wrung his hand and swore. He glared at the draugr and then ran toward the ladder, intending to follow Wulfe. The trapdoor slammed shut. Skylan beat on it and shouted for Wulfe to open it.

The trapdoor did not budge.

Cold and clammy sweat ran down Skylan's neck. He turned slowly to face the draugr. The hold was dark, but he had no need to light a lantern. The draugr gave off a ghastly light.

She pointed at the board.

Skylan walked slowly back, sat down.

"Why are you doing this to me, Draya?" he asked, his voice ragged. "Why are you tormenting me?"

The draugr pointed at the dragonbone. Slowly, his hand shaking, Skylan picked up the bone in his burned palm. Wincing at the pain, he moved the bone along the path, hardly looking to see where he placed it.

That game did not last long. Skylan was not a very good dragonbone player at the best of times. As Garn was always telling him, Skylan was too rash, too reckless, too eager to win. Now, his mental processes clouded by horror, Skylan made one unfortunate move after another, and the draugr soon swept away all his bones. Skylan prayed to Torval this would be the end of the game, that the draugr would release him from the nightmare. Instead she indicated she wanted to play again.

Skylan gave a groan.

"We will make a wager. If I win this game, we quit," he bargained. "You will go away and leave me in peace."

The draugr gazed at him with her lifeless eyes and said nothing. Skylan did not know if they had a bet or not. He could only hope. His terror was starting to wane, and he forced himself to concentrate on the game. He faced the draugr defiantly and rolled the first bone. Marking where it fell, he placed his bone on the path.

The draugr picked up five bones in her withered, bloodstained hand and made ready to toss them.

"What are you doing? That's cheating," Skylan said angrily. "You can't start by putting five bones into play."

The draugr threw the five bones onto the board. She picked them up, one by one, and moved them into position, then reached her hand across the board toward him.

Skylan shrank back from the horrible touch. The draugr picked up five of his bones and held them out to him. When he hesitated, unwilling to take them, she thrust them at him. Skylan held out his hand, shuddering as the draugr's icy nails brushed his skin.

He was apparently to throw five bones. He did so, and he placed them according to the fall. Play proceeded, with Skylan scrambling to try to figure out the new rules.

The dragonbone game had many variations. Every clan played by its own rules, some versions actually taking on the names of the clan that originated them, such as the Torgun Bone-Toss, the Heudjun Triple, and the Margen Cliff Fall. Skylan could only assume the draugr had made up her own variant, which, sadly, made the game exceedingly more complicated.

Competitive by nature, with a warrior's need to win, Skylan almost forgot he was battling a corpse. He took his time, thought over each move, and played an extremely good game. The draugr was skilled, as well. The game ended in a draw.

The draugr rose silently and walked into the darkness.

Skylan collapsed, falling onto the board, scattering the pieces. He was too exhausted to move, and Wulfe found him asleep like that.

The next night, the draugr came to play the game again.

The dragonship sailed on through the unrelenting fog. Skylan could not see the sun, and he kept track of the days by carving marks on the rail. The draugr came every night, and though Wulfe was terrified of the draugr and wished she would go away, the boy was at least consoled by the fact that Skylan no longer made him play dragonbones. After three nights of playing with the draugr, Skylan threw the board and pieces into the sea.

The next night the board and pieces were back in their usual place and so was the draugr. She now played one game and one game only. She almost always won, though sometimes Skylan was able to battle to a draw. He never defeated her.

She continued to play the Five-Bone variant. The draugr insisted on this and even made a sort of ceremony out of the start, lining up the five dragonbones in front of her, picking up each one with exaggerated deliberation, and throwing them down one at a time. She insisted on lining up Skylan's five dragonbones in front of him, watching him intently as he swept them up in his hand and gave them a careless toss.

Other than the nightly games, which Skylan came to dread with all his heart and soul, there was nothing to do on board the fog-bound ship except eat and sleep and talk to Wulfe. The boy was happy to relate the history of his eleven years. Skylan would have been happier if the boy had told the truth, but at least the version Wulfe recounted was entertaining.

"I've lived with the druids since I was four and they found me running with the wolves."

"Wolves? What were you doing with wolves?"

"They raised me," said Wulfe.

Skylan grinned. "Wolves raised you?"

"They were my family," Wulfe said with a sadness he had never quite managed to overcome. "One was my father."

Skylan snorted in disbelief.

"I'm not lying," Wulfe said.

"You expect me to believe your father was a wolf?"

"My father wasn't always a wolf. He was an Ugly One, like you. He was in the woods one day, stalking a deer, and not watching where he was going. He stepped inside a ring of mushrooms."

Skylan shook his head. All knew that a ring of mushrooms—a faery ring, as it was known—was a deadly trap set by the fae to capture men, one to be avoided at all costs.

"What happened?" he asked.

"He tried to escape, but the more he struggled, the deeper he sank. He was buried up to his neck. That night, the faeries dragged him out. They tied him up in cobweb and took him to their realm and made him one of their slaves. He was working in the palace of the faery queen when he met my mother. She was a princess and the most beautiful woman my father had ever seen. She had never met a mortal before, for the faery queen had kept her daughter hidden away from the Ugly Ones—"

"Why do you call us that?" Skylan interrupted.

"It's what the faeries call you," Wulfe explained.

"We're not ugly," Skylan protested.

"Compared to the faeries you are," said Wulfe.

"How do you know? Have you ever seen a faery?" Skylan challenged, laughing.

"I saw my mother," Wulfe said. "She is more beautiful than you can imagine. I saw my grandmamma, too, but she was hideous. Should I go on with my story?"

"Go ahead. I don't have anything better to do," Skylan said, sighing.

"My father fell in love with my mother and she fell in love with him. They kept their love a secret a long time, but then my mother discovered I was coming and she was terrified, for she knew the faery queen would be furious at the thought of her daughter bringing an Ugly One into the world. My parents tried to escape, but they were caught by my grandmamma's guards, terrible spiders that bound them up in cobweb.

"The queen locked my mother away and cast a curse upon my father and all his family, turning them into wolves. When I was born, my grandmamma gave me to my father and the wolf pack to raise. She forbade my mother to see me or have anything to do with me. My mother disobeyed. She would come to me in the night and hold me in her arms and sing to me."

A tear slid down Wulfe's cheek.

"My mother was so miserable that once she took me to the faery realm to introduce me to my grandmamma. She hoped that when the queen saw me, she would relent and forgive my mother and let me live with them. My grandmamma hated me. She said I was the ugliest of Ugly Ones. My mother wept and begged, but the queen threw me out. I lived with the wolves until the day the druids found me and took me away to live with them. I never saw my mother or father again after that."

"What was it like, living with the druids after being raised by wolves?" Skylan meant the question as a joke, but Wulfe took him seriously.

"I hated it," he said, but then he shrugged and added, "I think the druids hated it more. I was a lot of trouble. I walked on all fours, you see, and I tore off my clothes and I would crap on the floor. I ate only raw meat, and I ran away lots of times."

"You look and act like one of us now," Skylan observed dryly. "An Ugly One."

"Sometimes I do," Wulfe muttered. "Sometimes I don't." He thrust out his lower lip in a pout. "You think I'm lying, don't you?"

"I think you have a vivid imagination. You should be a bard—"

"Oh yeah? Watch this."

Wulfe jumped up and pulled off his robe, dragging it over his head. Dropping to the deck, he began to scamper about naked on all fours. Skylan stared in astonishment. The boy did not crawl on his hands and knees like a baby. He balanced on his hands and the balls of his feet and ran with his knees slightly bent, his rear end up and his head down. In this position, he moved faster than most people would have been able to manage on two legs.

"How do you do that?" Skylan asked.

"The wolves ran on all fours," said Wulfe. "I didn't know any different, you see. I thought I was one of them."

He looked downcast and stood up with a sigh. He did not seem the least bit uncomfortable or embarrassed about his nakedness. He was cold, however, and so he put on his robes again.

"Look at this if you don't believe me." Wulfe showed Skylan his hands.

The boy's palms were hard and covered with thick calluses, reminding Skylan of a dog's pads. He glanced at the boy's toes, which were unusually long. Skylan looked into Wulfe's strange yellow eyes, and he had a sudden, vivid picture of this boy running naked with the wolf pack.

"The druids named you Wulfe because . . ."

"They found me with the wolves, stupid," said Wulfe. He frowned at Skylan. "I've never told anyone that story. The elder said I mustn't. He said they'd hate me if I did. They would think I was moonstruck and they would be afraid of me and might hurt me. Do you think I'm moonstruck?"

"You think I'm a murderer, don't you?" said Skylan.

"Maybe," said Wulfe.

"Are you afraid of me?"

"A little."

"I guess I'm afraid of you a little," Skylan said with a wan smile. "But I won't hurt you."

"And I won't hurt you," said Wulfe earnestly.

Skylan almost started to laugh, then he looked at the boy with the strange yellow eyes who could run like a wolf on all fours, and he thought better of it.

They ate food that was damp from the fog, and when there was nothing else to do, they went to bed. Skylan watched Wulfe crawl round and round among the blankets, making a nest, before finally settling down. The boy fell asleep immediately, no tossing and turning. When he slept, his feet and hands twitched, and he made growling sounds. Skylan took to sleeping on deck.

He lay awake, listening to the water gliding beneath the keel, feeling the motion of the ship over the waves, and staring into the darkness that was thick and damp, and seemed to congeal on his skin.

The dragonship sailed on, ghostly in the fog.

CHAPTER

# 15

The fog bank, damp and chill, rolled in from the north, sweeping over the sea and moving onto land to shroud the village of Luda in a gray, dank mist. The fog came up so rapidly that it overtook those working in fields or pastures, blotting out the sun, obliterating landmarks. Many lost their way in the thick and blinding cloud, following the road east when they should have taken it west, blundering into forests that should not have been there, coming within a hairsbreadth of stepping off the side of a cliff.

Those in the village built bonfires in the streets and rang bells to guide the lost back home. Norgaard said a grateful prayer to Torval when the last wanderer stumbled safely into the village. People stood in their doorways and watched the tendrils of mist writhe past their houses and wondered uneasily what this unnatural weather portended. The Vindrasi were accustomed to fog, but only in the winter. No one could ever recall such a phenomenon occurring this time of year, especially after days of hot, glaring sun.

Among those caught by the fog were Garn and Aylaen. They, alone, did not mind it. The two had been working in the fields, but when the fog brought their work to an enforced halt, they slipped away to meet in a secluded grove.

Skylan's marriage had removed the last impediment to their happiness, or so Aylaen had finally managed to convince Garn. He knew Skylan did not love Draya, knew that his friend loved Aylaen. Even though Skylan's love was now hopeless, Garn could not quiet the feeling that he was betraying his friend by loving the woman he loved.

Aylaen had only laughed at his qualms and led him to what was known as Lovers' Grove. That day had been hot and cloudless. When they reached the grove, Aylaen unpinned the brooches on her dress and drew it off. She took off her smock, shook down her long hair, and stood naked before him.

"I love you," she said simply, and held out her hands to him.

Garn's passion overcame him. The two were now lovers, and not a day had passed since but that they managed to find time to slip away, take pleasure in each other's arms.

Aylaen had a secret motive for giving herself to Garn, one she didn't tell him. Since the man to whom she had once been all but betrothed was now married, Aylaen was again on the marriage market. Her stepfather, Sigurd, was shopping around for a husband for her. He would not even consider

Garn, who was an orphan with no property or wealth. But if Aylaen were to become pregnant with Garn's child, Sigurd would have no choice except to allow them to marry. He would be furious, but Aylaen didn't care. Let him rage. Let him beat her, even. She would have her reward. She would have Garn, and she would have his child. She was bitterly disappointed, after they'd been lovers for a fortnight, to feel the cramps that presaged her monthly bleeding.

She reflected that she had time. Even if Sigurd found a prospect, negotiations for a marriage sometimes dragged on for months.

The day the thick fog settled on the land, she and Garn smiled at each other and drew the mists over them like a woolly blanket. They lay twined together, keeping each other warm. Only when they heard the ringing of the bells—a clanging, tinny, desperate sound—did Garn realize that they would be missed, people would be worried about them. Norgaard might even send out search parties.

Aylaen tried to pull him down on top of her again.

"We don't have to go. Not yet," she pleaded.

"People are lost," Garn said. "What a strange sound the bells make in the fog," he added with a shiver, pulling on his trousers. "Not like bells at all. More like daemons clamoring."

"They sound like bells to me," muttered Aylaen angrily.

Garn helped her to her feet. She shook free of his grip and smoothed down her skirts over her bare legs. Then, seeing him smile, she relented and threw her arms around him and gave him one more passionate kiss. Holding fast to each other, the two followed the narrow path that led out of the grove. The fog was thick around them, and they were forced to grope their way through the woods.

"Our lives are like this," said Garn. "Shrouded in time, we exist only in the moment. Nothing lies ahead of us and nothing behind. If I turned around, I would lose my way. If I let go your hand, I would lose you. I could take a misstep and tumble off a precipice—"

"We're nowhere near a precipice," said Aylaen practically. "And we're not lost. This path leads straight to the road and once we hit the road, we turn right and take it back to the village. Dratted brambles!" She sucked the blood from a long jagged scratch on the back of her hand. "Stop talking nonsense and watch where you're going, Garn. You dragged me into a bush!"

They finally struck the road and turned right, but in this cloud-bound world, nothing looked familiar, and though Aylaen was confident they were headed for the village, she took comfort in the clanging of the bells and the calls and shouts of their clansmen.

The bonfires came in sight, orange smudges in a gray landscape, and Garn and Aylaen sighed in relief. Seeing Sigurd and her mother standing by the fire, Aylaen swiftly let go of Garn's hand.

"We mustn't be seen together. I'll meet you tomorrow, my love!"

Garn obediently fell behind, to let her hurry on ahead of him. She was heading toward the bonfire, walking slowly, for she was loath to encounter her stepfather, when a hand clutched her out of the mists.

"Aylaen! Here you are! I am so glad!" Treia whispered fervently. "I've been looking everywhere for you!"

Aylaen was startled. Her sister, usually calm and composed, was trembling. "Treia! What's wrong?"

"It's . . ." Treia hesitated, glancing around, seeing people watching them. "I can't see in the fog. You must be my eyes."

"Of course, Treia," said Aylaen, holding fast to her sister's hand.

"You took a wrong turn," she said after a moment. "This isn't the way to your house."

"I know. We're not going home. We're going to the shore," Treia said.

"Why there?" Aylaen asked, but her sister did not answer.

Her fingers dug into Aylaen's; her grip on her sister tightened. Aylaen wondered if perhaps men had gone out fishing and were lost in the fog at sea. But if that were the case, the people would be building bonfires on the shore to guide them home, and no one was doing that.

The sisters walked in silence. Treia refused to speak, and Aylaen's thoughts were on Garn, on the touch of his hands and the warmth of his kisses.

Treia startled her by saying abruptly, "You have taken Garn for your lover, haven't you?"

Aylaen didn't know how to respond. She would have been glad to confide her hopes and dreams to a sympathetic sister. Treia was far from that. She had always coldly rebuffed any attempts at closeness.

"I saw you two come out of the woods together." Treia cast Aylaen a scathing glance. "And the back of your dress is covered in leaves and dirt."

Aylaen's cheeks burned. She belatedly brushed off the telltale evidence.

"Sigurd will never let you marry him," Treia said.

"He will if I'm carrying Garn's child," Aylaen said, tossing her red hair.

Treia glanced at her sharply. "So that's the reason."

"And because I love him!" Aylaen added in blushing confusion. "I love Garn with all my heart."

"Whereas Garn loves you with his whole being. He'll soon come to realize what you've done, how you used him. You'll end up destroying him."

"You're only saying that because you're jealous!" Aylaen cried, stung by her sister's cruel words. "Because no one loves you!"

Treia paled. Her lips tightened. She angrily cast off Aylaen's hand and stalked off on her own.

"Treia, I'm sorry," said Aylaen remorsefully, catching up to her sister. "I didn't mean it. You'll find someone. I know you will."

"There is no need to patronize me," Treia retorted. "Sigurd tells me I am too old and half-blind."

"Sigurd has cow turd for brains!" Aylaen cried, burning with indignation.

Treia's mouth twitched. She rarely smiled, never laughed, but she almost did that time. Aylaen squeezed her sister's hand in apology, and the two walked together onto the dunes. The beach was eerily silent. The air was thick and weighed heavily on the still water. Wavelets left bits of foam on the sand.

The fog curled and slithered over the flat gray water. No need for bonfires. Those out fishing had seen the fog bank rolling across the sea and managed to make their way to shore in time. Treia and Aylaen were the only people on the beach, and Aylaen wondered uneasily why they had come.

Treia let go of her sister and stood gazing out into the fog. Her eyes squinted. She seemed frustrated.

"Can you see anything?" she asked Aylaen.

"What am I looking for?" Aylaen asked, and then stopped, astonished.

A dragonship glided out of the fog, seeming to materialize before Aylaen's eyes, taking shape and form from the mists.

"I see a ship," she said.

"Yes, I see it now, as well," said Treia.

The dragonship drew nearer. Aylaen scanned the decks and gasped, trembling. "Treia, there's no one on board. It's a ghost ship!"

"It is Skylan's ship, the *Venjekar,*" said Treia with implacable calm.

"But Skylan left here with many men," Aylaen said, dismayed. "And the Kai Priestess was with him. Where are they now? What terrible thing has happened? Why would the dragonship come back without them?"

"Fetch Norgaard," Treia told her.

Aylaen hesitated a moment; then, hiking up her skirts, she ran across the dunes, shouting wildly for the Chief.

Treia remained standing in the wet sand, gazing at the ship. "A ghost ship," she repeated. "So it is. The ghost of the might of the Vindrasi."

A crowd gathered on the beach and watched in silence as Garn and Bjorn and several other warriors waded out into the gray water to board the *Venjekar.* The warriors were armed, and they approached the ship warily. The Dragon Kahg would never permit an enemy to board his ship, but dragons were mortal. Kahg might be dead. This could be a trick—for all knew the story of the Olfet Clan.

Long ago, their dragonship had been attacked at sea by Cyclopes. The Cyclopes boarded the ship, killed the dragon and the crew, then sailed the ship to Vindrasi shores. People of the Olfet Clan spotted the ship floating on the waves. Seeing it empty and apparently adrift, they boarded it and were immediately set upon by the Cyclopes, who had been lying flat on the deck. The Cyclopes killed everyone, wiping out the Olfet Clan, leaving only a cautionary tale behind.

Garn grabbed hold of the hull and pulled himself up over the side slowly. He scanned the deck. The ship appeared to be deserted, no enemy lying in wait. The spiritbone hung in place. The eyes of the Dragon Kahg gazed fiercely into the fog. Motioning the other warriors to accompany him, Garn walked across the deck. He tried to be quiet, but the wooden boards creaked beneath his weight. The ship rocked as the warriors clambered aboard.

Finding a pile of blankets on the deck, Garn reached down to pick one up. He heard a noise and froze in place. The noise had come from below—a sound of feet scrabbling and a thud, as if someone, bumbling about in the murky darkness, had knocked over something.

Garn motioned for Bjorn and Erdmun. "Someone's down there!" he mouthed, pointing.

The three padded soft-footed to the sealed hatch. They stood over it, listening. The sound was not repeated. At Garn's gesture, Bjorn and Erdmun lifted their battle axes and took up positions on either side of the hatch. Garn grasped the trapdoor and gave a sudden jerk. Throwing it open, he sprang back, ready to fight.

"What? Who's there?" a voice called.

"Skylan!" Garn yelled, staring into the darkness. "Are you all right?"

Skylan, sword in hand, appeared at the foot of the ladder. His hair was tousled, his face creased from sleep. He gazed at his friend in groggy bewilderment. "Garn?" he said dazedly, lowering his sword. "Is that you? Or am I dreaming?"

Garn climbed down the ladder. "You are home, my friend!"

Skylan stared at him; then he dropped his sword and wiped his hand across his eyes.

"Thank Torval!" Skylan said fervently. "I did not think I would ever see you again!"

Garn regarded his friend in astonishment and concern. Skylan's arms and torso were covered with welts and jagged cuts. His face was bruised and battered; patches of hair and bits of scalp were sloughing off from an ugly wound on the back of his head.

"Skylan, where is everyone?" Garn asked. "What happened? Where is the Kai Priestess?"

Skylan shook his head. "Is my father here?"

"He's waiting onshore," said Garn.

"I must speak to him," Skylan said. He bent to pick up his sword, and that seemed to remind him of something, for he glanced around the hold.

"Wulfe?" he called out. "Where are you?"

There was no response, and Skylan turned to Garn. "Did you see a boy up on deck?"

"No," Garn said, mystified. "What boy?"

"He must be hiding," Skylan said, and he smiled. "Of course. It's your sword. You frighten him." He raised his voice. "These are my friends, Wulfe. They won't hurt you."

"Who is this Wulfe?" Garn asked.

"He's a strange kid. I think he's crazy, but he seems harmless. He was a good friend to me. He treated my wounds and nursed me through a fever. Let all men know he is under my protection."

Skylan called for Wulfe again. When he didn't answer, Skylan shrugged. "I guess he'll come out when he gets hungry."

He sighed and squared his shoulders, preparing for a difficult task. "And now I must tell my father and the rest of the people the terrible news."

"Draya?" asked Garn.

"She is dead," Skylan said. "They are all dead. Their bodies lie at the bottom of the Hesvolm Sea."

# CHAPTER 16

When we reached the Dragon Isles," Skylan said, "we did not beach the dragonship, but kept it in the water. There was something strange about this place I did not like. Draya felt the same, and she remained on board the ship while my men and I went to shore. When we walked onto the beach, I knew immediately that going to the Dragon Isles had been a terrible mistake."

Skylan paused to take a drink of ale. No one spoke. The Torgun gave him their full attention, listening in hushed, respectful silence, no one interrupting, no one expressing doubt or disbelief. Skylan was telling his tale well. Not surprising. He had spent so much time on board the dragonship rehearsing his lie, perfecting it, reciting it over and over, that he was almost starting to believe it himself.

"We came upon a strange imprint in the sand," Skylan continued. "We did not know at first what to make of it. The imprint was huge, as long as this hall, and it was not natural. I looked at it, looked at the shape. And then I knew. It was made by a foot. A foot as long as this hall and just as wide."

Skylan paused for effect and lowered his voice. "It was the footprint of a giant."

"A giant!" Erdmun laughed in disbelief, as did many of the young warriors.

The older warriors shouted angrily for silence.

"Do you laugh at Torval?" Norgaard asked sternly, glaring at Erdmun, who tried to hide from his Chief's wrath by ducking behind his older brother. "Torval gave the giants the Dragon Isles to live upon. In return, the giants guard the Hall of Vektia."

"I confess, Father, that I did not believe the old tales," said Skylan. "I should have listened to them."

In truth, it was Norgaard's stories about the giants of the Dragon Isles that had given Skylan the idea. Legend held that giants guarded the Hall of Vektia. No one had ever seen a giant, however, and many Vindrasi, especially the young, doubted the giants' existence.

The tale of giants was admirably suited for Skylan's purposes, however. His father believed in them, as did the older warriors. The fact that no one had seen a giant in many generations was easily explained. The giants appeared only when the Hall was threatened.

"The next moment," Skylan continued, "a spear, the size of a full-grown oak tree, flew from the sky and cut down three of my warriors. The giants came thundering out of the woods. They bore spears and clubs, but they needed no weapons. They had only to stomp their feet and my men died, crushed to bloody pulp. Most of my warriors fell before they ever knew what had happened to them."

"Why would the giants attack?" Norgaard demanded. "We have not broken any law—" He stopped in midsentence.

"As you have guessed, the Vektan Torque is the reason, Father," said Skylan. "I fought the monsters. Draya was on board the ship, trying to summon the Dragon Kahg. Before she could complete the spell, a giant grabbed hold of her and plucked her off the ship. I fought for her," Skylan added, subdued. At least that was the truth. "I tried to save her. The giant flung her, screaming, to the ground. Her back was broken. She could not move. I held her in my arms as she died."

Women wiped tears from their eyes. Men rubbed their noses. Aylaen wept. Norgaard was grim. Skylan did not look at Garn. It was Treia who broke the sorrow-laden silence. She seemed to be taking the sad news with calm equanimity.

"The giants killed the Kai Priestess. They killed your men. How came you to survive?"

Skylan had been waiting for this question.

"I wanted to die," he said somberly. "I wanted to be the one to lead my warriors before Torval. I was not given the chance."

He choked with shame and grief, and he had to stop to clear his throat. His emotions were real, if his tale was not. He *had* lost his men. He *had* been forced to watch Draya die horribly. He *had* tried to save his wife and failed. The true and the false began to blur in his mind.

"I challenged the giants, taunted them, dared them to fight me. But as we Vindrasi always leave one survivor in a battle to carry a warning to our enemies, so the giants left me alive. They sent me back with a message. Because Horg gave the Vektan Torque to our enemies, the gods have cursed us. We are not permitted to return to the Dragon Isles until we have recovered the sacred torque from the ogres."

This was the part of the lie that Skylan considered inspired. The Vindrasi nation would be roused to action. Skylan would recover the torque and redeem himself in the eyes of Torval. All his lies, his blunders, and mistakes would be forgiven him.

Drawing his sword, he held it high above his head. "I vow to Torval that by the next moonrise, the dragonships of the Vindrasi will sail. As Chief of Chiefs, I will lead our warriors to battle! We will find the ogres' lands, and we will put the monsters to the sword and take back our sacred torque! Then we will sail to the Dragon Isles and lay it at the feet of the gods!"

The Torgun cheered and stamped on the floor and pounded the tables with the flats of their hands. The hall thundered with their approval. Long years had passed since the Vindrasi had gone to war.

Only two people did not join in the wild enthusiasm. Aylaen stood with her hands at her side, her fists clenched. Garn, too, was somber. He said something to her, but she refused to look at him.

The Torgun gathered around Skylan, offering their condolences on his loss and vowing their support for his cause. The young warriors crowded near, vying with each other, each hoping they would be chosen to go on this journey that would be celebrated for generations in story and song.

Skylan turned away. He was in a dark mood, and he wanted them all to just leave him alone. He didn't know why he was upset. All was going well. His people believed him. His lie had been a success. But perhaps that was the problem. He had failed to save those he had pledged to protect, and now he was using them to gain what he wanted. He was like the craven warrior on the field of battle who hides beneath the corpses of his fallen comrades, praying his enemies do not find him.

Garn rested his hand on Skylan's arm.

"You don't look well," he said. "You should have Treia tend your head wound."

"I don't want some Bone Priestess praying over me," Skylan said. "I'm tired. I'm going home."

"I'll walk with you," Garn offered.

"I don't need a guide."

"I thought you might need a friend," Garn said quietly.

Skylan shook his head. "I can find my own way home."

He bade good night to his father and took his leave, walking out the door of the hall just as another man was walking in.

"What's this?" the man said heartily. "A celebration! I seem to have come at the right time!"

Skylan stopped dead. The man was Raegar. His eyelid flickered in a wink. He shoved past Skylan and entered the hall.

"Norgaard Ivorson!" Raegar shouted. "Even after all these years, I would know you anywhere! Let me embrace you, brother!"

Norgaard stared at the stranger, mystified; then he gasped. "Can it be Raegar?"

"The one and the same!" Raegar roared, grinning. "I have come home."

Treia knew Skylan was lying. The others were so gullible, swallowing that silly tale about giants. She didn't know why he had lied, but she could guess. It was to cover his crime and Draya's. The fact that between them they had conspired to murder Horg. Treia didn't know how. She didn't have proof. She had only suspicions. Once she knew for certain, she would go before the Kai, expose them both. The Kai would be shocked, of course, but they would also be grateful. So grateful they would choose Treia to be the new Kai Priestess.

Before now, Treia had never considered aspiring to such heights. Before now, she had known she didn't have a chance. None of the Priestesses liked her. Under normal circumstances, they would never consider selecting her.

Circumstances were not normal, however. Draya had named no successor. Even if she had, once the Kai discovered she had murdered Horg, robbed Torval of his judgment, the Kai would renounce her. It would be as if she had never been.

Treia's suspicions had been aroused by the fact that Horg had behaved strangely during the fight. She couldn't see all that well, but she had been able to recognize a sick man when she saw one. Horg had acted sick—clutching his belly, staggering about, retching. He had not taken any serious wounds, she was certain of that. People standing around her even commented on the fact. Treia thought it over and came to suspect that Horg had been poisoned. Her suspicions were confirmed when Draya had swiftly covered up the corpse, so that no one should see it, and then ordered the Dragon Kahg to get rid of the body.

Treia had considered voicing her suspicions, and she would have if anyone else had come forward. No one did, and she was forced to keep her doubts to herself. The people were satisfied with the decision of the gods. They had not liked Horg, and they did like Skylan. All that would change, though, once Treia had proof.

She slipped unnoticed out of the hall. Taking down a torch to light her way, she hastened through the empty streets, heading for the shore. She needed proof that Skylan was lying. No one would believe her otherwise.

The *Venjekar* rested on its keel on the beach. The wind had risen and shredded the fog. The moon was thin and pale; the stars seemed cold and distant. The sea was dark and stirred sullenly. As Treia boarded the dragonship, she felt the eyes of the Dragon Kahg on her.

Treia took down the spiritbone from where it hung on the figurehead, clasped it tightly in her hand, and boldly confronted the dragon.

Wulfe crouched in the hold, afraid to come out. The fierce warriors with their terrible swords and tree-killing axes had frightened him half out of his wits. He had run away to hide and stumbled over a stool, sending it crashing, which had brought the warriors down on top of him.

He found some small comfort in the fact that Skylan had been glad to see these men. They were his friends, not enemies. Skylan had called him to come out, but Wulfe was still too afraid. He remained hiding behind some barrels, relaxing only after they all left the ship.

He was now more hungry than afraid, but he feared if he went ashore alone, the warriors would find him and kill him. Skylan had told him lurid tales of what the Torgun had done to the ogres who had dared set foot on their land. Wulfe hoped Skylan would come back to fetch him, but the night wore on with no sign of his friend.

Wulfe decided to sleep on board the ship until the return of daylight, figuring that Skylan would certainly come for him then. He was almost ready to come out from behind the barrels when he heard the sound of someone walking on the deck, and that sent him scurrying back to his hiding place.

He heard someone talking to the dragon. It sounded like a woman—a real, live woman, not the draugr. The woman's voice was low, and Wulfe couldn't understand what she was saying. He could tell by her tone that she was addressing the dragon with reverence and respect.

The dragon did not respond.

The woman's tone changed, became sharper.

The dragon's silence continued.

The woman stomped her foot in frustration. Her tone was commanding.

Wulfe could sense the dragon's rising anger, and the boy shivered and wished the woman would take heed and leave. Perhaps she did notice after all, for she fell silent. She did not leave, however. Wulfe saw torchlight shining down into the hatch, and he realized in dismay that she was going to descend into the hold.

The woman climbed slowly down the ladder, moving hesitantly, holding the skirts of her robes in one hand and the torch in the other.

Wulfe recognized her by the robes.

It *was* the draugr. Coming for him.

He gave a piercing shriek and jumped out from behind the barrels, startling the draugr, who nearly dropped the torch. He dashed past the draugr, giving her a shove that sent her staggering backwards. He climbed two rungs of the ladder, then felt a hand seize him around the ankle.

Wulfe screamed and kept screaming, shrill and piercing, like the rabbit when the fox sank his teeth in its neck. He kicked frantically to free himself from the draugr's clutches. The draugr gave a yank, and he lost his grip on the ladder and tumbled down to lie on his back at the draugr's feet.

Except it wasn't a draugr. He could see that now. She was a living, breathing woman, and she stared down at him in astonishment.

"Stop shrieking," she snapped, and Wulfe stopped.

"Who are you? Where did you come from?" the woman asked.

Wulfe didn't like her. The elder said Wulfe had an animal's sense about people, perhaps because of the way they smelled. This woman did not carry iron, but she smelled of iron, as though her soul were made of iron.

No wonder the dragon had refused to answer her questions. Wulfe decided to do likewise. He kept his lips clamped tight and did not move.

"Are you dumb, boy?" The woman peered down at him through squinting eyes.

Wulfe shook his head.

"Not deaf, are you? Can you hear me? Do you speak our language?"

Wulfe nodded.

"Are you a friend of Skylan's?"

Again Wulfe nodded.

The woman's voice softened; her tone became soothing, as though she were trying to placate a snarling dog. "You don't need to be afraid. I am Skylan's friend, too."

She held out her hand. "I can take you to him, if you want. No one will hurt you. Not if you're with me."

Ignoring the outstretched hand, Wulfe scrambled to his feet, keeping his distance. "Can I have something to eat?"

The woman gave a tight, stiff smile. "So you *can* talk, after all. My name is Treia. What is your name?"

Names were powerful. Wulfe kept quiet.

The woman named Treia gave an exasperated sigh and motioned with her hand. "Wait for me up on deck. I'll join you in a moment."

Wulfe hesitated, then did as he was told. He stood on the deck, feeling oddly unsteady now that the ship was no longer moving. He could hear her rummaging about down below. He had no idea what she was looking for, and he didn't think she did either. He wished she would hurry.

Treia came back up the ladder. Her face was rigid. She seemed annoyed. When she saw Wulfe, she tried another smile, but didn't quite manage it.

"Come with me," she ordered.

She offered Wulfe her hand again. Again he didn't take it. Shrugging, she walked across the deck, and Wulfe trailed after her. She paused a moment to look up at the dragon.

The dragon had nothing to say, and Treia's lips compressed.

"How did you and Skylan meet?" she asked as they walked across the sand dunes. She had to glance around at him, for he walked several paces behind her, not liking to get too close.

Wulfe pretended he hadn't heard. He could see the roofs of longhouses silhouetted against the stars. Skylan had told him about the village, about his home, about his friends and his father and about the woman he loved. Wulfe hoped that this was not the woman. He didn't think it was. Skylan had told him she had hair the color of fire. This woman had hair the color of donkey piss.

The woman kept asking him questions, all of them about Skylan. Wulfe didn't believe her when she said she was Skylan's friend. If she was his friend, she wouldn't ask so many questions. He wished she would be quiet. Her voice was like being poked with a sharp stick.

They walked the streets. Wulfe's nose twitched, and his mouth watered. He could smell the meat and vegetables simmering in the stewpots.

"I'm really hungry," he said. "And I want to see Skylan."

Now it was Treia who did not answer him. She was peering down the street at a large building, the largest Wulfe had ever seen. The door to the building stood open—light poured out, and with it a hubbub of voices, lots of people talking all at once.

"Something has happened," said Treia.

She reached out and grabbed his arm, startling Wulfe, who hadn't been expecting that. His instinct was to pull away, but she was moving at a run toward the large building, dragging Wulfe behind. He thought maybe this was where he would find Skylan and maybe there would be something to eat, and so he let the woman keep hold of his arm, wondering why she felt the need to hang on to him. If she feared he would have trouble keeping up with her, she was wrong. He could run far faster than she could, especially on all fours.

Someday he would show her.

The Torgun crowded around Raegar, exclaiming and rejoicing, clapping him on the back, offering him drink and food, rearranging the benches, giving him a seat of honor.

Raegar embraced Norgaard, calling him "brother," and then asked, with easy good nature, "Where is my favorite cousin? Where is little Skylan?"

At this, everyone roared with laughter.

Skylan came forward. Raegar made a fine show of being astonished, proclaiming that this fine handsome young man could not be the scrawny little boy he remembered. He marveled to hear not only that this young man truly was Skylan, all grown up, but also that Skylan was now Chief of Chiefs of the Vindrasi nation.

Raegar embraced his cousin in a bear hug. "Don't worry. Your secret is safe!" Raegar whispered, his breath tickling Skylan's ear.

Grinning, Raegar slapped Skylan on the back and turned away to speak to Norgaard.

Skylan didn't find that very reassuring. All Raegar had done was remind Skylan that he had a secret and that Raegar knew it and could reveal it at any time. Skylan longed to go to bed, for the strain was exhausting. He couldn't.

He had to find a chance to talk to Raegar in private, discover why he had come to Luda.

Everyone wanted to know Raegar's story, and he was glad to tell it. He related how he had been wounded and near death and how his captors had healed him in order to sell him into slavery and how he had made a new life in the Southland. He was in the middle of the tale, with everyone listening eagerly, when Treia appeared in the doorway, holding Wulfe by the hand.

"Skylan," she said, interrupting Raegar's flow of talk, "this boy claims to know you."

Raegar stopped in the middle of a sentence. His mouth dropped open. He rose to his feet and took a step toward her, as though drawn by some invisible thread.

Treia blinked at him. He stared at her.

"I did not remember the women of the Torgun were so beautiful," he said. "Or else I would have crawled home on my hands and knees."

Treia's cheeks were flushed from running. Her blond hair had come loose from the elaborate braids and cascaded down around her shoulders. Her eyes glistened in the firelight; her breath came fast. None would have called Treia beautiful before this, but seeing her through the eyes of a stranger, they wondered where their own eyes had been all this time.

Treia's flush deepened. She blinked again at Raegar, trying to bring him into focus, and was about to reply to his compliment when Wulfe broke free of her grasp and made a lunge at the table. He seized a large bowl of stew, clasped it in both arms, and turned and dashed outside.

"What was that?" Norgaard asked, astonished. "An imp from the Nethervold?"

"The boy I told you about," said Skylan. "The one I found adrift in the sea. I warned you he was a little mad."

"More than a little, it seems," said Norgaard dryly. "Well, you had better go catch him before you lose him again."

"Cousin, I would first have a word with you," said Raegar, plucking at Skylan's sleeve. He drew him off into a shadowy corner.

"Yes, Cousin, what can I do for you?" Skylan asked pleasantly. Once they were out of earshot of the others, he glowered at Raegar. "What in the name of Hevis are you doing here? Why have you come?"

"I bring good news. I found a map that gives the location of the ogres' lands," Raegar said coolly, and he grinned. "Ah, I thought that would please you. The ogres are not far. A month's sailing, perhaps."

"That is good news," Skylan admitted. "I am grateful."

"There's another reason." Raegar glanced over his shoulder to the people laughing and talking. "Meeting you made me start thinking about my kin. I realized I had been away too long. It was time to come home."

As if he'd heard his nephew's words, Norgaard rose and called for silence. "We are all glad our clansman has returned home," he said. "I trust he will not soon leave us. This night has been long, starting in sorrow and ending in joy." He raised his drinking horn. "A toast to Raegar, who has come back from the dead."

The Torgun grinned at Raegar and lifted their drinking horns and drank.

Norgaard raised his horn to Skylan. "To our Chief of Chiefs and his safe return."

The Torgun drank this toast and then refilled their horns, all of them waiting eagerly for the toast they knew was coming.

"It is far too long since the Vindrasi have gone to war." Norgaard lifted his drinking horn high in the air. "To Torval and the destruction of our foe!"

The Torgun roared, "To Torval!" and drank.

"We have much work to do to prepare," said Norgaard, placing his empty horn on the table. "This meeting is ended."

Moving slowly and painfully, leaning heavily on his crutch, Norgaard limped over to Skylan and rested his hand on his son's shoulder.

"You have been through a terrible experience, my son," Norgaard said. His eyes were moist. "You handled it well. I am proud of you."

"Thank you, Father," said Skylan. His throat closed, choking on his lies.

People streamed out of the hall. Norgaard stood talking a moment with Raegar. Skylan made a hasty escape and plunged out the door. He nearly stumbled over Wulfe, who was squatting in the middle of the street, hunched over the bowl, shoveling food into his mouth with both hands. Skylan took down a flaring torch from the wall.

"Come with me," he said, grabbing Wulfe, who grabbed the bowl.

"Where are you taking me? To the ship?"

"To my home," said Skylan.

Wulfe planted his feet and stood firm. "I want to go back to the ship."

Skylan considered. Perhaps it would be best if Wulfe remained on board the ship. He would be less likely to talk to people than if he lived with Skylan in the village.

"Very well," said Skylan. "But you'll have to stay on the ship by yourself. I can't be with you."

"I won't be alone," said Wulfe. "The dragon is there."

"I didn't think you liked the dragon."

"I like him better. He wouldn't talk to that woman."

"What woman?"

"The woman who brought me."

"You mean Treia? She was talking to the dragon? What did they talk about?"

"You," said Wulfe, licking his fingers.

Skylan stopped, troubled and immediately suspicious. The only reason Treia would have to speak to the dragon would be to find out if Skylan was telling the truth. He glanced back over his shoulder. The Torgun were filing out of the hall, and some would be sure to come looking for him. Skylan doused his torch in a nearby bucket and ducked down a side street, hauling Wulfe with him.

"What did she say to the dragon?"

"I don't know," said Wulfe. "I couldn't hear. It doesn't matter, because the dragon wouldn't answer her. That made her mad, and she came down into the hold. She scared me. I thought she was the draugr. She was dressed like the draugr. She asked me questions."

"What questions?"

"Where I met you and where was I when I met you and who was with you and did I see the giants."

"What did you say?" Skylan waited nervously for the answer.

"Nothing," said Wulfe. "I don't like her."

"That's good!" said Skylan, relieved.

Wulfe used a piece of meat to scoop up gravy, running it around the side of the crockery bowl. "What did she mean about you fighting giants?"

Skylan paused. He'd known this moment was coming. He hadn't expected it to come so soon. He squatted down in front of the boy, looked him in the eyes.

"It's a story I made up. Wulfe, if Treia or anyone else asks you, tell them I found you adrift in the sea, lost in the fog."

"But you didn't," said Wulfe.

"I know. It's a lie, but it's a good lie, not a bad lie. Like the lie about the giants is a good lie. I told the lie because I want to protect the druids and your people on Apensia."

Wulfe looked puzzled by this. "You don't need to lie."

"Yes, I do. If my people found out that the druids killed my wife—"

Wulfe interrupted. "The druids didn't kill her. The druids don't kill people."

"I saw them drive a stake through her belly," Skylan said harshly. "Don't argue. Just listen! If my people ever find out what happened, they will sail to Apensia and use their swords to kill the elder and the others."

Wulfe smiled at his friend in reassurance. "They can't. The faeries won't let them. Your people would be the ones to die."

Skylan gazed out across the sea, dark in this dark night.

"Wulfe," said Skylan, "if my people hear the truth, I will die. They will kill me."

"I'll say you found me in the sea," said Wulfe.

# BOOK 4

# THE DRAGON ISLES

CHAPTER

# 1

The Vindrasi were going to war.

A month had passed since Skylan's return from his ill-fated voyage. The Vindrasi celebrated the summer solstice that launched the time of Skoval, the raiding season. The weather was hot and continued dry. Rain came in sporadic bursts, pelting the hard ground with huge drops that were of small benefit to languishing crops. The Vindrasi needed a week of gentle soaking rains. The Bone Priestesses offered prayers to Akaria, but the temperamental goddess did not see fit to respond.

Despite these ongoing concerns, Skylan was in good spirits. The time of his return had been dark and unhappy, but now that was over. His sun had risen once more, and hope for the future shone brightly. He moved from Luda to Vindraholm, took up residence in the house of the Chief of Chiefs, empty now that his wife was dead.

The funerals for the Heudjun dead had been hard, but he'd managed to get through them. If he was somber, people put it down to sorrow. Skylan expanded on the heroics of the warriors, describing the make-believe fight with the giants in detail. The Heudjun mourned their dead and honored them for their heroism and then made ready to go to war.

Draya's funeral was the most difficult. Skylan grieved for Draya with a grief compounded of guilt and remorse and self-recrimination. He tried to assuage her restless spirit and his conscience by giving the statue of Vindrash the lavish gift of a valuable turquoise necklace. The offering did not work. The draugr continued to plague him. Night after weary night, she came to Skylan before he slept and forced him to play dragonbones with her. He could not understand why she did this. It seemed her only purpose in walking this earth as a corpse was to play this game—a game he never won.

He had to admit the draugr had made him a better player. He kept hoping that if he finally beat the draugr, she would leave him alone, and thus he concentrated more on the game than on anything he'd ever done in his life. Previously he had always made his moves as the moment took him, rarely thinking more than one or two moves in advance. He had been quick to see his foe's weakness, but had generally failed to note her strength until it was too late.

The draugr was an excellent dragonbone player. Skylan had never gone up against such a skilled opponent. She was better than Garn, who had beaten everyone among the Torgun so often that now no one would play him. Skylan eventually realized that if he studied the way she played, the tactics she used to defeat him, he might learn something to his advantage. He began to do that, and he began to see that the game was far deeper and more complex than he had realized. He forced himself to be patient, to be observant, to think first before he acted. He still never won. But the matches more frequently ended in draws.

Skylan's next official duty, after presiding over the funerals, was to rally his people for war. Escorted by a troop of young warriors, he rode Blade or sailed in the *Venjekar* to meet with the other Clan Chiefs, convince them to give him warriors and what wealth they had to pay for the expedition against the ogres.

The Chiefs needed no convincing. All of them were eager to fight. The Vindrasi had long chafed under Horg's unwillingness to allow so much as a blood feud among kin. They were glad to have a Chief of Chiefs who was going to lead them into battle against their enemies.

Wulfe did not accompany Skylan on these journeys. Concerned and a little nervous at leaving the strange boy on his own, Skylan had tried to persuade him to go. But the warriors who escorted the Chief of Chiefs went heavily armed, and Wulfe could not bear to be around them. Skylan considered this aversion of the boy's to iron a silly notion, taught to him by the peace-loving druids. Skylan tried numerous times to persuade Wulfe that a stewpot was not his foe.

"How are you going to fight at my side in the shield-wall if you refuse to even touch a sword?" Skylan had asked the boy.

"I don't need a sword to fight," Wulfe had replied. "I won't be at your side in a battle, but I will be there to protect you. I saved your life. You belong to me."

The boy was intensely serious, and Skylan had smiled and reached out his hand to brush Wulfe's shaggy hair out of his eyes.

"You're a strange one," Skylan had said. "And someday I will teach you to use a sword."

While Wulfe remained behind, Raegar accompanied Skylan on his travels. His cousin had been true to his promise. He had kept Skylan's secret faithfully. And, as promised, he had brought Skylan a map, which he claimed revealed the location of the ogre nation. Skylan could not read, and therefore he could make nothing of the map himself. Skylan was forced to take his cousin at his word. He was forced to take Raegar at his word about a lot of things—one reason Skylan liked to keep Raegar close to him.

Raegar was at least a jovial companion, unlike Garn, who had turned into a killjoy, or so it seemed to Skylan. Garn always looked grave and somber; he was always wanting to "talk," which meant he wanted to lecture.

Skylan was convinced that Garn knew he was lying about the giants, about most everything, and in this, he was right. Garn knew Skylan was not telling the truth. Skylan was wrong about Garn wanting to lecture him, however. Concerned for his friend, Garn only wanted to find some way to help.

Skylan had another worry, and that was Treia.

She did not bother to conceal the fact that she thought Skylan was a liar. She did not confront him. She was like a snake, slinking about in the undergrowth, watching his every move, waiting for him to trip over a rock so she could sink her poisoned fangs into him. Skylan avoided her as much as possible, and that was one reason he was leaving for Luda tomorrow, when she was arriving here at Vindraholm for the Kai Moot.

Alarming news had reached Skylan. Word had it that the Kai were considering Treia for Kai Priestess. If she was thus honored by the gods, he would have to marry her! He took comfort in the fact that she would also be adverse to such a union. She disliked Skylan fully as much as he disliked her. And she had her eyes on his cousin.

Though Treia had left her stepfather's house and was living on her own in the lodging of the Bone Priestess, she was yet unmarried and was therefore under Sigurd's care and protection. Since Sigurd had given up trying to arrange a marriage for her, Treia decided in her own mind that the matter was now up to her. She made no secret of the fact that she had chosen her own future husband, and that her choice was Raegar. He continued to take a marked interest in Treia, singling her out over many other younger and prettier women who were vying to catch the notice of the tall, strong, and well-favored blond-bearded man.

Though Skylan was certain Treia did not want to be Kai Priestess, he did not trust the gods. Given his broken oath to Torval and the many lies he'd told since, the god might decide to punish Skylan by making this snake his wife. Skylan thought it best to head off danger. When he ended his triumphant journey to introduce himself to the clans, he traveled to Luda to speak to Aylaen.

"The Kai Moot will be held soon," he told her. "Treia will be attending. I want you to go with her."

Aylaen was going to draw water from a small spring, and Skylan offered to accompany her. The spring cut through a grove of ash, birch, hazel, laurel, and oak trees. Water from this spring was said to have healing properties, and though Treia had remarked scornfully that she did not believe this, her patients did.

The spring was located deep in the woods, near Owl Mother's house. Skylan thought back to the time the old crone had magically healed the wound when the boar had gored him. That same day, the ogres had arrived. The time seemed distant and remote, as if it might have happened in some other lifetime. Or to some other person. He remembered, suddenly, what Owl Mother had said to him on that day: *The thread of your wyrd snaps tonight. Tomorrow it will be spun anew.*

He was pondering her words and thinking that they had come true and wondering, with a shiver, how she'd known—when he realized that Aylaen was laughing.

"Did I say something funny?" he demanded irritably. He was not in the mood to be laughed at.

"Yes," said Aylaen. "You want me to attend a boring old Kai Moot! Why should I? I'm getting more than enough sleep now, thank you."

"I know the meeting will be dull and tedious," Skylan admitted. He took the bucket from her and knelt down to fill it at the sparkling stream. "But you have to attend. You have to tell them you want to become a Bone Priestess, and you want to do it in a hurry."

"But I *don't* want to become a Bone Priestess," Aylaen protested, still laughing. "I've seen what Treia has to put up with. People whining and complaining and asking her to do the impossible to make their lives better. I don't know where she finds the patience."

"You have to do this, Aylaen," Skylan insisted. "This is the only way for you to become Kai Priestess, and that is the only way we can be married."

"Skylan, you're not serious—"

"Hevis take me if I'm not!" Skylan said, glowering at her. "Why do you insist on mocking me? I am Chief of Chiefs. I want you to be my wife! You will do this, Aylaen. I command it!"

Aylaen flushed, hot blood rushing to her face. "You may order everyone else about, Skylan Ivorson, but not me! I do what I want and what I want is—"

"—the same thing I want," Skylan interrupted her impatiently. "You love me. I know it. Stop teasing me. I am a man now, not a boy. The time for such foolery is passed."

"I am not teasing you!" Aylaen said, her rage mounting, burning away reason. "Garn did not want me to tell you, but I have to! The truth is—"

"Garn!" Skylan exploded. "What has Garn to do with us? Look, if you're mad because you have to be Kai Priestess, I don't blame you. The position would be mostly ceremonial."

Skylan slid his hand around her waist and drew her close. "You will be spending most of your time raising our sons." He tried to kiss her.

"Skylan, let go of me." Aylaen averted her face, avoided his lips. "I have to be getting home. Mother will be needing my help with supper."

Skylan let go of her, but his expression was dark with anger. "I don't understand you, Aylaen. I know you love me—"

"—like a brother, Skylan," she said.

He glowered at this, but before he could say anything, she turned away and began to walk rapidly down the path, her skirts swishing around her ankles.

"The Kai would never make me their leader, Skylan," she said, flinging the words at him over her shoulder. "It would be an insult to all the other Priestesses. Those like my sister, who studied all her life."

"It is not up to the Kai," said Skylan, crashing through the brush after her. They had both forgotten their task. The water bucket remained beside the stream. "The gods make the choice."

"You know what I mean," said Aylaen impatiently.

"Besides, there is precedence."

"Precedence for what?"

"For making a woman who has never been a Bone Priestess the Kai Priestess."

Skylan had known he might be confronted by this very argument, though he had thought it would be raised by the Kai Moot, not by the woman he loved. He had gone to the Talgogroth to discuss the matter.

"Griselda the Man-Woman. Her deeds of heroism in battle impressed the gods so much, they told the Kai to make her Priestess, and they gave her in marriage to the son of Thorgunnd when he became Chief of Chiefs. Of course, you can't do what she did. You can't fight alongside the men—"

Skylan caught hold of Aylaen, and when she struggled, he clasped her tighter, refusing to let her go. He kissed her cheek and sought her lips.

"You will be my wife—"

"Skylan! Don't!" Aylaen shoved against him. "Let go of me!"

Skylan's desire flared inside him, burning his blood. He knew Aylaen wanted him. This show of reluctance was merely maidenly reserve. He pressed her against a tree with his body, while his hands, expert at such work, swiftly unpinned the brooches that held up her dress.

"Skylan, don't do this," she pleaded.

"You want this, Aylaen. You know you do. We're as good as married—" His hands slid down the front of her smock. He touched her breasts and groaned and thrust himself against her.

"Skylan!" someone shouted. "Skylan, where are you? I have a message for you!"

"It's only Garn," Skylan said huskily. He was pulling up her skirts. His need for her was painful, blinding him, like the Madness of Torval. "Keep quiet. He'll go away."

"Here!" Aylaen yelled. "Garn, over here!"

"Over where?" Garn called. He was close by.

Angrily, Skylan pushed back away from Aylaen. She hastily pinned the brooches in place and smoothed down her dress. Garn emerged from the shadows of the trees.

"Here you both are," he said, smiling and pretending not to notice Aylaen's flushed face and disheveled clothes and Skylan's scowl.

"What do you want?" Skylan demanded surlily.

"Owl Mother sent me to find you," said Garn. "She wants to talk to you. Something about a bargain you made with her."

"Since you are her errand boy, run back there and tell the crone I don't have time to deal with the whims of an old woman," Skylan told him. "Aylaen and I have things to talk about."

He put his arm possessively around Aylaen's waist and dragged her close.

"You better do as she wants, Skylan," Aylaen said, her voice shaking. "You shouldn't make Owl Mother angry."

"I'll stay with Aylaen," Garn offered.

Skylan hesitated, seething. He didn't want to leave, but at the same time, he didn't want to offend Owl Mother.

"Very well, I'll go. Talk some sense into Aylaen while you're at it, brother," Skylan told Garn. "She claims she doesn't want to be Kai Priestess, and that's the only way we can be married. Make her see reason."

He stomped off down the path, angrily shoving aside tree limbs. They could hear him smashing through the undergrowth.

"Oh, Garn!" Aylaen cried, sagging against him, hiding her face in her hands. "I was so frightened!"

He put his arm around her. "Hush, I know. I came to look for you. Treia told me you'd gone to the stream."

Aylaen looked up at him, blinking back tears. "Did you make up that story about Owl Mother? Oh, Garn, Skylan will find out you lied to him, and then he'll be furious with you!"

"He'll cool off by then. He'll realize he was wrong. Skylan loves you, Aylaen," Garn added, soothing her. "He would never do anything to hurt you."

"The old Skylan wouldn't," said Aylaen. "I don't know this new Skylan. You didn't see his face. You have to tell him the truth about us, Garn!"

"I know," Garn replied. "I will speak to him when we are on the voyage—"

Aylaen stared at him. "The voyage! But you're not going to war! You said you would ask him to leave you in charge when he left. Norgaard's health is failing. Someone needs to stay behind to guard the village."

"I said I would *consider* asking Skylan, Aylaen," Garn said gently. "I didn't say I would."

Aylaen's flush deepened. Her fists clenched, and she struck him on the chest. "You can't go! I won't let you! How could you do this to me?"

"Aylaen—"

"You will be killed!" She yelled at him in fury, refusing to listen to him. "And if you are, I will die! For I could not bear to live!"

She kissed him passionately. He kissed her, then pushed her away. "Skylan might see us—"

"I hope he does!" Aylaen cried fiercely. "I *want* him to see us! I want the world to see us!"

She began to sob uncontrollably. Garn took hold of her, stroking her hair and holding her until she quieted. She wiped her nose on her sleeve. He dried the tears from her cheeks.

Aylaen pressed her cheek against his shoulder and gazed up at him. "You will talk to Skylan. Tell him about us. Tell him we're going to be married. Tell him you're not going with him when he sails to war."

Garn sighed. "It's not that simple—"

"It can be, if you want it to be," said Aylaen. She drew back, frowning. "You do want us to be married, don't you?"

"You know I do. More than anything in the world." Garn kissed her on the forehead.

"Then tell that to Skylan," Aylaen urged.

"I will," Garn said, and he added quietly and sadly, almost to himself, "It won't be that simple."

Aylaen heard him, but she pretended not to.

Two others heard him—Wulfe and the naiad who guarded the spring.

Wulfe had made friends with all the fae who dwelt in the meadows, the woods, and the waters around the Torgun village. He spent his days roaming the woodlands, visiting with the fae folk. Though he liked Skylan's people, considering them far easier to live with than the druids, he was much more comfortable among the fae.

The boy had soon found living on the dragonship with only the dragon for company to be both boring and uncomfortable. The Dragon Kahg was not an amiable companion. He never spoke, and he always glared at Wulfe whenever he came on deck.

Skylan had not thought it wise to take the strange boy among the Heudjun, who were still getting used to their Chief of Chiefs, and he sent Wulfe to live in his father's dwelling. But Wulfe did not like the cramped, dark, and smoky house, and he was still a little afraid of the Torgun, who, unlike the druids, were given to strong emotions that they never bothered to hide.

At first their loud voices had frightened him. The boy had spent a great deal of time shivering beneath a table or hiding in a corner. Eventually he came to see that although the Vindrasi were loud, boisterous, and contentious, they were not dangerous. (Had Wulfe seen them at war, he would have changed his mind and gone away in terror of them.)

As it was, once he got over his fear, he found he liked the raucous laughter and the singing and round oaths. Best of all, unlike the druids, the Torgun had no interest in trying to educate Wulfe. Skylan had told the boy he had to work to earn his keep. Wulfe was quite willing to do this, and he'd gone to the fields to tend the crops or herd cattle with the other children.

This had not worked out. The children complained that Wulfe spent all his time talking to himself. (He was talking to the fae, but they did not know that.)

The boy did have a way with animals, and that, too, proved unfortunate. The sheep tended to follow him about and ended up trampling the crops. Horses came running across the fields when he called, behaving like silly colts when they were around him, lowering their heads to be rubbed and nuzzling his neck. Crows would land on his shoulder and eat grain out of his hand. Meadow larks would sing for him.

Eventually Wulfe found his own place among the Torgun. The dryads told him about Owl Mother. He sought her out, and the two became fast friends. Owl Mother soon discovered Wulfe's secrets. Gifted with fae magic herself, Owl Mother had taught Wulfe that while such powers could be used to harm, they were not inherently harmful. Wulfe had to practice, learning how to wield his magic as Skylan wielded his sword. The rest of the Torgun people thought the boy was crazy, but they considered him harmless. They did not know there was a dark side to Wulfe. They did not know about his daemons. Thus far, he'd had the strength to fight them off, a strength that rose out of his love for Skylan.

Wulfe only vaguely remembered his father, whose image was a mixture of the wolf he'd been by day and the human he'd become at night. He had adored his mother, and he was heartbroken when she had quit coming to see him. The fae were wayward in their passions, something Wulfe only dimly understood. His mother had loved her son with her whole being, until she found some new pleasure. She had probably by now forgotten his very existence.

Wulfe hungered for affection. The druidic elder had been kind to him, but Wulfe could tell the man had not loved him. The elder knew about the dark and dangerous daemons that lurked inside the boy. He had worked patiently to try to teach Wulfe self-restraint, self-discipline, self-control. Wulfe found these lessons hard to bear, and he had been overjoyed to discover that Skylan agreed with him. Skylan indulged Wulfe, let him do as he pleased. Wulfe, in turn, adored Skylan.

As much as Wulfe adored Skylan, he hated Treia. She had never given up trying to force him to tell her how he had met Skylan and what had happened on the voyage. Wulfe felt, with his animal instinct, that Treia was a threat to Skylan, and Wulfe took it upon himself to keep watch on her. He would often hide in the woods near her dwelling, observing her comings and goings, following her, listening in on her conversations, though he rarely understood much of what she talked about.

Wulfe hoped to hear her plotting to murder Skylan, in which case he would have an excuse to unleash his daemons, who were always urging him to do terrible things to her. But though Treia spoke of Skylan with scorn and disdain, she never said anything to indicate she meant him harm. Wulfe never gave up hope, however, and he continued to keep an eye on her.

In regard to the other people in Skylan's life, Wulfe felt sorry for Norgaard, who walked the twilight realm between life and death. Wulfe knew the old man wanted to die, to leave behind the crippled body and go to live in glory with his god. Wulfe was kind to Norgaard, who came to like the boy, finding him amusing.

Wulfe was at first disposed to hate Garn and Aylaen. He discovered their secret almost at once. He knew Skylan loved Aylaen, for Skylan was always talking about her, and Wulfe could not understand how she could love someone else.

Wulfe had hated them both for betraying Skylan, and he was considering telling Skylan everything. Wulfe loved gossip as much as any dryad, and he watched the couple and listened to them talk and eventually he came to realize that neither of them wanted to hurt Skylan. The secret of their love cast a long shadow over their lives. Wulfe also realized that if Skylan found out the truth, it would destroy him. And so Wulfe kept the secret.

He was lounging beside the stream, telling the naiad about the naiads who lived on the Isle of Apensia, when they were interrupted by the arrival of Skylan and Aylaen. Wulfe hid among the trees and settled down to eavesdrop on the two. The naiad of the spring, the dryads of the fir and birch trees, the hamadryads who inhabited the oak trees, and a passing satyr all gathered to laugh at the antics of the Ugly Ones.

They watched Skylan press his love on Aylaen, and they watched her struggle to resist him. The satyr did an imitation of Skylan, swaggering about on his hairy goat legs, shouting his love for the giggling dryads, shaking his bulging penis at them, and boasting of his prowess. The dryads laughed at the satyr, until he came too close to one of them, and then they jeered at him and threw acorns at the randy half-goat/half-man to drive him away.

Once the satyr was gone, the dryads and their sisters shook the boughs of their trees, spreading the gossip through the forest. The naiad—a lovely, languid creature—sang a song about the love of the Uglies and sent it bubbling and rippling over the stones. The song traveled downstream to her cousins, the oceanaids, who found it vastly amusing.

Wulfe didn't think it was funny. He thought it was sad. He could not comprehend how three people who loved each other could do such hurt to each other. Love was supposed to be good, bring happiness, and here it was making each of these people suffer, just as love had made his parents suffer.

# CHAPTER 2

Skylan fumed all the way to Owl Mother's dwelling. He did not understand women. Aylaen adored him, of course, but she had always been contrary. She enjoyed making his life miserable, delighting in teasing and taunting him. That had been fine when they were children, but the time for teasing was past. She should be sweet and loving, overjoyed to become his wife. She did not seem to realize that he could have any woman he wanted.

He could scarcely walk for the women who were hurling themselves at his feet. Every day, some father came to bargain with him to marry his daughter. Such a marriage would not last long. Once the Kai chose a new Priestess, the marriage would end in divorce. The former wife of a Chief of Chiefs would come away with a great many benefits, however, not the least of which might be a son. To be the Chief's concubine was no small prize, either.

Skylan had done Aylaen the courtesy of turning down these offers. Her refusal even to consider becoming a Bone Priestess angered him. She should have been glad for the chance. This would solve all their problems. Why was she being so stubborn?

Skylan had even secretly tried to change the law. As Chief of Chiefs, he had the power to proclaim new laws. Why not fix this one? He'd gone to the Talgogroth to ask if this would be possible. The answer had been a firm and irrefutable no.

"The marriage of the Kai Priestess and the Chief of Chiefs is more than a tradition, Skylan," the Talgogroth had told him. "It is a marriage of two halves of a clan, a nation. It is the marriage of every man and every woman. It is the marriage of the worldly and the godly, the marriage of faith and logic, the marriage of the sword and of the shield. The people would rise up in rebellion at the very thought of ending this tradition!"

Aylaen would have to be made to understand that this was serious. He would have to explain it to her. He would do so, the first chance he got. And he would tell her, too, that she should treat him with the proper respect. No more teasing. The two of them could hasten the wedding night. After all, as groom, he was the one who had the right to complain that his wife had not come to his bed a virgin, return her to her father, and seek damages for the insult.

"If I am the one to take her virginity, who is there to complain?" Skylan muttered to himself. He remembered the feel of her, the warmth of her breasts, the fragrance of her hair. He throbbed painfully.

He was lost in his lustful dreams, not paying attention, when the warning snarl of a wolf brought him back to the present with a jolt. He looked about, but could not see the wolf. He could hear its continuous low growl, however. Any moment it might jump on him, knock him down, and savage him, rip out his throat.

The growling came nearer. He reached instinctively for his sword, but he had been hoping to be engaged in more pleasant activities with Aylaen this afternoon, and he had left the sword behind. Skylan drew his knife and braced himself.

The growl became a gurgle of laughter. Wulfe leaped out of the underbrush and stood on the path, grinning at Skylan.

"I scared you!" the boy said.

Skylan did not lower the knife. "Where's the beast?"

"That was me!" said Wulfe.

"I don't believe you," said Skylan.

"Listen. I'll show you."

Wulfe crouched on all fours and began to make a growling sound, low in his throat. His lips curled back in a snarl. His eyes narrowed, gleaming yellow in the dappled sunlight.

"Stop it!" Skylan ordered uneasily. His skin crawled. "That's not funny. And don't do it again. People might mistake you for a real wolf and slit your throat."

"They could try," said Wulfe with another laugh.

Skylan shook his head. Though he thought the boy was half-crazy, Skylan liked him, perhaps because Wulfe was the one person who truly liked Skylan. Liked Skylan for his own sake, not because he was Chief of Chiefs.

Wulfe didn't want anything from Skylan. He didn't draw him off into corners to urge him to make deals that would favor a particular clan or support a particular cause. Wulfe did not offer bribes to look another way while a boundary stone was shifted or ask Skylan to pardon a cousin's uncle's brother for stealing a goat. At first, Skylan had been flattered to know he wielded such power. But lately the innumerable demands and requests, the subtle hints and veiled threats just made him tired, gave him a headache.

"What are you doing here?" Skylan asked.

"I came to see Owl Mother."

"I didn't know you knew Owl Mother."

"Oh, yes," said Wulfe complacently. "The dryads told me about her. Now we're good friends."

Skylan frowned. He didn't believe Wulfe when he claimed to be able to speak to dryads. Skylan believed in dryads, of course. Like all the Vindrasi, he asked the guardian of the tree to forgive him before he cut down her tree, and he left offerings for her to ease her grief. But no self-respecting person claimed to be able to see dryads or converse with them.

Skylan had too many other concerns to start up this argument again, and he let the matter drop.

"I am told Owl Mother wants to see me."

Wulfe raised his eyebrows. "She does?"

Skylan stopped to stare at the boy. "You mean she doesn't?"

Wulfe could tell Skylan was in a bad mood, and he answered warily, "Maybe."

"Garn said she wanted to see me."

"Garn hasn't been around all day. She could have told him some other time, though."

Seeing Skylan scowl, Wulfe added hurriedly, "Maybe I'm wrong. I'll go ask," and he raced off, shouting, "Owl Mother!" before Skylan could catch him.

Had Garn lied to him? It looked that way. Skylan was reflecting bitterly that he could no longer trust anyone, when he was confronted by Owl Mother, who sprang at him out of the brush.

"There you are," she snapped. "I've been waiting."

She whipped around, trotting along the winding path that led to her dwelling. She did not glance behind. Apparently she assumed Skylan would follow.

"Did you tell Garn to tell me that you wanted to see me?" Skylan demanded.

"Did I?" Owl Mother flung back over her shoulder.

"Didn't you?"

Owl Mother stopped so fast that Skylan had to do some fancy footwork to avoid bumping into her. "Does it matter?"

Skylan believed that it did matter, but he didn't want to prolong his conversation with the strange old crone.

"What do you want with me?"

"We made a bargain, you and I," said Owl Mother, poking his chest with her knotted finger. "The time I healed you, remember? You promised to do whatever I asked of you."

"I remember," said Skylan impatiently. "But I am Chief of Chiefs now. I have many responsibilities. The Vindrasi are going to war—"

"The Vindrasi are going to their doom." Owl Mother snorted.

They had reached the small clearing that surrounded her ramshackle house. Owl Mother pointed at a stool. "Sit down."

"What do you mean? The Vindrasi are going to their doom?" Skylan asked, still standing.

"Wulfe, fetch my chair," said Owl Mother.

Wulfe dashed into the house. He came back carrying a chair that was almost as big as he was. He had it hoisted over his head, making nothing of the weight, though the chair had thick arms and legs and a back that was decorated with fanciful carvings of magical beasts. He set the chair down opposite the stool. A tree stump stood between them.

Owl Mother sat down in her chair and made herself comfortable. "Wulfe, fetch the board and the bones."

Wulfe made another foray into the dwelling. He came back bearing a wooden board and a sack. He placed the board on the tree stump and dumped out the pieces. Skylan sucked in his breath. The hair prickled on his neck and arms. He stared at the board, feeling cold sweat trickling down his breast. He stared at the board and then at Owl Mother.

"I thought we might play a game of dragonbone," said Owl Mother with a sly smile.

"I don't have time for nonsense," said Skylan shakily. "I will chop wood for you, carry water, patch your roof or whatever chores need doing. I won't play this game."

Owl Mother began to hum a jarring tune. She pointed at Skylan's leg and a muscle in his thigh cramped, the pain so sharp and severe that his leg buckled. He gasped in agony and almost fell. He began to rub his thigh, trying to ease the cramp.

"That was where the boar gored you, isn't it?" Owl Mother chuckled, and stopped humming. "We made a bargain. I am fond of the game, and no one ever plays with me."

Skylan glared at her, but he realized he didn't have much choice. He limped over to where the board rested on the stump of the tree and, grimacing, sat down on the stool. He continued to rub his leg, which burned as if he'd been stabbed with a red-hot knife.

"I have first move," he said.

"Go ahead," said Owl Mother. "It doesn't matter to me. But then I'm not your dead wife."

Skylan paled, stared at her, startled. Then he flashed an angry glance at Wulfe, who flushed red and made a dash for the woods. Skylan felt called upon to explain.

"I don't know what lies the boy told you. The truth is I suffered from nightmares on board the ghost ship," said Skylan.

Owl Mother was busy sorting out the bones. "Wulfe says he saw the draugr."

"Wulfe says he talks to dryads."

Owl Mother arranged her bones in front of her. "Doesn't everyone?"

Skylan cast her a scathing glance. "It was a nightmare," he muttered.

Through force of habit, he picked up five dragonbones and started to throw them.

Owl Mother's hand clamped over his.

"Why do you do that?" she demanded.

"Do what?" Skylan felt his skin burn and grow cold all at the same time.

"Roll five bones. You're supposed to roll only one."

Skylan wrenched his hand out of her grip. "It's a variant I learned somewhere."

"From the draugr," said Owl Mother. Her eyes pierced him.

Skylan held the bones tightly in his hand, feeling the sharp corners prick his skin. He stared down at the board and did not answer.

"Five bones," Owl Mother said softly. "She always starts the game by rolling five bones?"

Skylan did not answer.

Owl Mother regarded him speculatively. "The dead walk this world for a reason. The draugr came to you, not seeking revenge for her death. She came to play a game of dragonbones. Didn't you ever think to wonder why?"

"It's a dream!" Skylan said. "I didn't wonder anything."

"You should. The draugr is trying to tell you something."

"Then why doesn't she just come out and say it?" Skylan cried angrily.

He flung the bones onto the ground and stood up, irresolute, thinking he would leave, only to sit back down. He ran his hand through his hair, wiped the sweat from his face, and spoke feverishly.

"She walks the earth and picks up dragonbones and sets swords aflame and slams shut trapdoors. She plays the game well enough to beat me every night. Why does she keep tormenting me? Why doesn't she tell me what she wants of me?"

He pounded the question into the log with his clenched fist, emphasizing every word with a blow, striking the log so hard, he bloodied the heel of his hand.

"Perhaps she cannot tell you. . . ."

Owl Mother paused, then said thoughtfully, "Or perhaps she is forbidden to tell you."

Skylan dug a splinter out of his hand. He was sucking on it when a thought came to him. He looked sharply at Owl Mother. "If I figure out what Draya wants with me, will she leave me in peace?"

Owl Mother shrugged. "Do I look like a draugr?" She added quickly, with a laugh, "Don't answer that!"

"But you know about draugrs," said Skylan. He leaned close to her, his voice soft and persuasive. "You are old and you are wise, Owl Mother. What do you think she means?"

"Save your honey words for young and pretty girls, Skylan Ivorson," Owl Mother told him, grinning. "They won't sweeten my vinegar."

She rose to her feet and shook down her skirts. "Now go away and leave me to my work. I've better things to do this afternoon than play games with you. Haul my chair back inside before you go, and now that I think of it, there *is* a leak in my roof that needs mending. . . ."

By the time Skylan finished Owl Mother's chores (she kept coming up with more), the sun was setting. The trees cast long shadows over the path that led back to the village. He walked with his head down, not paying attention to where he was going, his thoughts running on the draugr and the nightly games of dragonbones.

"Skylan," said Garn, coming to join him. "I want to apologize—"

"I've come from Owl Mother's," said Skylan.

"I know." Garn flushed. "I'm sorry—"

"What do you think of when you think of the number five?" Skylan asked abruptly.

"Five?" Garn repeated, startled.

"The number five," Skylan repeated.

"Every person has five fingers and five toes," said Garn.

Skylan considered this and shook his head. "The number has something to do with the dragonbone game."

Garn reflected. "There are five Dragons of Vektia."

"Five Dragons," Skylan repeated. "Anything else?"

"To do with the number five? No, not offhand."

"The Five Dragons. But if that's true, what's she trying to tell me about them?" Skylan wondered, frowning.

"Who's telling you? Owl Mother?" Garn asked.

"Owl Mother? What about her?" Skylan glanced at his friend. "Oh, I see what you're saying. No, not Owl Mother. Never mind. It doesn't matter."

"Skylan, there's something I want to talk to you about. Something important."

"Yes, what?" Skylan asked. He was preoccupied, thinking about the Five Dragons.

"I want you to leave me here when you go to war. I'll remain with Norgaard and those who stay behind to guard the village—"

Skylan stared at him, wondering if he'd heard him right. Then he broke into laughter.

"You are joking with me." Skylan clapped Garn on the shoulder. "A good jest. You fooled me completely. I actually thought you were serious. Now, I need to talk to you, and this *is* serious. I'm trying to convince Aylaen that she must become a Bone Priestess. She's being stubborn, as always, and I was thinking you could talk to her—"

"Skylan, I'm not joking," said Garn quietly. "I don't believe in this war. I don't want to be a part of it."

"I don't think I understand," Skylan said in dangerous tones.

"I think you do," Garn said gravely. "You and I both know that story you told about the giants and the Dragon Isles was a lie. The people believe you because they are eager to go to war. I don't, and I don't want to be a part of it. Men will be needed to guard the village. I will serve you better if I remain here."

"Old men like my father serve me by staying behind to guard the village," said Skylan angrily, ignoring the accusation that he'd lied. He could deny it, probably should deny it, but the truth was he *had* been lying and Garn knew it, so why go to all the bother? "Young, strong men stand by my side in the shield-wall! Or else they are cowards!"

Garn blanched at this, but by the expression on his face, he did not mean to back down.

"My friend," Skylan said, softening, "you must go. Not for me. For yourself. People will say you are afraid."

"Let them say what they want," Garn replied, but Skylan could see he was troubled.

"And there is another consideration," Skylan continued, seeing he'd found a chink in Garn's armor. "I speak frankly because you are my brother and because I want to help you. You are an orphan, Garn. You have lived for years on my father's charity. Norgaard loves you like a son. I love you like a brother. But you have nothing—no silver, no property, no cattle. Someday you will want to marry, and no father would seriously consider allowing such a worthless bastard as yourself to wed his daughter."

Skylan tempered his words with a grin, but Garn had gone very pale.

"Go on this voyage with me, Garn," Skylan said. "Your fortune will be made! The ogres' lands are rich, my friend! We will sail home with our ships stuffed with gold and silver and gems. You will be a wealthy man. Fathers will be parading their daughters naked before you. As for you not believing in this war, I don't believe it. You know that we must recover the sacred Vektan Torque. We cannot leave it in the hands of the ogres. You agree that is true, right?"

"Yes," said Garn.

Skylan had a sudden flash of insight. "There is some other reason you want to stay behind, something you're not telling me."

Garn swallowed and licked his lips and said huskily, "I tried to keep this from you—"

"It's my father!" Skylan interrupted. "Now I understand. You want to stay behind to help Norgaard."

Garn stared at him dumbly, unable to speak.

Skylan shook his head. "It won't do, my friend. My father would be furious with both of us if he suspected. He is a proud man. You know that."

"I had not thought of it that way," Garn admitted, and he sighed, "You are right."

"Therefore you will come," said Skylan. "You will stand by my side in the shield-wall. And you will earn so many silver bracelets for brave deeds that you will not be able to lift your arm."

"I will come," said Garn with a wan smile. "I will stand by your side in the shield-wall."

The two men embraced as brothers.

"My friend," said Skylan softly, "I want you to know something. I did try to save Draya's life. I fought to save her! I couldn't reach her in time. They hit me and kept hitting me. Her blood . . ." He found it hard to go on. Drawing a shaking breath, he said fervently, "If I could have saved her by giving up my life, I would have done so, Garn. I swear to Torval!"

Skylan clasped his amulet convulsively. "I swear!"

"I believe you, Skylan," said Garn.

"Good," said Skylan, embarrassed by his outburst. He wiped his hand over his eyes and nose and mouth and wished he'd kept quiet. "Good. Now go talk to Aylaen for me."

"Yes," said Garn with a long, heavy sigh. "I must go talk to Aylaen."

# CHAPTER 3

The Kai Moot lasted for several days. The Bone Priestesses and their acolytes locked themselves in the Great Hall of the Gods to discuss the many problems facing the Vindrasi nation. The proceedings were secret; the Bone Priestesses were forbidden to reveal the nature of the deliberations to anyone. Yet wives talked to husbands, sweethearts whispered to lovers, and almost every person in the Heudjun clan found some excuse to pass the Hall, hoping to hear something.

As was traditional, Skylan ordered warriors to stand guard at the door to stop those who might seek either to harm the Priestesses or unduly exert influence on them. The placing of the guards originally came about as a result of a disastrous incident at a Kai Moot during the time of the great Chief of Chiefs Grimwald Liefson. A clan known as the Laerad had been angered at the Chief's harsh punishment leveled against them for stealing cattle. In retaliation, they raided the Kai Moot and carried off the Kai Priestess, Grimwald's wife. The Laerad held her for ransom, demanding that the punishment be lifted.

Grimwald was furious at the abduction of his wife. He refused to negotiate and went to war against the Laerad. The two clans formed shield-walls. Grimwald was about to launch an attack when he saw, to his horror, that the Laerad had placed his wife in the front ranks. Grimwald was in agony. If he attacked, his wife would be the first one to die. If he retreated, the Laerad Clan would claim victory, and he would be seen as weak. Other Clan Chiefs would challenge his authority. No one would pay heed to his judgments.

The Kai Priestess knew her husband faced this terrible choice. She made the decision for him. She grabbed a sword from the warrior standing next to her and thrust the weapon into her own belly. She died on the battlefield as her husband watched in dismay.

Vowing to Torval that the Laerad Clan would pay for his beloved wife's death, Grimwald and his warriors attacked with such ferocity that the Laerad were utterly destroyed. Since that time, all Chiefs have placed guards at the doors of the Kai Moot.

The warriors Skylan chose were men of his own clan, among them Bjorn and his brother Erdmun. He chose these men, he said, to honor the Kai. The fact that the warriors stood with their backs against the door, which put them in a position to eavesdrop on the meeting, also played some part in his thinking, as it had in the thinking of every Chief of Chiefs before him.

Once they entered the Hall, the Priestesses were forbidden to leave until their business was concluded. This meant that they had to eat and sleep in the Great Hall, sometimes for days.

Led by Fria, the older women sought to conduct the Kai Moot in an atmosphere of calm. This proved impossible. Skylan learned from Bjorn that the Kai were in turmoil, finding it hard to cope with the series of disasters that had come tumbling down on their heads like boulders in a landslide: The loss of the sacred torque to the ogres. The loss of Desiria, the Goddess of Life, and the subsequent inability of the Priestesses to heal the sick and injured. The fury of the Sun Goddess and the terrible drought that was withering the crops. The tragic death of Draya, who had been loved and revered. The curse laid upon the Dragon Isles.

The grief-stricken Fria, mourning the loss of her dearest friend, proved unequal to the task of trying to quell the anger and assuage the mounting fears. Rumors flew. Some Priestesses said they had heard that all the gods were dead and that the Vindrasi were now alone and abandoned in the universe. Others countered angrily that this was not true, that they had been in communication with the gods and that they were still able to heal in the name of the goddess. Few believed them. The women shouted and screamed at each other. Fria tried to restore order, but no one paid any attention.

In this time of crisis, it was Treia who stepped forward and took charge. Her cold, dispassionate voice fell on them like a bucket of chill water thrown onto a pack of snapping bitches. The conflict ended abruptly, though the dogs continued to watch each other warily and occasionally showed their teeth.

Fria wanted those Priestesses who claimed to have healing powers to be put to a test. Treia rightly pointed out that such a test would serve nothing except to further fan the flames of discord. She suggested that the Kai leave the past to the past and deal with the dire events of the present. The Kai should select a new Kai Priestess.

Bjorn, standing guard at the door, was able to overhear what was said. He handed over his duties to his brother and went to report to Skylan in the Chief's dwelling in the city of Vindraholm. Skylan had not intended to return there until after the Kai Moot, but Aylaen had amazed him by coming to him, telling him meekly that she had changed her mind. She would attend the Kai Moot with Treia, as he wanted.

Skylan was overjoyed and congratulated Garn on persuading her. Garn swore he'd had nothing to do with it.

Garn was telling the truth. Aylaen had flown into a rage when he'd told her he was going to go with Skylan to war. She had called him a coward for not standing up to Skylan, and then she had run off and refused to see him.

Garn had no idea why she should suddenly change her mind about attending the Kai Moot, but he didn't like it. He had traveled to Vindraholm with Skylan, hoping to be able to talk with her, but Aylaen had gone out of her way to avoid him, and now she was shut up inside the Great Hall of the Gods.

Bjorn found Skylan and Garn together, sharing ale and making preparations for war. Wulfe was with them, sitting cross-legged on the floor near the door, which had been propped open to catch the late afternoon breeze. The boy was playing with the dragonbones from Skylan's game, stacking them up, one on top of the other, to see how high they would go before falling. He always laughed heartily whenever the bones tumbled down in a heap and went bounding about the floor.

Skylan didn't like to see Wulfe playing with the dragonbones. The sight reminded Skylan uncomfortably of the draugr, who continued to force him to play. After his talk with Owl Mother, Skylan had questioned the draugr, trying to find out what she wanted to tell him. All to no avail. The draugr always started every game by rolling five dragonbones. She almost always ended by claiming all his pieces.

Bjorn had to step over the tower Wulfe was building as he entered the door. "I have news," he said.

Skylan and Garn both stopped to listen. Judging by Bjorn's air of importance, the news was momentous. Skylan motioned Bjorn to sit. Garn handed him a foaming drinking horn.

Bjorn drank thirstily. Standing guard in the afternoon sunshine was hot work. He was about to launch into his tale, when Skylan asked him the question of the moment.

"Have they chosen the Kai Priestess?"

Bjorn shook his head, and Skylan breathed a sigh of relief. Bjorn went on to explain that since Draya had not named a successor, the Kai had to put up candidates. After much arguing, the Kai had at last settled on two: Fria, who had been Draya's best friend, and Treia, who had amazed everyone by putting herself forward.

Skylan alone was not surprised. He had guessed Treia was angling for the leadership, though he still could not understand why.

"Treia loathes me," said Skylan. "Why would she want to be my wife?"

"She doesn't," Wulfe called out.

The three young men turned to stare at him. Though Wulfe was almost always present whenever they were together, he had never before joined in their conversation. Bjorn jokingly termed the boy Skylan's pup, claiming that Wulfe was always to be found curled up at his master's feet.

"I suppose the naiad told you all about it," Skylan said with a wink at his friends.

Wulfe carefully placed a fourth dragonbone onto his little tower. "If Treia is named Kai Priestess, your cousin, Raegar, will challenge you to something called a . . . a . . ." He shrugged. "I forget."

"That's nonsense," said Bjorn, laughing, as did the others at the ridiculous notion. "Raegar doesn't have any reason to call for a Vutmana. No one would accept his right to issue such a challenge."

Skylan joined in the laughter, but his mirth was hollow. Raegar did have a reason to challenge Skylan. Raegar knew the truth about Draya's death.

"Still, it's a clever scheme, if you think about it," Bjorn said when the laughter had died down. "If Treia becomes Kai Priestess, she can determine the winner of the Vutmana."

"Torval determines the winner," Skylan said.

"That's true, of course." Bjorn gave a sly grin. "Yet the Kai Priestess can see to it that the god votes her way."

"I don't think you mean that, my friend," said Garn quietly.

Bjorn suddenly realized what he'd been saying. He looked stricken.

"Skylan, he's right. I didn't mean—," he protested.

"I know you didn't," Skylan said tersely, and he changed the subject. "What did the Kai decide? Is Treia to be Kai Priestess?"

Bjorn shook his head. "The Kai are split. Some want Fria to be Kai Priestess. Some want Treia. And there are some who don't want either of them."

"So what happens now?" Skylan asked.

"The Kai wait for a sign from the gods."

"What is the sign?"

Bjorn shook his head. "No one knows. With Draya, the sign was a comet streaking across the sky. The Kai before Draya, the sign came when Torval swallowed the moon."

"When will the sign be given?"

"Whenever the gods see fit to give it, I guess. Then, once they have the sign, the Kai must meet again to determine if it really was a sign and what it portends."

Skylan began to breathe easier. Nothing was going to happen immediately.

"In the meantime, Fria will stay in Vindraholm to minister to the people and Treia will sail with us," Bjorn stated.

Skylan thought of living in the close quarters on board ship with Treia, her squinting eyes always watching him, and he gave an inward groan. Raegar would be on board the ship, as well. Ah, well, as Norgaard always said, keep your friends close and your enemies closer.

Wulfe picked up the dragonbones and put them away and then went off to curl up in a corner to take a nap. Skylan poured another round of ale. He was bringing the drinking horn to his lips when he realized that Bjorn looked uneasy. He held the horn in his hand, his ale untasted.

"What's the matter?" Skylan asked. "Why aren't you drinking?"

"Something else happened in the Kai Moot," said Bjorn. He didn't look at Skylan as he spoke. "It's about Aylaen."

"I know already," said Skylan. "She asked to be made a Bone Priestess—"

"You need to hear me out, Skylan," said Bjorn. "The Kai refused. They said she was too old. She would have to be an acolyte, and that would take years and—"

"They can't do that!" Skylan said, leaping to his feet. "I'll force them—"

"Listen to me!" Bjorn said urgently. "Aylaen told them there was a way she could become a Bone Priestess without having to be an acolyte first. She claimed there was historical precedent."

Bjorn paused at this point to take a gulp of ale. He seemed to feel he needed it.

Skylan waited in suspense. "Yes, well?"

"She reminded them of Griselda the Man-Woman," said Bjorn.

Skylan's jaw sagged. He stared at Bjorn in disbelief.

"You can't be serious."

"Trust me, I could not have made this up," said Bjorn.

Skylan looked accusingly at Garn. "Did you know about this?"

Garn shook his head. "I had no idea!" He sounded as appalled as Skylan felt.

"What about Treia?" Skylan asked. "She would not approve."

"Treia said she did. She said she supported her sister in her decision. The Priestesses talked it over, and in the end they all agreed," said Bjorn. "Aylaen will become a man-woman and sail with us to war."

"No, she won't," said Skylan. "I will forbid it."

"I don't think you can," said Bjorn. "The Kai approved because Aylaen told them it was you who gave her the idea."

## CHAPTER 4

Skylan left in search of Aylaen, taking Garn with him. If both of them talked to her, they agreed that they might be able to make her see reason. They went to the Hall, only to hear from Erdmun that the Kai Moot had ended. A few Bone Priestesses remained, but Treia was not among them and Aylaen would be with her sister. One of the Priestesses said she thought Treia and Aylaen had gone to Fria's dwelling, where they had been invited to stay while they were in Vindraholm. Skylan and Garn walked to Fria's, only to learn that the sisters planned to sail back on the *Venjekar.* The young men hastened to the shore. The dragonship had already departed.

They went back to Skylan's dwelling. Bjorn had left to join his brother. Wulfe lay curled up asleep in a corner, his hands and feet twitching.

"I've been thinking, Garn," Skylan said. "Perhaps Aylaen is right. If this is the only way she can become a Bone Priestess, then she should undergo the ritual. She should come with us."

"You can't mean that," said Garn flatly.

"Aylaen is trained in both axe and sword. She was at the battle with the ogres, and she never flinched, even when a spear landed right beside her."

"She wasn't in the shield-wall, Skylan," Garn said grimly. "With men being disemboweled and brains splattering in her face."

"I will see to it that nothing happens to her," Skylan assured him. "I will put her with the warriors who guard Treia. Both women will have the Dragon Kahg to look out for them."

"She will still be in danger. Bone Priestesses are often killed," Garn said.

"I will order additional warriors to guard her—"

"—which means you must take men from the shield-wall, and that puts everyone in danger. You are going to imperil the entire mission for your own lust!"

Garn was pale; his eyes burned. "This scheme of yours will get Aylaen killed!"

He stalked out, slamming the door to Skylan's dwelling with such force that bits of it splintered.

Skylan sat down wearily in his chair. He could be rightfully accused of many crimes, but this was not one of them. He had mentioned the story of Griselda the Man-Woman to Aylaen only in passing. He had certainly never meant to suggest to Aylaen that she emulate the fabled female warrior!

Skylan left Vindraholm the next morning, sailing in a small boat back to Luda to prepare the *Venjekar* for war. Two dragonships, those belonging to the Svegund and Martegnan Clans, would meet them at Luda in two days. During the short journey across the bay, he mulled over what Garn had said. When he reached home, he went so far as to discuss the problem about Aylaen with Norgaard. The old Chief agreed completely with Garn and added a forceful argument of his own. None of the warriors would be comfortable fighting alongside a woman.

Yet, this was the only way Aylaen could become a Bone Priestess, the only way she could become Skylan's wife.

He was still undecided over what to do the night before they were to set sail. He lay awake, waiting tensely for the draugr to come for their game of dragonbones. She did not appear, however, and after a time, Skylan fell into an exhausted sleep.

He was in a battle, but not the shield-wall. His warriors were scattered all over the field, some fighting, some fleeing, others helpless from terror. He ran from one group to the other, urging them to fight the faceless enemy. Garn was at his right hand and Aylaen was on his left. All the time he was urging his men to fight, he was ordering her to go back to the ship. She wouldn't listen to him. And then the enemy was on them and he and Garn and Aylaen were fighting for their lives.

Skylan saw a flash of steel out of the corner of his eye and saw the faceless foe aiming a spear at Garn's back. Skylan shouted a warning, but Garn was battling two of the enemy in front of him and he did not hear. Skylan ran toward the spear thrower, his sword raised, when he heard a cry, and glancing back, he saw Aylaen slip in a pool of blood and fall to the ground. The enemy was on her. She struggled to regain her feet. Skylan would never reach her in time. The axe fell. . . .

Skylan woke, sweating and panting and shaking. His terror was real, and it took him long moments to realize he'd been dreaming. Flinging on his clothes, he grabbed a lighted torch and went to talk with Aylaen.

He came to Treia's dwelling. Sigurd had been furious when he heard that Aylaen was going to undergo the ritual of the man-woman. He had made life so unbearable for her that she had left, moved in with Treia. Skylan found the house dark. It was the dead of night. They would have been asleep for a long time.

Skylan banged on the door with his fist and shouted for Aylaen.

The door opened a crack.

"Who is that?" Treia asked, shielding her eyes against the flaring light.

"You know who it is!" Skylan said. "I want to talk to Aylaen."

"You cannot," said Treia. "She is in purification for her ritual. She cannot see or speak to anyone."

"She'll speak to me!" Skylan said, and he lunged at the door, prepared to shoulder his way inside.

Treia blocked the entrance with her body. "The gods forbid it."

"Get out of my way," said Skylan angrily, "or by Torval I will knock you down!"

Treia's lips twisted in a mocking smile. "You are too late," she said. "See for yourself."

She pointed at his feet.

Skylan kept his gaze fixed on her. "I don't believe you. Let me inside."

Treia shrugged, not caring whether he believed her or not. "You are too late," she repeated.

Skylan slowly and reluctantly looked to where she pointed. At first he couldn't see anything, and then he stared, sick with dismay at the sight of masses of beautiful, luxuriant, flame-red curls lying in a shining heap on the ground.

"We will join you on the ship at dawn," said Treia.

She shut the door in his face.

Skylan was tempted to batter the door down, but what would he do then? He picked up one of the shining curls and smoothed it between his fingers.

He let it fall to the ground and walked slowly home.

Skylan wasn't the only person roaming the woods that night. Wulfe had been visiting Owl Mother, telling her everything that had happened during the Kai Moot and after. The two worked as they talked. Wulfe ground leaves in a stone bowl. He tied bunches of lavender and hung them from the ceiling to dry, pausing often to sniff hungrily at the stewpot.

Owl Mother had little to say, but Wulfe knew she was listening to him, because every so often she would chuckle and talk about people sticking their heads into hornets' nests or wading hip-deep in bogs of their own making.

Wulfe talked until he didn't have any more to say. He teased the wyvern to make it snap its beak at him, for which he was scolded by Owl Mother, who fed him a bowl of stew and told him he was welcome to spend the night, if he didn't mind sleeping on the floor.

Wulfe thanked Owl Mother, but said he had to leave. The Torgun were sailing to war tomorrow, and Wulfe planned to go with them.

Owl Mother eyed him. "I'm surprised Skylan agreed to take you."

"He didn't," Wulfe said calmly. "He thinks I'm staying with you while he's gone. He won't know I'm on board until it's too late to send me back."

"The warriors will be armed with axes and swords and spears," said Owl Mother. "The ship will stink of iron."

"I know," Wulfe said, shuddering, "I don't want to go. But I have to. I've been thinking about it, you see, and I realized that Skylan is my geas."

Owl Mother grinned. "Your geas? What evil daemon laid such a thankless charge upon you as that young man?"

"No daemon laid it on me!" Wulfe protested indignantly. "I saved Skylan's life. His wyrd is in my care."

"You just take care of yourself," Owl Mother told him. She paused in her work and fixed him with her shrewd gaze. "And remember our lessons."

Wulfe nodded gravely. "I'll bring you back a present, Owl Mother. What would you like? A sack of rubies?"

"Bring yourself back," Owl Mother stated grumpily. "*And* that fool Skylan. He might end up being worth something someday." She snorted. "Geas indeed!"

Owl Mother walked with Wulfe to the door. She kissed him on his forehead, reminding him of his mother. Putting both hands on his shoulders, she looked him in the eyes.

"The druids meant well, Wulfe, but they were wrong. Your gift is just that—a gift, not a curse. Use it. Use it well. Use it sparingly. But use it. Don't be afraid. Do you understand?"

Wulfe gazed at her, wide-eyed. He wasn't sure he did understand, but he didn't want to hurt her feelings, and so he gave an abrupt nod and then hurried into the night.

Wulfe liked being out alone in the darkness. He had never been afraid of the dark, perhaps because night wasn't all that dark to him. The lambent gleam of moon and stars, mingled with the soft radiance of life that shone from trees and grass and flowers and animals, lit Wulfe's way. It had been nighttime when his father and his father's family had changed from their wolf forms into humans. And it had been night when his faery mother, in all her shimmering splendor, had come dancing through the darkness to sing lullabies to her child.

Walking through the forest, Wulfe saw the dryads slumbering in the boughs of their trees, and he bade them a silent farewell. He said good-bye to the naiad, who lay in her stream, her head pillowed on a smooth stone, the water running sensually over her naked body. She murmured in her sleep, and stretched out in languishing slumber. He encountered a pack of wolves, and he spoke to them politely, but they were hungry and searching for food and they had no time for him.

He took the path that led past Treia's dwelling. He always kept an eye on her, though at this time of night she would be asleep. He padded softly up to the door, put his ear to it, and listened. Not hearing anything, he started to continue on. Something jumped out at him, a hand grabbed hold of his arm, and another clapped over his mouth and dragged him into the underbrush.

"Wulfe! Ouch, damn it, don't bite me! It's Garn. Be quiet. I'm not going to hurt you. I thought I might find you sneaking about here tonight. I've seen you watching Treia's house before. What are you doing here?"

Wulfe stared at him in quivering silence and did not answer. He tensed, poised for flight the moment Garn let him loose.

"I guess it doesn't matter," said Garn, sighing. "The truth is, I've been waiting for you. I need you to do something for me."

Wulfe waited, not about to commit himself.

"I need to see Aylaen, and Treia won't let anyone inside," Garn continued. "She just sent Skylan away. I was thinking you might be able to sneak in without waking Treia, tell Aylaen I have to talk to her."

"I can do that," Wulfe said cautiously.

"*Will* you do it?" Garn asked, and he sounded wistful.

Wulfe thought it over and nodded. He waited with Garn, both of them silent, until Garn deemed that Treia must have gone back to bed. Wulfe sneaked across the clearing in front of the longhouse. He paused a moment to stare curiously at the tangle of red curls on the ground and then, shrugging to himself, continued on.

He pushed gently on the door, and it yielded to his touch. He slipped inside. The fire had been doused, the stewpot cleaned out and put away, for both women would be leaving tomorrow. Wulfe paused, trying to find his way around, when he saw Aylaen's head, pale and shimmering, floating disembodied in the darkness.

Wulfe was panic-stricken until he realized Aylaen was sitting on the floor with a blanket wrapped around her. She was not asleep. Her shadowed eyes stared at him.

"Wulfe?" she whispered, her voice muffled as though she had been crying. "What do you want? Skylan's not here. He left."

"Garn is here," Wulfe whispered back. "He's outside. He wants to talk to you."

Treia stirred in her sleep, muttering something. Aylaen clasped hold of Wulfe's wrist. Her fingers were cold and smooth, like he imagined the fingers of the draugr. He didn't like her touch, and he squirmed out of it. Treia settled back down. Aylaen gave a wistful sigh.

"Is he very angry with me?" she asked.

Wulfe shrugged. He had no way of knowing, nor did he particularly care.

"Tell him . . . No." Aylaen abruptly threw off the blanket and stood up. "I'll tell him."

She walked almost as softly as Wulfe. The two slipped out the door. Wulfe pointed to where Garn waited amidst the trees.

"Thank you," said Aylaen, and she added sharply, "You can run along now."

Wulfe trotted away obediently. When he'd gone a short distance, he turned around and doubled back, placing himself where he could see and hear.

"Skylan was wrong when he asked you to undergo the ritual, Aylaen," Garn was saying. "He knows that now. He made a mistake. You don't have to do this for him—"

"For him?" Aylaen repeated, amazed. She ran her hand over her shorn head. "I didn't do this for Skylan!"

"For the goddess then—," Garn said.

"I didn't do this for Vindrash, either," Aylaen said softly. She gazed at him. "Are you so blind? Don't you really know why I did it?"

Garn shook his head.

"For us!" Aylaen whispered, and she twined her arms around his neck and tried to kiss him.

Garn took hold of her arms, pushed her away. He frowned at her. "What do you mean?"

"I did this so we could be together," Aylaen explained. "Skylan didn't tell me to do this! He told me the story of Griselda, and that put the idea into my head."

"You lied to Treia, to the Kai," said Garn. "You said the goddess wanted you to do this!"

"It may have been Vindrash who put the idea into my head," Aylaen said defensively, unknowingly echoing Skylan's claim about Torval. "Who knows? Are you mad at me? I thought you would be pleased!"

"For what? That you could be killed—"

"And so could you! And if you died, I would die, for I could not live without you!"

"This is wrong," said Garn. "You can't go through with this, Aylaen. You're as bad as Skylan. Putting your own selfish wants first. How can I stand in the shield-wall and think of what I have to do to stay alive if I'm worried about you? I've been furious at Skylan, Aylaen. I thought this was his idea. I didn't know it was yours."

Treia came storming out of the dwelling. The lovers saw no one but each other, and they did not notice her. Wulfe did.

"Garn! Please!" Aylaen was clinging to him. "I did this for us. Because I love you. I never thought— I never meant— What are you going to do? Where are you going?"

"You have to tell your sister the truth," Garn said, trying to free himself.

"It is too late for that," said Treia.

The lovers sprang apart and turned guiltily to face her.

"She cannot tell the truth," Treia continued. "Not now. If the Kai found out my sister made all this up just so she could sleep with you, the Kai would think I was a willing participant in her lie. That would ruin my chances to become Kai Priestess. I will not let that happen."

"You can't stop me from telling them—," Garn began.

"Oh, yes, I can," said Treia calmly. "She inherits land from her father on the day she is married. I will tell Sigurd that you seduced Aylaen to force her into marriage because you wanted her wealth."

"Sigurd would kill him!" Aylaen gasped.

"Very probably," said Treia. She stood with her arms folded tightly across her breasts. "Aylaen, come back inside. We must rise early in the morning."

Garn looked grim. His fists clenched. He gazed at Aylaen, then turned and walked off into the darkness.

"Garn!" Aylaen cried. "Please . . . I'm sorry. . . ."

He did not look back.

"Come inside," Treia ordered with a dire glance about the woods. "Evil walks in the night."

"I'm not sleepy," said Aylaen, and her voice sounded muffled. "You go on. I'll be there in a moment."

Treia shrugged and walked off. Aylaen waited a moment; then she walked over to the Hall of Vindrash and went inside, shutting the door behind her.

Wulfe yawned. He was growing sleepy, and he still had to find a good hiding place on board ship. He had found two: the large empty chest the warriors had hauled aboard, meant to hold all the treasure they were certain they would be bringing back, and a pile of furs and blankets Treia had carried on board to be used for her bedding.

He was not worried about Treia finding him. She would be busy communing with the Dragon Kahg as the ships were setting sail. She would have no time to go poking about the bedding on the off chance a boy might be hiding there.

As for Skylan, he would be busy with his tasks. Wulfe had told Skylan he meant to stay with Owl Mother, and Skylan had no reason to doubt him. Skylan had yet to learn that he was Wulfe's geas, a charge that was usually magically laid on a person. In this instance, Wulfe had taken the geas upon himself.

Wulfe went loping down the path, trying to decide between the chest and the bedding, when his eye was caught by a flickering pinprick of light. He thought at first it was a will-o'-the-wisp. After his encounter with the draugr, Wulfe did not want to have any more dealings with restless dead, and he was about to take to his heels when a second glance revealed that the light was stationary, not moving.

Curious, Wulfe crept closer. Was everyone in the village up and about this night? He could move like his namesake through the underbrush, treading quietly on bare feet. As he drew nearer, the flame began to waver, and he saw that it came from a bundle of burning rushes, giving off smoke and a sweet smell. The fire illuminated a face. Wulfe recognized Raegar.

Wulfe hunkered down comfortably among the trees to watch. Raegar was on his knees in a clearing. In front of him was a large silver basin filled with water. The druids cared nothing for precious metals, and thus Wulfe had no way of knowing that such a basin was a thing of immense value. He knew only that it was metal, and therefore made his skin crawl, but he did admire the way it reflected the firelight.

Raegar held the rushes in one hand. With the other, he reached into a pouch he had strung onto his belt and drew out a small vial, the kind Owl Mother used to store her healing oils. Raegar drew out the vial's stopper with his teeth and spit it onto the ground. He dribbled the contents of the vial into the silver basin and then touched the burning rushes to the water.

Flames flared, lighting Raegar's face. Wulfe watched, enchanted, to see fire burning water. Raegar waited for the flames to die and then hunched over the basin. His lips moved. Wulfe could not hear what he was saying, for Raegar kept his voice low.

Wulfe lay on his belly on the ground, his chin propped in his hands, waiting for something exciting to happen. Perhaps a daemon to burst out of the bowl.

Nothing did. Raegar picked up the basin, dumped out the water, and thrust the basin into a sack. Using the flame of the burning rushes to light his way, he stood up and walked toward his dwelling.

Wulfe gave a shrug, and thinking he'd wasted enough time and that morning could not be far away, he hurried off.

All in all, it had been an eventful night.

As his mother had often told him, and as Wulfe had often observed, the Ugly Ones were very strange.

Aylaen sank to her knees on the dirt floor of the Hall of Vindrash. The outline of the base of the now broken and burned statue of Vindrash could be seen clearly in the dirt. Treia had brought a new statue of the goddess from Vindraholm and put it in the place of the old. The new statue was much smaller than the old one had been. It looked forlorn and shrunken to Aylaen.

She closed her eyes and imagined the old statue, the one that had frightened her as a child. She felt closer to that one.

"Blessed Vindrash, forgive me," Aylaen prayed. "Garn is right. I lied to the Kai. I lied to Treia. I lied to Skylan. I told them all I did this because I wanted to serve you, dedicate myself to your worship. I am sorry! I am so sorry! I did not think what it would mean. Garn is right. I will put men's lives in danger. I could imperil the mission!

"I came here to beg you to forgive me," Aylean said softly, "and to tell you that I will not go. I will remain here. Garn will sail away, and I will never see him again. I know that in my heart. But I would not be the cause of his death or any man's death. I could never forgive myself. Better this way. Tell me that I have your forgiveness, Vindrash!"

Aylaen remained kneeling in the darkness that was quiet and restful. Treia said that evil walked abroad in the night, but Aylaen did not believe that. She felt suddenly very close to the goddess. She pictured Vindrash holding shining wings over her, guarding and defending her. Aylean smiled and murmured a broken thank-you. She put her hand to the dirt floor, to start to rise. Her hand rested on metal, smooth and cool to the touch with a sharp edge that cut her finger.

Aylaen gave a little gasp of pain and looked more closely. The object shone in the moonlight, and she saw it was a sword. She gazed at it in wonder and awe. The sword had not been there before. She was certain of that.

Aylaen reached out her bleeding hand and gingerly picked up the sword by the hilt. The sword was lightweight, well-balanced. She knew enough about weapons from Garn and Skylan that she recognized this sword as being old, but superbly crafted. It seemed almost to have been made for her.

Aylaen lifted her wondering gaze to the heavens.

"Do you mean this, Vindrash? Is this your will?"

Aylaen picked up the sword reverently and took it back to the dwelling she shared with her sister.

Treia was awake, staring into the fire. She glanced at Aylean as she entered, and her eyebrows rose at the sight of the sword.

"What are you doing with that old thing?" she asked.

"Do you recognize it?" Aylaen asked. "Where did it come from?"

"Years ago some warrior had it made for Vindrash. He gave it to her as a grateful offering, saying she had appeared to him during a battle and given him the strength to defeat his foes. It used to stand beside the statue or so I remembered from the last time I was in the Hall, which was years ago. I thought it lost or perhaps the former Bone Priestess had gotten rid of it. Where did you find it?"

"I didn't find it," said Aylaen softly. "It found me."

# CHAPTER 5

The Goddess Aylis fought her daily battle with the Dark God Skoval, and drove him back. The Sea Goddess Akaria was placid and smooth. The Goddess of the Winds, Svanses, breathed on them gently. The day promised to be cloudless, fine. The gods were smiling on them. The Vindrasi were sailing to war.

The Torgun warriors boarded their dragonship, the *Venjekar*. Because they were the birth clan of the Chief of Chiefs, the Torgun had the honor of taking the lead. Each warrior placed his shield on the rack on the side of the ship, creating a colorful and formidable show of force. The *Venjekar* waited now for the arrival of the Bone Priestess, Treia, and her sister, Aylaen. Word that Aylaen was going to undertake the ritual of the Man-Woman had spread rapidly throughout the village, and everyone was avidly curious to see whether she would go through with her vow.

Neither Skylan nor Garn had any doubts. As Skylan had said gloomily to his friend, oak trees would dance in the forest before Aylaen changed her mind.

The warriors crowded the rail, calling out farewells or shouting last-minute instructions to friends and family. Raegar walked over to join Skylan, who was pacing the crowded deck, fuming over the delay. Skylan was not feeling particularly well-disposed toward his cousin these days, and he gave Raegar a dismissive glance and kept walking. Raegar noticed Skylan's ill humor, but put it down to a different cause.

"Do not worry, Cousin. Aylaen will not carry out her promise," Raegar said confidently. "Treia told me so herself. She's spent two days talking to her sister, trying to dissuade her. Aylaen is headstrong and wild, but she's not stupid."

Skylan shook his head and went to angrily berate a young warrior who had stowed his sea chest in the wrong place.

The sun climbed above the horizon and teetered on the ocean's flat surface like a bright coin. The ships should have set sail by now. If they didn't get under way soon, they would lose the fullness of the tide. Skylan was about to send a messenger to fetch Treia, when the Bone Priestess appeared, walking along the dunes. Aylaen walked behind her.

The entire Torgun Clan had gathered along the shoreline to bid farewell to their warriors. The mood was festive, everyone laughing and cheerful, certain that bad times were coming to an end. When word was whispered about that the two sisters were coming, all talk and clamor ceased.

Treia walked in front. Most of her possessions were already on board. As was customary, Skylan had given the Bone Priestess the cabin belowdeck for her own personal use, and she had stowed away her clothes and other necessities. She brought with her a small rosewood box containing vials of potions, unguents, and ointments she would use for healing, since the goddess was no longer around to answer her prayers. The jars and vials rattled as she walked. She trod carefully, peering down with her weak eyes to see where she was putting her feet. She did not want to fall and break her precious cargo.

Aylaen came a few paces behind. She walked with her head high, her face flushed, partly embarrassed, wholly defiant. She stared straight out in front of her, pretending to ignore the staring eyes, the gasps, the pitying cries from the women, the growls of disapproval from the men.

Her red curls were gone. She was almost bald. Treia had hacked off Aylaen's hair at the scalp line. Perhaps due to her poor eyesight, Treia had botched the job, leaving Aylaen with red tufts of hair sticking out of her head and bloody patches of skin.

Aylaen carried a shield that had belonged to her father, painted with his colors, blue and white. She carried her new sword.

She wore man's clothes, and surprisingly, they suited her. Aylaen was tall as most men, though more slender. She had altered the garments to fit her, and she liked the freedom and the comfort they afforded her. She wore leather armor studded with iron that had been her father's, and new boots, a gift from Treia.

At the sight of her daughter dressed like a man with no hair to speak of, Aylaen's mother ran to her and grabbed hold of her, weeping and begging her to stay.

"Mother, you are shaming me!" Aylaen said angrily, trying vainly to free herself from her mother's tearful pleas and clinging grasp.

Grim-faced, Treia walked back to deal with the situation. She said a few sharp words that left her mother pale and mute. Friends led the mother away with soothing words and irate glances for her two daughters.

"*She* is shamed! Hah!" Sigurd was on board the ship with the warriors. He glared at Aylaen, then turned his back and refused to look at her.

The entire village had been witness to his fury when word reached him of Aylaen's decision. He had stormed off to Norgaard to protest, demanding that the Clan Chief put a stop to this fool notion.

Norgaard had gone so far as to try to speak to Treia, who coldly rebuffed him. Aylaen had been called by the goddess to undergo this ritual. The Kai Moot had sanctioned her decision, and no one, not even her stepfather, could argue against the will of Vindrash.

Norgaard leaned heavily on his crutch, gritting his teeth against the pain in his leg, and wondered how much the goddess had to do with Aylaen's decision. Pain had not blurred his vision. Norgaard had been aware for a long time that Garn and Aylaen were lovers, and he wondered if it was Vindrash who had summoned Aylaen to war or her love for Garn.

And what would happen when Skylan found out, as he was sure to do on this voyage. Up until now, his own love had blinded him. Once he knew the truth, he would lose the two people he held most dear. Watching Aylaen walk in her man's boots across the dunes, Norgaard asked Torval to guard these three young people, whom he dearly loved. Three he feared in his heart he would not see again.

Treia walked up the gangplank. Skylan welcomed her with solemn if somewhat rushed ceremony. No one noticed. Everyone was staring at Aylaen.

She walked up the gangplank, her shield slung over her shoulder. The plank was wet, with men tramping back and forth through the water, hauling sea chests, rope, barrels of pitch and ale, and sacks of food on board. Aylaen had gone about midway when her new boots slipped. Arms flailing wildly, she toppled over and fell into the water.

The crowd hooted and laughed. Aylaen sat up in the shallow water. She was drenched. Her face burned in embarrassment. She looked for a moment as if she were tempted to curl up in a ball and sob. Her lips tightened. She rubbed the water from her eyes and stood up. Water poured off her. She walked up the gangplank, her jaw clenched, her head high.

She stepped onto the deck. The men watched in silence, stern and disapproving. Aylaen gave them all a sweeping glance of defiance. She went over to the rack, where the other warriors had hung their shields. She placed her shield alongside Garn's. She looked at him, gave him a small and tentative smile.

He lowered his eyes, shook his head, and turned away.

Skylan stared past her, out to sea, as he spoke. "I have ordered your sea chest stored below. You will sleep in the cabin with your sister."

Aylaen's eyes flashed. "I will sleep on the deck with the other warriors!"

Skylan fixed an exasperated gaze on her. "And will you also piss in the sea with the rest of the warriors?"

Aylaen flushed crimson; then she went fire white. Her emerald eyes sparked. "Yes, I will," she said clearly, and she began to unlace her trousers. "In fact, I think I have to go right now. . . ."

Skylan grabbed hold of her hands, scandalized. "What are you doing? Are you crazy?"

"I guess I must be," she said tremulously.

She looked up at him. He looked at her, and suddenly they both began to laugh. Aylaen's laughter was deep and rich; Skylan's loud and boisterous. The laughter bound their wyrds together, closer than they had been in years.

"Welcome aboard, Warrior," said Skylan. He bent close to her to whisper, "But, please, do not pee in public! Go below with your sister!"

"I promise," said Aylaen, smiling. "But I will sleep on deck with the other warriors."

"Have it your way," said Skylan. He reached out his hand, gave her head a rub. "By Torval, you look like a badly shorn sheep!"

Skylan turned to face the men on the ship and the crowd on shore. He raised his hands to silence the laughter and the talk.

"Hear me!" he called out. "This woman, Aylaen Adalbrand, has been called by the Goddess Vindrash to become a Bone Priestess. The Kai have judged she shall undergo the ritual known as the Man-Woman. Aylaen's journey is a holy one. The gods are watching her, and they are watching us, for all of us have been called upon to undertake this ritual with her. The curse of Vindrash on any man who disrespects the goddess's chosen!"

Aylaen gave Skylan a radiant smile. Some of the men continued to regard her with disapproval, but most looked ashamed of themselves. Bjorn and Erdmun asked to see her sword and offered to show her how to clean it to keep it from rusting. Only Garn was still angry. He shook his head and walked away.

Skylan wiped the sweat from his face. The sun beat down on the deck. He felt tired already, and they hadn't yet left the shoreline. Once out to sea, the air would blow fresh and cool. He would leave his problems and cares on the shore. He looked over at the other two dragonships bobbing in the water, their warriors lining the sides. All was in readiness. He turned to Treia.

"Bone Priestess, ask the Dragon Kahg to imbue the ship with his spirit and take us out to sea."

Treia placed her hand upon the spiritbone and spoke softly to the dragon. Kahg's eyes flared red. The carved wooden scales seemed to take on a metallic glitter in the sunshine. The ship glided away from the shoreline. The Torgun cheered.

The Vindrasi were going to war.

The women did not weep, though many knew they were seeing their menfolk for the last time. Tears were shameful, brought dishonor. The women cheered and held small babies high in the air to witness the grand moment. Boys ran into the water, waving and shouting, and dreaming of the time they would hang their shields over the side of the *Venjekar.*

The Torgun warriors stood proudly on the deck, pleased and excited, laughing and talking among themselves.

The Dragon Kahg thrust his head into the wind. The ship bounded over the waves, picking up speed.

Norgaard waved farewell. Skylan's gaze fell on his father, and his heart smote him. He had meant to apologize, meant to tell his father that he was sorry for everything, for breaking his vow, for taking away the chance to be Chief of Chiefs, and for more than that. Skylan thought unhappily of the times he had termed Norgaard an old granny—the times he had spoken of him disrespectfully, ignored his advice and counsel.

The wind blew strong and fresh. The waves broke beneath the keel. The sea spray splashed in his face. The dragon's eyes glowed. Skylan was no longer tired. He braced his feet on the swaying, rocking deck, drinking in the wind, tasting the salt on his lips.

I will apologize to my father when I come back, Skylan said to himself. When I come back a hero!

The Vindrasi were going to war.

# CHAPTER 6

The sea was smooth, ruffled by a light breeze. Fluffy clouds scudded through blue sky, casting shadows that glided over the water. Skylan, like everyone else on board, was in a good humor, enjoying the wind and water and freedom, looking forward to battle and glory and the rich rewards that would solve all their problems.

Skylan sat on a sea chest with Raegar, the map spread out between them, fluttering in the wind. Raegar pointed out the prominent landmarks as the ship sailed past them. The dragonships always sailed within sight of land if possible. The position of the sun by day and the stars by night gave them some idea of a ship's direction, but only by watching landmarks were the Vindrasi able to determine their exact position.

The Vindrasi never used maps. Skylan had never seen one. Since none could read or write, maps were useless to them. Skylan found it difficult to fathom how a bunch of lines could tell him where he was.

Raegar pointed out how the lines indicated landmarks.

"Imagine," said Raegar, "that this map is the board for the dragonbone game. You move your bones along the paths, using the 'landmarks' on the board as a guide. Our ship is the bone and we are moving along this path."

Raegar pointed to a squiggly dot on the map.

"We will soon sail past an island, which will be on our right hand," he said. "The Southlanders call it Gull Island because of the large numbers of seabirds that inhabit it."

Skylan knew the island, which the Vindrasi called White-Winged Rock, for if ships sailed too near it, the birds rose up from it in raucous alarm, white wings flapping.

The island soon came into view. The squawking of gulls filled the air as the birds flew about the dragonships, looking for food, the boldest diving down onto the deck to pick up a dropped morsel.

Skylan couldn't believe Raegar had known the island was coming just by looking at a dot. Still, he had to admit his cousin had been right.

The map had other features, which Raegar attempted to explain, but Skylan could not understand them, for these involved the use of a device known as a "compass" and some means of measuring the distance from the fixed star called the Eye of Torval by the Vindrasi, who believed that whenever Torval had to go to war in another part of heaven, he plucked out one of his eyes and set it in the sky to keep watch over his people.

"Because of such navigational techniques," Raegar continued, "the Southlanders can sail their ships far, far out to sea without having to keep close to land."

Skylan could not see much point to that. Treasure was found on land, not in the middle of the vast and dangerous ocean.

"Sailing across open water saves time," Raegar explained patiently. "You sail across the mouth of the fjord from Luda to Vindraholm. You don't follow the land all the way around. That would take days."

He showed on the map how a ship could cross the sea from one point of land to another, a trip that would normally take months, but which he claimed could be made in a week. Another advantage was that the ships would not have to make landfall every night, as did the dragonships. They could continue to sail even in the darkness and not lose their way.

Skylan had to admit he was impressed. "Can you teach me how to do this?"

Raegar grinned and shook his head. "Each ship's captain brings along men who are skilled in this science. They use special instruments to take readings of the stars and the sun, and every day they mark the ship's position on charts so that the captain always knows his ship's location whether he is within sight of land or not."

Skylan had always scoffed at learning. A warrior needed nothing more in this world than his sword and shield, the sea and a ship to make his fortune. Skylan studied the map, and his mind opened to new possibilities.

He thought about Raegar's comparison of the map to the board for the dragonbone game. Thinking of the game made him think of the draugr, and he smiled grimly to himself. He had thwarted the draugr, or so he hoped. He had left the dragonbone game board behind, and he had forbidden any of the warriors from bringing boards with them. He wanted their thoughts to be on war, not a game. A few had grumbled at this, but there were other games to play, and, in truth, the Torgun were too glad to be going to war to complain about the loss of something so trivial.

The sun began its downward dip. Bands of red and orange and violet streaked the sky and bloodied the sea. On land, shadows were closing in. Skylan needed to find a safe place in which to shelter the dragonships for the night. He remembered from the last time he had sailed these waters that nearby was a cove on a sparsely inhabited stretch of land that would suit his purpose. Raegar found it on the map and said the cove was not far away. They would reach it well before sunset.

Skylan began sorting out in his mind which men he would send ashore to refill the water barrels and which he would leave on board to guard the ship. A muffled shriek pierced his thoughts, sent him bounding up off the sea chest in alarm.

Wulfe came scampering up the ladder, running as if his life depended on it, which, perhaps it did, for Treia came right behind him. Her fists were clenched. She was livid with fury. Wulfe caught sight of Skylan and flung himself behind his friend, using him as a shield. Treia pointed an accusing finger. "I found him hiding in my bed!"

Everyone began laughing. Treia glared around at them, and they changed their laughter into coughs or clapped their hands over their mouths. Raegar came striding across the deck, angry and indignant, to scowl at Wulfe.

"This is no laughing matter, Cousin," Raegar said irately. "Something must be done about this young imp. He should not be aboard. He is unlucky."

The men were no longer laughing, which meant Skylan had a problem. If his warriors took it into their heads to decide the strange boy was bad luck, they would insist that Wulfe should be left behind when they next made landfall. While Skylan tried to think how to counter Raegar's claim, Aylaen provided the answer.

"The boy is part of Skylan's wyrd. If anything happens to Wulfe, a thread breaks."

The men thought this over. Their wyrd was bound up in Skylan's. The wyrd of every man is affected by the wyrd of others. If a thread snapped, the tapestry of life might start to unravel.

Raegar remained unconvinced. "I still think we should get rid of him, Cousin."

Annoyed at Raegar's daring to challenge him, Skylan said, frowning, "On this ship, I am not your cousin, Raegar. I am Chief of Chiefs, and you will address me with respect."

Raegar did not back down. His eyes locked with Skylan's like shields in the wall, both men shoving at each other, testing each other's defenses.

Treia smoothly intervened. "Raegar did not mean for you to harm the boy. But you must keep watch on him . . . *lord*."

She placed a subtle emphasis on the word, and Skylan suspected her of mocking him. He had to swallow it. He was the one at fault. Busy with preparations for sailing and worried about Aylaen, he had paid scant heed to Wulfe. He had assumed that the boy would not want anything to do with a ship sailing off to war. He remembered, too, that he was responsible for keeping peace on his ship, not an easy task when so many were forced to live together in a confined space. Above all, he could not afford to quarrel with his Bone Priestess.

"I apologize, Priestess," said Skylan stiffly. "I did not know the boy had sneaked aboard. You are right. I should have been keeping better watch on him. And now, you need to tell the dragon that it is time we made landfall."

Treia spoke to the Dragon Kahg, who presumably relayed the information to the other two dragons, for all the dragonships changed course and began to sail toward the land.

Once this was done, Skylan seized hold of Wulfe by the arm. "You should thank Aylaen for saving your ass."

"I had to come," said Wulfe defensively. "You are my geas."

"Whatever that is," Skylan muttered.

"I saved your life. I have to watch over you."

"I'm perfectly capable of watching over myself." Skylan glowered at him. "Keep out from underfoot. Don't bother the men, and stay away from Treia. Understand?"

Wulfe gave an emphatic nod, then added, grinning, "It's a good thing I came. You forgot your dragonbone board. I packed it up and brought it with me."

Skylan sucked in an irate breath. "I left the game behind on purpose!" He gave Wulfe a shake. "I didn't want to bring the draugr aboard this ship!"

"Owl Mother said you would try to get rid of the draugr," said Wulfe, wincing, "but that it wouldn't work. The draugr would come anyway. She said you need to find out what the draugr wants you to do. Only then will she stop coming."

The boy's eyes widened. "Are you going to throw me overboard?"

Skylan drew in a seething breath and waited a few moments for his rage to cool.

"I should," he said. "But Akaria would probably throw you back. As for the draugr"—he tried to shrug it off—"I have more important matters to worry about."

"Not according to Owl Mother you don't," Wulfe said.

"Now that you are aboard," Skylan continued grimly, ignoring that remark. "You must make yourself useful."

He paused, then said, "You will oil my sword."

Wulfe stared at him, horrified, and tried to pull away.

"I mean it!" said Skylan, keeping fast hold of the squirming boy. "You brought this on yourself. You will have duties while you're aboard, and one of them will be to oil my sword and keep the rust from forming. You will do this every day."

"It's iron!" Wulfe whimpered. "I can't touch it!"

"You should have thought of that before you sneaked aboard a warship," said Skylan coldly. "Now go."

He gave Wulfe a shove that sent the boy sprawling onto the deck. Wulfe picked himself up and looked at Skylan with pleading eyes, to see if he really meant it. Skylan glowered, and Wulfe turned away, smearing his nose with the back of his hand. He walked with dragging steps over to the sea chest where Skylan's armor and weapons were stored.

Wulfe glanced over his shoulder. He saw Skylan watching to make certain the boy obeyed his order. Treia was right. He'd let Wulfe run wild. The boy needed to be taught a lesson. Wulfe sniveled and gulped on his tears, then, squatting down, he reached out his hand for the beautiful embroidered sheepskin scabbard Skylan had purchased for Blood Dancer. Lanolin from the sheepskin would help keep the sword free from rust. Oiling the sword daily was also requisite. Rust was the bane of a warrior's existence. As Wulfe's hand closed over the scabbard, the boy's thin body gave a shudder so strong that Skylan saw it from across the deck.

Skylan turned away. He'd been too soft on the boy up until now. Letting him get away with this nonsense about touching iron. Skoval's balls! The boy claimed he couldn't even touch a stewpot! This would end here and now.

Skylan glanced about the ship. The warriors were seated on their sea chests, busy at various tasks, or talking and jesting. The men were in a good mood. Fortunately, by annoying Treia, Wulfe had managed to amuse the men, who were still sharing smothered laughter at the thought of the Bone Priestess finding a boy in her bed.

The men were also taking a more resigned view of Aylaen. Skylan's speech about Vindrash had impressed them. The Vindrasi would be dependent on the Dragon Goddess's goodwill in the upcoming battles, and they did not want to offend her. They were none of them comfortable having Aylaen around, however, treating her like a skunk that had wandered into the feast hall: careful not to make any sudden moves or poke at her or do anything to make her angry.

Seeing Wulfe hunched over the sword, Aylaen realized he must be feeling as lonely and friendless as herself, and she went to sit down beside him. He did not seem to notice her. He kept his back to her and to everyone. He gave a gulping sob every so often, and his shoulders shook. Aylaen thought nothing about it except perhaps that he was upset because Skylan had yelled at him.

She longed to talk to Garn, to try to make him understand, but he would not speak to her. To take her mind off their quarrel, she started to clean her new sword, which was sadly rusted. She rubbed the metal with the oiled cloth, working hard, scratching at spots of rust or dirt with her fingernail.

She noticed, as she worked on the sword, what she had not noticed before. The workmanship was extraordinary. Details began to emerge as she scrubbed away the dirt of years of neglect.

Although the sword was meant to ornament the altar of Vindrash, the maker had not insulted the goddess by making her sword lovely to look at but impractical. Aylaen pictured that early craftsman designing the sword for Vindrash herself, intending for her to use the weapon in battle. This was why the sword fit a woman's hand, why it was lighter in weight and delicate in design. As Aylaen worked, she could see runes on the blade, previously hidden by dirt and rust.

The hilt was made of ivory, and it was now yellow with age. She could see the faint outlines and feel the ridges left by what must have been ornate carvings, now worn smooth so that she could not tell what they had been. The weapon had seen battle. Odd for a weapon that Treia had dismissed as ceremonial.

Perhaps it was the hand of the goddess that wore down the hilt, Aylaen imagined, glad to lose herself in her daydreams. Vindrash had been pleased with the sword. She herself had used it in battle. And when the enemy gods had been defeated and peace had come to the world, Vindrash had put the sword away and forgotten about it. War had again come to heaven, but this time the gods had lost. Vindrash could not take up the sword herself. She had given it into the hands of one who would fight the battle for her. . . .

Aylaen's fanciful imaginings were cut short by a low moan. She looked over to see Skylan's lovely sheepskin scabbard smattered with blood.

"Wulfe, did you cut yourself?" she asked.

He turned away from her, hunching his shoulders, hiding his pain like a wounded animal. She rose to her feet and walked around to face him. His face twisted. His lips quivered, and his body shook.

Aylaen gently slid her hands beneath his hands and lifted them to the sunlight.

Wulfe's fingers were blistered, the flesh blackened and burned as though the sword he had been oiling were white-hot. He snatched his hand away and went back to his work. When he touched the metal, he gave a low moan. The flesh of his fingertips stuck to the blade and Aylaen smelled the stench of burning. She seized hold of his hand, jerking it from the metal.

"Don't let anyone see!" she said softly, taking the sword from him.

She hastily wrapped the boy's injured hands in the oiled cloth she had been using. Skylan glanced at them and frowned. Aylaen motioned with her head, and Skylan came over.

Shielding Wulfe with her body, keeping his hands hidden from the men, Aylaen removed the cloth.

Skylan stared at the boy in astonishment. The boy's fingers were burned, yet there was no fire on board ship, for fire was the most feared enemy of a dragonship. A blaze could consume the wooden planking in a matter of moments, and not even the Dragon Kahg would be able to save it or those on board.

"How did you burn yourself?" Skylan demanded.

Wulfe blubbered and refused to answer.

"It was the sword," said Aylaen, awed. "I . . . I saw it, Skylan. When he touched the metal, his fingers stuck to it and I could smell his flesh burning! Treia should treat him—"

"No!" said Skylan and Wulfe together.

"It was the iron!" The boy looked accusingly at Skylan. "I told you!"

"Give him to me," said Skylan. "I'll deal with him. Where is Treia?"

He looked around and saw Treia standing near the dragon's head, talking to Raegar. "Good. I'll take the boy below and bandage his hands. You keep your sister busy. Don't let her come down."

"Treia's far more happily occupied by Raegar than she would be with me," Aylaen said. "The wounds will putrefy if you don't put something on them.

At least you could use some of the unguent Treia made up for burns. I know where it is. I helped her pack it."

They hustled Wulfe down the ladder into the cool darkness of the hold. The cabin looked much different from when Skylan had occupied it on the nightmarish journey back from the ill-fated trip to Apensia. Sea chests were neatly stacked. The bedding was folded, smoothed. All was orderly and smelled of dried lavender.

"Shut the hatch," said Skylan.

Seeing Aylaen hesitate, he added, "We don't want Treia to come upon us without warning."

She didn't like the way Skylan was looking at her, but Aylaen did as he ordered. She pulled the trapdoor closed, leaving them in semidarkness as the faded light filtered in from between the chinks in the planking. He kept trying to catch her eye, but Aylaen avoided looking at him. She smeared the unguent gently on Wulfe's fingers. The boy flinched when she touched him, but he did not cry out. The unguent appeared to soothe him and he relaxed, watching in silence as she wound the bandages around his hands.

"If anyone asks, you cut yourself," Skylan admonished.

"It was the iron. It burned me," Wulfe insisted, staring perplexedly at the thick cloth lumps that were now his hands.

"No one believes iron could burn you. You cut yourself," said Skylan.

"Do you believe?" Wulfe asked, looking at him and Aylaen.

"I believe you," said Aylaen quietly. She glanced at Skylan. "I have to. I saw it with my own eyes."

"I believe you, too," said Skylan, sighing. "Satisfied?"

"I cut myself," Wulfe said.

"Now run along back up on deck."

"I'll go with him," said Aylaen, rising.

"Wulfe, go on," said Skylan. He escorted the boy to the ladder, helped him climb it, and opened the trapdoor.

"I cut my fingers," Wulfe announced loudly, climbing on deck.

Skylan shut the trapdoor and locked it. He hurried back down the ladder.

"I should go." Aylaen tried to sidle past him.

Skylan grabbed her around the waist and drew her close. "I thought I would hate the way you looked without your beautiful hair. At first I did hate it." He kissed her neck, not seeming to notice that she was pushing against him. "But now I find you are more desirable than ever."

He ran his hand over her shorn head and gazed at her tenderly. "No more teasing, Aylaen. I want you, and I know you feel the same. I like you in man's clothing. It is so much easier to manage than dresses and brooches and smocks. . . ."

One hand reached inside her shirt, fondling her breasts. He slid his other hand down her trousers.

"You did this for love of me," he murmured.

Aylaen struggled in Skylan's grip, but he would not let her go. She was exhausted; she had not been able to sleep for days. She was afraid, and she could not let anyone see her doubts, her fear. The men already thought ill of her. She was alone. Treia made no secret of the fact that she thought Aylaen was behaving like a spoiled brat. Aylaen could not turn for comfort to Garn, for he would not speak to her. She could not talk to Skylan, who refused to take her seriously, but kept willfully insisting she must be in love with him.

Aylaen was suddenly furious at all of them. She tasted the cruel words she was about to say on her lips, and they were sweet. Speaking them would hurt both Skylan and Garn. Good. She wanted to hurt them, as they had hurt her. Aylaen snapped, like the wyrd in the hands of one of the three sisters. She doubled her fists and struck Skylan in the chest. She struck hard, beating the words into him.

"I do not love you!" she cried angrily. "I love Garn! I did this to be with him!"

Skylan went livid. She knew, as she looked at him, that this was what his corpse would look like. His hands, cold and lifeless, fell at his side. His eyes were the only living thing in him, and they burned.

"Oh, Skylan, I'm sorry!" Aylaen reached out, as though the words hung between them and she could snatch them back.

Skylan stared at her, and now even the flame in his eyes died. He was nothing but deadly pallor and awful shadow.

"Don't look at me like that, Skylan!" Aylaen pleaded. "Please. I didn't mean—"

"How long?" he asked, his lips barely moving.

Aylaen could only shake her head.

"How long?" Skylan cried savagely, and he raised his hand as though he would strike her. "How long have you loved him?"

Aylaen said softly, "All my life!"

"Get out!" Skylan said. "Get out of my sight! I never want to see you again! Or Garn, either!"

Aylaen covered her face with her hands and began to sob. "Skylan, we never meant to hurt you. You have to believe that—"

"Believe you?" Skylan said, and he gave a terrible laugh. "Get out before I kill you!"

Foam flecked his lips. He was shaking, shivering with rage. He heard Aylaen stumbling across the deck.

"When we make landfall," said Skylan, not turning around, "you and Garn will take your things and leave this ship."

Everyone on board ship had heard the altercation. Their raised voices, particularly Skylan's, carried clearly. Garn was waiting for Aylaen. He helped her up out of the hold. The silence was awful. No one knew where to look or what to say.

The men moved away from them, gave the two room to pass. Aylaen sagged down onto a sea chest and lowered her face into her hands. Garn sat beside her, his arm around her shoulders. He avoided everyone, stared out across the leaden sea.

The dragonship was nearing the shore, and the men had work to do. Each went thankfully to his post, glad to be able to look somewhere else.

Skylan remained below in the darkness until he felt the motion of the ship slowing. His place was topside. He climbed the ladder, set foot on deck. Skylan cast one burning glance about the deck. His eyes warned every man to keep his distance.

Treia started to go to her sister, but Raegar stopped her. He whispered something to her, and she nodded and went over to speak to Skylan. He glowered at her, warning her to keep her mouth shut.

Treia paid no heed. "Aylaen must stay on board with me," she said.

Skylan's scowl darkened. He shook his head.

"You have no say in the matter," Treia told him. "Aylaen is my acolyte. The Kai commanded me to train her. Therefore, she must remain on board."

I have no say in the matter! Skylan's fury rose from his gut, surging hot and bitter into his mouth, nearly choking him. He snarled something, which Treia took for consent. She went to speak to Aylaen, who shook her head and clung to Garn. Both Garn and Treia talked to her, and at length, her head drooping, Aylaen gave in.

"Come with me," said Treia. "You should try to get some sleep."

Aylaen stood up. She looked down at Garn, and suddenly, casting a defiant glance at everyone, she put her hands to his face and kissed him on the mouth. "I love you," she said.

She refused her sister's help. Walking to the hold, she disappeared into the darkness below.

The three dragonships made landfall. The Vindrasi often used this cove as a first stop when setting out on voyages. The land was heavily wooded with streams that provided fresh drinking water. Skylan had stopped here on his last voyage. The charred wood from their fires lay in black lumps amid circles of stones.

Garn put on his chain mail, which had been a gift to him from Skylan. He took the shield that Norgaard had given him from the rack. He picked up his axe and his sea chest and walked over to where Skylan stood.

Skylan's arms were folded across his chest. He looked at Garn as though at a stranger.

"I am sorry, Skylan," Garn said. "We never meant to hurt you."

The blazing blue eyes burned Garn's words to ashes. Slowly and deliberately, Skylan turned his back and walked away.

Garn left the ship. All eyes were on him as he made his way to the dragonship belonging to the Martegnan. Out of the corner of his eye, Skylan watched his friend and brother leave the ship.

They were dead to him, these two he had loved and trusted. They were dead, and he would have to find a way to go on living without them.

## CHAPTER 7

Skylan longed to be able to crawl into sleep and hide there, licking his wounds. He ordered all the men ashore while he remained on board. Treia and Aylaen also stayed on board, holed up in the cabin. He hoped they knew better than to make an appearance. Night fell. His men doused their cook fires and went to sleep. He lay down on the deck and closed his eyes.

But it was not sleep who came. It was the draugr.

Draya stood over him, her pallid flesh drawn tight over her skull. She gazed down at him with sunken eyes. She pointed to the game board, which Wulfe had thoughtfully brought out before Skylan had angrily ordered him off the ship.

"Leave me alone," Skylan muttered with a courage born of not caring.

The draugr stood over him.

Skylan closed his eyes and tried to pretend the draugr was not there. The cold chill of death seeped around him, causing him to shiver, though the night was warm. He seemed to see her even through his closed eyelids.

The draugr sat down on a sea chest. She picked up the five bones and threw them on the board. It was his turn, but Skylan made no move to touch them. The draugr grabbed the bones and threw them again. Skylan sat there sullenly, not moving. The draugr again threw the bones.

Skylan realized that the draugr was prepared to do this all night. He grabbed the five bones and flung them onto the deck. The bones scattered everywhere. One landed on top of the hatch, leading down to the hold where Aylaen and Treia slept. One rolled across the deck to bump up beside Raegar's helm. One bounded off the carved wooden neck of the Dragon Kahg. One splashed into the sea. One came to rest at the feet of the draugr.

The draugr seized his shuddering hand and pried open his palm. She dropped five more bones into his hand and squeezed his fingers over the pieces, squeezing hard. He gasped in pain, and she finally released his hand. He saw his flesh had turned whitish blue, as from frostbite.

"I don't understand!" Skylan cried raggedly. "I don't know what you want from me! Five bones! Five Dragons of Vektia. Is that it?"

The draugr gazed at him and did not answer. Thinking only to get this over with, he threw the five bones.

He and the draugr played the dragonbone game, and for the first time, Skylan won.

It took him a moment to realize this. He won. He had beaten the draugr. She gazed at him and gave a nod, then went away.

"Garn was right," Skylan said. "Five bones. Five Dragons of Vektia." He started to go tell his friend, and then he remembered.

He had no friend.

Skylan lay down on deck. He stared into the stars and saw Aylaen's face and heard her voice. He saw her with Garn, the two of them making love, and his vitals curled with shame and burned with jealous rage. Only when the stars began to fade did he fall into a frayed-edged sleep to wake with a start from a dream of horror he could not remember.

The sun rose out of the sea, red and angry as Skylan's soul. The night had been hot and the morning was hotter. No wind blew. The men said the sun had swallowed it. Skylan went onshore to rouse everyone, shouting and kicking at any who were reluctant to rise. He could not find Wulfe. Bjorn said he had seen Wulfe run off down the beach.

The air was humid, hard to breathe. Clothing stuck to the body. Clouds of gnats appeared, flying into faces and into mouths. Pelicans flew over the waves in a straight line, their wings dipping and rising as one. Gulls circled overhead.

The men hurried on board the ships, all eager to go back out to sea, hoping to find a cooling breeze. Skylan saw Garn standing on board the deck of Martegnan's dragonship. Skylan pointedly looked away. He roamed the shore, searching for Wulfe.

Skylan shouted for him, a little worried that Wulfe might have run away. Skylan could not take time to go hunt him down. The men would not tolerate hanging about waiting for the boy to turn up. Most would be glad to hear he was gone.

Skylan gave one last shout.

"Here I am," said Wulfe, coming up behind him.

"Where have you been?" Skylan demanded. He seized hold of the boy by the arm, hurrying him along.

"Talking to my friends," said Wulfe.

"What friends? Never mind. You can tell me later. The ship is ready to sail."

"It can't," said Wulfe, shaking his head. "You have to stay here."

"Don't be ridiculous," Skylan said.

Wulfe grabbed Skylan's arm, hung on to it. "We can't go out there! The oceanaids warned me!"

Skylan grunted in disgust.

"I know you don't believe me—"

"You're right," Skylan said. He hauled Wulfe up the gangplank. He made a swift head count. Everyone was on board.

Treia had her hand on the spiritbone, communing with the Dragon Kahg. Aylaen stood beside her, presumably learning the ritual. Aylaen was not paying attention, however. She was haggard, her eyes swollen and red-rimmed. She cast one pleading look at Skylan. He met her look with a stone-cold gaze. She flushed. She had felt sorry for him, but now she was growing angry.

The three dragonships bobbed in the shallow water. Skylan waited impatiently for the Dragon Kahg to lead the ships out to sea. When nothing happened, Skylan walked over to see what was wrong.

"The Dragon Kahg will not leave unless you order him," Treia reported.

"What? Why?" Skylan asked.

Treia shrugged.

"I think I know why," Aylaen said. She gazed out over the water, seemed to look a long way off. "The Sea Goddess seeks revenge for the death of her sister. Akaria blames Torval and wants him to suffer as she suffers. Torval is angry and he is afraid, for Vindrash, whom he loves, has vanished and he fears she is lost to him forever." She glared at Skylan as she spoke.

Treia shook her head and brushed all that aside with a gesture of her hand. "What do you want to do, lord?"

"I want to sail!" Skylan said, exasperated, and the men cheered loudly in agreement.

Treia nodded. "The Dragon Kahg wants to know if you will take the responsibility for ordering him out to sea."

"I am Chief of Chiefs," Skylan said. "The decision is mine."

"Very well," said Treia, and she placed her hand upon the spiritbone.

The *Venjekar* set sail, gliding over the smooth and rippling water. The other dragonships followed.

The storm struck them shortly after High Sun.

The storm bore down upon them rapidly, giving them no time to head back inland. No man had seen anything like it. Black clouds shot through with purple lightning boiled up from the horizon and surged over the sea. The water went from calm to frenzied in the time between one beat of the heart and another.

The ship plunged and rocked. The seas broke over the hull and flooded the deck. Skylan ordered the men to carry their sea chests, their shields, and weapons and armor below so they would not be washed overboard. This proved difficult, for the men lost their footing on the canting deck. Some could do nothing but groan with seasickness and heave their guts over the side.

A gust of fierce wind spewed forth from the Storm Goddess's angry maw and came straight at them. The wind tore off the tops of the waves and spit foam into the air. The gust struck the *Venjekar* amidships, causing it to keel over. Men cried out and grabbed hold of ropes or the mast or each other, struggling to keep from falling off the deck that was almost perpendicular to the water. Skylan had nothing to hang on to, and he crashed up against the hull. Erdmun hurtled into him. A barrel rolled across the deck and slammed into them both.

For a terrifying moment, the ship seemed to hang between wind and water, and then the wind suddenly abated, like a sucked-in breath, and the ship abruptly righted itself, sending men and equipment sliding over the deck in the opposite direction.

"Did anyone fall overboard?" Skylan shouted, fighting to make himself heard against another blast of wind laced with stinging rain.

Not that it mattered, he thought grimly. If anyone did fall into that sea, he would be lost.

Skylan clung to the rack that held the shields and stared across the heaving, churning waves, trying to catch a glimpse of the other two ships. He could not see them due to the lancing rain and the sea spray and towering waves. Or perhaps he could not see them because they had gone under.

He glanced across the deck to the prow where Treia and Aylaen had been standing. They were gone, and his heart stopped. Then Raegar picked himself up and helped both the women to their feet. The big man must have caught hold of the two of them as they had gone flying, and he had managed to hang on to them, saving them from the waves.

"Take them below!" Skylan bellowed, and he jabbed his finger at the cabin.

Raegar either understood or he knew what he had to do. Fighting the wind, holding each woman around the waist, he struggled across the deck. Skylan, bent double, half-blinded by the pelting rain, went to help.

Lightning sizzled and thunder cracked. The wind fought them like a berserk warrior, coming at them from every direction. The Dragon Kahg would not allow the ship to sink, but he could not keep it from being tossed on the waves. Water crashed onto the deck, pulling and tugging at men's legs, seemingly intent on dragging them to their deaths.

Skylan managed to reach the hold. He tried to lift the hatch. The wind buffeted him, and he could not manage on his own. Raegar let go of his charges. Treia crouched on her hands and knees, her wet hair streaming over her eyes. Aylaen started to join her sister, and then she gave a wild cry and ran to the ship's side.

"Garn!" she screamed, leaning perilously over the rail.

Skylan looked out and saw Garn's face and arms and hands riding the surface of a rising wave. And then the white water broke over him and he was gone.

"Garn!" Aylaen cried again, and Skylan realized she meant to dive into the water. He leaped to stop her. The motion of the ship sent him careening into her, and he dragged her off the rail.

"Keep hold of her!" Skylan shouted at Raegar.

Skylan stared into the blue-black, foam-flecked waves. He saw nothing for long moments, and then Garn, gasping for air, burst out of the water. Garn saw the dragonship, and in the space between one wave and another, one lightning strike and another, he tried to swim toward it.

Skylan marked Garn's location. Climbing up onto the rail, Skylan dived into the water.

He plunged into sudden quiet, an almost soothing contrast from the chaotic noise of roaring wind and booming thunder. The water was dark and murky, and he could not find the surface. He floundered beneath the waves, not knowing if he was on his head or his heels, his lungs burning. Then he saw lightning flare, and he swam toward it. His head broke free of the water. He gasped for breath and searched for Garn.

Men lined the rail, shouting and pointing. Skylan began to swim in that direction. A wave carried him up, and he saw Garn below him. The wave flung him down on his friend, practically right on top of him. The two grappled, each trying desperately to hold on to the other. The sea dragged them both below.

Skylan managed to grab a tangle of Garn's hair. He wrapped his arm beneath his friend's chin and kicked toward the surface. Garn's strength was flagging. He was almost finished, and he had sense enough to go limp in Skylan's grip, not struggle against him in a panic that would have drowned them both.

Skylan's lungs seemed ready to burst. He was going to have to breathe, even if it meant breathing in his death—when his head broke free. He gulped air. Keeping Garn's head above water, Skylan plowed doggedly through the waves. He seemed to be making little progress. If he managed to claw his way forward by an arm's length, a wave dragged him back six.

And then a wave carried him and Garn so near the ship that Skylan's outstretched hand touched the hands of men leaning over, in peril of their own lives, to grab hold. The sea swept them apart and water closed over his head. Skylan despaired. His arms ached and his legs and lungs burned. He could not hold on to Garn much longer.

He surfaced again, hauling Garn out of the water with him. Garn had lost consciousness. His eyes were closed, his mouth open. He was dead weight in Skylan's arms.

Perhaps he was dead in Skylan's arms.

I should let him go, save myself, Skylan thought. Anger raged inside him. This was a battle with Akaria, and he'd be damned if he was going to let the goddess win. He began, once more, to swim toward the *Venjekar,* though it seemed farther away now than ever.

Then a wave lifted the two men up and, as if in a fit of pique, hurled them toward the ship. Skylan feared for a horrible moment that he and Garn were going to be smashed against the hull. The wave carried them up and over the rail and cast them like immense fish onto the deck. Skylan slammed painfully into the mast and came to rest in the water that was sloshing over the deck. Garn lay beside him. He was not breathing.

The men seized hold of Garn and carried him below. They laid him on his belly and began the task of pounding his back and pumping his arms to force the water out of his lungs.

Skylan crawled across the deck to the rudder, with some idea of trying to steer the ship inland. But the rudder was gone, broken off. Only a stump of jagged wood left behind jutted out.

Skylan wished in that moment that the gray waves had closed over his head. He reminded himself that he was Chief of Chiefs and he was the one who had ordered the ship to sea. He staggered across the deck awash with water up to his ankles. Grabbing hold of the men, he told them to find rope and tie themselves to the mast, the prow, anything they could find. He sent men who were severely injured—and there were many of those—down to the cabin for Treia to treat.

Finally, Skylan went below himself. Water kept running into his eyes, blinding him. He wiped it away and saw that it was blood.

Lightning flared. The ship rocked wildly. Skylan shut the hatch and made sure it was sealed, then descended the ladder and looked around the cabin. It was hard to see in the darkness.

"Garn?" Skylan called out. His mouth was parched from the salt water; his throat hurt.

"Here," Garn answered weakly. "You saved my life. Thank you."

"You're one of my men," Skylan said shortly. He could make out Aylaen, crouching near him. "Wulfe?"

"I'm here!" Wulfe's voice quavered. He was terrified.

"Treia?"

"I am safe and well, lord," Treia replied, cold and calm as always. Skylan could not help but smile, though his smile was grim. At least some things did not change.

Fifteen men were on the deck, tied to anything that would hold them. He took a count of the men down here and discovered, to his relief, that they had not lost anyone.

Skylan was not feeling grateful to the gods, however. He was bitter and resentful, and he wondered if what Aylaen had said was true. The gods should be united against the foe. Why were they wasting time fighting among themselves? He and his men were nothing more than bones tossed down onto some heavenly game board.

The Five Dragons of Vektia. Five pieces thrown onto a game board. A heavenly game. Five dragons. Moving the pieces about the board. It was like . . . it was like . . .

Skylan frowned. He'd had a flash of understanding. If only he could think . . . but the thought slid away from him—or rather, was washed away.

He went back up on deck and lashed himself to the mast. He crouched on the deck and listened to the creaking and groaning of the ship's timbers. He and his people would be safe on board until the planks began to give way under the constant battering. And then not even the dragon could save them.

Skylan had no idea how long the storm lasted. There was no day, only one horrible night that seemed to go on and on. The ship rocked and tossed and swooped up and plunged down and wallowed and foundered, and after a time Skylan came to wish that the ship would simply sink and put an end to the misery.

He was wet and shivering. His head hurt and the old wound in his leg throbbed. Periodically he risked standing up and fought his way down to the cabin. The stench was horrible. Men were seasick, lying in their own vomit. The cabin stank of waste. They were drinking rainwater that poured down between the cracks from the deck above, catching it in drinking horns that were handed around. Skylan checked on those who were injured. Treia reported dourly that they were alive and that was the best they could hope for. He glanced at Aylaen, who sat beside Garn. They were asleep in each other's arms.

Skylan looked at them for a long time as the ship lurched beneath him. He finally went back up on the deck, tied himself again to the mast. He slept and woke and slept and woke. Once he found Wulfe curled up at his side like a mongrel dog.

And then one day Skylan woke up abruptly. He lay a moment, confused, wondering what had wakened him.

Silence.

No howling wind. No crashing waves. No booming thunder. He looked into the night sky and saw stars.

The storm was over. The *Venjekar* had survived.

# CHAPTER 8

Skylan scrambled to his feet. His limbs were stiff from disuse, his feet numb and cold. Around him, other men were rousing, peering around in the darkness, whispering their heartfelt thanks to Torval. The sun rose, a pale orb, pinkish red, floating in and out of tendrils of mist that writhed about the surface of the sea and made the dragon's head ghostly.

Skylan was uncomfortably reminded of his voyage back from Apensia, except then the fog had been dark and thick, and these mists were airy, almost ethereal, and tinged with glowing light.

The people emerged from the hold. They stood on the deck and stared out at the mist-covered sea that was smooth and calm.

"The goddess is still angry," said Aylaen. "She is just worn out."

Skylan tried to see the other dragonships, but he could not see past the dragon's head. The mists parted as the ship sailed into them, closed behind.

He ordered the men to call out, and they hallooed across the water and banged their weapons on their shields.

No one answered. Skylan posted a lookout. Raegar quickly volunteered. He stood at the rail most of the day, staring into the mists, trying to penetrate them. Once he offered to climb up the dragon's carved figurehead to try to obtain a better view. Skylan refused, saying that he doubted it would bear Raegar's weight, especially after the pounding it had taken during the storm. Wulfe offered to make the climb, but Raegar said that he didn't want to risk the boy's life.

Skylan thought no more of this until he happened, a short time later, to see Raegar peering out into the mists. Raegar turned around, a worried expression on his face, and caught Skylan watching him. He shrugged, shook his head, and walked off. Skylan found this concern odd. If his ship had survived, there was a good chance the others had. It was not surprising they had been separated. They would meet again at the rendezvous. Perhaps Raegar was concerned about some friend, though as far as Skylan knew, Raegar had not made friends among the other clans. Skylan doubted Raegar could have named a single man. Why, then, was he taking the loss so hard?

Skylan asked Treia to speak to the Dragon Kahg, ask him what had happened to the other dragonships. He also needed to know if the dragon knew their location and where they were bound, for the ship was sailing on a course that, according to the position of the sun, was taking them to the east.

Treia tried to talk to the dragon with no success. Kahg would not respond. Skylan asked if the Dragon Kahg was angry with him, and Treia replied in wry tones that she considered it quite likely.

The *Venjekar* had survived, but just barely, and Skylan was not sure how much longer the ship could remain afloat. They were taking on water; they had lost the rudder. The men could drink their fill of rainwater, but the food had either washed overboard or was soaked in brine and inedible. Their bellies were empty and cramping. They managed to assuage the worst of their hunger by catching a few fish. The fish were bony, and they had to eat them raw. Warriors could not survive long on such a diet.

Treia begged the Dragon Kahg to take them inland. Again the dragon refused. He did not alter course, but continued sailing in an easterly direction. Kahg was taking them somewhere, and wherever that was, he was making haste. Seawater churned beneath the bow and flowed around the keel in a long creamy wake.

Skylan was frustrated, but there was nothing he could do. He paced the deck or stood by the prow, staring into the mists. His men, who had been overjoyed to survive the storm, were now grumbling and muttering. Some remembered that it was Skylan who had ordered the dragon out to sea.

"We are in strange waters. The dragon will head for land by nightfall," Skylan told them. "He will be forced to."

Dragons could see in darkness, but not even a dragon's piercing eyes could detect the sharp rocks lying beneath the water that could rip open a ship's belly or sandbars on which a ship could founder. Only in waters the dragon knew well would he risk sailing after dark or in thick fog, as he had when he'd brought Skylan home.

The sun sank; the mist glowed orange with the dying flame. Darkness fell, and the moon was ghostly in the mists that lay clammy fingers on the skin and writhed about the deck. The dragon continued to sail east.

Of course, Erdmun would remember the *Durtmundor,* the famous ghost ship whose crew had killed a whale, a sea creature sacred to Akaria, and been cursed by the goddess to forever sail the seas, lamenting their fate.

"Maybe we're a ghost ship," Erdmun said to his listeners, crouching on their sea chests. "Maybe we're all dead and we just don't know it."

Skylan walked over to Erdmun, yanked him to his feet, and punched him in the face. Erdmun stumbled backwards, fell over the chest, and landed on his rump.

"Did you feel that?" Skylan demanded, standing over him with clenched fists.

Edmund mumbled something and spit blood.

"Good," said Skylan. "Then you're not dead."

He walked off. He saw, in passing, Garn smile and give an almost imperceptible shake of his head. Skylan's steps slowed. All his life, he had turned to Garn for counsel and advice. Skylan never needed that counsel more than he needed it now. He saw Garn watching him, silently asking for Skylan's forgiveness.

But Skylan couldn't forgive. How could Aylaen love Garn? She was supposed to love Skylan. She was *meant* to love Skylan. He was Chief of Chiefs. He was a courageous warrior. He possessed land and cattle and a fine horse and a sword worth a chief's ransom. Garn was nobody, a pauper, living on Norgaard's charity. Women—other women—loved Skylan. No woman had ever loved Garn.

No woman except Aylaen.

Let Garn choke on his counsel! Skylan thought. I have no need of it. I am, after all, Chief of Chiefs. He walked to the stern, putting the length of the ship between himself and Garn. Skylan set the watch and then flung himself moodily down on the deck, hoping to get some sleep.

Wulfe came pattering over. "I'm hungry. When are we going to eat?"

Skylan scowled at him. The boy had barely a stitch on. "Where are your clothes?"

"They were wet," said Wulfe. "And they itched."

"Go put some clothes on," Skylan said. "You'll freeze."

"I'm not cold." Wulfe sat down beside him. "Did you see? Your draugr's guiding the ship."

Skylan snorted. "Go tell your ghost tales to Erdmun," he muttered, clasping his arms around his chest, trying to make himself comfortable. The draugr had not visited him since the night before the storm. He had hoped he was rid of her.

"But she is," Wulfe insisted. "See for yourself."

Skylan sighed, and just to shut the boy up, he raised himself onto one elbow and looked to the front of the ship.

The draugr stood beside the spiritbone, her hand on the dragon's carved neck, just as Skylan remembered seeing Draya on the day of her death.

The dragon's eyes shone red in the mists. Draya's face shimmered white. Skylan shuddered.

"Where is she taking us?"

"I don't know," Wulfe said. "I asked the oceanaids where we were, but they won't tell me. They jeer at me and say we're cursed."

"We are not cursed," Skylan said wrathfully, and he raised his voice for all to hear him—all, including his dead wife. "We are not cursed! Torval brought us safely through the storm. He has us in his care. He will bring us home."

He glared at Wulfe. "Go put some clothes on!"

Skylan threw himself back down on the deck. He shut his eyes, squeezed them tight, so that they would not fly open and stare at the draugr.

"Skylan," said a gentle voice. "May I talk to you?"

"What do you want?" Skylan asked harshly. He did not have to open his eyes. The voice was like a sword slicing through his gut.

"I know you can never forgive me, Skylan," Aylaen said. "I understand, though it makes me sad, for you are my friend, my brother—"

Skylan's eyes flared open. Aylaen flinched at the raw pain she saw there. She reached out her hand.

"Don't," he said, his fury burning.

Aylaen let her hand fall. "I know you can never forgive me," she repeated, "but I hope you can forgive Garn—"

"Why do you love him?" Skylan demanded.

"Why do *you* love him?" Aylaen countered.

"I'm asking you," he said sullenly.

Aylaen smiled. "I'll tell you why *you* love Garn. You love him because he is wise and good and kind. You love him because his courage is not a banner that he waves in your face. His courage gives him the strength to do grubbing work in the fields day after day. His courage is patient and gentle with Norgaard when he is twisted up in pain. His courage led him to dive into the sea during the storm to try to save a man he didn't even know. You love him for all those reasons, Skylan. And that is why *I* love him."

Skylan grabbed hold of her, held her tightly. "But I want you to love me!"

"You have always had everything you wanted in life, Skylan," Aylaen said, gently and sadly. "But not this time."

"Freilis take you, then! Freilis take you both!"

Skylan shoved her away and lay back down. He closed his eyes, did not look at her. He sensed her lingering for a moment, hoping he would relent. Skylan would never do that. His aching heart, his bitter jealousy, his wounded pride twisted around inside him like a nest of baby vipers. He knew he should cut off their heads, for the longer he nursed them, the stronger and more powerful and more poisonous they would become. He could not help himself, however. He fed the snakes the milk of hatred.

"Skylan!" Erdmun was shaking him. "Skylan, wake up!"

"I'm awake," Skylan mumbled, trying to crawl out of the hole of deep sleep. "What is it?" He sat up, yawning and scratching at the beard sprouting on his chin. He hated going without shaving. It made him feel unclean.

"I sighted land," said Erdmun, who had been standing lookout.

Skylan was on his feet, awake in an instant. He looked swiftly and uneasily in the direction of the dragon's head and breathed a sigh of relief to see that the draugr was gone. The mists were gone, as well. A red slit on the horizon presaged the sun, whose light was already spreading a pinkish glow in the sky.

"Wake the others," said Skylan.

"I wouldn't if I were you," said Erdmun. "Not yet."

Skylan cast him a frowning glance. "Why not?"

Erdmun pointed.

Two immense rock formations jutted up out of the water. The rocks stood opposite each other, leaving a space between large enough for a dragonship. The rocks were not a natural foundation. They were the remains of an immense stone arch that had been built centuries before. The top of the arch had long ago broken and fallen into the sea. All that remained were the pillars that had supported it, and they were so eroded by wind and wave that only the Vindrasi remembered from their legends and stories and songs what they had been.

"You see why I told you not to wake the men?" Erdmun said gloomily. His lip was swollen from where Skylan had hit him. "What are we going to do? The Dragon Kahg has brought us to the one place you warned us we should not go! We *are* cursed!"

The Arch of Vektia, gateway to the Dragon Isles.

The men were alarmed and frightened, and they urged Skylan to tell the dragon to turn the ship around so that they would not be attacked by giants. Skylan couldn't very well tell the men they had nothing to fear, that he'd made up the entire tale. There was no curse. There were no giants. There had been no battle on the Dragon Isles.

Once his initial shock had passed, Skylan felt a vast sense of relief. He was grateful to the Dragon Kahg, who had known what he was doing all the time. Skylan had been on the Dragon Isles before. There was plenty of game. There were trees that could be cut down, used to make a new rudder.

The ship had, admittedly, been blown a vast distance off course. But even with the delay, there were still several months of good sailing weather ahead of them. Time enough to meet up with the other dragonships and find the ogres' lands.

Now, all Skylan had to do was fix his lie. The dragonship was sailing straight toward the arch, and some of the men were threatening to jump overboard rather than risk the wrath of the gods.

Raegar came up to the rail, leaned his elbow on it. "Strange that the dragon should bring us to the Dragon Isles," he said in a low voice.

He moved closer. He pitched his voice for only Skylan to hear. "Don't fret, Cousin. You did what you had to do. You saved Draya's reputation, as well as your own. The gods understand and forgive. As for why the Dragon Kahg brought us here, consider this—the dragon would not have done so if Torval had not commanded it."

Skylan leaned on the rail, watching the pillars draw nearer, and considered his cousin's words.

"That is true," Skylan was forced to concede.

Except he knew it wasn't. The dragon had not brought them here. Draya had. She had been standing beside the dragon, guiding him.

The men needed food. They needed to make repairs to the ship, which was slowly sinking beneath them. Skylan stood mulling it over and was only gradually aware that Raegar had departed and Garn was at his side.

Skylan started to walk off.

"You don't need to speak to me," said Garn quietly. "Just listen. I came to warn you. Raegar is acting strangely. He spends most of his time scanning the sea, as though he's searching for something."

"He's looking for the other dragonships," Skylan replied curtly. "Nothing strange in that."

"Just keep an eye on him," said Garn, and he moved away.

Skylan looked around the ship. The men lined the rail, eyeing the pillars and arguing about whether they should land on the Dragon Isles, a moot point, for the dragon seemed intent on carrying them there. Raegar was not among the crowd. He was standing by the rail, gazing out to sea, and he was smiling.

"Raegar!" Skylan called.

He jerked his head around, startled to find he was being watched.

"Any sign of the other ships?" Skylan asked.

Raegar was wary. His eyes narrowed. "What ships?"

"The two dragonships, of course," said Skylan, puzzled by the response.

"Ah!" Raegar's face cleared. He gave a shrug and a sorrowful shake of his head. "I've seen nothing of them, I'm afraid."

He crossed the deck to join the other men.

Skylan wiped the sweat from his face and ran his hand through his hair to feel the cool air on his scalp. Things were getting far too complicated. Skylan looked at the pillars, and he longed to tell Garn everything.

Tell him I lied when I said I had been to the Dragon Isles before. Tell him it was not Torval nor yet the dragon who brought us here to these sacred isles. It was the draugr, the walking corpse of my dead wife. My wife who haunts my dreams and forces me to play dragonbones night after night for a reason I cannot fathom. I would tell Garn the truth about Raegar, how I met him, how he owned slaves, how he was going to abduct Draya, how he seemed perfectly content to never come back home and then he came back home.

Garn would be able to explain it. He would know what it all meant.

I saved him from drowning. Now the waters are closing over my head. I need him to save me.

Skylan looked at his friend and even took a step toward him. At that moment, Aylaen walked over to Garn. Their hands twined together. They gazed into each other's eyes. In that moment, they were the only two people in the world. In that moment, each existed only for the other.

The snakes inside Skylan twisted.

"Listen to me!" Skylan shouted, and the men ceased their arguments.

"Torval himself has brought us to this blessed haven, where we can rest and eat our fill and repair our ship. We will offer prayers of thanks to Torval and to Vindrash for bringing us safely through the storm. And we will vow to the gods that we will not return to our homes until we have recovered the Vektan Torque."

The warriors discussed this among themselves and at last agreed that Skylan must be right. The dragon would not have brought them here if there were a curse.

In spite of all that, they might not have agreed so readily, but that no man could stomach more raw fish.

# CHAPTER 9

The *Venjekar* swept between the Pillars of Vektia and entered the Bay of the Pillars. The water here was aqua blue, many shades lighter than the dark blue of the sea. The Dragon Kahg did not diminish his speed. Dragons and men had traveled here since the beginning of time. The only sandbar was clearly visible—a narrow strip of brownish-white sand adorned by a single wind-stunted tree. The dragonship sailed around the sandbar and through the deep water, heading for the shore.

And then, without warning, came the sickening sound of splintering wood. The ship's forward momentum stopped abruptly. Everything and everyone kept going. Men slammed into the hull. Those, like Skylan, who had been leaning on the rail flew over the side and landed in the water.

The *Venjekar* had run aground.

Skylan bobbed to the surface. The water was calm and shallow. He could not touch the bottom, but he could see it beneath his boots. He could also see the sandbar and the wrecked dragonship. Beside him, Wulfe was coughing, spitting out water, and looking indignant.

"Can you swim?" Skylan asked.

Wulfe nodded.

"Then head to shore," Skylan ordered.

From his vantage point in the water, he could see that returning to the ship was useless. The dragonship perched at an odd angle on a narrow strip of sand, the keel buried deep. Even if the ship had sustained no major damage, freeing it would be an immense task.

The tide would make a difference. Skylan had no way of knowing if it was rising or falling, but if they were at low tide, the high tide might float the dragonship off the sandbar.

He swam back to the ship to tell the others to disembark. Skylan glanced at the dragon's head. He couldn't help but think that this disaster served the dragon right. Kahg had allowed the draugr to bring them here and then dump them on a sandbar. The eyes of the Dragon Kahg were hooded. Treading water, Skylan could see only a narrow red glint of light, and the light looked angry.

"Unload everything!" Skylan yelled up at those still on board. "Lighten the weight!"

Garn understood, and he and Aylaen and Bjorn began gathering up weapons and shields and the supplies that had survived the storm. They lowered sea chests and barrels over the side. Skylan and those in the water began ferrying them to shore. When the last barrel had been thrown into the water, Bjorn jumped in. Garn and Aylaen went to persuade Treia that she should leave. She clung to the rail, shaking her head violently.

"She can't swim!" Garn called.

"Toss her down. I'll catch her!" Skylan cried, and before Treia could protest, Garn picked her up and lowered her over the side.

Treia fell into Skylan's arms with a gasp and grabbed him around the neck with a clutch that nearly strangled him.

"Let loose and stop kicking!" he ordered. "You're going to drown us both!"

"The spiritbone!" Treia spluttered, clawing at him in panic.

"I have it, Treia!" Aylaen called out.

Skylan took Treia to the shore. Men were sorting through the supplies, cleaning the salt water off their weapons.

Skylan stripped off his shirt and was spreading it out in the sand to dry when Aylaen came hastening up to him. He glowered, warning her away. As always, she ignored him.

"Raegar's missing," she said.

Skylan frowned at her, then shrugged. "He's around. Probably off in the bushes taking a crap."

"No, he's not, Skylan," said Aylaen insistently. "I've looked. Treia's looked, and so have Garn and some of the others. Raegar's not here. He's not anywhere. And there's something else. Erdmun says he saw Raegar fall into the water. No one's seen him since."

Aylaen drew in a shaking breath. "I . . . we're afraid he may have drowned."

Skylan snorted. "The water's not that deep. Raegar would have to work really hard to drown in it."

"Raegar was standing at the stern, not the prow like the rest of us. Erdmun says Raegar fell into the deep water on the other side of the sandbar. And he told Treia he couldn't swim."

Skylan instituted another search. He sent men into the thick stands of wind-stunted pine trees and others back out into the sea to search the clear waters of the bay. He and Erdmun swam back to the sandbar, boarded the dragonship, and walked to the stern.

"He was standing here looking out to sea when the ship struck," said Erdmun. "He pitched over headfirst."

"Did you see what happened to him? Hear him cry or shout?" Skylan asked.

Erdmun shook his head and pointed to a large swelling purple bump on his forehead. "I was knocked off my feet. I think I must have blacked out a moment, so I didn't hear anything."

Skylan stared down into the dark blue water.

The sea was fathoms deep here, not shallow as it was on the other side of the sandbar. Raegar was a large man, big-boned, heavy, and muscular. He would have sunk like a sack of boulders.

Skylan shook his head and said a silent prayer to Torval for his cousin's soul. Raegar had returned from the dead, and now he'd gone back there. Torval be with him. Skylan and Erdmun swam back to shore.

Aylaen looked hopefully at Skylan. He shook his head. "No sign of him."

Treia crouched in the sand, her thin arms wrapped around herself, her nails digging into her flesh. She said nothing. She did not weep. She stared with burning eyes and livid face out to sea.

Aylaen tried to comfort her. "Treia, I'm so sorry. Raegar was a good man—"

Treia stiffened, went rigid. She flashed a bitter glance at Aylaen, a glance that was like a blow. Treia stood up and walked off across the sand, her wet robes trailing behind her.

The men watched in uncomfortable silence, uncertain what to do or say.

"Go with your sister," Skylan told Aylaen. "She shouldn't be wandering around here alone. Garn, go with them. Take your weapons."

Garn picked up his axe and shield and hastened off after Aylaen.

Skylan faced the men. "Raegar was our clansman. We grieve his loss. There will be time later to honor the dead. Now we must think of the living."

He sent a few men to scout the area and find fresh water and hunt for deer or rabbits. The rest went to work building shelters amid the pine trees, cleaning and oiling the weapons, and rolling chain mail in the sand to rid it of rust.

"I will go to the Hall of Vektia, to pay our respects to Vindrash," said Skylan. "I will thank her for guiding us here."

"You shouldn't go alone," Bjorn objected. "It's not safe. Someone should go with you."

"We're on the Dragon Isles. We are known here," Skylan returned.

"But you said that Vindrash was angry with us for having lost the sacred torque—"

"I'm going alone," Skylan stated in a grim tone that silenced further argument from Bjorn or anyone else.

Skylan knew he was acting recklessly, venturing off on his own. He could not risk bringing a companion, however, for he did not plan to pay his respects to Vindrash. He planned to humble himself before her, fall down on his knees, beg her forgiveness. The draugr had guided him here, perhaps for this very reason. Skylan hoped that if Vindrash forgave him, she could persuade the draugr to quit tormenting him.

He armed himself with his fine sword and picked up his shield. He thought of Raegar as he buckled on Blood Dancer, which had been Raegar's gift. Skylan was truly grieved at the loss of the big, jovial man, but he was also a little relieved. Raegar alone knew the truth about what had happened to Skylan on the Isle of Apensia, and that secret was now drowned in the dark blue depths of the ocean.

Thinking this, Skylan was assailed by guilt. The last thing he needed was to be plagued by Raegar's angry ghost! Skylan put his hand on the hilt of the sword his cousin had given him and asked his shade's forgiveness. He vowed to give Raegar a rich grave gift on their return.

The terrain surrounding the bay was flat, a mixture of sand and dirt dotted by groves of pine trees, clumps of sage, and tough, bristly grass. The place had changed little in two years, since the last time he had come to the Dragon Isles with Norgaard to make the Torgun's offering to the Dragon Goddess. A poor offering, for they had gone on few raids, and those had not been particularly profitable.

No trail led to the Hall of Vektia, despite the fact that the Vindrasi came here often. Wind and water swept away all traces. Skylan remembered the way, however. The Hall was not difficult to find. A man standing on the beach faced the rising sun, turned to his left, and walked a gently rising slope until he came to the Hall, which stood on the highest point of the large island, atop a cliff overlooking the sea.

Caught up in the tangle of his trouble, Skylan walked with his head down, not paying particular attention to his surroundings. If memory served, the ground rose gently until he reached the Hall. He was startled, therefore, to come suddenly upon a small lake.

He did not remember a lake, and he wondered irritably if he'd come the wrong way. Upon closer examination, he saw that this wasn't a lake. A large depression had been deep enough to catch and hold rainwater. The same storm that had raked them at sea must have struck the Dragon Isles. That would account for the formation of the new sandbar and the formation of this oddly shaped body of water. He walked along the edge, idly speculating on what had made the odd-looking depression. Reaching the end, he was disconcerted to see, some distance away, another depression filled with water, roughly the same size and shape as the first.

"Skylan! Wait for me!"

Skylan turned to see Wulfe chasing after him.

"Did you know the draugr is following you?" Wulfe announced, coming to fall into step alongside Skylan.

Skylan placed his hand on the hilt of his sword and turned to look.

The draugr was walking along behind him, her feet leaving no mark on the sandy soil. The draugr came to a halt when she saw Skylan turn to confront her. She did not come closer, but stood gazing at him fixedly.

Skylan broke out in a cold and clammy sweat. "I am going to the Hall of Vektia," he told the corpse. "I'm going to beg Vindrash to forgive me. I will do whatever she asks of me to make amends to you, Draya! I swear this by Torval!"

He hoped the draugr would see that he was in earnest and leave him alone. Draya remained, standing on the ground, leaving no mark.

"I'm doing what you want!" Skylan cried. "This is why you brought me here, isn't it?"

"No," said the draugr. "It is not."

Bright white light burned like a star in the draugr's breast, and the corpse burst apart, exploding in a ball of fire like a lightning-struck tree. The blast hurled Skylan to the ground. He lay on his face in the sand, blinking dazzled eyes. He lay at the feet of a dragon.

The feet of a goddess.

Shimmering wings extended outward from the enormous body. The long graceful tail thudded on the ground, causing it to shake and quiver. The gilded mane bristled. The dragon's head on its curved neck swayed menacingly above Skylan. The mouth gaped, saliva dripped from the fangs, spattered on his face like the blood that had spewed from Draya's mouth in her death throes. The dragon's eyes were large and flared red orange.

Wulfe gave a terrified screech and took to his heels. Skylan wanted to run away like the boy, but he couldn't move. He had heard all his life about men who were paralyzed with fear, and now he understood. A bitter taste filled his mouth. He shook as with fever chills. When he tried to speak, his throat clogged.

"Vindrash," Skylan begged wretchedly, "forgive me!"

"I am not the forgiving sort," said the goddess, and Skylan flinched.

"Fortunately for you, Skylan Ivorson," Vindrash continued, "Torval is forgiving, though you have done much to offend him. You broke your oath to your father by declaring yourself Chief of Chiefs. You broke your oath to Draya to honor and love and protect her. And oath-breaking is the least of your sins. You plotted to have your wife, a Kai Priestess, abducted. To cover your crimes, you told more lies, claiming you were attacked by giants on the Dragon Isles. Worse, you swore to the truth of your lies by invoking Torval's name, bringing shame and dishonor on yourself *and* your god."

Skylan felt each accusation thud into him like a spear.

Vindrash's harsh tone softened. "Torval grieves for you. He thinks well of you, Skylan Ivorson. And because Torval thinks well of you, he has decided you will be given a chance to redeem yourself."

"I am grateful to Torval," Skylan said, weak with relief. "I will do whatever the god asks of me! I swear!"

"Another oath?" Vindrash snorted. "Stand up, Skylan Ivorson. Look around. What do you see?"

Skylan rose to his feet. The goddess's radiance blinded him, but gradually his eyes grew accustomed to the shining light. He looked about, wondering what marvels Torval was about reveal.

Skylan was disappointed to see only what he had seen before: stands of pine trees, grassy terrain, the large, irregular depressions in the earth, one here, one there, another farther on, another after that, looking for all the world like footprints . . . gigantic footprints . . . the footprints . . . of giants . . .

Skylan remembered his lie.

*We came upon a strange imprint in the sand. . . . It was made by a foot. A foot as long as this hall and just as wide.*

Skylan sank to his knees and stared at the goddess in horror.

"You have been ravaged by guilt over your lies," said Vindrash, gently mocking. "Torval is merciful and he will ease your conscience—"

The Dragon Goddess smiled down on Skylan.

"—by making your lie the truth."

CHAPTER

# 10

The Dragon Goddess spread her wings and sprang into the air. The shadow of her wings glided over five giants walking slowly across the land, looking about as if searching for their foe. Skylan was tempted to cry out, beg for mercy. He clamped his lips on the words. When he was a child and Norgaard had whipped him in punishment for some infraction, if Skylan sniveled, Norgaard only whipped him harder.

I deserve this punishment, Skylan thought, staring at the giants in dismay. He had never seen or imagined creatures like those he watched bearing down on him.

The giants in Skylan's lie had been those of fable and song, enormous humans, dull-witted and stupid, who dressed in bearskins and carried spears the size of oak trees.

The giants of the Dragon Isles were human in appearance, taller than a full-grown oak and thin as a post. They seemed to be made of skin-covered bone held together by catgut. They had huge hands with long splayed fingers, and enormous feet with long toes. They sprang off their toes as they walked, jumping high into the air, landing lightly as spiders. Their movements were slow, but they covered huge chunks of ground.

Their heads were small, like spiders, and swiveled on long necks. They had small bright eyes and small mouths and long, silky hair. They wore nothing but cloth twined about their privates. They carried what looked to be a child's toy: two large stones hanging from each end of a length of rope.

But this was no toy. One of the giants began to dexterously twirl the rope in his hand, causing the two stones to whip about with destructive force. The giant struck several pine trees with the stones. The pines seemed to explode, limbs snapping and branches flying. Skylan pictured the stones whirling among his men, smashing them to bits.

*My men died, crushed to bloody pulp.*

Skylan turned and ran back toward the bay, thinking as he ran. In his lie, he had told how Draya had tried to summon the Dragon Kahg only to be carried off by a giant. The dragon could fight these monsters. Skylan had to reach the camp before the giants did.

Skylan passed the hunting party on his way. A sharp command brought the men dashing after him. He arrived in camp to find the men already armed and prepared for a fight.

Winded from his run, Skylan had to pause a moment to find breath enough to speak. He kept his eye on the east. The giants had been moving fast. They would be here soon.

"We're about to be attacked," Skylan gasped. "By giants."

"Then what you said is true!" Erdmun cried. "Torval's curse is upon us! We're not wanted here! We should not have come!"

"Torval's curse upon you if you don't shut your mouth!" Skylan said furiously. "We don't have time for wailing and whining. I need Treia. She must summon the Dragon Kahg to help us fight these creatures."

Skylan cast a glance about the gathering on the beach. He saw Aylaen and Garn, but they were alone.

"Where is Treia?" he demanded.

"We thought she was with you!" Aylaen said, her voice quavering.

"With me?" Skylan stared at her. "Why would you think that?"

"She said she was going to go with you to the Hall of Vektia." Aylaen faltered and grew pale. "Vindrash save us! Treia is out there . . . by herself. . . ."

"Skoval's balls!" Skylan swore. "I never saw her. When did she leave? How long ago?" He glared at Garn. "I ordered you to guard her! Why did you let her go off alone?"

"He didn't, Skylan," Aylaen said defensively. "Treia said she felt faint. I stayed with her while Garn went to fetch water. When Garn left, Treia said she had sent him away on purpose. She was going to the Hall to pray for Raegar. I begged her not to go, but she assured me she would be safe. She said she would meet you. I couldn't stop her. She was gone by the time Garn came back."

"I set out after her," Garn added. "I picked up her trail and yours. And then I ran into Wulfe, who was yelling about a dragon. I didn't believe him, but the boy was clearly frightened, and I feared something had happened to you. I made the decision to come back to arm the men. I was going to bring them to your aid."

"You did the right thing," Skylan muttered. Garn always does the right thing. I'm the one who constantly fouls up.

Now he had five tree-snapping giants bearing down on them and no Bone Priestess and no way to summon the dragon.

Unless . . .

Skylan looked at Aylaen. "Did Treia take the spiritbone with her?"

"No, I have it. . . ." Aylaen realized what he was about to say next and she vehemently shook her head. "I can't, Skylan! You can't ask me!"

"I'm not asking," said Skylan grimly. "I'm ordering. Treia has been training you to be a Bone Priestess. You know the ritual. You have to summon the Dragon Kahg. Otherwise we're going to be smashed to pudding."

"You don't understand—" Aylaen swallowed.

"I understand that we're all going to be killed if you don't summon the dragon!" Skylan yelled.

"Don't shout at her," Garn said angrily.

"You shut up!" Skylan glared at him. "Aylaen?"

"I lied, Skylan!" Aylaen's eyes shimmered with tears. "I lied to you. I lied to the Kai. I didn't come because I wanted to be a Bone Priestess. I came because . . ."

"I know why you came," said Skylan bitterly.

He wanted to hit things and break things and punch things. He wanted to rail against the wyrd that had wrapped them in this coil. He wanted to cry like a little child. He couldn't do any of that. He was Chief of Chiefs. His people were depending on him.

Skylan walked over to Aylaen. He took hold of her hands and clasped them firmly. She kept her head lowered.

"Look at me. Look at me," he repeated when she refused.

Aylaen raised her eyes.

"You lied to the Kai, to Treia, to me. You lied to the gods."

Skylan paused. He longed to confess, tell her that he, too, had lied, told lie upon lie. He didn't dare. He was the Torgun War Chief, their leader. His men had to have faith in him; otherwise, they were doomed.

"Perhaps this is the way the gods will redeem you, Aylaen. By making your lie the truth."

Skylan drew in a deep breath, then went on. "Treia has been training you. You know the ritual—"

"No, I don't!" Aylaen cried. "I saw Treia perform the ritual once, and that was months ago when the ogres attacked! She tried to explain it to me while we were on board the ship, but I didn't pay attention. I never thought I'd have to . . . The dragon has never spoken to me—"

"Try, Aylaen," Skylan urged. "That's all I'm asking. Pray to Torval. Ask for his help."

"Why should he help me when I lied to him?" Aylaen asked miserably.

"Because the wyrd of the gods is bound up in ours," Garn told her. "Because even the gods are afraid."

Could that be true? Skylan wondered suddenly. He didn't know whether to be comforted by that thought or not. He wanted to ask Garn what he meant. He wanted to have a long talk with his friend. After the battle, I will tell Garn everything, Skylan resolved. I will ask him to forgive me. No wonder that Aylaen loves him. She was right. She loves him as I love him. He deserves our love. I am a cheat and a liar and a fraud. I do not.

"I will try," Aylaen said softly. "I will pray to Torval to forgive me."

"And I will pray that Torval forgives at least one of us," Skylan said beneath his breath.

Aylaen drew the spiritbone from the embroidered leather bag in which it was kept when it was removed from the dragonship. She went down on her knees in the sand and started speaking the words to the ritual. She spoke slowly and hesitantly, starting and backing up and repeating herself, and then she stopped altogether.

"I can't remember!" Aylaen clutched the bone, shaking it in frustration.

"Take your time," Garn counseled.

The ground shook, as when thunder fell from heaven and rolled across the land. Or when huge stones thumped the ground.

"Just don't take too much time," Skylan said.

Aylaen bit her lip and began to recite the ritual again.

Skylan watched Aylaen a moment longer, then glanced at Garn. "Stay with her."

Garn nodded. Skylan turned to find his men, under Sigurd's direction, forming a shield-wall. He glared at them in exasperation.

"Are you mad? All bunched together like that, a giant could take you all out with one blow! We have to spread out! We're not going to win this battle with swords and shields. Fetch the spears, as many as you can carry. I don't care if you can't throw. The targets are big enough so that even you, Alfric, can't very well miss."

Alfric the One-Eyed grinned. During a spear-chucking contest, he was renowned for having missed the mark by such a wide margin that he'd wounded one of the judges.

"Take cover in the pine trees," Skylan continued. "Just make sure you keep within shouting distance of each other."

"What do we aim for?" Erdmun asked, bewildered. "Their eyes?"

"Their balls," said Skylan.

Erdmun gave a nervous snicker.

"I'm not kidding," said Skylan grimly.

The men scattered, running to grab the spears that had been salvaged from the dragonship. Skylan realized suddenly that someone else besides Treia was missing.

"Where's Wulfe?" Skylan turned to Garn. "You said you saw him."

"He ran off before I could grab him," said Garn. "I think he was more frightened of me than of the dragon."

Ugly Ones armed with swords and axes, stinking of iron.

Skylan shouted Wulfe's name, but there was no answer, and eventually he gave up. The ground was shaking from the thudding of the stones almost continually now. Men cried out that they could see the giants coming.

Skylan took up four spears, two in each hand. He walked back to where Aylaen knelt in the sand, holding the spiritbone in her hands, turning it round and round in unhappy confusion.

Skylan thrust the spears into the ground between himself and Garn.

"You and I will guard Aylaen."

The gods are afraid.

Their wyrd is bound up in ours.

The gods had once believed they were all-powerful, all-knowing. The gods had once believed they were immortal.

Nothing lives forever. Not even the gods.

Creation destroys. Destruction creates.

Fire burns down the pine tree, but the heat of the flames causes a cone bearing the seeds of new life to burst, scattering the seeds on the blackened ground where they put down roots and become the pine tree, which burns in the fire. . . .

Holding the spiritbone in her hands, Aylaen held the wyrds of them all: gods, men, dragons. Their threads woven together, the fabric stronger than a single thread. Her thread as strong as Torval's thread. His thread as fragile as hers.

"The dragonbone game!" Aylaen murmured.

"What about it?" Skylan turned from watching for the enemy to stare at her intently. "What about the dragonbone game?"

Aylaen looked up, startled by his tone.

"I remembered something Treia told me! The ritual to summon the dragon is based on the dragonbone game. That's how the priestesses remember it."

The ground trembled, shuddered. Men were running for cover.

"The dragonbone game," Skylan repeated. An odd, exultant light shone in his blue eyes. "The ritual . . . I wonder . . ."

"Wonder what?" Aylaen asked, puzzled.

He shook his head.

"We need the dragon," he said curtly.

Aylaen did not know the ritual, but she knew the dragonbone game. She oftentimes won big. When she lost, she lost spectacularly, her pieces swept clean off the board. Though she was not reckless like Skylan, she was a risk-taker, not afraid to make bold moves.

Aylaen thrust the spiritbone into the sand and shut her eyes so that she would not see the giants and lose her concentration. Skylan and Garn, the two people she loved best in the world, were with her, guarding her, protecting her.

And the gods are with all of us. Our wyrds are woven together. . . .

# CHAPTER 11

Treia felt the ground shake, but she paid little heed to it. If she had turned around and looked behind her, even her weak eyes would have seen the giants, striding with terrible purpose toward the beach. She did not look around. She did not look ahead. What was the use? It was all a blur anyway. She stared down at her feet to see the ground on which she walked, and even then she didn't see that much for the bitter, burning tears.

Treia could not have said where she was going. She had left the camp for one reason and that was to escape: to escape her sister, of whom Treia had always been jealous; to escape Skylan, whom she loathed and despised; to escape the pitying stares of the rest of the Torgun, pitying the spinster who had lost her last chance for a husband.

Raegar was lost, drowned, dead. The only man she had ever loved. The only man who had ever loved her or was likely to love her.

Treia's grief tore at her, shredded her. She could not bear the pain of her loss. She could not bear her sister's attempts to offer comfort or Skylan's triumph.

Pity for the spinster. Pity for the Bone Priestess of an impoverished clan, a Bone Priestess who must spend her days in lonely solitude, lancing boils on people's asses.

Raegar had given her love and something more: hope for a better life. He had fanned the flames of her ambition, given her reason to dare think she might rise to heights she had never before imagined. And now he was dead and her dreams had drowned with him.

It was only when Treia at last raised her head to cast a dreary look about that she saw the Hall of Vektia, a large wooden blur for her at this distance. She thought wearily she might as well go to the Hall as anywhere else, and she kept walking.

She was to have been Kai Priestess. Raegar would have been Chief of Chiefs.

"I know a secret about Skylan," Raegar had told Treia. "A secret that when I reveal it will cause the Vindrasi to clamor for his death."

Treia had urged him to tell her this terrible secret. Raegar had refused.

"The time is not right. I will wait until the raid on the ogres, after Skylan has recovered the Vektan Torque."

Raegar had been particular about the torque's recovery.

"For all his faults," Raegar had said, "Skylan is a valiant and courageous warrior. The men like and admire him. They will follow him through fire and blood. Let him lead us to victory, let him think he has won the gods' favor, let him think he stands on top of the world. His fall from such heights will hurt all the more."

Treia had agreed. She would have agreed to anything Raegar had suggested. Well, almost anything. She had not agreed to let him become her lover, though he had tried his best to convince her to lie with him.

She wanted to. At night, she dreamed of Raegar's touch, his kisses. But in the bright, cold light of day, she remembered Horg and his hands groping her, pulling up her skirts, thrusting his fat fingers inside her, grunting and sweating like a hog. She remembered her shame when Draya had walked in on them and her ardor would turn to revulsion. She could not bear for any man, not even Raegar, to touch her like that.

And now, no man would. Her eyes blurred with tears, she tripped and fell. She did not get up, but lay on the ground outside the Hall, sobbing uncontrollably, more in rage than with grief. Rage against the gods for having given her hope with one hand and snatched it back with the other. Finally, too exhausted to cry anymore, she dragged herself on toward the Hall of Vektia.

She did not know why she was going there, for she did not believe Vindrash could help her. Treia did not, at times, believe in Vindrash.

The flagstone path came to an end. Treia stared down at it and then lifted her eyes. The Hall swam before her. She stared dully at the stairs leading up to the main entrance and, not knowing what else to do, she began to climb them.

She had been to the Hall once before this. When Draya had made her yearly pilgrimage, she had brought several Bone Priestesses and acolytes with her. One year Treia had been chosen. She had been sixteen, and, for a change, she had been excited and pleased at the idea of the adventure.

Unfortunately, the voyage had proved boring and tedious. She had been cooped up in the cabin, forced to attend to Draya, who had been seasick at the start of the voyage and, when she was well, spent the rest of the voyage praying with the Bone Priestesses. When the women were not praying, they spent their time talking about what they were going to pray for.

Treia had been looking forward to the Hall, for she had heard stories of its grandeur. When she saw it, she was impressed, taken with the beauty and intricacies of the wood carvings of dragons that decorated the outside and awed by the immense statue of Vindrash and the dragons who served her. But after spending hours on her knees, she came to loathe the Hall, the statue, even the dragons. She had been glad when she was finally able to leave, even though that meant tending again to a seasick Draya.

Treia remembered that there would likely be the spirits of guardian dragons inside the Hall, and she almost turned and fled, rather than have to face them. But she was too tired to go anywhere else and, besides, for her there was nowhere else to go.

"If a dragon says so much as a word to me, I'll scratch its eyes out," Treia muttered.

The great double doors, adorned with carvings of Vindrash and the World Tree, were generally kept closed. Treia would have to seek admittance from the dragons. She was about to do so when she noticed that the doors were slightly ajar.

That was odd, but Treia was thankful. She hoped she could sneak in unnoticed, avoid, for at least a time, being accosted by a dragon.

The Sun Goddess entered the Hall with Treia, casting a slanting band of light across the Hall's wooden floor. The light spread like rising water to the feet of the statue of Vindrash and there it stopped, as though in awe, leaving the statue in darkness.

The Hall appeared, at first glance, to be empty. The dragons were not around, apparently. Treia was uneasy. Due to her poor eyesight and the play of light and shadow, she could not see much, but she had the sense that all was not right.

"Hello?" Treia called out sternly. "Is anyone here?"

To her amazement, she heard someone groan.

The sound came from the direction of the statue of Vindrash. Treia advanced slowly and cautiously, following the path of the slanting sunlight. Then she saw why Aylis, the Sun Goddess, had been loath to advance. The ancient statue of Vindrash, said to have been been made of wood taken from the World Tree, lay on the floor. This statue of the Dragon Goddess was unique, in that it did not portray Vindrash in her warlike attitude, as did all other statues, with spread wings and striking claws. This statue showed Vindrash in repose, lying prone, with one eye closed and one eye open, to show that even in sleep, Vindrash kept watch over her people.

Except that her watch had failed. The head of the statue had been struck from the body. The statue's trunk had been hacked to pieces.

The groan sounded again, louder. She squinted her eyes and saw a huddled form lying beside what was left of the statue of Vindrash. Treia was no coward. The blood of generations of Vindrasi warriors ran in her veins. Spotting a jewel-encrusted urn lying on the floor, Treia picked it up and, holding it in her hands like a club, she drew nearer. A man lay on his side on the floor, his back to her.

"Don't move!" Treia warned. "I would just as soon bash in your skull as not."

The groaning stopped. The man raised his head, turned to stare at her in astonishment. "Treia?"

Treia dropped the urn. Clapping her hands over her mouth, she sank to her knees.

The man sat up and held out his hands. "Treia, it's me! Raegar."

She flung herself into his arms, kissing him and crying and babbling incoherently. He held her and soothed her, stroking her hair, kissing her gently, then more passionately.

"Treia!" Raegar groaned again, this time with the pain of desire. "You are mine. You are meant to be mine. The gods saved me from death to bring us together!"

Treia asked no questions. She didn't care how he came to be in the Hall of Vektia or why.

Overwhelmed with joy at the miracle of his return, Treia clung to him, kissed him fiercely, clasped him, held him. His hands hiked up her skirts. He lowered himself on top of her, fumbling at the fastening of his trousers. She opened herself to him. He was gentle, at first, mindful of her virginity. She urged him with broken words to take her and he did so, thrusting hard, almost savagely. She reveled in the pain and only a small moan escaped her when he withdrew and lay limply on top of her.

She smiled at him tremulously. Raegar seemed to become suddenly aware of what he had done. He sat up, hastily lacing his pants.

"Treia, I am sorry. I didn't mean to do that. I was so happy to see you. I never thought . . ."

Raegar covered his face with his hands, hiding his tears. Treia gathered him close. The two clung to each other.

"I feared you had drowned," she whispered.

Raegar wiped his tears with his hand, drew his sleeve across his nose. His eyes, red with weeping, were wide with awe and wonder.

"I did drown, Treia," he said, and he shuddered at the memory. "I could not hold my breath. I opened my mouth and water flowed in and . . . and the next thing I knew I was here in this great Hall."

He looked around, bewildered, then focused on her. "And you are with me, my love, my own. It is a miracle!"

"Vindrash brought you here," said Treia. "She brought you back to me."

Raegar looked at her strangely. "No, my dear. I do not think it was Vindrash."

Treia gave a little laugh. "Well, of course it was Vindrash. Who else could it have been who brought you to her Hall?"

Raegar gazed at her intently, and he said solemnly, "Death was my punishment, Treia."

"Punishment for what? I don't understand." Treia's voice hardened. She drew back from him, wary and suspicious. "What do you mean?"

Raegar took hold of her hands and held them in reassurance. "Vindrash did not save me." He cast a meaningful glance at what was left of the statue. "Vindrash has lost the power to save herself, let alone anyone else. You know that, Treia. You know in your heart I am right."

Treia eyed him skeptically, her face cold, expressionless.

Raegar opened her palms, kissed them. "I am being punished for keeping Skylan's guilty secret. For not revealing what I know to be the truth. We were going to wait, but I must purge my soul."

Treia smiled and relaxed in his arms. She nestled close to Raegar, twining her legs around his, and felt him grow hard against her.

"Tell me the truth," Treia said with fierce joy. "Tell me all you know about Skylan."

Raegar clasped her to him as they lay tangled at the feet of Vindrash, and making love to her again, he told Treia exactly what she wanted to hear.

Raegar didn't know it, but he was also telling Wulfe.

Frightened half out of his wits by the sudden appearance of the dragon and the giants, Wulfe had dropped to all fours and run as fast as he could. He felt bad about leaving Skylan to face his foes alone, but he had not felt bad enough to stay.

"The gods hate the fae," Wulfe's mother had always told him. "The gods are always looking for ways to harm us. Gods are never to be trusted."

Faced with an angry goddess, Wulfe ran.

Unfortunately, his next encounter proved even more terrifying. Fleeing the Dragon Goddess, he ran headlong into menacing Ugly Ones. Never mind that he knew these Ugly Ones, who were Skylan's friends. Garn spoke gently to Wulfe, trying to calm him down. The horrible stench of iron—always equated in Wulfe's nostrils with the smell of death—was sickening. Caught between gods and iron, he ran from both.

He eventually grew tired. His run slowed to a lope. His hands were cut and blistered; his feet hurt. He panted for breath, his flanks heaving, and his tongue lolling. He was thirsty and lonely and utterly lost and now the ground was shaking. He had no idea how to find his way back to Skylan. He was in despair, and he came upon Treia.

Wulfe did not trust Treia, but at least she was not a vengeful goddess. She carried no iron, and she would be able to lead him back to Skylan. Wulfe did not make himself known to Treia, because she was acting strangely—talking to herself, wringing her hands, moaning, and clutching at her head. He followed her at a safe distance, trotting along silently behind.

She led him to an immense building, very beautiful in Wulfe's eyes. He watched Treia enter. Wulfe settled down to wait for her to return. Hearing her give a startled cry, and wondering what had happened, Wulfe went in after her. He slipped inside the door, which she had left ajar, and there he saw Treia and, to his astonishment, he saw Raegar.

Wulfe was alarmed at first, fearing he'd come upon yet another draugr, but then he reflected that even Treia wouldn't be likely to rut with a corpse. The more Wulfe watched the two, the more he was convinced that Raegar was very much alive.

Wulfe did not like Raegar any more than he liked Treia. Having spied on both of them, Wulfe knew that they both hated Skylan, and Wulfe hated the two of them for that reason.

The boy settled himself behind one of the many wooden posts that supported the vaulted ceiling and watched without much interest the man and woman in the throes of their passion. Growing bored, he glanced about the Hall. He saw bloodstains. He shivered, wondering what terrible thing had happened here, and then he saw what Treia had failed to see: tracks of wet boots clearly visible on the dust-covered floor of the Hall.

The tracks were recent. Wulfe touched a print with his fingers and could still feel the dampness. The water on the boots had turned the dust to mud, leaving a clear imprint behind. The foot that made that print was very large, as large as Raegar's. The boots had walked all over the floor, to and fro, back and forth. Pacing, waiting.

And there were other footprints, different footprints, dry footprints, these made by two sets of boots, one slightly larger than the second, though neither so large as Raegar's. The two Dry Boots had come in and gone out again. They had not walked around the hall. At one point, Wulfe noticed, Wet Boots had stood facing Dry Boots.

Wulfe had heard Raegar claim to Treia that his coming to the Hall was a miracle. The fact was, he'd walked into the Hall on his own two wet feet. And while he was in the Hall, he'd met two pairs of dry feet. Nothing miraculous about that. So why make up the story? And why let everyone think he'd drowned when he hadn't? And to whom did the dry feet belong?

Treia and Raegar finally ended their lovemaking, for which Wulfe was grateful. The two began talking and Wulfe pricked his ears, hoping to hear the answers to his questions. But the two were only plotting against Skylan again, which was nothing new.

The two talked, and then they began to rut again. Wulfe rolled his eyes in frustration. He'd known nymphs and satyrs whose appetites were not so voracious. Wulfe yawned and scratched himself. He was thirsty, his belly hurt from being empty, and he wondered what had become of Skylan.

Seeing Treia and Raegar completely occupied with each other, Wulfe left the Hall, going off in search of water first and then to find Skylan to see if he could answer his questions about Raegar.

# CHAPTER 12

Aylaen held the spiritbone of the Dragon Kahg in her hands. She kept her gaze fixed on the bone, concentrating on the ritual, visualizing the dragonbone game in her mind and trying to blot out the terror that was thundering through her. She gathered up a handful of sand and let it trickle down over the dragon bone.

In the game, the gods make the first move.

"Vindrash, hear my prayer," Aylaen said softly.

Mortals make the second move.

"Tell the Dragon Kahg of our desperate need."

Fate has the third move. Gods and mortals, each bound by their own wyrd, each bound to the other.

Aylaen drew the rune that represented the wyrd in the sand. She remembered the rune because it was on the game piece, a piece important in play, for its movement is random and can disrupt the strategies of both men and gods.

Aylaen laid the dragonbone down on the rune and took up more sand. She let it fall over the bone.

So far, so good. This was all part of the ritual. But what came next? In the game, the pieces moved along winding trails, leading to birth, death, victory, loss, journey, status, marriage, home, children, crossing paths, meeting, parting, meeting again, parting forever.

"The ritual is ever changing," Alyaen remembered Treia telling her. "The ritual involves my wyrd, the gods' wryd, the dragon's wryd, and what we are now, what we were then, where we have been, where we are going."

There was something about moving and turning the bone, pushing and taking and holding and forcing.

"This part is very complicated," Treia had said. "It takes years to learn."

"Vindrash, I don't have years!" Aylaen cried in despair. "I have only now and the people I love and they are depending on me and I lied to you. I am sorry. Forgive me!"

Aylaen let more sand fall over the spiritbone. "I love Garn, Vindrash, as you love Torval. I seek your blessing, though I do not deserve it. I ask that you send your dragon to fight for us this day!"

Aylaen picked up the spiritbone, and with all her strength and all her might and all her love and desperation and fear, she cast it high into the air. The spiritbone rose, then, twisting and turning, it began to fall. Aylaen's heart fell with it, for she knew she had failed.

The spiritbone spun round and round, faster and faster, and first it was one bone and then it was twelve bones and then it was a hundred bones bursting from the spiritbone.

As fast as forked lightning, the Dragon Kahg came into being. Formed of sand, he was whitish in color, his scales hard as rock, hard as the mountain that had stood for countless eons, before time and the elements reduced the mountain to a grain.

The Dragon Kahg materialized in front of the five giants, who came to an uncertain halt. They glowered at the dragon. The stone weapons swung from their hands.

Aylaen sent up a prayer of heartfelt gratitude. She did not have time to be proud of her accomplishment or to wonder that she, who had lied about becoming a Bone Priestess, had been able to summon the dragon.

"Good work," Skylan said. He thrust a spear into her hand. "Now be ready to fight."

The Dragon Kahg was confused. He had been overwhelmed with relief to have found his goddess, Vindrash. She had explained to the dragon that she was in fear of her life and that she had needed her enemies to believe she was dead. Not even the dragons who worshipped her could know the truth. She had asked the Dragon Kahg to keep her secret, and he had been proud to do so.

He had obeyed her commands. He had carried Skylan from Apensia back to Luda. He had watched with considerable amusement to see Vindrash disguise herself as the draugr of Skylan's dead wife, Draya. Kahg knew why Vindrash played at dragonbones with Skylan. The dragon knew the game was serious, the stakes were life and death. Kahg understood and sympathized with the goddess, who was bound by Torval's edict regarding the Five Bones. Ever since Hevis had basely sought to use the Five to attack another god, all the gods had been forbidden to speak of them to a mortal. Vindrash had to find a way to tell Skylan about the Five, without actually coming out and telling him.

Thus far, all had been going as planned. And then disaster.

Vindrash had felt the growing fury of the Sea Goddess, Akaria, and she had warned Kahg that sailing was dangerous. The hothead Skylan had paid no heed to the warning. The Dragon Kahg might have taken it upon himself to refuse to sail, but Vindrash was determined to teach Skylan a lesson, and she had ordered him to sea.

He had lost contact with the other two dragons, an alarming situation, for dragons are able to commune mentally. Kahg could find no trace of them, and Vindrash claimed she could not locate them either. Dragons were mortal beings and it was possible they could have been killed, but she did not think so. Kahg had the feeling she knew the truth of what had happened to the dragons and their ships. If so, the goddess was keeping her knowledge to herself.

When the Sea Goddess had finally exhausted her fury, the Dragon Kahg discovered that the winds of her rage had blown them close to the Dragon Isles. Vindrash ordered him to take the half-starved, weary Torgun to what he believed would be safe refuge on the isle, only to run aground on a hidden sandbar. And now he discovered that the Torgun were about to be attacked by their own guardians.

The Dragon Kahg was further troubled by the fact that although he had repeatedly alerted the goddess to the presence of a strange ship shadowing them, Vindrash had not seemed to care. The ship had dogged them all the way from Luda, keeping below the horizon line, staying out of their sight. Even when the Sea Goddess caught the ship in her tempest, the ship had survived. The winds of divine fury that had blown the *Venjekar* off course blew the strange ship to the Dragon Isles, as well.

The Dragon Kahg had tried to persuade Vindrash to take an interest in the ship, but she persisted in ignoring it. And now, the Dragon Kahg knew why.

He had been hovering about his spiritbone, eager to be summoned, when he heard Garn's words.

*The gods are afraid.*

Kahg had known Vindrash was afraid for her life, but Kahg had not really understood the depth of her fear. He had not truly understood the danger, not even after the attack on the Hall of Vektia, not even with the death of Desiria. Now, at last, Kahg could visualize the might of the foes arrayed against them. The dragon was appalled.

The gods were falling victim to fear. They were a family, these gods. A clan of immortals, not much different, neither better nor worse than the humans who revered them. The Gods of the Vindrasi quarreled and bickered, lusted and loved. They were either preoccupied with their own pleasure or were embroiled in plots to disrupt the pleasure of the others. The world to them was a shining ball they had come across while at play and they had amused themselves down through the centuries by tossing it back and forth between them.

But now came gods who wanted to take away the ball.

And not only that, these gods planned to destroy their foes in the process.

Kahg was starting to think the gods had lost their minds to panic. How else could the dragon explain the fact that Torval had ordered the guardians of the Dragon Isles to attack the very people they should have been guarding?

And so the Dragon Kahg did not attack the giants. He sought to reason with them.

# CHAPTER 13

Skylan gave an exultant shout when he saw the Dragon Kahg appear, large and menacing. The gaunt and spiderlike giants had been bounding across the sandy grassland, twisting and twirling their strange weapons, occasionally slamming the round stone heads into the ground as they came leaping to attack.

The Torgun warriors were shocked and shaken at the sight of these strange creatures. Jaws sagged, faces paled, eyes bulged. Some cried out to Torval to save them. They were ready to attack when Aylaen shouted for them to halt.

"Stop the men! Don't let them harm the giants!" she cried. "The Dragon Kahg says that there has been some mistake. The giants are the Hall's guardians. Kahg's going to talk to them—"

"Talk?" Skylan couldn't believe he'd heard right. "They're trying to kill us—"

One of the giants let loose his strange weapon, flinging it at the dragon. The rope with the two large stones attached at either end flew through the air and wrapped around the dragon's neck. The stones whipped about, striking the Dragon Kahg in the head, the two blows so hard that Skylan could clearly hear the cracking of bone.

Blood spurted from the dragon's smashed and mangled jawbone, raining down on the warriors who had taken refuge in the dragon's shadow, and who were now running for their lives. Roaring in pain, Kahg fell into the bay, landing with a splash in the shallow water, narrowly missing crushing the dragonship with his massive tail.

The dragon lay thrashing about feebly in the water, seriously, perhaps fatally wounded. Blood-tinged waves, churned up by his flailings, rolled onto the shore, washing about the boots of the warriors.

The dragon had not stopped the giants' attack, but he had at least given the warriors time to recover from their initial shock. The loss of their dragon filled them with rage. The warriors did not wait for Skylan's order. Each man grasped his spear, taking his time with his aim, trying to find a vulnerable spot on the grotesque bodies.

Alfric the One-Eyed flung his spear and hit the giant in the shin. The spear appeared about the size of a knitting needle compared to the giant, but it pierced his flesh. Blood poured down the giant's leg, and he gave a yelp of pain, even as the spear bounced off the shinbone and fell to the sand. The warriors were heartened by the fact that the enemy could bleed, and the Torgun attacked, flinging their spears first, and then making daring forays, running beneath the feet of the giants to recover their spears or to strike at the foe with axes and swords.

The deadly stones whirled above them, making a horrid buzzing sound as they whipped through the air and shaking the ground when they slammed down with bone-crushing force. Men died beneath the stones, died with only time for a horror-stricken scream before the stone smashed into them, their bodies disintegrating into gruesome blobs.

Skylan hefted his spear. Taking his own advice, he aimed for the giant's testicles.

He started to pray to Torval to guide his hand, then thought better of it. Why should the god heed his prayer? Torval had inflicted this punishment upon him. Torval expected Skylan to deal with it. Yet, perhaps Torval relented, for Skylan's spear soared straight and true and struck the giant in the groin. The giant let out a shrill shriek and, dropping his weapons, clasped his splay-fingered hands over his privates.

"Close in! Get close to them!" Skylan shouted.

The smashing stones were lethal, but Skylan had noticed that the giants were careful to keep them far from their own bodies. The reason became obvious. The giants dared not strike at warriors who were close to them for fear of hitting themselves.

The warriors rushed to surround the giants. Bjorn and Erdmun stabbed at their heels and jabbed their spears into the muscles of their calves. Sigurd hacked at the back of an ankle with his axe, hoping to slice through a tendon to cripple the creature. The giants howled in pain and hopped about on their spindly legs, trying to stomp the warriors beneath their feet. The giants were thin-skinned, their wounds bled copiously, and soon the Torgun warriors were covered with blood.

Skylan hurled his last spear and then drew his sword, prepared to join the assault. All the giants were limping, but it seemed none was ready to give up the fight. They struck furiously at the warriors with their stone weapons, the stones bashing and thudding into the ground. Sklyan started forward when Garn grabbed his arm.

"Where's Aylaen?"

"Here beside me!" Skylan cried, only to look to see that she wasn't.

Aylaen fought courageously and with skill. Realizing she could not effectively throw the heavy spear with strength and accuracy, she ran at one of the giants and jabbed the spear's head into a tender part of the giant's foot, just below the ankle. Howling in pain, the giant kicked his foot, trying to shake her loose. Aylaen held on grimly, though the giant flung her about like a rag doll, eventually hurling her into the sand.

The giant tried to stomp her with his bloody foot. Skylan and Garn attacked the giant with sword and axe, and managed to distract the giant from Aylaen, who regained her feet. She was covered with blood, part of it hers, most of it the giant's. She drew her sword, ready to return to battle, only to suddenly stop and look behind her, over her shoulder.

The wounded Dragon Kahg was dissolving. His shattered head, sparkling sandy scales, flaring red eyes, spikey mane, powerful legs, smashing tail, and translucent wings were all crumbling, pouring into the sea like the grains from a broken hourglass.

"The spiritbone!" Aylaen cried and, dropping her sword, she ran toward the dragon.

A wounded dragon can heal himself only by returning to his lair in the Realm of Fire, where he can rest while spirit and body fuse together. In promise that he will return, the dragon leaves behind his spiritbone. During battle, a Bone Priestess is supposed to focus her attention on the dragon, to the exclusion of everything else going on around her, one reason why warriors are assigned to guard her. If the dragon is wounded and forced to retreat back to his realm, his physical form disintegrates rapidly. The Bone Priestess has to be ready to recover the spiritbone, marking the location where it falls in order to find it.

The Dragon Kahg had departed to his realm, hopefully to recover, leaving behind an enormous mound of sand. The white spiritbone was clearly visible atop the mound. Heedless of her danger, knowing only that she must recover the spiritbone, Aylaen ran across a beach pocked with deep holes bored into the sand by the smashing stones.

Skylan and Garn both left off attacking the giants to run after Aylaen. Skylan was the swifter of the two and he outpaced Garn. Aylaen splashed into the water. She was ahead of him, Garn was behind. Skylan heard the heart-stopping whirring sound made by the stones and he looked up to see the stones hurtling through the air, one aimed at Garn, the other at Aylaen. Skylan had Blood Dancer in his hands. He could save one of his friends, but not the other.

Skylan looked back at Garn in agony. Garn, as always, understood. He pointed at Aylaen.

Skylan watched the stone fly at her. He would have one chance and one only. He waited, timing his stroke. The rope looked thick as a tree trunk and he would have to cut completely through it. He swung as hard as he could, putting his back and his shoulders and his prayers into the stroke. Blood Dancer sliced through the rope. He dropped his sword and flung himself on Aylaen, dragging her down into the water. The stone whistled harmlessly over their heads to land with a drenching splash in the sea.

Aylaen had not seen him coming, and she was shaken by the fall. She sat up, choking and coughing and spitting seawater.

Skylan leaped to his feet and looked, his heart in his mouth, at Garn. His friend lay on the beach.

Heedless of the giants, Skylan ran to his friend and flung himself down into the sand beside him. He searched anxiously for a wound, and he did not see any. Then Garn looked up at him.

Skylan saw the shadow of death in his eyes.

"Where does it hurt?" he demanded.

"It doesn't," Garn said, frowning, puzzled. "I can't feel my legs. I can't feel anything."

Skylan saw the blood seeping out from underneath his friend's body, and he knew that Garn's body was broken. The dream came back to him. Only then it was Draya who had been slain by the giants.

*She could not move. I held her in my arms as she died.*

"You can't leave me!" Skylan said fiercely, making it an order. He took hold of Garn's limp and unresponsive hand. "I need you!"

Garn smiled. "Not . . . much choice . . ."

He coughed, his breathing labored. He could no longer talk, and he asked the question with his eyes. *Aylaen?*

"She is safe," said Skylan. "You saved her life."

He wrapped the palm and fingers of Garn's hand around the hilt of his axe and held them there, so that Garn would come before Torval holding his weapon.

Garn's breathing slowed to nothing. His eyes stared into the sun and did not blink.

Skylan fought back the tears. Garn had died a warrior's death. He did not want to dishonor his friend with blubberings and wailings, but the tears came, hot and burning, down his cheeks.

He heard, behind him, a heart-piercing moan.

"Aylaen—" Sklyan turned to comfort her.

"You killed him!" Aylaen screamed and she struck him across the face.

She hit him again, bruising his cheek and splitting his lip. He tasted blood.

"You were jealous of him and you killed him!" she cried in a frenzy of grief and rage, hitting Skylan, pounding on him, beating him with her fists and kicking him. "You killed him!"

He bowed his head before the onslaught, did nothing to defend himself. Bjorn and Erdmun had to leave the battle to drag her off him.

Wulfe saw the giants from a distance. He heard the cries and shouts, he smelled the blood and iron. He would have run away from the battle, but he recognized the foe from his mother's lullaby-tales. They were known as Flesh-Spinners and though he had never seen them, he hated them.

The giants were fae, wicked fae, shunned and despised by the faery folk because, during the First War, the Flesh-Spinners had turned against their own kind and fought alongside the Ugly Ones. The faery folk had never forgiven the Flesh-Spinners for their treachery or for the fact that they believed the giants continued to slavishly serve the gods of the Ugly Ones.

According to the fae, the Flesh-Spinners had been giants who bestrode creation, scattering stars like seeds throughout the universe and spinning their own flesh on enormous wheels, using the threads formed of their bodies to form the fabric of worlds. The faery folk populated these worlds and loved and cared for them.

But then came the gods of the Ugly Ones. They saw the beautiful worlds and wanted them. They praised the work, and the Flesh-Spinners grew proud and haughty, refusing to believe the fae when they warned the Flesh-

Spinners that the gods were trying to trick them. The Flesh-Spinners believed the lies of the gods and ended up giving them the worlds. The fae were furious, and they cursed the Flesh-Spinners, so that their flesh would never again grow back. They could make no more worlds.

Angry at the fae, the Flesh-Spinners sided with the gods and fought against the fae during the First War, only to discover that after they had helped win the war, the Ugly Ones and their gods reviled the Flesh-Spinners and drove them away. Tormented by the fae, the Flesh-Spinners hid in their lairs, whining and sulking over their hard fate until the God Torval came to them with an offer. He needed guards for the Hall of Vektia, and he promised to give the Flesh-Spinners a home on the Dragon Isles, a home where the fae would not attack them, for the fae were in awe of the dragons and would not live near them. The Flesh-Spinners agreed and moved their small tribe to Vektia, where they came to revere Torval and obeyed him in all things.

Wulfe remembered only bits and pieces of this history, but he knew one part for certain: All fae everywhere hated the Flesh-Spinners. His inner daemons had no trouble convincing Wulfe that it was his duty to attack them.

Wulfe hastened toward the battle, his dislike of iron overcome by the thrill of being able to avenge the faery folk on these wicked fae and help Skylan in the bargain.

Wulfe had been studying his magic with Owl Mother. No one had ever before tried to teach him how to use his magic. The druids did not understand the magic, but realizing how dangerous such power could be in the hands of a child, they sought to suppress it, their fond hope being that by teaching him self-discipline the boy's human side would learn to subdue the chaotic influence of the fae.

Owl Mother had taught him the basic fundamentals. She had said he would never be as powerful as his faery mother had been, but that he would be far more powerful than Owl Mother, who had only a smidgen of fae blood in her. (Wulfe had been eager to hear how that could be, but Owl Mother had refused to tell him.) At first he'd been afraid that lessons in magic would be dull and tedious, like learning to read and write.

Her lessons had proved far more fun and interesting. He was looking forward eagerly to trying them out.

Wulfe sped toward the shore, racing over the sand on all fours. He considered as he ran his best plan for attack. At first he thought he would grab sunbeams and throw them at the giants. He liked this idea, for the fiery beams would burn holes in the giants' flesh. Then he remembered Owl Mother's first lesson: Use nature when you can, especially when around Skylan and his kind.

"Like the druids, the Ugly Ones fear fae magic because they do not understand it. They will come to fear you if they think you are using magic, even to help them. Use your magic to call upon nature to help you, and the Ugly Ones will always find the means to explain it away."

If Wulfe had been in a forest, he would have asked the dryads to fight the Flesh-Spinners by rousing their trees to attack them. The pine trees were spindly, and he did not think they would be of much help. He might call upon the oceanaids, but he feared that if they rose up in fury, the deluge would drown not only the Flesh-Spinners, but also Skylan and the other Ugly Ones.

Wulfe was close enough now that he could see the carnage. The stench of blood and iron sickened him. He trembled in every limb, and wished he hadn't come. He could always turn and flee, but the sight of the Flesh-Spinners brought back to him the memory of his mother's voice, her burning hatred. It was now his burning need to make her proud of him. If only he could think how. . . .

A seagull circled overhead, squawking in annoyance. The hungry bird had spotted a dead fish washed up on the beach, but every time the bird dived for it, a giant would lash out his foot or a man would swing his axe and drive the bird away. Wulfe began to sing, as Owl Mother had taught him, using the music and the notes to form a net of enchantment that he flung over the bird.

*Peck their flesh.*
*Peck their eyes out!*
*They steal your fish*
*and suck your eggs and kill your young.*
*The giants, the Flesh-Spinners!*

Wulfe remembered to add the last hastily, realizing that the enraged bird might attack everyone in sight. The seagull gave a raucous call and within moments was joined by flocks of gulls, screaming in hatred, flying down to peck at the eyes of the giants, diving at their heads, tearing at their hair.

The Torgun warriors were at first astonished and startled by this unexpected help, but then someone called out that the Sea Goddess had sent the birds to fight for them, and the warriors redoubled their efforts, attacking the giants with renewed vigor. His fear forgotten, Wulfe enjoyed the spectacle, and he began to run around and flap his arms and shriek, playing at being one of the birds.

The Flesh-Spinners were not cowards, but they were bullies. The fight had been fun when they were smashing Ugly Ones into globs of jelly. But now all the giants were wounded, one of their number so seriously that he had very nearly fallen to the ground, which would have been disastrous, for then the evil Ugly Ones would have swarmed him and cut him with their horrid iron. The hordes of squawking, pecking gulls were an added nuisance. The Flesh-Spinners gave up the fight, and wrapping their arms around their injured comrade, they helped him hobble from the field, snapping their fingers angrily at the gulls, who continued to plague them.

Wulfe quit singing and dashing about. Panting for breath, he was pleased with himself and was just thinking he would go find Skylan and tell him what he'd done when someone grabbed hold of him painfully by the hair.

Wulfe thought it was a giant, and he yelped and twisted in a panic. Then he saw that it was Raegar who had hold of him. Raegar and Treia were staring at Wulfe as though he was a snake they'd found coiled up in their path.

"You summoned those birds! You are *fae*!" Treia hissed the word between her teeth and her lips.

Raegar's grip tangled in Wulfe's hair, hurting him.

"He is an imp. He is demon spawn," said Raegar, glowering. "A child of evil."

"Then so are you!" Wulfe cried, glowering at Raegar from beneath shaggy bangs. "You use magic! The other night at your house, I saw the strange lights. And you didn't drown. What you said back in the Hall was a lie—"

Raegar gave Wulfe's hair a brutal yank. Raegar clapped one hand over Wulfe's mouth. Grabbing Wulfe around the waist, he hoisted the boy off his feet.

"He was in the Hall. He's been spying on us," Raegar said to Treia. "Probably on Skylan's orders."

Treia was watching the retreating giants. Now she looked back around.

"He saw us in the Hall?"

"He overheard us, at least," said Raegar. "You can't let him go back to camp. He'll warn Skylan, and my cousin will have time to think up even more lies."

"What do we do with the wretched little beast?" Treia asked, her lip curling.

"I will take him back with me," said Raegar.

"But we were going back to camp together," Treia protested.

"We don't dare let him loose. I'll take him back and then—" Raegar bent close to Treia and whispered in her ear.

Treia listened intently, then asked, "And where will you be?"

"Waiting for you, my love," Raegar said, and, keeping hold of the squirming Wulfe, he kissed Treia. "Waiting to make you my wife. Chief of Chiefs and Kai Priestess."

She slid her arms around him, returned his kiss hungrily. She yearned near him, wanting more. Raegar gently put her from him. "You had better go. Now that the battle has ended, they will come searching for you. Skylan mustn't see me. He must have no hint of the doom that is about to befall him."

Treia gazed at him adoringly, obviously unwilling to leave him. "I will see you soon. . . ."

"You will," he promised.

Treia gave him one last swift kiss, then turned and, keeping her head lowered, watching where she walked, she headed toward the beach. Raegar stood in the shadows of the scrub trees, holding on to Wulfe and watching Treia.

Wulfe took advantage of the man's preoccupation to bite him.

"You little bastard!" Raegar swore, and he flung Wulfe onto the ground.

Wulfe was on all fours in an instant, starting to scamper away. Raegar lashed out with his foot, kicked the boy in the midriff, and Wulfe curled up, clutching his stomach and moaning with pain.

"Demon spawn," Raegar said grimly.

He lashed out with his foot again. Wulfe saw the blow coming, and he flung up his arms to protect his head, but it didn't help. Light burst behind his eyes, and then all was darkness.

# CHAPTER 14

The Torgun went about the sad task of honoring their dead. Four men had fallen to the giants, including Garn and Alfric the One-Eyed. A pulverizing blow had caught Alfric on his blind side. He'd never seen it coming. The gruesome remains of the two others lay at the bottom of a large depression that had been punched in the sand by the smashing stones. The sight of the mangled mess that had once been men was so horrible that Sigurd, a hardened warrior of many bloody battles, fell to his knees, puking.

They decided to leave what was left of the two where they were. The tide was rising, and the seawater would soon fill the holes with sand, mercifully covering the ghastly remains.

The warriors made Alfric ready for his journey to Torval. They covered his smashed skull and shattered body with his shield and placed his axe in his hand so that Torval would know he had died valiantly in battle.

The men would have done the same for Garn, but Skylan ordered them away. Aylaen would tend to Garn, as she would have done if she had been his wife. He could give her that poor comfort at least.

"The dead are at rest," Skylan said to the others. "We are alive, and we must take thought for ourselves."

Skylan sent men to cut pine trees for funeral pyres. He ordered men out hunting. He himself led a group to the dragonship. The ship had to be manned and ready to sail when the incoming tide floated it off the sandbar.

The wounded dragon had returned to his realm, either to heal or to die. The warriors would have to sail the ship themselves. Skylan and his men hoisted the sail and fit the oars into the oarlocks, ready to row it into shore when the water lifted the keel and set it free. Since dragons were mortal and could be slain in battle, the Vindrasi carried oars and sails aboard their ships, so that a ship bereft of its dragon would not be stranded on the sea. His plan was to sail the ship to the beach, where they could repair the damage.

Skylan left Aylaen in Treia's care. The Bone Priestess had walked into camp shortly after the battle. When he asked her where she had been, she said that she had been praying in the Hall of Vektia and lost track of time. He asked her if she had seen Wulfe. Treia said caustically that since Skylan had brought the brat, he should keep better charge of him.

If Skylan had paid more attention to Treia, he would have noticed a smoldering triumph in her weak eyes. But Skylan paid no attention to Treia or to anyone. He was like the warrior who stands alone against his foes, braced for the assault he knows is coming, waiting to be overrun by his anguish, his grief, and his terrible guilt.

Aylaen had been right when she accused Skylan of killing Garn. Skylan had not wielded the weapon, but he was responsible for his friend's death. Torval had made Skylan's lie the truth, and Garn had died.

The warriors were shocked at Aylaen's accusations and tried to convince her she was wrong. Bjorn described how the giant had swung the huge round stone and struck Garn a glancing blow, breaking his back. Erdmun told her how Skylan had saved her life at risk of his own, standing in the path of the swinging stone to slice the rope with his sword.

"If anyone was responsible for Garn's death, it was you, Aylaen," Sigurd told his stepdaughter. "If you had remained home as was seemly—"

"—then we would all be dead." Skylan said. "Aylaen summoned the Dragon Kahg. His intervention bought us time to ready our attack. No man will say a word against her."

Aylaen had not thanked him for his defense. She had not spoken a word to him or to anyone. Her face pale and set, she went about the task of preparing Garn's body for the funeral. She closed the staring eyes, washed the blood from his body. She shaved his face and combed and plaited his hair. She scrubbed his clothes, for he must not go before Torval looking like a beggar. When she was finished, the men built a pyre for Alfric and Garn and laid their bodies on top. Aylaen placed Garn's axe in his hand. When all was done, Aylaen remained beside the pyre.

Treia came to stand beside her. "I understand you summoned the dragon."

Aylaen nodded. She did not take her eyes off Garn. "You were not here. . . ."

Treia's lips pursed. Her arms were folded across her chest, and her fingers drummed in annoyance.

"I am here now," she said. "You may return the spiritbone to me."

Aylaen shook her head. "I don't have it."

"Then where is it?" Treia asked, alarmed. "I left it with you! Is it lost? What happened to it?"

"I summoned the Dragon Kahg. He was wounded in the battle and went back to the Realm of Fire. He vanished, and his body collapsed into a pile of sand. I saw the spiritbone. . . ." Aylaen spoke in a dull, uncaring monotone. "I saw it shining white in the mound of sand . . . I went to recover it. . . ."

She fell silent. Her hand stroked Garn's cheek. He lay on the pyre in quiet repose, his lips curved in that last sad smile.

"Where did the spiritbone fall?" Treia demanded. "Where did you last see it?"

Aylaen made no reply. Treia started to ask Aylaen again, then realizing she would not receive an answer, she shook her head in frustration. Treia ordered those on shore to help her search. The men formed a line and waded out into the water, each man walking arm's distance from his neighbor. They moved slowly, carefully searching the sandy bottom at their feet.

Treia kilted up her skirts and waded into the water herself, peering and poking and feeling about the sand, cursing her weak eyesight.

"The bone is white," Treia told the men repeatedly, though they knew well what it looked like. "Aylaen said she could see it from the shore! It should not be difficult to find. Look around the mound of sand."

But the tide had been steadily rising and the wind increasing, blowing from offshore, stirring up rolling waves. The seawater took immense bites out of the large mound of sand that had been Kahg's physical form. Sand swirled about the feet of the searchers. Whenever a man reached down to grab something, a wave surged around him, washing away whatever it was he thought he had found.

Eventually Treia waded back to shore and shook Aylaen from her grief. Then she marched her to the water's edge. "Where did you last see it?"

Aylaen stared into the water and then slowly shook her head. "It is not there." She shrugged and added bitterly, "Maybe it never was."

She went back to Garn. She lay down on the pyre, rested her head on his chest, and clasped her arms around him. Her eyes burned. She shed no tears.

The searchers came back in defeat. Shivering in her wet clothes, Treia stared out to sea. Her face was pinched, her mouth compressed. She could feel the men staring at her, and she knew what they were thinking. The dragon and the Bone Priestess who summoned the dragon formed a bond that was not easily broken.

A wounded dragon would often retreat back to his own world in order to heal his injuries in the quiet sanctity of his lair, leaving his spiritbone behind in the care of the Bone Priestess. The Priestess used the spiritbone to judge the extent of the dragon's injuries and could use her prayers to Vindrash to aid in the dragon's recovery. Thus a spiritbone that was lost would find a way to return to the Bone Priestess unless . . .

The dragon didn't want to be found.

Treia had to face the bitter knowledge that the Dragon Kahg had answered the summons of her sister, when so many times the dragon had either ignored or refused to heed Treia. And now the spiritbone was lost and would not be found. The men would blame her.

Treia's thin lips twitched.

Unless they had someone else to blame. . . .

## CHAPTER 15

The *Venjekar* floated off the sandbar. Skylan and his men sailed the ship to shore, not an easy task, considering they had no rudder. Men ran out to help drag the ship up onto the beach. Lying on the shore on its side, its broken rudder sticking out at an odd angle, the *Venjekar* was an object of pity, a wounded animal waiting to be put out of its misery.

Night had fallen by the time this was done. The hunting party had returned with a deer. The men ate and then slumped down on the deck of the dragonship and slept.

Skylan was bone-tired himself, but he would not rest until Garn's spirit had been freed to start upon its journey. He took upon himself the task of keeping watch over the dead during the night to keep away any evil spirits who might disturb them. They would set fire to funeral pyres at dawn, burning the bodies, freeing the spirits of Garn and Alfric and the other two warriors who had died. The spirits would travel with the Sun Goddess. Aylis would light their way to Torval's Hall.

Treia finally persuaded Aylaen to leave the body.

"You shame Garn with this show of grief," Treia scolded her sister. "He will take his leave of you in the morning. Do you want him to see you pale and sorrowful like this?"

Aylaen gazed down at Garn, who was lying on the pyre beneath the stars. Skylan stood beside the pyre, prepared to take up his vigil. Aylaen turned her gaze upon him. The piercing blade of her rage sank deep. She allowed Treia to take her to the dragonship.

Skylan went down into the sand on his knees beside the pyre. The long night stretched ahead of him, a night of bitter self-recrimination. He looked at Garn's ashen face, the lips already darkening, the flesh sinking into the bones, and he remembered the time they had killed the boar and the time they had fought the ogres and the time Skylan had dived into the sea to save his friend, his brother. . . .

Skylan wept, heaving, racking sobs that tore at his chest. Sobs that were silent, stifled, for fear his men should hear. For fear Garn's spirit would hear.

When Skylan had no more tears to cry, either for himself or his friend, his sobbing ceased. He knelt in the sand. The wind blew off the sea, and the waves crashed to shore endlessly behind him, wetting him with sea spray. He whispered a prayer to Vindrash.

He felt, in answer, the touch of a cold hand.

He looked up to see Draya standing over him and behind her, above her, within her, the shining wings and sparkling scaled body and stern-eyed face of the Dragon Goddess.

"You are the draugr," said Skylan. "The corpse of my wife. You forced me to play the dragonbone game."

"I did," said Vindrash. "Do you know why?"

"I think so," said Skylan slowly. "The Priestesses designed the game to help them remember the ritual to summon the dragons. The five bones you throw at the beginning have something to do with the Five Dragons. But I don't understand—"

"True," said the goddess. "You don't understand. And because of the Curse of Hevis, I am forbidden to tell you." The dragon's tongue flickered from between her teeth. "I did enjoy our games, however. Though I doubt you did."

Skylan smiled bleakly. "Wulfe tells me the druids do not sanction murder. He said the druids did not kill my wife. The boy spoke the truth, didn't he?"

"Draya vowed to give herself to me, and she kept her vow. She knew she had done wrong by poisoning Horg. She had usurped Torval's right to judge him, and she accepted her punishment. She drank her death willingly and died at peace. She gave her body to me, so that I could use it to hide from my enemies."

"As she repented, so do I." Skylan looked directly into the bright, shining light. "I ask you to forgive me, Vindrash. I ask Torval's forgiveness."

"We forgive you." The dragon sighed. "Can you forgive us?"

"What do you mean? The gods have no need for man's forgiveness," Skylan said, bewildered. "The gods do not make mistakes."

Vindrash fanned her wings. He felt the wind brush his cheek, a harsh, brooding breath.

"You called upon me for a reason, Skylan Ivorson," the goddess said. "What do you want of me?"

Skylan rested his hands upon his knees. He looked up at the goddess and said, "Take my life, Blessed Vindrash. Let my body rest upon that pyre. Let the fire consume my flesh. Let Garn live, for it is my fault that he died."

Vindrash smiled gently, then shook her head. "Torval does not want your death, Skylan Ivorson. Torval wants your life. He wants a sword that has passed through fire and water. He wants a sword whose bright, fierce light can be seen throughout heaven."

"Am I that sword?" Skylan asked in wonder.

Vindrash laughed. The universe rang with her laughter. Her laugh made the stars tremble and silenced the ocean's roar. She bent her dragon head on her curved neck, darting toward Skylan, the fangs glistening and her reptile tongue dancing. He fell back before her, cringing.

"You? A sword of the gods?" Vindrash said scornfully. "You are a knife to gut fish!"

Skylan flushed at the insult. Lowering his head to avoid the goddess's mocking eyes, he saw that Garn's hand had slipped from the handle of his axe. The body was stiffening, the muscles growing rigid. Skylan pressed his hand over Garn's cold flesh, trying to shape it around the handle of the axe.

Garn's eyes opened. He gazed up at Skylan.

"Look to the south!" he said urgently.

Skylan dropped the hand, sprang back. Had yet another draugr come to haunt him?

"Look to the south!" Garn insisted.

Skylan turned his head.

Winged serpents, silver and shining, huge as rivers, slid through the night, their bodies masking the stars. The serpents were seven in number, and they came from the south, their bodies rippling like silver ribbon. Their slitted eyes glowed with flame, and the fire of their terrible purpose was aimed at Vindrash.

Skylan recalled Vindrash saying she had been hiding from her foes. Foes who had now found her. His hand reached for his sword.

"Goddess!" Skylan cried, and pointed.

The Dragon Goddess saw her danger. She roared her defiance and shouted for help. The Sea Goddess, nursing her anger, refused to do battle. The Sun Goddess fled to the other side of the world. The moon vanished behind a cloud. The stars disappeared. The waves diminished, dwindled to frightened ripples.

Vindrash faced this terrible foe alone.

The war was not of Skylan's making. He could say it was none of his concern. He was angry at the gods. Torval had reviled him. Vindrash had mocked him. Akaria had nearly drowned him. Aylis had scorched him. The foe they fought must be terrible, for even the gods had fled. Skylan would do well to follow their example.

Skylan was suddenly ashamed. He was ashamed of the cowardly gods. He was ashamed of himself. He did not know who or what these dread serpents were. He knew only that they meant to destroy Vindrash. And by attacking his goddess, they attacked him.

Vindrash spread her wings and sprang into the air to face her foes that were diving down on her from the clouds. Scarcely knowing what he was doing, thinking only that he would not be left on the ground to watch the battle in the skies, Skylan jumped upon the pyre and seized hold of the dragon's clawed hind foot.

Vindrash stared down in astonishment to see Skylan clinging desperately to a massive claw with one hand. He held Blood Dancer in the other. She had no time to speak, for her foes were closing on her rapidly. She seemed to smile in grim approval, however, and then she twitched her leg and flung Skylan up amongst the stars.

He hung in the dark sky for a terrifying moment, watching the sea and the shore turning beneath him, and then he landed upon a sandy beach beneath chalk-white cliffs. He recognized this place. He had been here before, though he could not remember when or where it was.

The dragon flew to meet the serpents, breathing fire and lightning and lashing at them with her ripping claws. Skylan heard a shout and turned to see Torval come striding down from the north, roaring in anger and swinging his massive battle axe.

Hearing Torval's challenge, three of the serpents broke off the fight with the dragon and swarmed down to do battle with the god. Torval was no longer the strong warrior who had fought and bested the Great Dragon Ilyrion. He was an old man, the same old man Skylan had met cooking fish by the shore. His hair was long and gray, his beardless chin grizzled. His face was seamed and creased and wrinkled like the folds of mountains, the crevices of valleys. His eyes burned with fire; his armor outshone the coward sun. His axe gleamed brighter silver than the base moon.

Torval glowered at Skylan. "What do you want?"

"I thought you might need to gut some fish," Skylan replied coolly.

Torval threw back his head and roared.

"Back to back, then," said Torval, grinning. "Heel to heel."

Skylan put his back to the god's back and braced his heels against the god's. The immense serpents flew at them. Slitted eyes glowed. Their toothless maws gaped. Their wings seemed small for their bodies and were positioned near the front. And then Skylan saw why, as one of the serpents battling Vindrash twisted his body to lash at her with his tail.

Blood dripped onto Skylan's upturned face. He watched in rage to see the serpent's tail slice through the dragon's scales, opening a gash in her body. Another vicious lash from a tail tore through one of the dragon's feet, sheering off a claw.

Skylan wrenched his gaze from the embattled dragon and focused on his own danger. The three serpents were circling the two warriors, who held sword and axe raised to meet them, shifting their stances to keep the enemy in sight.

"They will strike in a rush," Torval told Skylan. "Aim for the—"

A serpent darted at Skylan. The slitted eyes grew large as the serpent drew near. Its maw gaped wide, as though it would swallow him whole. Skylan knew a moment's sheer, panicked terror, and then he felt the god's back against his, solid and reassuring. Skylan let the serpent get close, and then he swung his sword, putting all the strength of his body and his soul into the blow.

The sword sliced through the serpent's neck, cut off the head. Blood spurted. The head went spinning off into the night. Skylan gave a triumphant shout that ended in a strangled gargle of horror. Two heads sprouted from the severed neck. Two maws gaped. Four slitted eyes fixed their fiery gaze on him.

"—heart," Torval finished dryly. "That's the only way you can kill the slimy worms."

Skylan wondered where the heart of these slithering monsters was located. He was about to ask, then he saw a serpent streaking down on the god and he called out a warning. "Your left, lord!"

Torval shifted his stance. Shouting defiance, the god swung the blade of his axe in a flaring arc, striking the serpent near the wings, cutting the creature in half. Blood rained down on them. The two halves of the serpents twitched and writhed and then two heads sprouted, two tails lashed. Two serpents sprang into being.

"Bah!" Torval swore and spit blood. "I missed. Look to your right, young dog!"

The heart must be near the wings, Skylan guessed, and he hoped grimly he guessed right, for the two-headed serpent was winging around to attack him again. It dived from the sky. Skylan waited, braced and ready to strike. At the last moment, when it seemed both gaping maws were about to snap off his head, he ducked down into a crouch. The serpent's forward momentum carried it above his head. Skylan gripped his sword in both hands, and aiming his strike at the body right between the small, rapidly beating wings, he thrust the sword deep.

Blood ran down the groove in the sword that had given Blood Dancer its name. The blood drenched Skylan's arms and hands, making the sword slippery and difficult to hold. He tightened his grasp and jabbed upward. Impaled upon the sword's blade, the serpent screamed in pain and fury, twisting its body, trying to free itself, and ended up driving the blade deeper, right into the heart.

The serpent died, but in its death throes, it struck a final blow. Its tail whipped around and caught Skylan across the chest. With a blast like spiked lightning, the tail sliced open flesh and muscle, laying bare the bone. The pain was searing, excruciating. Skylan's heart, jolted by the shock, pounded erratically. Blood Dancer slipped from his hand. He could not catch his breath, and he fell to the ground, only there was no ground. He fell and kept falling, spiraling downward. He saw Torval continuing to battle his foes. Vindrash had a torn wing and was struggling to remain airborne.

"Retreat, my lady!" Torval shouted. "I will cover you!"

He redoubled his attack, slashing furiously. Several serpents lay dead at his feet, including the one Skylan had slain, and the others were keeping their distance. Vindrash folded her wings around her mauled body and dived headfirst into the sea. Two serpents sped after her, trying to catch her, but at the last moment, the Sea Goddess relented. An enormous wave rose up to receive Vindrash and carry her safely into the depths of the ocean, where, it seemed, the serpents were loath to follow.

Skylan landed on the ground, the soft sand absorbing his fall. The last he saw of Torval, the god was swinging his axe tirelessly, felling serpents who now swarmed him.

The world went black as night for Skylan for a moment, and then it was bright as dawn. He found himself lying on his face in front of Garn's bier. The warriors were gathered around him. Treia stood over him, gazing down on him. Vindictive, triumphant, she was about to swallow him whole.

"Skylan Ivorson," Treia said, pointing her finger at him, "you have heard the charges against you. You have heard me denounce you before men and the gods as a liar, a cheat, and a murderer. Because of you, good men are dead and the Dragon Kahg has abandoned us. What do you say to this, Skylan Ivorson?"

Skylan gazed up at her in bewilderment. He had been fighting the battle with Torval, yet he must have been here, as well, for he remembered, dimly, Treia summoning the warriors when they woke that morning. He remembered her telling them of his crimes. How he had conspired with Draya to murder Horg and rob Torval of his judgment. He had then rid himself of Draya, for fear she would expose him. He had plotted with a slaver to abduct Draya and take her to the Southland. His plot had been foiled by the druids, who had murdered Draya and changed Skylan's men into rabbits. When Bjorn demanded angrily how Treia knew all this, where had she come by her knowledge, she had claimed she had been told by Vindrash.

Skylan knew that was not true. Vindrash had forgiven him. It was Treia who lied. He smiled bitterly. Convicted by a lie. How fitting.

Perhaps the battle had been a dream. He looked down at his chest and saw an angry red weal slashed across his naked breast.

The battle with the gods had been real. He was living the nightmare.

"What do you say, Skylan Ivorson?" Treia cried.

She regarded him smugly, eager to see him twist and wriggle, struggle to try to free himself.

Skylan lifted his head. He drew a deep breath and spoke quietly and calmly. "I say that you have spoken the truth."

# CHAPTER 16

Treia seemed disappointed. His calm confession sucked the air out of her.

"We cannot trust this man. He may yet try to escape justice," she said. "Bind him and take him on board the dragonship. Lock him in the hold. We will carry him back to Vindraholm for the Vutmana."

"He is god-cursed!" Sigurd said. He drew his axe. "Let us kill him now!"

The men growled their agreement.

"Skylan is guilty of robbing Torval of his judgment!" Treia cast a flashing-eyed, sweeping glance around the circle. "Would you risk angering the god by doing the same?"

Sigurd glowered at his stepdaughter, trying to intimidate her. Treia faced him, unafraid. Sigurd, muttering, flung his axe into the sand and picked up a length of rope.

Skylan held out his hands, wrists together. He was prepared to accept his punishment, yet he could not help but flinch when he saw that Aylaen was among those who came to bind him.

She wrapped the rope around his wrists and leaned over to hiss in his ear, "I saw the battle in heaven. I heard Vindrash speak to you. The gods may forgive you, but I do not. I will always hate you!"

She gave the rope a yank, pulled it tight. The rope bit into his flesh, but it was her words, not the rope, that drew blood. Aylaen walked away and went to stand beside the pyre. Men held flaming torches, ready to set it alight.

They bound Skylan's legs. He could not move his hands or arms, and they had to drag him to his feet.

"At least let me stay to bid farewell to my friend," Skylan asked.

The warriors jeered at him.

"Garn's spirit would curse us all if we allowed you to be present at his funeral," Bjorn said.

They hauled Skylan off down the beach. With his legs hobbled, he could not walk. He stumbled, fell. The men did not give him a chance to stand, but dragged him through the sand.

The morning was hot and breathless. No air stirred. The sun beat upon the shore. Heat rose in shimmering waves. The sea was flat. The tide had gone out. The shallow water stirred sluggishly beneath an oily film. The men carried him onto the wounded dragonship. Bjorn and Erdmun picked him up by the arms and legs and threw him down the ladder and into the darkness of the hold. They tossed down a skin containing fresh water and shut the trapdoor.

He heard the scraping sound as the men hauled over something heavy—probably one of the water barrels—and placed it on top of the door to keep him from escaping.

Skylan lay where he fell, too weary and dispirited to rise. The ropes were tight and cut into him. The wound on his chest burned. His body hurt, but the pain in his heart was far greater. Garn was dead, and Aylaen might as well have been. She was dead to him.

And what had become of Wulfe? He should have been back by now. Something had happened to the boy. He was probably dead.

I will be dead before long.

Oddly, the thought of death didn't frighten Skylan. He almost welcomed it. His heart and soul had died already.

He heard the men begin to sing the death-song, and he caught a whiff of smoke. Skylan crawled across the floor and peered through one of the gaps in the planking.

The men tossed torches onto the pyres. The wood, daubed with pitch, caught fire immediately. Smoke rolled from the pyres. Skylan could smell burning flesh.

The smoke hung in the breathless air, forming a blinding cloud that set men gagging and ended the death-songs. Tendrils of smoke crept in through the slats in the wood. Skylan coughed. The smoke stung his eyes. He blinked his burning eyes and stared out between the gaps in the planks.

The men, their mouths and noses covered against the smoke, stood around the pyres, waiting for the spirits to depart. That would happen only when the pyres collapsed and the bodies were consumed.

The men choked and coughed. Their clothes were drenched with sweat from the intense heat and caked with ashes and soot. The smoke grew too thick for Skylan to see. He was thirsty, his mouth parched and his throat clogged. He hobbled across the deck to the waterskin. He managed to pick it up with his bound hands and lifted it to his lips. He was about to drink when he happened to glance through another gap.

He dropped the waterskin.

A ship rode at anchor in the deep water near the sandbar. The ship was huge, with three decks, three banks of oars, two masts near the center and a smaller foremast near the front. The rowers sat idle, watching men streaming down a gangplank, landing on the sandbar. The men were warriors. Each man wore a helm with wing flaps that covered his cheeks and armor made of overlapping strips of shining metal. The segmented armor protected each man's shoulders, his upper arms, his breast and the back. Strips of leather studded with metal formed a skirt that protected the warrior's groin and thighs. Each man carried a sword and a large rectangular shield.

Skylan lurched toward the gap and stared out. His eyes stung from the smoke, and he blinked and wiped them and stared again. He could not believe what he was seeing.

The shields bore the image of a winged serpent.

The moment each warrior landed on the sandbar, he ran to join the ranks of his fellows. No man spoke. All was done swiftly and in disciplined silence. An officer gave a signal, and the men plunged into the shallow water and began wading toward the shore, holding their swords and their shields above their heads.

This was an ambush. The enemy was bearing down on Skylan's men. Skylan hobbled back to the other side of the hold. He moved too fast, lost his balance, and fell. Cursing, he crawled over and put his eye to the gap.

Smoke covered the beach. He could not see his men, and they would not be able to see the threat bearing down on them from the sea. No man would be armed, out of respect for the dead. Their weapons and their shields were stacked in the sand, along with their helms and armor.

Skylan yelled a warning. The thick air swallowed his shouts. With the crackling of the flames and the popping of sizzling flesh, no one could hear him. He swore again, frustrated, and frantically tried to undo the knots at his ankles. He worked at them until his fingers bled, to no avail. They were tied tight. He shuffled over to the bottom of the ladder and stared at the hatch. He had heard them roll the heavy barrel atop it, but perhaps, if he could get his shoulders under it, he might be able to lift it.

He managed to climb the ladder by hooking his elbows, his arms still bound at the wrists, over the rungs and pulling his feet up a rung at a time. Sweat poured from his face. He gasped for breath from the exertion. He maneuvered himself into position, his head bowed, and pressed his shoulder against the hatch and heaved.

The hatch did not budge. Skylan tried again, straining against the hatch, shoving with his legs. His feet slipped. With his hands bound, he could not hang on, and he fell to the floor.

He started to pray to Torval to help him, and then he remembered the god battling the winged serpents, fighting for his life. Torval had his own problems. Skylan was on his own.

His people were on their own.

The first the Torgun knew they were under attack was when they saw the ranks of the enemy coming at them out of the smoke. The Torgun ran to grab their weapons, but they were intercepted by soldiers. The Vindrasi fought with their bare hands, but the soldiers struck them with the flat of their blades or bashed them with their shields until they fell unconscious.

Skylan, watching in agony, heard the officers shout repeatedly, "Take them alive! We want prisoners, not corpses!"

Skylan tried to see Aylaen. She would fight. He knew she would. He pressed his face against the gap, cursing the smoke that obliterated his view.

Suddenly, he realized he had his own problems. The sound of heavy boots thudded on the deck above him. The enemy had boarded the dragonship. He heard men running across the deck, taking up positions.

"You men, move that barrel," a commanding voice ordered, a voice that sounded vaguely familiar. "The hold is below. We'll stow the brat down there."

Skylan stood at the bottom of the ladder. He would not be taken alive. He heard the barrel scrape as the men hauled it off the hatch.

The trapdoor opened. Sunlight tinged with smoke streamed down on Skylan. He looked up to see an unusually tall man with broad shoulders and powerful arms clad in the shining segmented armor. The man wore a helm, as did the other warriors Skylan had seen. His helm was decorated with red feathers, perhaps denoting him as an officer.

Skylan stood with fists clenched, ready to fight. The officer gazed down at him.

"Well, well, well," the man said with a chuckle. "If it isn't little Skylan."

Skylan's fists uncurled; his hands went limp. He stared, squinting into the sunlight, trying to see clearly. "Raegar?"

"The same." Raegar chuckled. "Once more, Cousin, I have returned from the dead."

Raegar removed the feather-crested helm. He had shaved off his beard and his long blond hair. His bald scalp was white, a contrast to the sun-tanned skin of his face. The tattoo of a winged serpent ran across the crown of his head from front to back. The serpent's red tongue flicked down almost to the center of the forehead. Raegar regarded Skylan with amusement.

"I hear Treia told your men about you," he remarked. "They were planning to take you back to Vindraholm, force you to fight the Vutmana."

Raegar squatted down on his haunches. "I've done you a favor, Cousin. Where you are going, you won't have to fight."

"Treacherous coward!" Skylan swore at him. "You betrayed your own people!"

Raegar shook his head. "The Torgun are not my people anymore, Cousin. These are my people." He gestured to the warriors around him. "They have been for a long time."

Skylan clenched his fists. "I challenge you! Fight me!"

Raegar threw back his head and gave a loud roar of laughter, as did the men who had gathered around the hold.

Skylan burned with fury. "All of you!" he shouted. "I will take on all of you. Your swords. My bare hands!"

The soldiers thought this funny, and they laughed louder, saying something about "caged beasts."

"While that might prove amusing, especially to my men, the Tribune would not like it," said Raegar. "You see, Cousin, you're his property. A valuable commodity. The Tribune would be most displeased if you were damaged."

Skylan began to understand. It was like peering through the slits in the planks. He could only see a part of the truth, but for the moment, that was enough. His gut shriveled. Death did not frighten him. This did.

"What do you mean?"

"By Aelon, you are dense, Cousin," said Raegar. "Fortunately no one in Oran is in the market for brains, these days. Only brawn. How shall I put it? Instead of calling you Chief of Chiefs, Skylan Ivorson, from now on, men will call you Slave of Slaves!"

The soldiers grinned appreciatively at their commander's jest.

Raegar glanced around at them and frowned. "Are the other warriors secure? Was anyone slain?"

"No, Revered One. The men were taken without a fight. A few had to be knocked unconscious, but they will recover."

"What of the two sisters?"

The blood pounded in Skylan's ears. He had to calm himself to hear the answer.

The soldier grinned. "One fought like a catamount. It took three of us to subdue her, and we have the scratches to prove it! We finally threw a sack over her head, half-stifling her, and eventually she calmed down. The other female did not fight us. She is half-blind, it seems. Still, I do not trust her. There's something strange about her. She's more dangerous than her wildcat sister, or so I would guess."

"What of the spiritbone?" Raegar demanded. "Did you recover it?"

"We found no bones except those of the dead men, Revered One. The woman claimed it was lost."

Raegar scowled, displeased. "She is lying. She must be hiding it somewhere."

"What do we do with the prisoners, Revered One?"

"The women are to be conveyed to the Tribune's ship. Bring the men on board the dragonship. Chain them to the oars. How long will repairs take?"

"Not long, Revered One. We should be able to sail when the tide returns."

"Good. Get to work."

"What about the brat? What do we do with him?"

Raegar glanced down into the hold. "Toss him down there with little Skylan."

The soldier shouted, and two men came forward, bearing Wulfe between them. One side of his face was bruised, one eye swollen shut. The soldiers flung him into the hold. Wulfe landed sprawled on the deck, and he blinked up at Skylan groggily.

"I'm sorry," Wulfe said. "I was going to warn you."

"It's all right," said Skylan quietly. He looked up at Raegar, who was shutting the trapdoor. "You have come back from the dead two times, Raegar. When you and I meet, that will be the end. There won't be a third."

"When you and I meet, Cousin, you will be on the auction block, and I will be collecting my share of your selling price," Raegar replied.

He dropped the trapdoor shut. Skylan heard the barrel being rolled over it.

He closed his eyes and slumped down on the deck. He gazed into the darkness, trying to see a way out, but there was only darkness. He put his hand to the amulet, Torval's axe, he wore around his neck. The silver was cold to the touch. He let his hand fall. He wondered suddenly what had become of his sword, Blood Dancer. The last he had seen, the sword was spiraling down through the heavens. Much like himself.

"Someone's here," Wulfe said tensely.

Skylan opened his eyes, bracing for a fight.

Garn, dressed in his armor and carrying his sword and shield, stood before him.

Skylan was not surprised to see his friend, his brother. Nothing surprised him anymore.

"Can you forgive me?" Skylan asked.

Garn smiled. "There is nothing to forgive. Our wyrds were bound together, but the thread of my days ran out."

"It is not fair! You cannot leave me now," said Skylan wearily. "Not when I most need you. What will become of our people?"

"I see a long journey, Skylan. I see death and despair. I see hope. I see a dark end and a bright beginning."

"Why can't you ever just give me a straight answer?" Skylan asked, and he smiled.

Garn's spirit began to fade. "Farewell, Skylan. We will meet in Torval's Hall, and you will tell me of your exploits."

Skylan held up his bound hands. "I do not think I will get past his door, my friend."

"Do not be so certain," Garn said, his voice dwindling. "The thread of your wyrd is strong. You alone can break it."

Skylan sank back. He could hear the sounds of his men being herded onto the deck, hear the rattle of chains and the shuffling of feet.

"Warriors of the Vindrasi!" Raegar shouted. "Your gods are dead. I am going to tell you of a new god. A powerful god, Aelon, Lord of the New Dawn."

Wulfe shook his head. "He's lying. Your gods aren't dead. Vindrash was badly wounded, but she survived. Torval fought his way back to his Hall. He summoned the souls of the dead warriors, and they drove back the serpents."

Skylan stared at him, mystified. "How could you possibly know all that?"

"The oceanaids told me," said Wulfe. He yawned. "I'm bored. Do you want to play dragonbone? I'll move your pieces for you, since your hands are tied."

I am in chains. My warriors are prisoners. Aylaen has been taken from me. The spiritbone is lost, the Dragon Kahg wounded, perhaps dead. All because of me, because of my own arrogance and stupidity, my lies and oath-breaking.

Skylan slumped in despair. He did not want to play the game. He wanted to throw the board and pieces and himself in the sea. Let the dark water close over his head. He sank back against the timber and felt something jab him painfully in the buttocks. Skylan swore and shifted about to see what had poked him.

Sunlight gleamed on the blade of a small knife, the type used to gut fish.

Skylan picked up the knife, slender and brittle as hope, and secreted it in his boot. Making sure it was hidden, he turned to Wulfe.

"Roll five bones," said Skylan.

# POSTSCRIPT

Sent by fire, water, and oil, to the Watcher in the Temple of the New Dawn with orders to deliver to Acronis, Tribune.

To Acronis, Honored Tribune of the Twenty-four, Commander of the Navy of his Imperial Majesty, Emperor Dunumadi. Greetings!

I have momentous news. Our glorious god, Aelon, has blessed us far beyond my expectations. My men and I, disguised as traders, had landed on the shores of my homeland. We had made camp and were going to commence our mission to capture one of the Bone Priestesses when the god gave to me a great gift. Aelon dropped into my lap my arrogant and foolish young pup of a cousin, Skylan Ivorson, who, it turns out, is now married to Draya, Kai Priestess, the most powerful priestess of the Vindrasi.

And, by Aelon's blessing, my stupid young cousin happens to loathe his new bride!

Praise be to Aelon. He has heard our prayers and answered them. I hope that I may soon present the Bringer with the Kai Priestess of the Vindrasi and that we will be able to "persuade" Draya to tell us what she knows of the dragonbone that Aelon, in his wisdom, caused us to find when we attacked the Hall of Vektia.

I will write again when I have firmed up the details of my plan.

I remain as always your servant in the blessed service of Aelon, Lord of Light, etc., and so forth, Raegar, Warrior Priest of Battle's Glory.

Sent by fire, water, and oil, to the Watcher in the Temple of the New Dawn the next night.

To Acronis, Honored Tribune of the Twenty-four, Commander of the Navy of his Imperial Majesty, Emperor Dunumadi. Greetings!

All is arranged. I have devised a plan to abduct the Kai Priestess. My stupid young cousin will deliver her into our hands, at which time I can slay him if you command it, Master.

I venture to suggest, however, we keep him alive. He is a godsend to us—a young hothead who will happily lead the Vindrasi people to ruination. If we kill him, the Vindrasi will merely choose another Chief of Chiefs, and this time they might select a wise old fox, not a yapping young kit.

My cousin is to bring the Kai Priestess to the Isle of Apensia. I chose this place because it will also give us the opportunity to strike a blow at the pagans who rule that island, reveal to them the awful power of the God of the New Dawn, and bring these heathens into the fold. (Either that or, as Aelon commands, slay the corrupt lest they corrupt others!)

I remain as always your servant in the blessed service of Aelon, Lord of Light, etc. and so forth, Raegar, Priest of Battle's Glory.

Sent by fire, water, and oil, to the Watcher in the Temple of the New Dawn some time later.

To Acronis, Honored Tribune of the Twenty-four, Commander of the Navy of his Imperial Majesty, Emperor Dunumadi. Greetings!

Again, I humbly apologize to your lordship for the disaster that befell my men and me on the Isle of Apensia. Clearly, these druids are very dangerous people and must be eradicated. However, all that for another time.

I have, as you commanded, returned to the Torgun. My kinsmen were overjoyed to see me, and they have welcomed me back with open arms, with the possible exception of my young cousin, who fears that at any moment I will betray him.

Through Aelon's blessing, the Torgun's Bone Priestess is a spinster named Treia, who is hungry for a man. She is not ill-favored and she is near my age, so none of my kinsmen were surprised to see me take an interest in her.

In truth, I find her to be an intriguing woman. She and I have much in common, and it is no punishment to me to spend time with her. Perhaps I flatter myself, but I have no doubt that I can make her do anything I want.

My cousin, the so-called Chief of Chiefs, is preparing to undertake a voyage to the ogre nation to retrieve the dragonbone. I will send you notice of our departure that you may be ready to intercept their ships. We can then recover the Vektan Torque ourselves, which will give us two of these valuable dragonbones.

I remain as always your servant in the blessed service of Aelon, Lord of Light, etc. and so forth, Raegar, Priest of Battle's Glory.

Sent by fire, water, and oil, to the Watcher in the Temple of the New Dawn, done in haste, slightly garbled.

Acronis! Praise Aelon that you came safely through that terrible storm and that you managed to keep track of us! I have escaped the dragonship, faking my own death by drowning. I am in the Hall of their dead goddess. Send men to meet me. I have a plan.

Raegar

# AFTERWORD

## Brian Thomsen
## In Memoriam

As *Bones of the Dragon* was going to press, Tracy and I were shocked to learn that our friend and the editor of this book, Brian Thomsen, had died unexpectedly of heart failure. Brian was only fifty-four, far too young to be taken from us.

Tracy and I first met Brian back in the mid-1990s when he came to work for TSR, Inc., the publisher of *Dungeons & Dragons,* in Lake Geneva. He became head of the book department. We soon learned that Brian was an editor who loved his authors and who wanted to see them be successful. Editing wasn't just a job to Brian, it was a passion.

At one point in time, back in the late 1990s, TSR, Inc., was going through financial problems. I was writing a book for the Dragonlance series, called *The Soulforge,* the tale of the early years of one of the series' most popular characters, the wizard Raistlin Majere.

Since I lived close to the company headquarters, I called Brian to tell him I had finished the book and would bring the manuscript into his office. He suggested instead that I meet him for lunch in a local café and bring the manuscript with me.

Over lunch, he confided that he was worried about the company's finances. He was afraid they might declare bankruptcy and, in that case, if the manuscript was in his office, it might be seized as an asset of the company. He didn't want that to happen. He said he would keep it with him until the situation improved. I later found out he carried it around in his car!

The company did manage to carry on and *The Soulforge* was published. Brian would later joke that he was probably the only person ever to keep Raistlin Majere locked up in the trunk!

Brian remained my friend and mentor for years after he left TSR, Inc., to return to New York. He became a freelance editor for Tor Books, where he delighted in developing plans for his authors. One day he called me to say that he had an idea for me. He suggested I write a series of novels about dragons and that the first book be titled *Mistress of Dragons.* He said he thought that Tor would be interested in this series.

I was thrilled to have the opportunity. I asked him if he had any ideas on what the series should be about.

"No," said Brian airily. "I'll leave that up to you. I know you'll come up with something great. Oh, and by the way, I'll need a synopsis for three books in two weeks."

Generally it takes me months to come up with a plot for a series, but I was excited about this and I worked furiously. In two weeks I had developed the outline for what would become one of my favorite series about dragons, Dragonvarld, published by Tor Books. The first book was titled, as Brian suggested, *Mistress of Dragons*.

When Tracy and I began working on the complex plot for Dragonships, we first thought of Brian, and we were pleased and excited when Tor became our publisher, with Brian as our editor. He provided invaluable guidance for the series. He was involved in all aspects of this book, from the wonderful art for the jacket to offering advice on the characters.

After he edited *Bones of the Dragon,* he called to tell us how much he enjoyed it. He also added, laughing, that the proofreader had liked it! Brian was enthusiastic about Dragonships, and both Tracy and I are deeply saddened by the fact that he will not be with us to guide our books through to completion.

Tracy and I would like to dedicate the series, Dragonships, to our friend, editor, and mentor, Brian Thomsen, with love and respect and admiration.

—Margaret Weis and Tracy Hickman
September 25, 2008